Read... ...3 *series*

'An original action-packed international thriller with tension and danger on every page. Rob Sinclair is a writer of immense power' – **Michael Wood, author of** ***For Reasons Unknown***

'Timely, gripping and utterly shocking . . . one of the most intense and engrossing thrillers of the last decade'

'Perfect for thriller lovers and fans of *I Am Pilgrim, Orphan X*'

'Another excellent read from Rob Sinclair. Couldn't tear myself away from it from start to finish'

'Could not put down this book'

17. 'Powerful and hard-hitting psychological thriller'

'Took my breath away with its sheer energy and fast-paced narrative . . . I lived and breathed every moment'

'Fast-paced, all-action thriller which keeps you on the edge of your seat'

By Rob Sinclair

Rob Sinclair specialised in forensic fraud investigations at a global accounting firm for thirteen years. He began writing in 2009 following a promise to his wife, an avid reader, that he could pen an 'unputdownable' thriller. Since then, Rob has sold over half a million copies of his critically acclaimed thrillers in both the Enemy and James Ryker series. His work has received widespread critical acclaim, with many reviewers and readers likening his work to authors at the very top of the genre, including Lee Child and Vince Flynn.

Originally from the north-east of England, Rob has lived and worked in a number of fast-paced cities, including New York, and is now settled in the West Midlands with his wife and young sons.

FUGITIVE
13

ROB SINCLAIR

ORION

An Orion paperback

First published in Great Britain in 2019
by Orion Fiction,
This paperback edition published in 2019
by Orion Fiction,
an imprint of The Orion Publishing Group Ltd,
Carmelite House, 50 Victoria Embankment
London EC4Y 0DZ

An Hachette UK company

1 3 5 7 9 10 8 6 4 2

A CIP catalogue record for this book
is available from the British Library.

ISBN 9781409175964

Typeset by Born Group

Printed and bound in Great Britain by Clays Ltd, Elcograf S.p.A.

MIX
Paper from
responsible sources
FSC® C104740

www.orionbooks.co.uk

For my mum and dad

ONE

Sevilla, Spain

The windowless room was a chilly sixteen degrees and the skin on Wahid's bare arms prickled as he sat, alone, on the hard metal chair, in his prison issue cotton t-shirt and trousers. The only door to the room was directly in front of him, across the plain metal table that, like his chair, was bolted to the floor. Thick cuffs clasped Wahid's hands together. A chain ran down from his wrists to the cuffs around his ankles. The small amount of flex was long enough when he was sitting, but caused him to stoop uncomfortably and shuffle demeaningly when walking. Just one of many indignities designed to make him feel weak and defeated.

As Wahid stared straight ahead at the closed door, wondering what questions today's trip from his cell would include, he heard footsteps the other side. Two sets. One set was cushioned – a guard, they all wore the same thick rubber-soled boots. The other footsteps made a sharper click-clack sound. Hard soles on the concrete floor. Not a guard, but someone else. A smartly dressed someone else.

Locks clicked and churned. Wahid thought through all of the people who'd been to see him in this place over the last twelve months. Which face would it be today? Which approach would they come at him with? Aggressive, conciliatory, understanding, accusatory? Whatever tactic they tried, all they had were their words, and Wahid was confident that this time would be no different.

The door swung open. Wahid caught a glimpse of the hand of the guard who'd opened it, but he didn't make a move to come inside. The fresh face of a young man Wahid didn't recognise appeared in the doorway. An unexpected visitor. Wahid was immediately intrigued. Confidence and arrogance seeped from the man despite his youthful appearance. He stepped inside, hands behind his back, his eyes fixed on Wahid, both men unblinking. The door closed with a thud. Locks clicked back into place. The man didn't say a word. Wahid didn't move, but his curiosity bubbled away, even though he was also now wary.

Something about this visit already felt different, wrong, even before the man glanced up to where one of the two CCTV cameras in the room was located. After a couple of seconds the little red light beneath the lenses flicked off. The lens shrivelled back inside its black plastic casing. The man switched his gaze to the other camera, which shut down too, before turning his attention to the four-foot-wide two-way mirror that took up most of one wall. In a flash the glare on the mirror noticeably reduced as the glass was blacked out from the other side.

Wahid's eyes narrowed. The man finally looked at Wahid once more.

'And now we can talk,' he said.

He slapped a newspaper down onto the table. A UK tabloid. Wahid first glanced at the date. Today's paper. Then his eyes fell upon the headline – *Muchas Gracias, España* – and the grainy image that accompanied it. A grainy image of Wahid. Despite himself, he frowned. The reaction drew a smile from the man.

'Congratulations,' he said. 'You're dead.'

Fifteen minutes passed. The man who'd introduced himself as Eric Neumayer was sitting opposite Wahid. Neumayer's manner remained confident yet relaxed. Almost snide, with a plastered crooked half-smile. The man certainly wasn't like any of the other visitors Wahid had had here, yet Wahid hadn't said a single word since his arrival, despite his growing curiosity at the situation. Combined with his apparent authority – the switched-off cameras and the blacked-out glass – it was made clear to Wahid that Neumayer wanted to do the talking, not the other way round.

'Do you understand what I'm saying to you?' Neumayer asked.

Once again Wahid held his tongue.

'The whole world believes you're dead now.'

Or so the headline said. Wahid, aka Ismail Obbadi, the infamous terrorist caught red-handed on Spanish soil by MI6 more than twelve months before, had been killed in a brawl at a maximum-security jail in southern Spain.

'The Spanish government have had enough of you. They don't want to put you on trial, and neither does anyone else. They want rid of you. Within twenty-four hours you'll be on a plane out of Europe for good. You'll be sent directly to a black site. Zed site. Have you heard of that? I'm not kidding when I say it makes Guantanamo look like a luxury resort.'

Wahid's mind whirred. Could the governments of Western European countries really be so corrupt and deceitful as to concoct such lies to their public?

The answer was simple. Of course they could.

'I'm sure I don't need to explain what will happen to you when you get there,' Neumayer said. 'The lengths we're prepared to go to in order to get you to talk.'

3

'We?' Wahid said.

That smile on Neumayer's face rose slightly at Wahid's decision to speak. He hadn't yet stated who he worked for, even though it was pretty damn obvious.

'Does the accent not give it away?' Neumayer said.

MI6, Wahid would bet, but once again chose to say nothing.

'There'll be no stop to the torture. Not until you tell them about your brother. And the others at the Farm.'

Wahid clenched his fists under the table. His brother, Talatashar, number thirteen, was still on the loose. Talatashar was the reason that many of Wahid's brothers were now dead, and why Wahid himself would soon become a plaything of the British government. He could only hope the authorities never caught up with that vermin. He wanted his own people to get there first.

Neumayer looked up to the two cameras which remained switched off. Wahid's eyes narrowed again. He had so many questions for the man sitting in front of him, but he wouldn't ask them. He couldn't show any weakness.

'I'm not expecting you to open up to me here,' Neumayer said. 'And besides, to do so would be pointless.'

Neumayer paused as if for dramatic effect.

'But I do have a message for you, from the man I work for.'

Another pause. The crooked smile on Neumayer's face dropped away. He squinted and leaned forward.

'Shadow Hand.'

The two words rattled in Wahid's head. Two simple words that meant so much. Did Neumayer have any idea of the true nature of what he'd just said?

That look on his face suggested he probably did.

Then what was this? A threat? Or was it possible that Neumayer actually was an ally? That he was working for the same people as Wahid?

4

Or was the threat, in fact, coming from his own people?

Wahid had never talked in the twelve months of his captivity. Hadn't given away a single piece of intelligence. But now the authorities were shipping him out of jail to a black site – perhaps he was nothing but a liability. Once a shining example of the capabilities of his people, Wahid – number one – was now simply a problem.

Whatever the answer, it didn't matter. Wahid knew what he had to do.

Neumayer opened his mouth to speak again.

Before a word passed his lips, Wahid roared, leaped up and hurled his whole body across the table. Neumayer twisted backward, trying to find a counter, but the element of surprise was enough to give Wahid the upper hand. The two men crashed to the ground. Neumayer was young and sprightly, but Wahid had been trained in close quarters combat since he was just a boy, and he'd always been top of the class at the Farm.

Despite Neumayer's attempts to gain ground in the scuffle, Wahid seamlessly wormed onto his back. Neumayer's lean body was on top, the chain between Wahid's cuffs wrapped around Neumayer's throat.

Wahid tugged and pulled on the chains, his body tensed, the muscles on his arms rippling and bulging. Neumayer gasped for air, jolted and bucked. He threw fists and elbows into Wahid's side.

An alarm blared. How did they know? Had they been watching all along, or had Neumayer somehow triggered the alert?

Barely a second later the door burst open and two uniformed guards barrelled inside, weapons drawn, shouting instructions in a convoluted mess of Spanish and half-baked English.

Neumayer screamed at the guards, as best he could with the metal crushing his throat.

5

There was a loud pop as one of the guards fired his dart gun. A painful jab on Wahid's thigh. Another pop. Another jab in his shoulder. A wave of numbness quickly spread across his limbs. He only had a few seconds before he was out cold.

He tugged even harder on the chains. Wrapped the links around his wrist to shorten the flex further. The grip was now so tight the metal cut into his skin. Blood poured down his hands and arms. With one final effort, Wahid mustered all the strength he could and shouted out again with pure venom and hatred as he jerked sharply on the chains. There was a sickening crunch. Wahid didn't know if he'd snapped the spine or crushed the windpipe. Maybe both.

Neumayer's body gave a final fateful shudder, then he went still.

Wahid heaved a long sigh, his body slumped. His vision blurred before turning black.

TWO

Alexandria, Egypt

'You have nothing to worry about,' Aydin Torkal said to the man crumpled by his feet. 'By tomorrow morning you'll be at home with your family. No harm will come to you. As long as you do as I've said.'

The man didn't respond. He couldn't talk with the tape covering his mouth. Instead he huffed through his nostrils and glared defiantly into Aydin's eyes.

Aydin leaned forward and slowly pressed the needle into the man's neck. He pushed down on the plunger. When all five millimetres of the liquid was inside the man's bloodstream, Aydin pulled the needle out and placed the syringe into the clear plastic bag by his side. He sat for a few moments as the man slowly drifted off. When Aydin was sure he was uncon- scious, he pulled the balaclava off his head and placed that too in the plastic bag. He'd dispose of both later.

He opened the van's back doors, looked across the street. No one was in sight.

Satisfied, he grabbed the backpack and stepped out into the glorious afternoon sunshine.

A few hundred yards from where he'd left the van, Aydin walked along the coastal road with the rippling blue waters of the Mediterranean off to his left. On the opposite side was modern-day Alexandria, a sprawling urban mass with lofty apartment blocks and hotels rising up by the side of the road, that every now and then gave a glimpse of the city's rich and spectacular ancient past. At the mouth of the eastern harbour in the near distance the Citadel of Qaitbay sat in pride of place, the fifteenth-century defensive fortress partly built from the ruins of the ancient wonder that the city was most famous for: the Lighthouse of Alexandria. Just like the lighthouse, Aydin had been broken into pieces, but after twelve months in the shadows, he was now back – a different beast altogether from the young man the world had come to know as Talatashar.

He turned off the coastal road onto a wide paved street with a mishmash of run-down sandstone apartments and the occasional modern glass-rich office block. On a late Sunday afternoon the street was quiet. Across the tops of the buildings a call to prayer sounded out through loudspeakers from all directions.

Aydin carried on past a glass-canopied entrance to a four-storey office block. A small plaque by the entrance noted the tenant of the building as Alexandria Technology Systems. ATS. Aydin turned into a narrow alley that ran alongside the building. He passed a line of over-spilling industrial waste bins, then stopped at an innocuous-looking metal-panelled door. There were no handles or visible locks. Just a small, discreet security pad attached to the wall. Aydin kept his head low as he came to a stop. The baseball cap, emblazoned with the logo of the security company the man in the van worked for, did its job of hiding his face from the camera he knew was located above his head.

Aydin flipped the plastic case up from the security pad and pressed his thumb onto the sensor. After a second a green light flashed to show the silicon thumbprint stuck over his own had been accepted.

8

Next, he input the six-digit code. A moment later the door hissed open an inch. Aydin pushed the door further open and stepped through.

Inside, faint blue strip lights along the bottom edges of the corridor walls trailed into the distance, illuminating the passage like a runway. Aydin closed the door behind him and stayed on the spot for a few moments to allow his eyes to adjust to the dull light.

He'd been inside the offices of ATS twice before, but only ever through the front entrance as an apparent customer. Having obtained and perused the blueprints for the three-year-old building at length, however, the space in front of him felt familiar. He looked at his watch. The time was approaching five thirty. He had until seven p.m. before the change of security for the night. The day guards would perform one last sweep before the end of their shifts, leaving their posts at roughly six forty-five. If all went to plan, Aydin would be back on the outside well before then.

Happy that the corridor in front of him was clear, Aydin cautiously made his way along, once again keeping his head low so that the many cameras couldn't make out his face. If one of the guards was watching the camera feeds, they'd see only the baseball cap and the uniform, and together with the name tag and Aydin's size and frame, the guards would surely assume he was Hakim Mahi – the guard who lay unconscious in Aydin's van, whose night shift started with the change of guard at seven.

Aydin stopped outside a closed door. Unlike most of the others on the corridor, that led into meeting rooms and offices, this one wasn't frosted glass, but solid. Mahi and the other guards didn't have access to this space.

Aydin looked left and right. Still nothing. He slipped the tablet from his backpack, attached the cable to the USB port, then carefully prised the keypad away from the wall to reveal the wires at the back. After attaching his cable into the maintenance port at the back of the keypad he fixed his eyes on the tablet screen as the software kicked into action and flashed through countless permutations for the eight-digit code to open the door.

One digit after another the code was read. The hack would leave a clear digital footprint, but gaining physical access to this room was the only way to get to the servers inside. He'd tried every back door he could to remotely hack ATS's systems, but had failed at every attempt.

Aydin's nerves continued to build as he waited. His eyes settled on the door further along the corridor that led to the large central foyer. He was sure he'd just seen a shadow moving across the frosted glass. One of the guards?

His hand brushed down to the gun holstered on his hip. He didn't want to use it, to hurt the guards, but he was prepared to do whatever it took.

A clicking sound made him flinch. He quickly realised it was only the door unlocking. It had taken close to five minutes, but the riskiest part was over. Aydin pushed the door open, and packed the equipment back inside his bag. He refitted the keypad back on the wall as best he could, then stepped through into the black space beyond.

He put on the night vision goggles he'd brought, then gave himself a few seconds to allow his eyes to properly adjust. When he was happy, he moved off down the metal staircase. He could relax now, if only a little. There were no cameras in the basement, and no one would be coming down here. Not tonight.

At the bottom of the stairs Aydin continued through the cool corridor. The floor and walls were rough concrete, everything purely functional. At the end of the corridor was a single metal door. Another keypad. This one only needed a simple four-digit code. After all, not many people ever got this far.

Less than two minutes later the door was open and Aydin moved inside, already fishing in his backpack for the equipment he needed to take a complete image of ATS's most off-limits server drives.

THREE

At six forty Aydin climbed the stairs. He only had five minutes to make himself scarce. The imaging had taken longer than expected, but now he had what he needed. The backpack over his shoulders felt as it had done before, yet he now had over two terabytes of data crammed onto the external drives he was carrying. Much of the data he'd stolen was likely encrypted, and getting through those layers of security would be an even tougher step than what he'd just been through, but at least he'd have time and privacy for it. Right now, he didn't have either of those. He had to get out, and quick.

He reached the top and the blue-lit corridor, heading back towards the exit. He was only a few yards away when there was a noise behind him. A door opening? One of the guards? It had to be. Completing his rounds early, most likely.

'Hey,' the guard shouted out. Not a hostile shout, more one of greeting. 'Hey, Hakim.'

Aydin almost smiled to himself. Would the simple subterfuge be enough to save him?

'Where you going?'

'Cigarette,' Aydin said, without turning round, and without breaking stride.

'You're early.'

Aydin said nothing, just carried on walking.

'What's in the backpack?' the guard shouted out, the tone more neutral, almost questioning now.

Not that Aydin believed the cover was completely blown. It was more likely the guard's scepticism was for another reason – how could the lowly paid security guards not be tempted, given the nature of the data stored at ATS?

Aydin stopped, his range of options narrowing by the second. The door to the outside was three yards away. He had to get there.

Aydin spun and drew the Colt handgun from his hip. He fired. The warning shot sent the guard scuttling back into the room he'd come from. Aydin burst towards the door. Released the lock. Crashed out into the alley and moved into a sprint.

The alarm sounded.

Not only would the guards on duty be after him in a flash, but the call would no doubt go straight to the local police too. He had to get back to the van before they got to him.

Aydin bounded to the end of the alley and skidded round the corner to head away from the front entrance of ATS. He heard the shouts behind him, but didn't dare look back. He knew the guards were armed, but dodging between parked cars and the odd pedestrian, he seriously doubted they'd shoot unless they were absolutely sure.

He took a quick left. Then a right. Then another left, and found himself edging into the old town, busy with tourists and locals heading out to cafes and restaurants. He barged his way through, deliberately aiming for and flattening a young couple. He needed the distraction. More shouts around him. But this time it was just the concerned yelps of pedestrians.

Up ahead he spotted two uniformed police officers. One had a radio handset up to his mouth. He locked eyes with Aydin.

'Stop him!' he shouted out.

His colleague drew his gun. Aydin ducked and darted off to his right. No gunshots came. Two yards away was another alley. He burst into it and started sprinting, though he could already feel the build-up of lactic acid in his muscles. He was only a little over halfway back to the van, and there was no way he could continue at full pelt.

The end of the alley neared. His muscles burned, he was losing pace. He risked a glance behind, saw a guard and the two police officers just turning in. They were a good ten seconds behind, but Aydin needed more. He fired another warning shot. The bullet ricocheted off a metal fire escape and caused all three of the men to falter and cower.

Distracted, Aydin clattered into someone ahead of him, only spotting it was another policeman as the gun flew from his grip. The strap of his backpack snapped and the bag tumbled across the tarmac. Aydin landed on the cop, knocking the wind from him, and saving Aydin from more painful contact with the ground. It also meant, luckily, that there was barely a scuffle. Aydin craned his neck and crashed his forehead onto the top of the policeman's nose. Blood spurted, and with the policeman dazed and fighting for breath, Aydin clambered back to his feet.

Behind him, the three other men were quickly closing in. Aydin scooped up the gun and fired again. This time they returned fire and a bullet whizzed past Aydin's ear. Time to step things up. Aydin took a fraction of a second to aim. The bullet sank into the thigh of the security guard, sending him crashing to the ground. Aydin grabbed his backpack and carried on running, only realising as his legs got going again that he'd badly twisted an ankle in the earlier fall. It wouldn't stop him now. Finding every last ounce of energy and strength, he hobbled along as fast as he could. Took the next right, then a left − now well clear of the chasing pack.

The van was right there. He threw open the back doors and climbed inside, caught in two minds. He could fire up the engine and speed away. But no. There was another option. He quickly rifled through the medical kit in the back. Hakim Mahi was still sleeping soundly. Not for long. Aydin snipped away the cable ties. Pulled the tape from his mouth. Grabbed the shot of adrenaline. Lifted the needle and slammed it down into Mahi's heart. The guard jolted upright almost instantly, took a huge inhale of breath, his eyes bulging. Aydin didn't give him a beat more than that. He kicked him out of the van. Mahi tumbled to the ground. Aydin grabbed the doors and was swinging them shut when the first of the policemen careered around the corner, gun drawn. He immediately spotted Mahi.

'Hands up!' the policeman screamed.

As he jumped from the back of the van into the driver's seat, Aydin heard Mahi's confused protests. The engine fired up on the first attempt and Aydin slammed the gear stick into first and thumped his foot onto the accelerator. The van lurched forward, only narrowly missing the parked car in front as Aydin shot out into the road. The police opened fire. Aydin ducked as bullets hammered into the back of the van.

He swung the van round the first corner. Was soon into fourth gear as the needle swept beyond a hundred km/h on the cramped city streets. He took a series of lefts and rights, his eyes busy the whole time.

After thirty seconds he realised there were no flashes of blue behind. None ahead either. He slowed the pace. Drove more measuredly for two minutes as he headed onto quieter streets. Finally he turned into the abandoned three-storey car park adjoining a derelict industrial area near the western harbour. He parked the van on the middle floor, stripped off the guard's uniform and put on his own casual clothes. He put the uniform and the plastic bag with the other items he needed to dispose of into his backpack, then stepped out and jumped onto the motorbike he'd parked up earlier.

Seconds later, he was outside again, casually riding the Yamaha along the coastal road, heading out of the city for good. Up ahead, the blood-red sun was setting in the distance, its edges merging at the horizon with the shimmering blue of the sea.

FOUR

Kabul, Afghanistan

Rachel Cox had commanded or overseen countless armed extractions and assaults in her time as a field agent for SIS — the British secret intelligence service, more commonly referred to as MI6. But never before had she taken control of such an exercise while sitting alone in a rusted-out 1980s Toyota Corolla. Was that called blending in, or something to do with the never-ending austerity back home?

She had no visual of the upcoming raid, only a running commentary from the three-man assault team — known to her simply as Blue One, Blue Two and Blue Three — run through a minuscule wireless earpiece. The building that Blue Team was about to enter was fifty yards further up the run-down street in front of Cox — a small private compound in a semi-rural area on the outskirts of Kabul. Surrounded by a seven-foot-high rendered perimeter wall, the two-storey house within the compound was big enough to be called a mansion, had it not been in such a dire state of disrepair.

With her headscarf on, and sitting low in her seat, Cox was about as inconspicuous in her surroundings as she could be, given her light, freckled skin and green eyes — and the fact that she was an unaccompanied adult female. Yet every time someone walked past the parked car she felt her nerves ratchet several notches, one hand always on the Glock handgun balanced on the seat between her legs — a precaution she hoped she wouldn't need. Not if Blue Team did its job anyway. But this was her op, based on her intel, and she needed to be there, not sitting in some cushy safe house several miles away.

'Blue One in position,' came the crackling voice in her ear.

'Blue Two, Blue Three — ready.'

Cox gripped the steering wheel tightly, trying to channel the anxiety away through white knuckles. 'Blue One, go on your command,' she said.

A short pause, then came the follow-up command in her ear: 'Blue Team go, go, go!'

There was an echoing bang as charges erupted both in the near distance and in Cox's ear. A plume of smoke billowed into the sky as she listened to the shouted instructions of the raiding team. A brief rattle of gunfire. Cox frowned. Blue Team were armed, but they hadn't been sent to eliminate the three targets — known for the operation as Alpha, Beta and Gamma — only to capture them. So who was shooting?

'Target Gamma is down!' shouted Blue Two seconds later.

Cox growled in frustration. 'What about the others?'

No answer. More shouting. More gunfire. Cox spotted two people running down the street towards her. A man and a woman. After an initial wave of panic, Cox realised they were just two terrified pedestrians who'd heard the commotion — in the wrong place at the wrong time. They carried on past her car without so much as a backward glance.

'Target Beta detained,' came the out-of-breath voice of Blue Three. 'Alpha on the run.'

'Shit.' Cox turned the key and the Corolla's aged engine grumbled to life. Concentrating too hard on the sounds in her ear she pulled out into the road without checking and was nearly side-swiped by a passing four-by-four. The driver honked at her and shook his fist angrily but carried on ahead, before taking a left turn at the compound and disappearing.

Cox took a deep breath, checked her mirrors properly, then sped up, heading for the double gates at the entrance to the compound.

'Target Beta locked and loaded,' shouted Blue Three. Which meant the guy was out of the compound and already in the van.

'Update on Alpha?' Cox asked.

No response.

'Update on Alpha?'

'He's coming your way!'

The next moment the gate in front of Cox swung open and Alpha – aka Kasim Noor, their primary target – barefooted and wearing only khaki shorts and a white t-shirt, came bursting out. He locked eyes with Cox. Reached behind his back . . .

Cox thumped her foot onto the accelerator and the Corolla's engine whined as the rusty beast bolted forward. Noor tried his best to dodge the speeding car. He didn't make it. Cox slammed on the brakes to avoid crashing into the compound's walls. The front bumper smacked into Noor's legs, sent him clattering onto the Corolla's bonnet. He slid off and landed in a crumpled heap by the passenger side.

Cox jumped from the car, Glock held out. Noor was moaning and writhing on the ground, but he'd live.

'Stay down!' Cox yelled, pointing the gun at him.

Another chorus of gunfire from the compound.

'Get Beta out of there!' Cox shouted. They couldn't afford to lose another target. Blue Team's van was the other side of the compound. The intention was to transport all three detainees together, but clearly events weren't going to plan.

'But Blue One and Blue Two are still inside,' came Three's response.

19

'Just get him to the extraction point.'

'Yes, ma'am.'

Noor was trying to sit up, his furious eyes on Cox.

'Don't you fucking move. Or I'll shoot your damn balls off.'

'Nice,' called Blue One, his bulky mass – even wider with his combat fatigues and equipment on – jolted as he came running out of the open gate of the compound. He moved up to Cox's side, lifted the semi-automatic from his shoulder and smacked the butt of the weapon down onto Noor's face.

'We need to go,' he said. 'Now.'

'Damn right. Where's Blue Two?'

Blue One indicated. Cox looked back over and saw him coming through the gates too, dragging another man by his neck, his feet scuffing along the dusty ground.

'What the hell?'

'We don't know who he is,' Blue One said, 'but he was taking pot shots at us. He's coming too.'

Cox groaned. She was in charge of the extraction. She could have stood her ground and argued that one, but frankly, leaving the unknown man behind could prove a bigger risk than taking him with them. The main issue right then wasn't taking the extra prisoner along for the ride, it was that Blue Three had already scarpered in the van with Beta.

'OK, load them up,' Cox said, looking up at Blue One.

The deep ridges in his forehead folded over even more than they normally did.

'You have a better idea?' Cox asked.

He growled, opened the back doors of the Corolla then cable-tied Noor's wrists, before scooping up the barely conscious man and climbing cumbersomely inside the car, pulling Noor into the seat beside him. Blue Two pushed and shoved the other man to the ground, clasped his wrists together with cable ties, then crammed him into the back with Noor and Blue One before jumping into the front. Cox put her foot down and the weak engine did its best to pull the now-hefty load along.

'Where are you guys?' Blue Three's voice crackled.

'On our way. We'll see you there,' Cox said.

She looked in her rear-view mirror. The two prisoners were conscious, but their eyes were rolling. Cox's stare found Blue One's.

'What the hell happened in there?' Cox asked, her tone not particularly friendly.

She didn't know the identities of any of the ops team, who they really worked for, what their backgrounds were. That was often the case with operations like this one. Unless the UK government had authority from the local government for their action, then it was necessary to operate at arm's length. That meant using outside contractors and mercenaries, whether British or foreign, to do the dirty field work. It also meant accepting varying degrees of competence, aptitude and, of course, attitude. She'd only met Blue Team two days ago and had been impressed with them in planning the op, but she was now wondering whether – like so many ex-military guys – they became too trigger happy in the heat of the moment.

'There was nothing we could do,' Blue One said, his face stern and giving away no emotion. 'Gamma pulled the gun first. It was him or me.'

'You could have shot him in the fucking leg,' Cox said.

'I did. The first two times. These bastards don't know when to give up.'

He threw an elbow into Noor's gut as though in recompense for his fighting back.

'Still, we got three targets, eh?' said Blue Three.

Cox looked over and saw the wry smirk on his face. The problem was, if the unknown was just an innocent civilian, it

21

was Cox who would be reprimanded. The former commandos would just head off to their next job for whomever.

It only took another five minutes before the overloaded Toyota was rolling into the abandoned car park of an ageing industrial unit. As they approached, the rusted loading doors of the warehouse in the far corner were rolled open to reveal a gleaming black Ford Transit van, which two other men Cox hadn't met before would use to take the prisoners to a little-used airbase near the border for their onward travel to which-ever black site her boss, Henry Flannigan, had designated.

Parked up next to the Ford Transit was the considerably more decrepit van that Blue Team had earlier arrived in. Blue Three was by the loading doors. He approached Cox's window.

'Quite a crowd you've got there,' he said, studying the car's passengers and smiling.

'Tell me about it. Where's Beta?'

'Ready to go.'

'OK. Get these two in there with him.'

Blue Three nodded. Blue Two got out of the car and the two bulky men pulled the prisoners from the back of the Corolla.

'Say bye-bye to the motherland,' Blue Three heckled as he dragged Noor to the waiting Transit. Perhaps he shouldn't have been so flippant. Or perhaps they shouldn't have over-estimated his injuries, because in a sudden flash of movement, Noor twisted his way out of Blue Three's grasp, swivelled and took the mercenary's legs from under him with a swiping kick. As the big man was falling, Noor, hands still tied behind his back, reached out and pulled the holstered sidearm from Three's belt . . .

Cox glanced to Blue One, stepping from the car, gun in hand.

'No!' she screamed.

Bang, bang, bang. Three shots in quick succession. All were direct hits.

Noor's lifeless body collapsed. Cox glared over at Blue One. Didn't even bother to start the argument. The determined look on his face suggested he wouldn't listen to a word she said anyway.

'One out of three,' she said. 'I'll know who not to call next time.'

Blue One gave an angry huff.

'Get the other one in the van,' she said. 'Then you can all go home.'

Blue One grunted. 'What about him?' He pointed down to Noor's corpse.

'Not much we can do with him like that, is there? Take him home with you. Leave him for the vultures. Your choice.'

Doing her best to contain her anger, Cox sank back down into the driver's seat, turned the wheel and spun the car round, then put her foot down, kicking up dust as the Corolla sped away.

FIVE

'You're so young, Nilay,' her uncle Kamil said. Nilay cringed at the words. She hated people saying things like that to her, as though her youth made her dumber than they were. 'You have so much life ahead of you. Why do you want to do this?'

'I have to do this, uncle. Aydin is my brother. I have to know what happened to him. My father too.'

They strolled along the European bank of the Bosphorus, in the Ortaköy neighbourhood, a trendy and cosmopolitan area of the city whose literal translation was 'middle village'. They'd just been for lunch in a new Lebanese restaurant her uncle had recommended, and her belly was as full of food as her mind was of questions.

Nilay stopped and leaned on the railings. Looked up ahead where the Ortaköy mosque sat beneath the Bosphorus bridge.

'It's beautiful here,' Nilay said, staring at the twin minarets of the neo-baroque structure.

'But if you scratch the surface . . . Not everything is as it first appears.'

Nilay didn't question the strange statement. Was he referring to Istanbul and Turkey, or to the fate of her brother and father?

She'd only been nine years old when her father had disappeared from their London home one night, taking Aydin with him. Now twenty-one, she could still remember the morning after

24

with incredible clarity and detail. Her first reaction, when her mother had torn through the apartment screaming that her boy had gone, had been one of gleeful delight. She'd never got along with Aydin all that well. There'd been no particular reason, other than typical sibling rivalry.

That fleeting thought had lasted only a few seconds, and memory of that naive reaction now, many years later, made Nilay feel huge guilt. She'd quickly learned, even as a nine-year-old, that Aydin's disappearance was a terrible thing for the family. It had torn her mother apart, and she'd never been quite the same since. When she'd discovered her own husband had kidnapped Aydin, and taken him to Afghanistan to join some rebel jihadi outfit, it destroyed her.

Or so the story went.

But Nilay needed to know the full story, the whole truth.

Neither Aydin nor Ergun Torkal had been heard of since that day. At least not by Nilay or her mother. But did Kamil, Ergun's brother, know something?

'You'd tell me if you knew anything, wouldn't you?' Nilay said, looking her uncle in the eye.

He held her gaze for a few seconds.

'He'd be so proud of you now,' Kamil said. 'If he could see the amazing young woman you've become. But you should be looking to the future, not the past. Getting married, starting a family. You're a beautiful woman.'

She saw the pride in Kamil's eyes and looked away, riled. Yes, she was young and pretty and female, but she was as bright as anyone else. She would find the truth, one way or another, and certainly wouldn't be fobbed off by her ageing uncle's witless charm, or by anyone else who couldn't see past her looks and her gender.

'I know they went to Kabul,' Nilay said. 'The British police confirmed that. Who did they go to see? Did my father ever tell you of his plans? You must know something.'

Kamil pulled away from the railings and began to walk off, edging closer to the bridge in the near distance.

'Uncle!' Nilay said. She grabbed his shoulder to stop him. 'I'm not going to give in. I will find out. I have to. Not just for Aydin, but for my mother. The thought that one day she might see her son again is about the only thing that keeps her going.'

'No. You're wrong there. What keeps her going is you. Forget about Aydin. He's gone. Even if he's still alive he's not the boy you remember any more.'

Again Nilay wondered exactly what Kamil meant by that.

'Make the right choice, Nilay. Have a good life. I beg you not to go so deep that you can't get out.'

'I've already made my choice. There is no turning back now. Please, if you can help me, you have to.'

Kamil turned away and sighed.

'If you really are determined to do this, then . . . Well, it's not much, but I can give you a name. A place. You won't find all you need there, but it could be a start.'

Nilay felt a sudden swell of emotion. Anger, resentment, that her uncle had been so reticent to help her, even though he so clearly knew more than he let on. But also optimism. All she needed was a way in. A starting point. If that's what he could give, then she would take it.

'Please, uncle. Tell me. I have to know.'

SIX

Mosul, Iraq

Several weeks later the conversation with her uncle in Istanbul played over and over in Nilay's mind as she sat at the back of the hall and listened to the imam spouting his bile and hatred. There were more than fifty people crammed into the room, surrounded by crumbling stone walls, a ceiling with gaping holes, which gave a clear view to the blue sky above, filled with dust and debris from the perpetual bombardment of the city.

Behind the imam stood two soldiers – or militants? – dressed all in black, AK-47 rifles over their shoulders. On the pockmarked wall behind them the outstretched black-and-white flag of ISIS – Islamic State of Iraq and al-Sham – took pride of place.

The imam finally stopped speaking, stepped away from the podium. The crowd murmured in appreciation, then people began to get to their feet. The two soldiers remained on stage as the crowd filed back outside. Nilay didn't move. She sat as calmly as she could, her gaze on the younger, more handsome of the two soldiers as the other spectators slowly filtered out.

She became more nervous by the second, and a large part of her was desperate to get up and follow the others out. But she couldn't do that. Just being here, among these people, wasn't enough any more. She had to get closer, and there was only one way to do that, even though the thought of what was to come terrified her.

27

Even in her short time in Mosul, Nilay had seen how poorly women were treated by ISIS. Far from equal, women weren't just second-class citizens to the men, they were little more than animals. Forced marriage and sexual subjugation was just the beginning. She knew only too well that many of the men used women to satisfy a sadistic side. At the most extreme, ISIS's war on the Yazidi people was both terrifying and unrelenting. Men and children were butchered at will. The women unlucky enough to survive the slaughter were only kept alive to be used as slaves. Nilay and the other women were sometimes required to look after them – to clean them, feed them, and bandage their wounds. Nilay truly had seen the most horrific side of humanity in this place.

Looking at the soldier in front of her, she couldn't believe that he could be so cruel as to be a part of that. Yet, living among these people, she knew how brainwashed and how desensitised to violence they'd all become. Including herself, she realised.

That thought petrified her almost as much as anything else.

Yet she really didn't have a choice, she had to make the next move. She'd come here for a reason: for Aydin. And she wouldn't turn back now.

When Nilay was the last remaining spectator, she got to her feet. The soldiers both looked over in her direction. Not a particularly friendly look on their faces. She walked towards them. At first her legs were wobbly, but she fought against it and idled over, not looking either of them in the eye for more than a fleeting second, though making sure her target knew it was him she wanted to speak to, and not his friend.

The men got the message. The companion slapped his comrade on the back, then turned and walked away. Nilay moved right up to the man, her head bowed. She stopped, looked up into his dark eyes to see a confident smile on his face. Nilay smiled back, with just enough meekness to make him feel in charge – and just enough eagerness to show him her intentions. She knew in that instant that she had him.

Step one complete.

SEVEN

Kabul, Afghanistan

The wood-panelled room in the MI6 safe house was a depressing throwback to the corporate offices of the 1970s, Cox thought. She was surprised not to see a sign on the door demanding staff don flares and a perm in order to enter. She leaned back in the creaky swivel chair and stared at the laptop balanced awkwardly on the narrow work surface, which was clearly designed long before personal computers were the norm.

Cox sighed and looked out of the windows that were covered in grit and sand from the high winds that had bombarded the city the night before. The sun was shining outside now, though Cox was glad to be back on the inside following the botched operation earlier in the day.

The desk phone rang. Cox answered.

'It's me,' Henry Flannigan said in his usual gruff tone.

Flannigan was Cox's level four boss back at Vauxhall Cross in London. She felt sure she knew what this call was about.

'Have you seen?' he asked.

'Seen what?'

'Are you at your computer?'

'Yeah.'

'Check the news. Where have you been, Cox? I thought you of all people would have been all over this.'

'What? I—'

'Call me back. We need a secure line.'

The line went dead. She navigated to the BBC News website and immediately spotted the picture of Ismail Obbadi, aka Wahid. Killed in police custody in Spain?

'What the . . .'

Cox grabbed her mobile phone from her bag. Realised she had a message from Flannigan on there too, requesting a white line call. The safe house was as secure, eavesdropping wise, as it could be, but there was always the chance that the telephone line was somehow compromised. A white line call remained the most secure means of telecommunication – a voice over IP line that was encrypted through a secure real-time transport protocol, or SRTP for short. It meant that both of the devices on either end of the conversation were encrypted, as was the line itself. Not completely foolproof, but far better than using regular telephone lines.

It took a few seconds for the call to connect on Cox's laptop. She didn't bother with any pleasantries.

'Please tell me it's not true,' Cox said.

'You would rather Wahid lived a long and prosperous life?'

'I didn't say that. But I'd rather there was a chance that we could get him to talk, and we certainly can't do that if he's buried in the ground.'

'Yeah, about that? I could say the same thing about Kasim Noor.'

Cox scoffed. Good news travelled fast.

'Noor pulled a gun. There was nothing we could have done. And we still bagged two of them.'

'But only one we actually wanted. What the hell were you thinking? You lost two of your targets so you just picked up some random guy off the street to make up for it?'

'He's not a random guy. He was there with Noor and the others. And he was armed. Once we've ID'd him I'm sure we'll realise this was actually a slice of good fortune.'

31

'Chance'll be a fine thing.'

'But what about Wahid? I can't believe—'

'It's not true. Wahid is still alive.'

Cox took a long inhale. Relief, though it wasn't because she felt Wahid deserved to live. His name and face was recognisable to nearly every person in the West as the leader of a violent terrorist group that had very nearly inflicted catastrophic carnage in cities across Europe last year. Cox had played a huge hand in stopping those attacks, with the help of one of the members of the group – Aydin Torkal, also know as Talatashar.

Unfortunately for Aydin, the press and the authorities hadn't been quite so impressed with his heroics as they had been with Cox's. As far as the world was concerned, Aydin was still one of *them*. A terrorist sleeper no longer dormant – a fugitive at large, at the top of both the FBI and Interpol's most wanted lists. In the aftermath Cox, although she hadn't been formally named in the press, had been nicknamed 'Plain Jane'. A covert MI6 operative who, to the outside world, was portrayed as a kind of female James Bond. How disappointed the public would be to know the truth, Cox thought. She was no action hero, as demonstrated that morning.

'Then why the charade?' Cox asked. 'You've just faked the death of the most recognisable terrorist on the planet.'

'Because Wahid would never tell us what we need him to any other way.'

By which Cox took to mean routine questioning had got nowhere with Wahid. Torture however . . .

'Wahid standing trial would be nothing more than a media circus,' Flannigan said. 'It would make him a martyr. It's the last thing we need.'

Part of Cox wanted to dispute that claim, to argue that trust in the justice system should be unbreakable. But just like Flannigan, she didn't really believe that. As far as she was concerned people like Wahid didn't deserve to have the same rights as other human beings. They forfeited that when they chose to murder innocent people at will. Which was why she felt little guilt at having sent those two men from that morning's raid off to UK black sites.

'Who takes him now?' Cox asked.

'We do. The Spanish authorities couldn't wait to get rid of him, to be honest. He's going to Zed site.'

'Algeria,' Cox said, shutting her eyes. Zed site remained one of the most notorious black sites on the planet. At least to the few people who knew of its existence. To most others it was simply legend.

'He'll arrive later today.'

It wasn't too long ago that Flannigan had been set on taking Aydin there too. Cox had set in motion an escape plan for him to ensure *that* place wasn't his fate. She'd seen some good in Aydin. Her trust had been rewarded, as Aydin had played a huge hand in stopping Wahid and the others. A small part of her now felt jittery that Wahid was to be taken there. Could Wahid concoct an escape too? Surely that couldn't be allowed to happen . . .

'The reason I was calling . . .' Flannigan trailed off, and Cox stayed silent, waiting for him to spit out whatever he was trying to say. 'You've been out there for twelve months, Cox. You need to stop punishing yourself.'

'That's not what I'm doing here.'

'No? You're Plain Jane. A national hero. You shouldn't be stuck in some backwater office scraping the barrel for lowlifes—'

'That's not what I'm doing here!' Cox blasted.

'Then what *are* you doing there?' Flannigan asked.

'I'm trying to finish what I started.'

And she wouldn't stop until she'd achieved that aim. Aydin and Wahid had both grown up and been groomed at a place known only as 'the Farm'. A group of fifteen children, mostly runaways or orphans, or kids kidnapped from enemies, had been raised at the Farm and trained in all manner of combat, arms and terrorism skills. Thirteen of the fifteen had survived the training. Most of those thirteen were now dead. Some were in jail. Aydin was the only one still on the loose. But that wasn't where the story ended. The people behind the Farm were still out there, and they weren't going to stop now. There were likely other groups of children, already being trained in similar places. Identifying the people who set up the Farm, and tracing them, had to be the best way of cracking the whole operation. That remained Cox's number one aim, even if progress in the last few months had almost ground to a halt.

'I can't let another group of kids be brought up like that. It has to stop.'

'And it will,' Flannigan said. 'We'll get Wahid to talk. We'll tear down the entire infrastructure that created him and the others.'

'I know you will. But getting Wahid to talk is not my job.'

'It could be. Come to Algeria.'

'Is that an order or a request?'

Flannigan sighed. 'A request. I'm heading there too. You can be part of this. You know these people better than anyone. Maybe you can break through to Wahid.'

Cox didn't give an immediate answer. She had to admit, the idea of going face to face with that monster held a certain appeal. She had so many questions for Wahid. But in truth she didn't want to bear witness to what was to come for him. Not that she particularly cared what they did to him there, they could tear him limb from limb for all she minded, but that didn't mean she wanted to see it.

'No. I'm sorry,' she said.

'If you change your mind . . .'

'Yeah, I know.'

There was a moment's silence, Cox felt strangely awkward.

'I've got to go,' Cox said.

'OK. But we're not finished on Noor. We'll talk properly about what happened when I have your report.'

'Of course.'

Cox ended the call. She spent a short time perusing the many news articles about Wahid's death, then sat and stared out of the window, thinking through her conversation with Flannigan, and whether she'd made the right choice.

A faint ping from her computer caught her attention. She looked at the screen: an incoming email. On her private account, rather than work. The sender's name was listed simply as '13' and the address was a random string of numbers and letters. The email subject was Shadow Hand.

Cox frowned and opened the email. The message was brief.

They're lying to you. Watch your back.
AT

AT. Aydin Torkal? Cox, feeling her heart lurch, looked around the empty room. She didn't know why. She was all alone. Yet a shiver ran through her as though she'd just seen a ghost. Like she was being watched. Which, she guessed, she was. She glanced over to the tiny camera up in the corner of the room. She quickly deleted the email. Removed it from her deleted items too. Her heart drummed faster and faster in her chest as she struggled to work out the meaning of the message.

Was it really Aydin, or just a trap? For months her work and her activity had been heavily scrutinised both by Flannigan and his superiors. Even though Aydin had helped to bring an end to the plans of terror he and his brothers had concocted,

35

he'd still been vilified in the press the world over. He was a wanted fugitive. The one that got away. No one had explicitly said it to Cox's face, but she felt sure that someone, somewhere, within MI6 believed she was responsible for Aydin being on the loose, that she was still in contact with him.

Was this email the first test of that theory?

She should tell Flannigan. He trusted her. She trusted him. As much as she trusted anyone else, anyway.

No. She decided she couldn't. Not yet. Instead she opened a new email. Typed in the email address that she'd memorised moments before. Sent a response.

We should meet.

She hit send. A moment later she received a 'send failed' notification. The email address was no longer valid.

EIGHT

Cairo, Egypt

Aydin quickly deleted the email account then closed down the browser window on his laptop, thinking about what he should do next. He only hoped he'd given Rachel Cox sufficient food for thought. He didn't have anywhere near enough answers himself yet, but perhaps with a little direction, she could still help him.

The road trip from Alexandria to the country's capital had taken several hours, and it was deep into night-time before Aydin had arrived back at his apartment in central Cairo the previous night. The top floor single-room studio was about as basic and worn as the rest of the building that housed it, but it did have private access to the building's roof terrace, which Aydin was now sitting on – a simple white plastic chair on top of terracotta tiles, scorching hot from the endless daytime sun.

In front of him he had a glimpse of the sprawling Tahrir Square in the distance. Also known as Martyr Square, he recalled seeing the large open space on the news, crammed with protesters, both during the 2011 revolution, and 2013 coup d'état. How different it must be to make a difference as one of many, rather than alone, he mused.

A *ping* on his laptop stole Aydin from his thoughts. He looked at the screen to see the video feed from the front door of his apartment. The building may have been old and decrepit, but Aydin hadn't held back with security and technology. He saw the bald head of a plump man standing outside his apartment. Mr Ahmadi. His landlord. Ahmadi pressed on the buzzer again.

Aydin sighed and closed the laptop then headed across the roof tiles to the staircase. Inside his apartment he glanced quickly over to the bank of computer terminals that were whirring away in the corner of the room inside a built-in cupboard. Since arriving back in Cairo he'd downloaded the data from one of the two hard drives, and had begun the lengthy hacking operation to gain access to the encrypted data. All was going smoothly so far, though he'd likely need at least another couple of days before he could start to filter through the information, looking for what he needed.

Another buzz from the front door followed by a loud knock. Aydin quickly shut the cupboards. He slipped on a skullcap, and stuck the beard in place. Until three days ago the beard had been real. Just a basic disguise to try and hide his true identity. He was on the run after all. Not that in Cairo he'd ever had any hint of trouble. He knew, though, that the UK and other European intelligence agencies were still out there, looking for him. In Cairo he blended, and he'd done as much as he could to keep a low profile. Until the run-in at ATS last night, that is. But it was clear that sooner or later, if he was to find the answers he needed about the Farm, and why he'd been taken there by his father, he'd have to come back out in the open. He wouldn't hide forever.

He'd shaved off the beard, clipped his hair, in order to make himself a more convincing lookalike of Mahi in Alexandria. He'd regrow the beard in time, but for now the fake would have to do when he was face to face with people who *knew* him in Cairo.

Aydin opened the door a few inches and peered out.

'*As salām 'alaykum,*' Aydin said in greeting.

Ahmadi already looked a little put out, his brow creased in a frown.

'*Wa 'alaykum as salām,*' Ahmadi said with little feeling. 'You're back.'

'Just last night,' Aydin said.

'I thought maybe you'd run off. You still owe me for last month's rent.'

'You'll get it today. I promise.'

One of the many problems of renting from a somewhat legitimate landlord was that Aydin had to expect a certain amount of nosiness. In a perfect world he would have stayed completely off the grid, either a secluded house in the middle of the countryside or hopping to different discreet motels every few days. The reality was either of those scenarios were entirely impractical. Yes he was on the run, but renting the apartment in Cairo, as well as the ones he'd had in Aleppo and Kabul over the last twelve months, not only gave him some semblance of normality as he continued his search and his quest for answers, but allowed him to put time and money to good use.

For starters there was no way he could lug all of his computer equipment about with him every few days, and the more places he stayed, the bigger the trail he left behind.

It was now a year since he'd thwarted his brothers' attacks in Europe, and day by day he was getting closer to the truth as to who was behind the Farm. If he could crack the data he'd taken from ATS, he felt like the pieces would finally start to fall together.

Ahmadi craned his neck to look beyond into the apartment.

'I saw someone else coming in here last night.'

'There's no one else. Just me.'

'It didn't look much like you.' Ahmadi stared at the beard but didn't say anything.

'Ah. Yes, that was just a friend. He didn't stay long.'

Ahmadi still didn't look convinced. 'You're not supposed to have anyone else staying here. Extra heads mean extra money.'

'I understand. There's no one staying here but me.'

Aydin went to shut the door. There was a series of beeps and blips from inside the cupboard. Aydin tensed. Not just because he saw Ahmadi's beady eyes narrow further, but because he knew what the sounds indicated. A problem.

Ahmadi thrust his foot into the doorway.

'What was that?'

'Just my computer,' Aydin said.

Just wanting to get the nosy landlord away, Aydin quickly retreated into the apartment, grabbed a stash of cash from his backpack and counted out enough to keep Ahmadi off his back for a few weeks. Doing so would seriously deplete his dwindling cash reserves, but perhaps the peace of mind was worth it.

'Here. That should be enough for now?'

Aydin pushed the notes into Ahmadi's hands. He looked at the money suspiciously, and Aydin thought he was about to say something else. In the end he just snorted, took his foot away and then turned round.

Aydin pushed the door shut and rushed over to the cupboard. He flung open the doors. Saw the error messages on the screen.

'No!' he shouted.

He tore the hard drive away. The error messages continued to flash up and scroll. *Fatal error. Auto data deletion enacted.* And other similarly nauseating notifications.

The encrypted data must have contained a failsafe. A booby trap that would tear it all to shreds if it got into the wrong hands. The hard drive was burning hot in his hand, as though

40

the malware was literally frying the circuit boards. He dropped the device down onto the desk. Typed away on the keyboard. No response. The whole system was frozen.

He bent down, pulled out all the plugs. Was there anything left to salvage? He still had one intact hard drive from ATS, and he'd also backed up his research onto a separate drive, but if he lost the main terminals, then he wasn't sure where he'd go next. He certainly didn't have the money to start over.

Another buzz from the door stole Aydin's attention. He took out his phone and navigated into the app. Sure enough Ahmadi was on the other side of the door once again. Aydin sighed, got to his feet. His gaze flicked from the door to the screen as he moved over. He paused. Ahmadi glanced to his side. Once. Then again. His movements were nervy and jittery.

Aydin stared at the picture. There was no one else in view of the camera. But Aydin was certain Ahmadi wasn't alone.

Together with the fried hard drive, Aydin knew exactly what was happening. The data from ATS had left a trail. A trail right to Aydin's apartment. Someone had found him.

NINE

Another knock at the door. Another glance by Ahmadi over his shoulder.

'Hey,' Ahmadi shouted from the other side of the door. 'It's just me. I need to ask you something else.'

A lie. Aydin rushed through the apartment. Grabbed the second of the drives with the ATS data. Grabbed the backup drive too with all his research and files. The remaining cash. The Turkish passport. The Colt handgun. He threw them all into a backpack. Another buzz and knock on the door. Aydin looked over to his computer equipment. He'd inbuilt a kill switch that would delete everything on there should he become compromised. Well, it looked like that had happened. Even though it was possible the malware on the ATS drive had already eaten through everything, he wanted to be sure.

He bent down to push the plugs back in place. It should only take the system thirty seconds to reboot. Then he heard the *click-click* of the lock on the front door. His eyes shot back to the phone screen. Ahmadi was now standing back from the door. A tall casually dressed man was in front of him, busily picking the lock.

No time.

Aydin jumped up, ran for the stairs to the roof. He'd reached the first step when the front door burst open. There wasn't a second's respite before the man opened fire with a handgun. Bullets raked the staircase wall as Aydin bounded up. Dust and grit filled his eyes and mouth. Coughing to clear his throat, he reached the top and pushed down on the handle, then darted out into the sunshine. He spun round, kicked shut the door, flicked over the outer bolt that he'd put in place for this very purpose.

A moment later there was a slam as the man on the inside threw himself at the closed door. The door would hold. For now. But Aydin needed to get away. He raced over to the far side of the rooftop where a metal staircase ran down the side of the building to a small wraparound balcony on the second floor. He peered over the edge, then jerked back when he saw the dark-clothed man down there, looking up.

No gunshots came, so maybe he hadn't been seen. Still, Aydin was a sitting duck if he stayed on the roof.

He turned and sprinted in the opposite direction. Flinched and ducked when he heard a muffled gunshot. The man in the apartment. Trying to blast his way out.

Aydin jumped up onto the top of the two-foot perimeter wall, took one glance below, then flung himself forward . . .

He landed on the roof of the next building, one storey below, with a thud, rolling into the fall as best he could, to avoid the jarring to his joints. In a flash he was back on his feet, sprinting across a much larger rooftop, dodging between air-conditioning vents and maintenance huts. A crash behind him. No doubt the man had blasted his way through the door locks. There was shouting.

Aydin didn't dare look behind. He climbed a small metal ladder to reach the top of a maintenance unit. Raced across the top and readied for another leap. A gunshot behind him caused a moment of distraction. He wasn't hit, but the sound of the flying bullet so close caused him to lose focus for a split second. Off balance, he more stumbled than jumped over the edge of the building, completely losing his momentum. His body slammed into the brick side wall of the building. He had just enough time to reach up and dig his fingers around the lip of the roof.

The muscles in his arms strained. His shoulder sockets burned. He grimaced and gritted his teeth, used all the strength he had to heave himself up and onto the roof.

Another gunshot. A nearby ricochet. Rather than jump to his feet Aydin rolled, over and over, pushing himself further from the building's edge, hoping his low profile would give him sufficient cover from the shooters.

He was given no chance to dwell. Another gunshot boomed. He risked a glance to see one of the men readying to jump to the rooftop Aydin was on. Behind him, the man who'd been at Aydin's door had a handgun held up close to his face as he took aim.

Aydin rolled over one more time, toppled over an unseen edge. His body fell half a storey and smashed into the tiled roof garden below. A woman jumped up from a sunbed and screamed. Aydin got painfully back to his feet. Finally decided to pull out his own gun. He rushed for the woman. She cowered and screamed even louder. He wasn't going to touch her. Just hoped the close distance would provide the smallest amount of cover.

Once he'd passed her, he burst across the open space that was cluttered with pot plants of various shapes and sizes, crashed through a bamboo screen and came to an abrupt halt on the edge of the roof. He peered down to the street below. He was still five storeys up. He couldn't go down. He looked across to the next building that rose several floors higher. No way could he get to the roof of that one. But he had to move.

There was a boom behind Aydin. He threw himself down. Wasn't sure if the bullet knocked the Colt from his hand or if it had simply come loose as he'd fallen. The gun clattered down to the street below. Aydin rose up, scrambled back a few feet, then dashed forward and leaped. More gunshots as he flew through the air. A bullet whizzed past him, but the next sank into his side. He lifted his arms to protect his face as he crashed through the window of the building opposite. There was a painful scrape on his thigh, across his arm. He rolled into a heap among the shards of glass on a plush carpeted floor. A hotel bedroom. It was empty.

Aydin grimaced in pain. He looked down. Blood seeped through his clothes. He had at least two deep gashes, plus the gunshot to the side. But he couldn't stop to tend to his wounds. He cried out as he clambered back to his feet. He looked to the bedroom door.

Before he knew it an unseen figure came hurtling through the window and smashed into him. Aydin tumbled back to the ground, crying out in pain again. The man rained punches onto Aydin's face. But Aydin hauled up his thigh, sinking the kneecap into the man's groin. The man grimaced and Aydin heaved him up and off him.

They were both on their feet. Squaring off, hunched over and circling each other like wrestlers in a ring. This was the man Aydin had seen outside, on the roof. He wasn't old, maybe late twenties but with a smooth shaved head, thick stubble and a furrowed brow that gave him a menacing appearance. Aydin's gaze flicked to the man's hand. No gun now. Just a shard of glass. Had he lost his gun somewhere in the room? The man flicked his arm out. Aydin jerked back and to the side, avoiding the slashing blow. The man came forward with the glass a second time. Aydin sidestepped, grabbed the flying wrist, twisted the arm and pushed the hand forward, palm towards wrist. The man cried out and his hand opened reflexively, dropping the glass. Aydin didn't stop. He pushed the hand further, heard the crack as the man's wrist snapped.

The man cried out again, but he wasn't done either. He swivelled, caught Aydin on his knee with a roundhouse kick. Aydin's leg buckled inward. He could do nothing to stop himself falling. The man jumped on top. Threw his injured forearm down onto Aydin's throat, using his body weight to crush Aydin's windpipe. With his good hand he thumped Aydin in the side, aiming for the fresh wound there. Aydin cried out. His vision blurred from the pain. The man hit him again and again. Aydin choked and rasped but he was drifting.

His hands searched out to the sides. Trying to find and grasp a piece of glass. He couldn't see what he was doing and the fragments simply scraped and cut the skin and flesh on his hands and arms.

He finally managed to grab on to a piece. He threw his arm up. Plunged the sharpened glass into the man's eye with a horrific squelch. Aydin expected – hoped – for immediate respite. It didn't come. In fact, the man's focus and determination ratcheted up a level. Panicked, Aydin drew out the glass and stabbed again. Again. Again. Blood poured. Spurted. Aydin thrust the glass into the man's neck. He gurgled. Aydin took the shard out and stabbed again. The man's eyes widened. The pressure on Aydin's neck finally lifted. He shoved the man off and he rolled into a heap on the blood-soaked floor, gurgling and spluttering. Aydin jumped on top. Lifted the man's head.

'Who are you?' Aydin screamed.

The man choked on blood, tried to say something.

'Who sent you?' Aydin shouted.

The man's head lolled. His gurgling stopped. He was dead.

TEN

Aydin quickly checked the man's pockets. Nothing. No wallet. No ID. He growled in frustration. He had no doubt the data stolen from ATS had led the wolves to his door. But just who were they? Police? Intelligence? Or something more sinister. There was no time to dwell. The second shooter was still out there.

Aydin got to his feet and tentatively crept to the window. Risked a glance out and over to the adjacent rooftop. No sign of the second man. But Aydin didn't believe he'd scarpered. He had to get away before another attack was launched.

He rushed into the en-suite bathroom. Did a pretty lousy job of washing the blood from his face, hands and arms. Grabbed the crisp white bathrobe hanging on a hook on the back of the open door. Went to his backpack and took out the lighter. He moved over to the curtains and held the inch-high flame at the corner. It only took a couple of seconds for the fire to start spreading up. Aydin stepped to the opposite curtain. Lit the edge. Then he pulled the bedsheets over the edge of the mattress and lit those too. Within a few seconds flames were leaping up the walls and across the ceiling, and the intense heat caused Aydin's face to sting.

The fire alarm wailed. Ceiling sprinklers kicked in. The immature fire wouldn't spread far with the water cascading down, but at least the alarm would provide the distraction he needed.

Aydin slipped the robe over his blood-soaked clothes, being careful not to get any crimson on the outside of the white material. Out in the corridor he could hear doors opening and closing. Footsteps. Disgruntled moans and groans of the other guests. Aydin moved over to the door and looked through the peephole. If the hotel's fire response was good, it wouldn't take management long to pinpoint the source of the alarm, or to discover the dead body in the room. Aydin had to move.

He opened the door and looked out before stepping into the corridor behind a middle-aged couple. Three doors further down a younger couple, northern European, were just coming out of their room. The man was slim, only a couple of inches taller than Aydin. Aydin glanced behind him. There was no one else there. He dropped his pace slightly. The two couples in front edged away. He got to the young couple's door just a fraction of a second before it self-closed. He pushed his hand across to stop the latch from catching. Checked again behind him, then to the couple to make sure they didn't have a sudden change of heart and turn back. No. Up ahead, Aydin could hear shouting. Hotel staff, corralling the guests. Explaining this wasn't a drill. The foursome in front picked up their pace, eager to make it out. Aydin slipped into the room. Took only a few seconds to grab a clean pair of jeans and a t-shirt, which he stuffed into his backpack. He didn't have time to change now, but with the blood on his own gear, he'd need to before long.

He moved back out into the corridor and quickly regathered with the groups of people descending the stairs. Aydin kept his head down, staying as close as he could to the people in front, not risking making eye contact with anyone. He'd sense a threat, if there was one.

He was soon among the crowds in the hotel's main expansive foyer. Outside the glass-fronted entrance a fire engine screeched to a halt. On seeing the flashing lights the guests' panic levels heightened, their movements quickening. Aydin stayed in step with them, herding towards the doors that would take him back into the open. He heard more sirens outside and briefly looked up to see two police cars pulling to a stop outside. That was not what he needed.

As he glanced down he noticed the red on the bathrobe. He hadn't yet had a chance to inspect the wound on his leg, or the others on his body, but blood had seeped not just through his jeans but through the thick towelling of the robe too. His heart beat faster. The exit was a few steps away, but if the police saw him, robe over his clothes, blood all over, they'd surely stop him.

Aydin moved more quickly, gently brushing past people in an effort to get to the exit. He heard one or two hushed questions, comments about his bloodied appearance. His legs twitched, readying him for action. As he stepped through the doorway onto the pavement outside, his eyes locked with those of a policeman for a split second. The policeman's eyes narrowed. Had his hand closed around the grip of the pistol holstered on his hip?

Then a shout from somewhere inside the foyer. Aydin didn't look to see what it was. A guest falling in the melee perhaps? A skirmish of some sort. Maybe someone had already found the dead body. Either way, the policeman's attention was grabbed. Aydin ducked right and walked as fast as he could, away from the hotel, away from the police, away from the crowds. He looked behind him. No one was paying him any attention. Still no sign of the second shooter either. Perhaps the police had scared him off. For now.

Aydin turned into a side alley and stopped. Stripped off the robe. Then ran, as best he could with his debilitating wounds.

Despite his injuries, it didn't take long before he'd lost himself in the labyrinth of streets in the old town. He was sure there was no one on his tail. He'd escaped the clutches of whoever had come after him. Quite who they were, he didn't know, but he didn't like close shaves. He'd left a clear marker now. A trail that could be followed. After twelve months in the shadows, his time was running out.

One thing was for sure. His stay in Egypt was over. With the remaining stolen data from ATS weighing heavy in his backpack, it was time to plan the long journey east.

ELEVEN

Mosul, Iraq

Life in the caliphate was as outdated, horrific and barbaric as Nilay had feared. She'd very deliberately thrown herself into the middle of the hornet's nest. After all, what better way to find what she needed than from the inside? She had to believe that the end goal was worth the considerable risk.

Only one month after first meeting Sajad, the two of them had been 'married'. The role she was playing was, in many ways, simple, even if being there made her question her own morality on a daily basis. Still, the few young Western women who flocked to ISIS were openly welcomed, and outnumbered several times over by men in the ranks. Women like Nilay were in high demand, and for the most part she was treated well – at least humanely. Certainly much better than the poor Yazidis, and other women who'd been captured.

Nilay soon found that acquiescence was the route to a life of relative safety.

But she wasn't in Iraq just to acquiesce.

A further month after her marriage to Sajad, the Battle of Mosul had begun, as alliance forces tried in vain to regain control of the beleaguered ISIS-held city. Nightly air raids were the norm as Turkish warplanes bombarded militant strongholds. Outnumbered and out-powered, the caliphate was quickly losing control, but not confidence.

Nilay, unlike the deluded ISIS soldiers all around her, knew that it was only a matter of time before the Western-backed Iraqi forces regained the city. She had to get what she needed before then – before the very people who could provide her answers in this city were wiped out. She just had to hope and pray that she wouldn't be killed alongside them.

She walked in the sunshine down a street of yellow rubble, next to her friend, Yolanda, a twenty-year-old from Belgium. Both had their burqas on – a requirement laid down by the elders – and Nilay was sweltering in the heat. Burned-out jeeps and cars lay abandoned on what used to be the road. Up ahead an ISIS roadblock stretched across, blocking anyone from leaving the war zone and entering the booby-trapped no-man's-land that led to the Iraqi army's base camps. To do so was punishable by death, if the booby traps didn't get you first.

Not even two weeks ago, one of Nilay's few companions in the commune, a young Austrian girl, had been beaten to death in the street, in front of her so-called husband, for trying to sneak out of the ISIS-controlled area in the night. Nilay had been made to watch. Everyone had. The rules were clear. The punishments too.

As they approached the roadblock, Nilay noticed the armed men there take notice, as though she was about to make a mad dash for freedom. They needn't have worried. She wasn't that stupid. And she couldn't leave yet. Not until she had what she needed.

They turned right and were soon at the grocery stall where there was already a queue of four other women in plain black dress waiting to be served. It reminded Nilay of a book she'd read as a teenager – The Handmaid's Tale – about a dystopian future where women were second-class citizens. The 'handmaids', who belonged to their male masters, all wore identical dress and would go out on the streets under close watch of armed guards to carry out daily chores. Even the whispered conversations the women had when out and about bore a resemblance to the rebellious images Nilay remembered from that book. Not that the women in Mosul were all rebellious as such, but Nilay was slowly learning which were more open than others. Yolanda was one such woman.

They approached the stall and moved to the far corner, looking over the selection of ground spices.

'The three women who came in last night,' Nilay said, just loud enough for Yolanda to hear. 'Where were they from?'

Yolanda looked away, checking no one was listening.

'They're Iraqis,' Yolanda whispered in her thick accent. 'Their husbands were killed in an attack on a convoy. There were several families trying to escape to the other side.'

Nilay knew that Yolanda had been tasked with looking after the women, preparing them for their new ordeals. In most ways, Nilay would have described Yolanda as normal, but for the fact that somehow she'd been radicalised online back in her native Belgium. She'd had an online 'marriage' ceremony with the ISIS soldier she was now living with before finally fleeing her parents' home aged nineteen. Although Yolanda had never said so, Nilay sensed the life in Mosul was quite different to the one she'd been sold.

'Were there any children?' Nilay asked.

'Some were killed. The others . . . I don't know.' Yolanda looked down. Went to shuffle away.

'What is it?' Nilay said, grabbing Yolanda's arm. 'Where did they take the children?'

Yolanda snatched her arm back. One or two of the other women glanced over but then quickly got back to what they were doing.

'Not here,' Yolanda said.

Nilay decided to drop the subject and both went about getting the supplies they needed. Soon after, they were heading back along the same bomb-destroyed streets.

'So?' Nilay asked.

'So what?'

'The children? Why do the children always disappear?'

'Why do you think? They give them guns. They strap bombs on them.' Yolanda spoke these words with a certain bitterness that Nilay hadn't heard before. Nilay thought about playing it cool, but no . . . Push on, she decided.

'They wouldn't sacrifice them all so easily. And even if it's only for cannon fodder, the elders must still train them. So where?'

'You're asking a lot of questions.'

'Because I trust you.'

The two women turned to face one another.

'I'm looking for someone too,' Nilay said. She was aware of the story of Yolanda's younger sister. When Yolanda had first fled to Iraq, she'd been promised there'd be a space for her sister too, then only fourteen years old. ISIS had eventually managed to get their claws into the young girl and she'd run away from home, but she'd disappeared en route, somewhere in Eastern Europe, and no one had heard from her for over six months.

'Who?' Yolanda asked.

'My brother. He was taken from our home when he was a young boy. Before I came.'

Nilay's heart was now drumming in her chest. She'd never told anyone her own story, nor even made any mention of Aydin to Sajad or Yolanda, or anyone else.

'You think he's a soldier now? Is that why you're here?'

'It's partly why I'm here.'

'What's his name?'

Nilay thought about answering that but decided against it. 'I need to find him. That's why I'm asking these questions.'

Yolanda sighed. 'I honestly don't know much. But I've heard rumours. Of a place. The Farm. Maybe that's where they all go, maybe it's not. Maybe your brother was there.'

The Farm. Not the first time Nilay had heard that term. What had at first seemed like a dark fairy tale she'd now firmly decided held real truth.

They took a right turn and walked the short distance to the bombed-out apartment block where Nilay and Sajad and two dozen other people had been staying for the last few weeks. Yolanda lived in the next block along which was similarly decrepit.

'You won't say anything, will you?' Nilay asked when they stopped outside the entrance.'

'If I don't say anything, how will it help you to find your brother?'

Nilay grabbed Yolanda's arm again. 'Please. I don't know if it's safe. For me, or him. Even you.'

Yolanda didn't say a word. Nilay let go. 'I'm sorry.'

'I'll see you tomorrow.' Yolanda turned and walked off and, as she watched her friend, Nilay had to try hard to hold back her tears.

Had she just ruined everything?

She entered the building through the exposed stone entrance and clambered up the staircase, avoiding the loose stone and rubble underfoot as best she could. On her floor, she pushed open the creaky wooden door to the apartment and stepped inside. The TV was on. It amazed her that despite the destruction in the city, many mod cons remained: TV, radio, mobile phone signal, even occasional internet. After all, the so-called caliphate's strength relied heavily on spreading its hateful propaganda far and wide using technology; a working mobile phone with enough signal to send videos was as powerful to ISIS as a battle tank.

Which worked to Nilay's advantage in many ways.

Through conversations with women like Yolanda, along with her own computer-based research, she was slowly building a picture of the place often referred to as 'the Farm'. All of her files were on a single thumb drive she kept hidden in the bedroom. Sajad had no idea what Nilay got up to when he was out toting his gun around. Her treachery actually made living with him all the more bearable – and so did the thought of crossing him and his comrades without their knowledge.

Nilay spotted Sajad sitting on the worn sofa in what passed as the living room. He was hunched over, watching a news report on the tiny TV, the image on the screen grainy and flickering.

'Where've you been?' he said grumpily, not looking up.

'To get fresh food.'

'I expected you to be home,' he said.

He looked up to her, an angry scowl on his face.

'I'm sorry,' she said. 'I'm here now.'

'Go to the bedroom. I don't have all day. I need to be back out in less than an hour.'

Nilay inwardly cringed, but showed no reaction on her face.

'Of course,' she said, turning and heading towards the bed.

TWELVE

Half an hour later Nilay was on her side of the bed, facing away from Sajad as he smoked. Did he notice her shaking with disgust every time he had sex with her? she wondered. He'd never said so, had never even intimated that he was dissatisfied with her in the bedroom. She wasn't sure how much longer she could keep the pretence up. She'd made up her mind that the sacrifice of her body was worth it to discover the answers she needed, but it didn't make the act any easier.

If she had the chance to start over, would she search for a different path?

'There's a young boy I saw today in the square,' Nilay said, pushing the thought to the side like she did so well now. 'His name's Akram, do you know him?'

Sajad shuffled in the bed. It had actually been the day before that she'd seen Akram, but what was the difference to Sajad?

'I heard about him, yes.'

'He's from London. His mother was killed two nights ago by the bombs. He's all alone now.'

Colloquially some of the residents referred to their enclave as 'Little Britain', for the unusually high number of people who'd originated in the UK. But in truth the origins of its people was far more diverse: France, Spain, Belgium, the Caribbean, Turkey, Egypt, Australia. ISIS's venom had poisoned all corners of the globe it seemed, and there was no shortage of disillusioned young men who welcomed the idea of carrying out their violent fantasies in the real world. Plus disillusioned young women like Yolanda who were conned into believing being the wife of an ISIS soldier was something glorious.

'What will happen to him now?' Nilay said 'He's only eight years old. He has no one.'

The boy and his mother had only been in Mosul for a few weeks. She hadn't married any of the fighters before she'd been killed. Nobody would care about the boy now, and Nilay genuinely felt sorry for him. But she also hoped she could use his position as bait. More than once she'd had the intimation that Sajad was well informed about the training of young recruits. But what did he know specifically of the Farm?

'He's not your concern,' Sajad said. Nilay turned over in the bed and caught his gaze. He was still glowing from the aftermath of intercourse; if ever there was a time to gently pry, this was surely it.

'No? Then what are we fighting for here, if not for the future of the children?'

'He'll be fine.'

Sajad looked away.

'But how do you know he'll be fine? He needs a parent. I could look after him. We could look after him.'

'No,' Sajad said. 'There really is no need. It's already been arranged.'

'What has?'

'That's enough. I told you already, it's not your concern.'

'The Farm. Is that where they're sending him?'

Sajad's eyes narrowed. He didn't need to ask the question.

'I've only heard people talk about it. Rumours. They say the Farm is where some of the children are taken. The ones with most potential. Is it true? Does it exist?'

58

'You should be careful who you talk to.'

'But is it real?'

Sajad said nothing. He got up and stretched his hands up into the air. Nilay shivered, looking at his naked body. Not because his body was in any way disgusting, but for what it represented to her.

Nilay snapped herself back into focus.

'I heard that Aziz al-Addad is known as the Teacher there,' Nilay said. 'Have you met him?'

Sajad turned to her. The look on his face now was one of outright suspicion. Anger.

'I'm sorry,' she said, bowing her head.

'I said already, stop listening to stupid rumours. You'll get yourself and others hurt.'

That was enough warning for her. For now. She'd opened the door at least, but now wasn't the time to head through it.

Gunshots outside. The rat-a-tat of automatic weapons. Sajad glared at Nilay then grabbed his boxer shorts from the floor and headed to the window. He peered out. First across the street to where the sound of gunfire was coming from, then into the sky.

He spun round, a mixture of concern and anger on his face.

'The Turks. They're back.'

He grabbed his fatigues from the floor, hurriedly threw them on. Nilay got up from the bed, dressed quickly as the distant sounds of the jet engines grew louder and louder. She knew from experience that if you could hear them, it was already too late.

The men outside shouted and threw orders at each other. Seconds later there was a chorus of bangs and booms. RPGs and anti-aircraft guns trying to shoot the jets down.

Nilay was still pulling her dress over her head when a huge explosion erupted nearby. The whole building rocked and swayed. Windows shattered. Dust and grit burst into the bedroom, knocking Nilay to the floor.

Her ears were ringing. She coughed and spluttered.

'Sajad!' she shouted.

She tried to get to her feet. She could see nothing in front of her. Another explosion. She soon found herself back on the floor, choking on dust, her vision gone, her mind distant and foggy.

'Nilay!'

She heard his voice. Felt the tug on her arm.

'We have to get underground.'

He pulled her up and together they fought their way through the debris. Nilay could see nothing, the cloud of dust was too thick. They used their hands to guide them down the stairs to the outside. The explosions, further away now, carried on. The rattling gunfire was non-stop.

By the time they made it to the street, the dust was just starting to settle. Men with guns were running in every direction. Women and children were crying and cowering, looking for shelter. The building next to theirs was completely destroyed. People were staring zombie-like at the mess, screaming. Dozens of people lived there. Or had, at least.

'Yolanda,' Nilay said, quietly, and felt a wave of genuine sadness. There was no sign of her outside the building. There was only one other place she'd be.

'No time,' Sajad shouted, 'come on!'

He grabbed her arm and pulled her along. She ran with him. Looked up to the sky. It was clear blue above. Not a wisp of cloud. No sign of the jets. But she knew they'd be back.

As they moved along she could hear screaming, getting louder. Another building reduced to a pile of rubble. A crater in the road. Blood-soaked bodies lay strewn on the streets. Dismembered limbs. A woman was wandering around in aimless circles, covered in blood, her left arm dangled off her shoulder by a thread of skin. Nilay gulped down the bile in her throat.

She heard the whoosh of air above.

'Get down!' Sajad screamed.

The explosion tore Nilay from Sajad's grasp, threw her into the air. She tumbled, but had no idea of direction. She came to a crashing halt against a wall, or maybe the ground. Once again she could see nothing. Could only hear the screams and the echoing gunfire as she drifted into unconsciousness.

Nilay had no idea how long she was out for. When her eyes finally opened, she was lying on the sunken roof of a red car. Smoke billowed up from the building across the way. The gunfire continued, but sounded more distant now. At first she heard no voices, no shouting, no footsteps. Painfully, she pushed herself up onto an elbow. She didn't seem to be seriously injured, just disorientated.

'Sajad!' she shouted out as best she could, though her voice sounded weak and croaky. She looked around. Spotted the body, face down on the pavement ten yards away.

'Sajad!' Nilay shouted again, surprised at the grief that washed over her. Where did that come from?

She jumped down from the car, stumbled on the ground and fell into a heap. It was an effort just to stand. Aching, she headed over to him.

Shouting behind her. Screaming. Gunfire. Closer than before. She crouched behind the back of the car. Seconds later a black-clad figure came skidding round a corner, clutching an assault rifle. An ISIS fighter. Nilay didn't recognise him, but he was young, only a teenager.

A moment later two green-fatigued men came from round the same corner. Both were armed, and both bore the green, black and red insignia of the Iraqi Army. One of the men lifted his weapon, fired three times. The young man in front jolted and skidded into a crumpled heap on the ground just yards from Nilay.

She was frozen to the spot. She stared over at the man on the ground. He was still breathing and staring right at her. She heard more heavy footsteps. Looked up to see a whole line of men in green huddling at the end of the street, weapons drawn, scanning the area ahead and what remained of the buildings around them. They edged forward. Eight of them. Ten. Twelve.

Another burst of black as an ISIS fighter bounded out into the open from his hiding place. He opened fire and bullets raked the ground. Two Iraqi soldiers fell but the attack was short-lived, and the insurgent was soon on the ground in a pool of his own blood.

Nilay was shaking with fear. The Iraqi soldiers continued to edge forward. She could try to run. She could try to hide. But would they just shoot her if they saw her doing that? She wasn't one of them, not really, but the Iraqis didn't know that.

There was another option. A risk, but wasn't everything? She lifted her hands into the air.

'Please, don't shoot me. Please!'

She slowly rose up from behind the car. The soldiers all stopped and trained their weapons on her. She felt sick at the sight. Even though she clearly wasn't a soldier, would they suspect she was a suicide bomber?

'Thank God,' she said, emotion getting the better of her. 'Thank God you're here. Please. You have to help me.'

Shakily, she sank down onto her knees, keeping her hands high in the air. Two soldiers crept forward to her as tears, black from grit, rolled down her face.

THIRTEEN

Liverpool, England

Monday morning and the weather in Liverpool was typically crap. The sky was a single sheet of dark grey and the rain pelted down, forming a layer of surface water on every road and pavement around. Leo Thornhill stomped along the paving slabs, the splash-back as his rubber-soled boots pounded the ground reached up past his knees. His oversized raincoat was at least doing the job of keeping the water off his body though he was beginning to worry that the contents of his backpack would soon be sodden. The material itself was water resistant, but it surely wasn't made for this kind of rain?

Leo took a right onto Prescott road, a wide street with mostly run-down red-brick terraced houses stretching away in both directions. Up ahead, by a busy crossroads where a giant Tesco superstore had been surreptitiously plonked, was the overcrowded bus stop. Except today it was even busier than usual.

Leo pulled the hood further over his head to avoid the water dripping off the peak of his baseball cap and down his neck, then carried on to the bus stop. There was no chance of a space under the shelter so he stood in the wet and waited, the patter of rain from the overflowing gutters of the nearby terrace loud in his ears.

It only took two minutes for the green double-decker number ten bus to appear in the distance. A few of the waiting crowd groaned in relief.

As the bus came to a stop there was a brief melee as the eager passengers momentarily forget their inbuilt British queuing etiquette and pushed and shoved each other to get on first and out of the driving rain. Leo stayed back. As miserable as it was out in the rain, a few more seconds wouldn't cause any lasting damage – he hoped.

Eventually, second to last, Leo stepped on board, paid in cash, nodded to the driver then carried on through the busy lower deck. There were still a small number of seats remaining and Leo slipped the backpack from his shoulders and took one by the window. He knew that within a couple more stops it would be standing room only as the bus neared the city centre, so was glad to have found a seat at all.

The bus pulled away. At the next stop a couple of hundred yards down the road, a further crowd of more than ten got on. The seat next to Leo was taken by a middle-aged woman in a see-through plastic mac, who was on the wrong side of wide. She squeezed into the seat, bumping and jostling against Leo to fit in. She didn't offer any kind of apology. Leo said nothing. Just stared out the window.

After the next stop, as predicted, there were no seats remaining, and six people were left standing. When the bus pulled off Leo reached down to his backpack and unzipped it a few inches, did a quick check that everything was in place and untainted by the rain. It was. He zipped it back up and used his feet to push the bag further under the seat in front, out of the way.

They were fast approaching the next stop. Leo leaned across the woman and pressed the red stop button that gave a faint tinkle to alert the driver.

'Excuse me, please,' he said to the woman when the bus began to slow. She turned and glared at him like he was an obnoxious fool then grunted and shuffled to get herself up.

Leo thanked her then eased his way through the standing crowd to the front.

'Hey!' came the shout from behind him. Leo turned and saw it was the woman. 'Hey, mister. Wasn't that your bag?'

Leo pursed his lips, shook his head. 'Not mine,' he said.

The bus came to a stop. Leo turned and the doors wheezed open and he had to push past the waiting group outside who were all overeager to get on. Once clear, Leo walked a few brisk steps then stopped under the awning of a cafe. He turned and watched as the last of the waiting passengers – a young mum with a double-decker pushchair – somehow managed to cram herself inside. A part of Leo hoped that maybe there wasn't any room for her or her babies, but she managed to get on. The bus's indicator flashed, the red brake lights flicked off, and the double-decker slowly pulled back into the road with a roar of its plucky diesel engine.

Leo fished his phone from his pocket. Navigated to the self-made app. Pressed the red button . . .

FOURTEEN

Kabul, Afghanistan

Having deleted the mysterious email, Cox spent the next two hours sitting in the lounge of the safe house, staring into space in front of her, occasionally out of the window, just thinking, as the sun made its slow march towards the horizon. Doing so got her nowhere. She simply couldn't decide whether or not telling anyone about the email, and who she believed it was from, was the best thing to do.

If she chose not to, would her superiors tolerate her holding back potential key information from them again? She'd never been one to shy away from putting her own neck on the line to do what she saw as the *right* thing. But was withholding information about Aydin Torkal really the right thing to do? Either for him or for anyone else?

Failing to find an answer, Cox grumbled to herself, got up from the sofa and moved to the kitchenette for some food. She opened the fridge door.

'Damn it!'

She'd forgotten she was out of everything save for bottled water, some crappy cheese that had turned deep yellow around the edges, and a mound of cooked meat and rice that she'd bought from a deli three days before, and which she was still making her way through. She wasn't sure she could

66

take that again, and so grabbed her keys and headed for the door.

With a headscarf on and her press lanyard and passport in her pocket should anyone happen to stop her and question her presence in the city, Cox exited the apartment building out onto the wide paved street on the edges of Khair Khāna — for the most part an area much like those found in any large city in the world, with glassy, high-rise offices, hotels and apartment buildings, together with shops and restaurants aplenty. Yet despite its relative normality, the threat of violence was never far away, whichever part of Kabul you were in. Less than two weeks ago twelve people had been killed in a suicide bomb attack at a mosque in Khair Khāna, just a couple of hundred yards from where Cox was walking. However sensible you were, and however well you knew the area, there was always the outside chance of finding yourself in the wrong place at the wrong time.

That said, the area was, compared to others, surprisingly untouched by the inner fighting that had blighted the country over the past two decades and that had seen much of Kabul destroyed — largely due to Khair Khāna's geographic position in the north-west of the city, with rebel groups including the Taliban having been based in and launching their many attacks from the south, the other side of the Kabul River that dissected the city.

Sticking to the wide, traffic-heavy streets, Cox walked down to where there was a large shopping mall, one corner of which contained a traditional food market. As she walked through the tall glass doors into the large open space, the smell of the wide array of food immediately hit her, and with each step she took, another scent or flavour tickled her nose; spices, fruit, vegetables, freshly cooked traditional breads, rice, kebabs cooking on hot griddles. Cox's stomach rumbled away as she settled on a stall where several dozen foot-long lamb kebabs sizzled away on cast-iron griddles heated by coal.

She smiled at the vendor and was about to ask for one of his specialities when she was distracted by someone else. Beyond the kebab seller stood a man with his back to her, at a spice stall across the way. He wore a smart linen shirt, khaki trousers. He wasn't particularly tall, but stocky in the frame. The man's skin was far lighter than those around him.

Cox muttered an apology to the vendor then edged round the counter, trying to keep her eyes on the man she'd seen. Even from the back, he was familiar to her.

She moved round the corner as a large group of men walked by and temporarily blocked her view of him. By the time she'd reached the spice stall he had already gone.

Cox stopped, looked left and right. No sign of him at all in the busy market now. Yet she was sure about what she'd seen.

Distracted, Cox forgot all about the food, and kept her eyes busy as she moved through the crowds and back to the main doors. Outside, the low sun cast a deep orange glow over the buildings in front of her. Long shadows stretched far down the street. She took a breath. Turned to her left, and almost stepped right into him.

'Flannigan!' Cox stepped back. 'What the hell is going on?'

Henry Flannigan looked unfazed by her startled reaction.

He held a finger up to his lips. Looked over her shoulder, as if checking she were alone. Cox, her nervousness peaking, cast her eyes around too. There was no one else there. At least no one paying them any attention. Flannigan nodded for her to follow. She had so many questions, but she also knew when to keep her mouth shut.

She followed her boss along the city streets, back the way she'd come minutes earlier. Except they didn't go to the safe house. Flannigan soon led Cox away from the main roads, into a secluded back alley. Cox followed. Anyone else in the world and she'd have run a mile. But this was Flannigan.

They stopped behind two stinking, industrial-sized bins, out of sight of the street further down. Cox remained a couple of steps from her boss.

Flannigan reached into his pocket and pulled out a small wand metal detector. Flannigan raised his eyebrows. As if asking for her permission. Cox nodded, though by now she was as angry by his charade as she was confused. He came forward with the wand. Took his time to sweep it over her body. After a minute or so he stepped back, satisfied, and put the wand away.

He held up his hands, open palms facing her. Cox nodded again. Flannigan performed a brisk search of her body. Working up and down her legs, her arms, her torso. Flitting through her pockets. He took her phone. Cox didn't protest. Just remained passive the whole time. She understood what he was doing, even if she didn't know why, yet she felt violated still. Did he not trust her? Because of that email? she wondered.

After he'd finished he stepped back, stuck his hands in his pockets.

'Now we can talk,' he said.

'Damn fucking right we can. What the—'

He held up a hand to stop her rant.

'Why don't we go and get one of those kebabs. They looked bloody amazing.'

Cox paused. Thinking through her response.

'You're right. They are. But you're paying.'

She turned on her heel and strode down the alley back to the road.

FIFTEEN

Cox sat with her back to the wall in the seating area within the market. The tables around them were filled with locals drinking tea and coffee and eating the delicacies on offer from the nearby stalls. Flannigan was to Cox's left, on the corner of the table. Neither of them wanted to turn their backs to the people around them, it seemed.

'What was with the pretence?' Cox asked, her tone and her manner as cool as the untouched grilled meat in front of her.

Flannigan put a chunk of meat into his mouth and held Cox's eye as he chewed.

'What pretence?' he finally said, his continued nonchalance riling Cox further.

'We white-lined a couple of hours ago. You must already have been in Kabul.'

'I never said otherwise.'

Cox huffed her disapproval.

'You need to tell me what's going on,' Cox said.

'I could say the same thing to you.'

'Meaning what, exactly?'

Flannigan said nothing to that, though Cox wondered again whether the issue was that email. But like she'd said, Flannigan must already have been in Kabul by then so what was going on? Cox looked around at the other people sitting nearby. She was positive, whatever his agenda, that Flannigan wouldn't have travelled to Kabul alone. So where were his security?

Cox spied a well-groomed man in his thirties, dark hair, thick beard, who was sitting with a coffee and a broadsheet newspaper. He'd looked at Cox more than once in the last couple of minutes. Was that just because she and Flannigan stood out among the crowd? There were close to two dozen other people within Cox's field of vision. Any of them could have been planted there by Flannigan, Cox knew. Even the young couple off to her right with the soundly sleeping baby. Either that thing was comatose or it was just a prop.

Or perhaps Cox was just reading too much into the situation.

The situation. What the hell was the situation anyway?

'I'm guessing you've heard about Liverpool?'

'Liverpool?'

'Jesus, do you even get news here.'

'Yes. But I'm not glued to the TV all day every day.'

Flannigan sighed. 'A bomb exploded on a bus in the centre of Liverpool this morning.'

Cox's mouth opened but she said nothing. She was as shocked as she was horrified.

'We don't know how many are dead yet, nor who's behind it. No one has claimed it.'

Cox shook her head in disbelief.

'But we will get to the bottom of it,' Flannigan said. 'I have to ask you, Cox, and I need a truthful answer. Do you know where Aydin Torkal is?'

'You can't possibly think he—'

Flannigan's fist drummed the table lightly. 'Do you know where he is?' Not even a touch of friendliness in his tone.

'No.'

'Have you had any contact with him at all?'

'No.' The answer – or was it a lie? – came out without any forethought.

Flannigan bent down and fished in the plastic shopping bag he'd brought with him. He drew out a printout of an online news article.

He put the piece of paper on the table. Cox didn't pick it up, just scanned over the story. A robbery at a high-tech company in Alexandria, Egypt. Two snapshots of the uniformed suspect, though in both of the grainy images the man's head was down and his face covered by a baseball cap.

'What is this?'

'Alexandria Technology Services. You heard of it?'

'No.'

'Which figures. Neither had I until this happened yesterday. Turns out ATS is a satellite team. One of ours.'

'Someone robbed MI6?'

Flannigan winced at her words. But she didn't believe anyone within earshot – other than his stooges – had a clue what they were talking about. Otherwise they wouldn't be having the conversation there at all. He'd already swept her for bugs or other listening devices, so he was clearly being ultra-cautious. Though she did now wonder: was he, for whatever reason, recording their conversation?

'Basically, yes.'

'And what exactly does ATS do?' Cox asked.

'That information is beyond your pay grade.'

'And yours?'

Flannigan shrugged.

'Then why are you bothering to tell me this at all?'

'Take a closer look at those pictures.'

Cox did so. She could already guess what his next question would be.

72

'So now whenever there's a problem in the world, Aydin Torkal becomes suspect number one.'

'I'll ignore your flippancy. Do you recognise the man in the picture?'

'Recognise what? His uniform? The cap covering his face? You think that's Aydin?'

Flannigan nodded.

'Based on what, exactly?' Cox's tone was now even sharper than it had been before. 'His slender shoulders? The shape of his thighs? I can see the same as you in this picture, which is bugger all. It's a person, not an octopus, but that's about it. It could be anyone.'

'No. That's not it. It's a man. Even though the shots are from above we can also tell his height by matching against what's around him. We can tell the size of his hands. His feet. The length of his arms. We also have descriptions given to us by the security guards and police who chased him from the scene.'

'So he got away?'

'Clearly. Otherwise we wouldn't be having this conversation.'

'You think I knew about this?'

Flannigan didn't say anything.

Cox stared at the pictures again. 'You really believe this is Aydin?'

'Everything we have about the description is consistent.'

'And how many other men in the world fit that description?'

'A more apt question would be how many men in the world fit that description and have both the cause to infiltrate an MI6 facility and also the skills to achieve that aim without getting caught.'

'What makes you think Aydin has a cause to infiltrate an MI6 facility? He has no quarrel with us.'

'Is that your professional opinion, or do you know that for a fact?'

Cox didn't answer the question. She didn't believe either answer she gave would satisfy Flannigan.

'And you can't be telling me he robbed ATS in Alexandria then immediately hopped on a plane to England to launch a bomb attack in Liverpool.'

Flannigan's face turned even more sour. 'Again, is that your professional opinion?'

Cox sighed. 'Why are you talking to me like this? Why are you here at all?'

'Isn't it obvious? Somebody, somewhere within MI6 isn't playing ball.'

'You think that's me?'

'I think it could be anyone.'

'What about you? You're the one who's come here on the sly, who's had me checked for devices. Perhaps it's you with the hidden agenda.'

Flannigan gave Cox a long, cold glare. She looked away first.

'What would Aydin want from ATS?' Cox asked.

'I told you already, it's beyond your remit to know what they do. It's questionable whether I should even have told you about them.'

'Well if you only give me half the story, then I'm afraid you can only ever expect half an answer.'

Flannigan raised an eyebrow. Took the last cube of meat from his plate. He indicated Cox's untouched plate.

'You not eating that?' he said with a full mouth.

'Lost my appetite.'

He shrugged. Fished into his plastic bag again. A senior MI6 officer walking around Kabul with top secret documents in nothing more than a supermarket carrier bag. Was that called hiding in plain sight?

'I haven't been entirely forthcoming with you about Wahid,' Flannigan said.

He placed the bundle of papers on the table, but put his forearms over them so Cox couldn't yet see any of the content.

'So he's not gone to Zed site?' Cox said, sounding calm though her anger was rising again. How many more lies and deceits?

'No, he damn well has gone there. But the events leading up to that point are a bit . . . well, *murky*.'

Flannigan looked around him now, as though for the first time concerned about eavesdroppers.

'Have you ever come across an Eric Neumayer?'

Cox briefly wracked her brain.

'No,' she said. 'Not that I recall.'

'He's dead.'

Flannigan paused, as if expecting Cox to respond to that blunt statement. She didn't.

'Eric Neumayer was a low-level analyst at Vauxhall Cross. Twenty-six years old. He was Wahid's final visitor before he was shipped out of Spanish jail. Wahid killed him.'

Cox scoffed. Flannigan looked put out by the reaction.

'How the hell could that even happen?' she said. 'In a maximum-security jail.'

'That's one of the big unanswered questions. Neumayer was given clearance way above his station. He went to that meeting with Wahid alone. He had authorisation for a complete blackout.'

'The Spanish authorities agreed to that?'

'They didn't have a choice. No cameras, no witnesses inside the room, no one viewing from outside. It was only when the prison guards heard screaming that they knew something was up.'

'That's a bloody suicide mission. Who sent him there?'

'That's what we're still trying to figure out. Maybe it was Neumayer himself who concocted it. All we know is

75

the sign-off documentation was forged with Roger Miles's signature.'

Cox gulped. Was that why suspicion had come her way? Miles was a level six director. One of the bigwigs. It wasn't that long ago that she herself had forged his authorisation to gain approval for heightened surveillance to help track down Aydin and his brothers. What was Neumayer's motive for the trickery?

'You have to believe I had nothing to do with this,' Cox blurted out, immediately disappointed that she'd felt the need to say that.

'No. Again, if I thought you did, then we wouldn't be having this conversation.'

'Yet you still haven't explained why we *are* having this conversation.'

'The thing is, and only two other people in the world know this.' Flannigan glanced around again. 'We actually do have audio of the conversation between Neumayer and Wahid.'

Cox's mouth dropped open. 'You said it was a blackout.'

'It was.'

'Then how—'

'Neumayer still had a phone on him. An MI6 issue. The whole conversation was recorded. Whether he knew that or not, I really can't be sure.'

Flannigan's words swirled in Cox's mind. Did he mean that all MI6 phones automatically recorded everything, all of the time? She wouldn't put it past the organisation to do something like that. Or had Neumayer set the device to record himself? Or had some other party bugged him? Cox thought about asking the questions, though she was sure she wouldn't be given full answers.

'The sound quality is poor. I've listened to it myself a dozen times the last twenty-four hours and there're still parts I can't decipher.'

Flannigan took his arms away from the papers on the table. Pushed them across to Cox. The papers were a transcript of the meeting between Wahid and Neumayer. She tried to picture the scene. Wahid: captive and in his prison garb, yet still filled with arrogance, such was his manner on the recording. The young MI6 agent: confident and astute, and seemingly in charge of the situation, judging by his language. But completely out of his depth in reality.

Cox read through, her heart now pounding in her chest.

But I do have a message for you, from the man I work for.

Cox tensed up as she read the line. She could imagine the edginess in the room at that point.

Shadow Hand.

The transcript ended, just like that. Cox remained frozen for a few seconds, staring down at the last two words on the page. The same two words that had formed the title of the email she'd received hours earlier.

She flicked the page over, double-checking there was nothing more.

'That's it?' Cox asked.

Flannigan's eyes narrowed. 'What more were you expecting?'

'I . . . I don't know. But . . .'

Cox again tried to put herself into that room. To imagine what Wahid's reaction was to hearing those two words. They must have meant something to him.

'I appreciate perhaps the impact isn't quite the same, just reading the words rather than hearing them. But I can tell you, the audio is not pleasant. Whatever *that* means, it got Neumayer killed.'

Cox sat back, she shook her head. She really didn't know what to say.

'One minute the conversation is ongoing. Then Neumayer blurts out this phrase: *Shadow Hand.* The next second Wahid jumps over the table and throttles the poor guy to death.'

Cox still said nothing. Once again her mind went back to the email she'd received. It had to be Aydin. But what was *Shadow Hand*, and how did he even know about it? Then she recalled the other words from the email.

They're lying to you. Watch your back.

Who the hell were *they*?

'I'm only going to ask this one time,' Flannigan said. His tone remained sharp, almost accusatory. Cox waited for the question. 'Do you know what Shadow Hand is?'

'No,' Cox said. 'I've no idea.'

Flannigan reached across the table and scooped up the papers then put them back into his carrier bag.

'You hear anything at all – about this, about Liverpool, about ATS, about Aydin – you come straight to me, OK? The only conclusion I can come to is there's someone within MI6 working against us all. We need to find them.'

'Absolutely.'

'Watch your back, Cox. You never know who's watching.'

Flannigan held Cox's gaze as the words swam in her mind. He got to his feet.

'Get back to your work. I'll be in touch. And if you change your mind about going to Zed site . . .'

Cox nodded. She had to admit, her curiosity was now piqued. Going face to face with Wahid to get to the bottom of what had happened was, on one level, more appealing all of a sudden. But no, she couldn't.

'I'll let you know,' she said.

Flannigan nodded, then turned on his heel and walked away.

Four tables across, the young couple with the baby got to their feet just as Flannigan passed. They set off in stride behind him. Cox shook her head in disbelief. Convenient timing? She really didn't know any more.

78

Flannigan was soon out of sight, but Cox didn't move. Her brain was too busy. Her appetite was still missing, but she ate the now cold meat anyway, giving her weary brain more time to think.

When she'd finished the food she finally got up from the table and, discreetly scouring everyone around her as she moved, made her way to the exit.

There wasn't much she liked about Flannigan's un-announced visit, in particular that it seemed Flannigan didn't fully trust her – even though that was largely justified, she guessed. Regardless, her brain was now a confused mess. One thing she did know was where she needed to go next.

One way or another, she had to find Aydin Torkal.

SIXTEEN

Mosul, Iraq

The room wasn't exactly a prison cell, though Nilay didn't know how best to describe it, because it certainly wasn't homely. On the first floor of a sandstone building somewhere on the Iraq government-controlled side of Mosul, the room had a single small window with wire-mesh glass. Rusted steel bars surrounded the frame on the outside. The roughly eight-foot-square room had plain, white-painted walls, a scratched concrete floor. There was a rickety metal single bed with a two-inch-thick springless mattress. The wooden door had a thick lock, though it hadn't yet been utilised in the six days Nilay had been there. She was free to roam the bland space outside her room which consisted of a small communal area with TV and kitchenette, plus a bathroom with toilets, showers and sinks for three people. There were eight other similar rooms on Nilay's floor, though only three of them were occupied – each with a young woman who'd been rescued – or was it captured? – from ISIS.

She wasn't a prisoner as such, not a suspected enemy or terrorist. Yet she wasn't exactly trusted either, nor was she allowed to leave. There was only one exit off the floor. A thick metal door – usually locked – led to a small security enclosure where there were always two uniformed guards on duty. Another locked door at the far end of the enclosure led to a stairwell and the way outside.

Could Nilay and the others break out if they really wanted to? Very possibly. But Nilay really didn't know what was outside. And until she did, she was going nowhere.

There was a rap on the door.

'Come in,' Nilay said.

The door opened to a smartly dressed middle-aged man with dark skin and a thick moustache which clashed with the lack of hair on the top of his shiny head. He called himself Dr Mhawi. Nilay had spent several hours each day in the makeshift interview room being questioned by Mhawi and the others. They were amenable enough to her, it never felt like an interrogation, but Nilay still felt she didn't quite know what their agenda was, or what her fate would be if the answers she gave to their questions weren't to their satisfaction. Nor did Nilay know any of the other three women who were currently staying. And what had happened to all the other people from her neighbourhood in Mosul, Yolanda included?

'Good morning,' Mhawi said in Arabic, with an unconvincing smile.

'You want to talk to me again?' Nilay answered back in his tongue.

For days they'd grilled her on who she was, where she'd come from, how she'd come to be part of the ISIS faction in Mosul. As well as what she knew of their leaders, their locations, their tactics and their plans. Nilay had, of course, already planned answers to her own background well before the attack. She had never intended on living a life with ISIS in the long run, and one of the obvious exit routes had always been to turn herself in to the Iraqi authorities one way or another, so she'd had to make sure she had a convincing story of how she'd come to be part of ISIS, against her will.

Accordingly, she'd told the interviewers her real first name, and a half-true story, but had never given her full identity or true nationality. The last thing she wanted was to be carted off back to England. If that happened, she had no doubt she'd be placed on every terrorist watch list there was in her home country. She'd never be able to leave the British Isles again.

Instead she claimed to be from Turkey, which was, after all, her family's home country, and she could speak the language almost fluently, and knew enough of the country to make up a decent story. Enough to get by the Iraqi authorities anyway, who didn't have a single word of the language and new little of the place. She spoke to Mhawi and the others using her own broken Arabic, and a forced broken English.

'Not today,' Mhawi said. She noticed the outline of one of the uniformed guards standing out in the corridor behind him. 'Actually, it's time for you to go.'

The way he said it caused Nilay to tense. The guard came into full view. Nilay's heart skipped a beat at the presence of the stocky man, the gun on his hip. Her brain fired with grim thoughts. Could she fight back? She'd never had even basic combat training, but if she were fighting for her life . . .

'Where are you taking me?' Nilay asked, getting up from the bed and taking a step back, closer to the outside wall, as though the extra distance would protect her if the guard came for her. If she could get the gun . . .

'Somewhere safe.' Mhawi held his hands up in the air. 'You don't need to be afraid.'

But Nilay didn't trust him. Not really. For all she knew they were about to cart her off to a real jail – and she knew the ones in Mosul were a far cry from the cushy jails of Western Europe. Or worse, they'd take her to some off-the-map interrogation site like the ones Sajad had told her about, where the Iraqis would have free rein to torture her to get the information they thought she had about their enemies.

'I've told you everything I know,' Nilay said.

Mhawi must have sensed Nilay's unease, because rather than argue the point, he turned and took two steps back, out into the corridor, where he summoned a third as yet unseen person.

Only when Nilay saw the casually dressed young woman did she begin to relax. The light-skinned woman, freckled nose and cheeks and mousy brown hair, had a welcoming smile on her face.

'You don't need to worry, Nilay,' the woman said in English. A West Midlands accent, Nilay thought. 'You're coming with me.'

'Where are you taking me,' Nilay asked, as the woman, who called herself Abi Garrett, drove the banged-up Ford through dust-filled city streets.

'To a safe house,' Abi said, looking straight ahead. 'A hostel. There are other women and children there. Like you they've lost their husbands, their families or their homes, one way or another. You'll be looked after for a while, until we can reconnect you with family, or until you can find somewhere else to live.'

The answer sounded genuine enough, and Nilay hadn't yet had any sense from Abi that she was anything but the charity worker she claimed to be. She certainly didn't seem like some spook playing a role, yet Nilay wouldn't fully relax just yet.

'It must have been awful for you,' Abi said.

Nilay bowed her head. Tears welled and she wiped at her face with her forearm. There was no doubt she was overcome with relief that perhaps the hardest part of her journey – living with ISIS – was finally over, but part of the reaction was undoubtedly sadness and grief at the thought that she'd already sacrificed so much.

Abi looked over as Nilay wiped her eyes, but said nothing.

'It was more than awful,' Nilay said.

The story she'd told to Mhawi, and which Abi obviously had heard too, was how she'd been studying in Iraq but had been kidnapped by ISIS and forced into marriage with Sajad. It was a similar story to what Nilay had seen in real life countless

83

times recently. Wherever the women she'd met fell on the broad spectrum of acquiescence and rebellion, all had a similar glint. Fear, but also hatred.

'Your . . . husband—'

'He's dead. And good riddance.' Nilay looked out of the passenger window, surprised that behind the bitterness in her words, there was also more than a sliver of sadness that Sajad was dead. She'd told herself any feelings towards him were nothing more than some kind of Stockholm syndrome. But was that really the truth?

'They can't harm you any more,' Abi said.

Nilay had nothing to say to that. They stopped at a crossroads. Further ahead was an army checkpoint where several soldiers in their fatigues patrolled with assault rifles in their hands. When the lights were green Abi slowly rolled the car forward, towards the parked jeeps and the wooden fences topped with barbed wire that provided the cordon.

The guards got into position as the car approached. Abi brought the Ford to a stop and wound down the window. She took her British passport from her purse along with the ID badge that identified her as working for the charity Believe. Nilay had never heard of it before today. Now she wanted to find out more.

There was a brief exchange in Arabic between Abi and the soldier, who ducked his head into the car and glared defiantly at Nilay as Abi explained the situation. Nilay remained calm throughout, largely because Abi herself seemed so relaxed. Eventually the soldier straightened up and indicated to his colleagues who nodded and lifted up the red-and-white barrier to let the car pass.

Nilay glanced over to Abi as they drove through.

'Why are you here?' Nilay asked with genuine curiosity.

'Because people like you need people like me,' Abi said as she put her foot down and the car picked up speed.

Nilay felt slightly guilty at the response. What would Abi think if she knew the truth? What would the Iraqi authorities do with her then?

'I grew up with everything a child could need,' Abi said. 'My parents weren't rich, but we had money. A nice house, we went on holidays to hot countries. They paid my way through university.'

'And this is where you ended up?'

'It was time for me to give something back.' Abi gave Nilay a hard look. Nilay couldn't quite read what it meant. 'I had it so easy all my life. But here, it's a horror show. I told myself if I could help even just one person to have a better life, then I'd have made a difference.'

'How long have you been here?'

'In Iraq for over a year, but with Believe for over six.' Abi shook her head. 'I'm not sure how I'd fit back into my old life now.'

And Nilay felt she knew what Abi meant by that. It had only been a few months since Nilay had been a graduate in London with a promising array of career options in front of her. Instead she'd chosen a very different path to her friends. Yet, unlike Abi, she hadn't travelled to a war zone to help others. Only to help herself. She felt a flash of guilt about that. But only a flash. Because she still had a job to do out here, and although armed with what she'd already found out about the Farm – even if her research was in a pile of rubble in Mosul – perhaps she'd just found a way to carry on her work.

'Where were you before Iraq?' Nilay asked.

'A few places, but mainly Syria.'

'You worked for the same charity in Syria?'

'For more than four years. In Aleppo mostly.'

Nilay clenched her fists – a quiet triumph – as a thought sparked in her mind.

Abi took a left turn and after a hundred yards pulled the car to the side of the road outside a five-storey building whose stone

85

walls were pockmarked with bullet holes. A battered sign above the main entrance showed the building had once been a hotel. It was clear that the building was now in disrepair, but it was a whole lot better than what Nilay had become used to recently.

'We're here,' Abi said, looking up at the building.

Nilay noted there was no sign of any guards or soldiers here. Just a matronly woman with a broad smile on her face who came out through the front entrance and walked over to the car.

Nilay stayed in her seat. Gave a big sigh. Abi put her hand on Nilay's knee and looked at her purposefully.

'I know you're nervous,' she said. 'But there are a lot of good people here. You'll be safe. The fighting is miles away. It's time to look to the future now. For a way to rebuild your life.'

Nilay didn't doubt that. And she didn't doubt that the hostel or safe house, or whatever it was called, was indeed safe. But her idea of looking to the future was quite different to what Abi was thinking. Even before she'd stepped from the car, Nilay had already decided she wouldn't stay long. She already had another clear destination, another step on her arduous journey in mind.

SEVENTEEN

Cairo, Egypt

As much as Aydin wanted nothing more than to leave Cairo, it simply wasn't possible for him to travel without first seeking medical attention for his wounds. In his blood-soaked clothes, he'd lain low in the bowels of Qahirat al-Maez – remnants of the old walled city around the grand Citadel of Cairo – for several hours until nightfall before breaking in to the basement of a convenience store. Not ideal, what he really needed was a pharmacy or a health clinic closed up for the night, but the store would have to do. The priority was to tend to his wounds, in whatever way possible.

The dank basement was nearly pitch-black, with the only illumination coming through a small slit window at the far end where a thread of orange light from the street light outside peeked through. Just enough light for Aydin to make out the store room in front of him lined with shelves crammed with goods for the store upstairs.

He set about finding what he needed. The crate of bottled water was the easiest find. Then salt. Sugar. Basic essentials. But the store room didn't have everything he needed. Aydin downed a half-litre bottle of water before hobbling painfully through the space to the stairs that led up to the shop. The bare wood stairs creaked and strained under his weight and

Aydin moved as slowly and carefully as he could, all the time listening out for sounds from above. He reached the top of the stairs where there was a closed but unlocked door.

Other than the most basic of medicines – paracetamol, ibuprofen and the like – there were no other medical supplies in the shop. Not even basic gauze to wrap his wounds. Disheartened, Aydin grabbed two boxes of painkillers. They were better than nothing. The store did, however, hold a wealth of random odds and sods. Household cleaning supplies, hardware, tools, kitchen utensils, tins and packets of food, but nothing fresh. Aydin took some of the food, a length of rubber tubing, some industrial sticky tape, and a marinade syringe.

He moved back down the stairs to the basement. Stopped dead when he heard a squeaking floorboard above. After a few seconds of silence Aydin felt confident to take another step. Somehow, he slipped . . .

He grabbed hold of the handrail, stomped his foot down to get traction. Dropped the packaged syringe which clattered down the steps to the bottom.

Aydin – eyes wide – held his breath and waited for the reaction to the noise he'd made.

Sure enough he heard more creaks from up above. Soft footsteps. The click as a light was turned on. Aydin quietly retreated into the basement, gathered up all of the items he'd collected. He'd wanted to stay in the basement a while – he was getting more tired, his mind was loose and foggy. He needed shelter and the chance to recuperate. But he might have blown that opportunity now.

Standing at the door to the outside, the backpack with the supplies clutched at his front, Aydin was about to head out when he took pause. All seemed strangely quiet above once more. Then the sound of running water – coming from the waste pipe outside the door he was standing by. Aydin relaxed a little. Just a nocturnal toilet visit. When he heard the fading footsteps above again a moment later, he knew he was in the clear.

Aydin stripped off his bloodied clothes and shivered as the cool air hit his skin. He used another bottle of water and a kitchen cloth to clear dried blood from him, and to wash away fresh blood still seeping from the wounds so he could properly inspect the damage.

As well as various scrapes and bruises, he had two large gashes. One on his right thigh, about three inches long, and one on his left biceps, slightly smaller. The most troubling wound, however, was the bullet he'd taken to the side, which he couldn't properly see. That one worried him the most. The awkward location meant it was near impossible for him to reach.

Aydin opened up a pack of granulated sugar, sat on the hard stone floor and poured granules into the wound on his leg. His whole body tensed and shook as the shock of pain swept through him. If he'd been anywhere else he'd have screamed out too, but by clenching his teeth as tight as he could he managed to hold it in.

He continued to grimace and writhe as the sugar crystals dissolved into the open flesh. Despite the immense pain, Aydin knew the sugar would greatly assist the healing process and help prevent infection by drawing liquid from the wounded tissue, lowering the water available for bacterial growth. The resulting lower pH would further help fight infection and aid recovery by promoting dilation of small blood vessels, and flooding the area with white blood cells – the body's natural defence against disease and infection.

That was the theory at least. Though Aydin wasn't sure he could take two more hits like the one he'd just had on his leg. He grabbed a packet of paracetamol, put six in his mouth and chewed through them as he carefully poured sugar into the wound on his arm. Once again he was sent to the brink as pain consumed him.

Finally, when he'd given himself a few minutes to recover, he used a pair of pliers and did his best to dig into the wound on his side. Let out intermittent stifled yelps of pain. Managed to grasp the slug of metal and wrench it out. Hand shaking almost out of control, he looked at the mangled bullet in the plier's pincers. It looked to be intact, but he knew there could well be fragments remaining. He could do nothing about that now. He did his best to get sugar into the wound, lying down on his hip on the cold floor so that the granules wouldn't fall out.

After a few minutes, when the pain had once again begun to subside, he took the tape and covered the three wounds over. Not the most ideal dressing by far, but at least it would stop further blood loss. Before long he'd have to apply stitches, but that would require finding the right kit. His more immediate concern had been stemming the blood loss and stopping the onset of infection.

Now he needed to replace those lost fluids. Aydin took a bottle of water and the packet of salt and put a measure of the crystals into the liquid. He replaced the cap and shook until all of the salt had dissolved. Next he took the rubber tubing, and used the tape to secure the rubber to the plastic rim. Finally he took the syringe from the packet. The needle was far thicker than a regular medical syringe, but it would have to do. He took the plunger out of the syringe and again used the tape to secure the syringe needle to the other end of the rubber tube.

He coaxed a vein in his right arm. Took a deep breath, then jabbed the thick needle into his flesh, once again clenching

90

his jaw at the shock of pain that coursed up his arm and into his neck and down his spine.

He took several deep breaths, then turned the bottle upside down and the water glugged out and filled the rubber tube. Aydin winced as the cold liquid entered his bloodstream, causing him to shiver. But the worst was over. He sat back against a crate full of cat litter boxes, the upturned bottle in his hand, as exhaustion finally got the better of him and his eyes slowly closed.

EIGHTEEN

A loud crash woke Aydin from his delirium-induced sleep. His eyes shot open. Despite his grogginess it only took him a fraction of a second to recall where he was. He glanced over to his right where a teenage girl was standing, open-mouthed at the bottom of the basement stairs, the messy pile of flattened cardboard boxes that she'd just dropped lying by her feet.

The girl – wearing a pair of jeans, a thin black jumper, a blue apron over the top – turned on her heel to run.

'No!' Aydin shouted out. 'Please. I need your help.'

Perhaps it was the desperation in his voice that caused her to rethink. Or was it the state she could see he was in, sitting there in his boxers, his taped-up wounds on display, a bloodied pile of clothes next to him.

When she turned back round, her face was covered in panic. Tears welled in her eyes.

'Please,' Aydin said. 'I'm hurt. I just needed somewhere to stay.'

She didn't say anything. That was at least better than her screaming the house down.

'What's your name?' he asked her, grimacing as he sat himself up.

'Layla,' the girl said.

'How old are you?'

'Sixteen.'

'Who else is here?'

She glanced up the stairs. 'My father. He's in bed. He'll be up any minute.'

Was that the truth? Or just a warning to Aydin?

'I won't cause any trouble. I was desperate. I promise, I'll pay you for the things I used.'

'How did you get in here?'

'The basement door was unlocked.'

Layla frowned at that but didn't say anything.

'What happened to you?'

'I was attacked.'

Her rabbit-like eyes not leaving Aydin, Layla back-stepped up the stairs.

'I should tell my father. If you need help, he'll know what to do. He can call a doctor.'

'No!' Aydin said, his voice raised but being careful not to move from the spot. The last thing he wanted was to obviously flinch and send her into a further panic. He had no intention of harming her. Not unless doing so was an absolute last resort for his escape. 'Please. Don't do that. In my backpack, there's some money. Take as much as you want.'

She was looking less and less certain now. But Aydin didn't believe she was about to run screaming. She was too scared for that.

'Do you have any medicine?' Aydin asked. 'Antibiotics. Painkillers.'

'We have some in the shop.'

'Could you get me some? Please. And some chewing gum. My mouth is like a swamp. Then I promise I'll be gone. You'll never see me again.'

93

A look of resolve broke out on her face. Perhaps because he'd just offered her a chance to get out of the basement and away from him.

'OK. Wait there,' she said. 'I'll only be a minute.'

She turned and headed up the stairs, her footsteps quick but soft. She glanced over her shoulder every other step to make sure he wasn't following.

When she was out of sight, Aydin burst into action, as best he could. He ripped the syringe from his arm and hauled his heavy body up, and shouted out in pain. His wounds were plugged and somewhat treated but they'd still be seriously debilitating for the next few days, and he needed to find something far stronger than paracetamol to quell the pain.

He grabbed the clean clothes from his backpack, quickly pulled them on. Above him he heard the creaking floorboards again. Muffled voices. A conversation becoming more heated. Layla and her father.

Aydin looked at the rolls of banknotes in his bag. Before long he'd need to acquire more. He could barely afford to give any up now, but he'd meant what he said to Layla. He had no cause to steal from them, nor did he want them to go straight to the police, even though he had to assume that was the most likely end result now.

He put some money on top of the crate of cat litter, then headed for the basement exit. He opened the door and glanced outside. It was light, but the long shadows of the sun in the cramped city streets suggested it was early, and it was still quiet. Aydin took one last look around the basement. Still no sign of Layla or her father, though he could hear stamping footsteps from somewhere inside.

Aydin climbed the stairs, kept his head down as he walked away with purpose. Within a few seconds he was well out of sight of the shop, moving deeper into the twisting city streets once more.

He briefly wondered what Layla would think when she returned to the basement to see he'd gone. He'd never know if she really had gone to get him help, or if she'd simply cried foul. He hoped it was the former. That not everyone in the world was out to get him.

As Aydin walked into a small but quaint city square, he spotted a clock tower ahead of him. Seven a.m. Which explained why the streets were still so quiet. He continued walking, heading across the city, the overbearing structure of the centuries-old Mosque-Madrassa of Sultan Hassan off to his right. In a shop window he caught sight of his reflection – he looked a state. Like a zombie, his face an insipid yellow. With his cap pulled low over his face, Aydin kept his head down and drew little attention from the few pedestrians around him.

Then he spotted two policemen on early morning patrol. Aydin was on a collision course with them, and he decided against an abrupt change of direction. Instead, he kept his pace steady as he neared them, not daring to look up to see where their attention was focused.

As they got closer, his eyes on their legs, he noticed the step of the policeman on the left slow down. Then the other slowed too. Somewhere in the distance a police siren echoed across the rooftops. Despite his injuries, Aydin's body primed itself for action. Had Layla called the police after all?

By the time Aydin was a step away from the policemen, they'd stopped walking altogether. He looked up at them. They were both eyeballing him. He just gave a slight smile and nod then carried on past as causally as he could.

'Hey!' one of them shouted out.

Aydin didn't falter in his step, just kept on going, though his body was ready to uncoil.

'Hey, you, stop!'

Aydin could make a run for it, but the last thing he needed in his state was another foot-chase. Better to play cool and wait for an opportunity. Or hope for some good fortune. He was surely due some.

Aydin stopped and turned.

'Let me see some ID,' the older and plumper of the two officers said as he stepped forward towards Aydin. His companion had his hand on his sidearm.

'Sorry? I speak only a little Masri,' Aydin said in his best bad accent as he shook his head and cupped a hand to his ear.

The officers exchanged a look.

'ID. Passport,' the policeman said, in broken English now. 'You need to show me.'

'Is there a problem?' Aydin said, following suit by switching tongue too.

'Where you from?'

'Turkey.'

Another look.

Aydin slipped the backpack off his shoulders. Noticed the second officer flinch. His hand twitched on the grip of his holstered weapon.

Aydin had no gun on him any more, but he was still cautious about the officers seeing inside the backpack, so he carefully opened the bag and took out the passport. He handed it over to the older policeman who glared at it suspiciously for a few seconds.

'You here on a vacation?' the officer asked.

'Studying,' Aydin said.

'What happened to you?' the other officer said, looking Aydin up and down.

Aydin tried to process an answer but his brain was mush. The distant siren was getting louder. The officer glared down at the passport again, as though he was mulling over what to do or say next. Then came the noise of a revving engine, and a moment later a patrol car came speeding around a corner. Both policeman, Aydin too, glanced to the speeding car.

Aydin looked to the gun of the policeman nearest to him. The guy was barely two steps away. Aydin planned the move. He'd grab the gun, swipe the officer off his feet and crash his heel into his face to put him out of the fight. He'd deliver a leg shot to the second officer before turning the gun to the speeding car. It'd take him only a few heartbeats to turn the tables on them, to give himself the chance to get away.

He was a breath from taking the first step. But then the police car screamed past them. The policemen, quite casually, turned their attention back to Aydin. Then their radios crackled to life. The older officer put his radio to his ear. Didn't say a word. When he'd heard enough he put the radio down and handed the passport back to Aydin. And that was it. The policemen looked at each other, then hurriedly set off in the direction the car had just gone in.

Aydin waited until they'd turned the corner in front of him before he heaved a huge sigh of relief.

Minutes later, with no further impediment, he'd reached the large multi-storey public car park where he'd left a battered old Fiat several days earlier. The door was unlocked. The keys in the glove box. He pushed the key into the ignition. The engine rattled to life.

Soon after, Aydin was heading out of the city for good.

NINETEEN

Port Said, Egypt

Nightfall had once again descended by the time Aydin reached Port Said. The city of some six hundred thousand inhabitants contained Egypt's busiest port, and the second busiest container seaport in the whole of the Arab world. Less than an hour before arriving Aydin had been blessed with his second stroke of luck that day when he'd happened upon a vet's surgery closed for the evening. His raid of the premises had been anything but subtle, and with the alarm blaring he'd given himself just thirty seconds to grab what he needed before running. The morphine-based painkillers he'd found were a world away from paracetamol, but he still needed equipment to properly stitch and dress his wounds. That would have to wait.

Drowsy from the debilitating effects of his wounds and the drugs coursing through his blood, Aydin, under the cover of darkness, scaled the mesh security fence that ran round the perimeter of the industrial port, then traipsed his way through the sprawling space.

Thousands of shipping containers were stacked here, there and everywhere. Articulated lorries grumbled and roared back and forth, bringing containers for the departing ships, and taking away those that had just arrived. Massive cranes with rows of bright white lights whisked containers from the port and raised them onto the waiting cargo ships. Men in yellow and orange hi-vis jackets scuttled back and forth, while security patrols with assault rifles roamed around half-heartedly.

The sheer scale of the place and the bustling activity provided ample cover for Aydin as he assuredly made his way through the complex towards the docks, sticking to the shadows that the stacked containers and sporadic low-rise buildings provided as best he could.

A monstrous red cargo ship loomed in front of him. Row upon row of containers were already sitting atop the massive structure. Aydin crouched down behind a stack of containers, spying on the hub of activity in front of him. Several metal gangways stretched from the towering structure down onto the port. The two at the stern of the ship were clearly the most in use as the ship was readied for departure.

Aydin waited for his opportunity then jumped out behind a lorry and dashed after it as it drove on towards the ship. When he was alongside the ship's bow Aydin darted off to the right, pulling to a stop by the thick leg of a towering yellow crane, panting heavily, his whole body aching from just a few seconds of exertion.

Ahead of him engines whirred, blips came and went from reversing vehicles and from the cranes. Containers crashed into place. Men shouted out instructions at each other. None of them suspected Aydin's presence.

When he was once again sure all eyes were elsewhere, Aydin broke cover once more and rushed for the water. The sound of the sea lapping against the dock and the ship's hull grew louder. An unused metal gangway clung to the side of the vessel. The end of the gangway was at least four feet from the edge of the dock and sat above the dock level by about the same amount. As he moved, Aydin heard the hissing air brakes of a truck somewhere behind him. Took the peak in noise as his opportunity.

He jumped over the edge of the dock and landed on the gangway with a thud. He immediately spun round, to survey the area. Noted he was still unseen and unheard above the din, despite the clattering noise he'd made. Out in the open, speed was his best option, and he quickly ascended the rickety steps, ignoring the throbbing in his body. When he reached the ship's deck he crouched down and peered around the open space in front of him. The cranes worked overhead but the deck was all but deserted. Aydin quickly scuttled off to his right, heading to the very end of the bow. On either side of the ship, free-fall lifeboats hung in position, ready for deployment. Aydin climbed over the side of one, lifted the fabric cover and slunk inside.

Two hours later, with Aydin fighting off his body's desire to succumb to sleep, the ship eventually edged away from the port, and Aydin finally felt able to relax. The events of the last two days had catapulted him onto a course from which there was no return, and yet he'd had no time until now to really consider exactly what was happening.

Two days ago he'd felt like he was on top. He'd come away from ATS in Alexandria unscathed and carrying the data that he believed would finally give him the truth of what had happened to cause his father to kidnap his only son and send him to a terrorist training camp thousands of miles from home. Now he wondered whether all of the effort – and all of the hope – had been in vain.

He still couldn't be sure exactly who had come after him in Cairo. What he had to believe was that they wouldn't stop looking for him just because he'd successfully skipped out of Egypt. The people he was up against were powerful and all-seeing, and with each step he'd taken in the last twelve months he'd come closer to breaking open their secrets.

He'd been told his father was dead. The target of a drone strike because of his affiliations to an Al-Qaeda cell. Aydin wasn't sure he believed that any more. First there'd been Spain. Wahid's words as the two of them fought in the midst of his brothers' attacks in Europe.

Your father will be so disappointed.

Vague words at best, but the taunting nature in which Wahid had delivered them meant something, Aydin believed. Or was it hoped? If his father really was still alive, Aydin would do anything and everything to track him down.

But second was the information Aydin had already found about Shadow Hand. Information that potentially turned his whole view of the Farm upside down. With the ATS data, he had to hope he could find the truth, and halt the atrocities taking place at the Farm for good.

Aydin sighed and lay back against the hard, fibreglass hull of the lifeboat. With the adrenaline that had fuelled him and spurred him on earlier now gone, the pain was once again taking over. He slipped some more tablets down and drained half a bottle of water. He only had three more bottles for the trip, plus the paltry snacks he'd taken from Layla's shop.

In two days he'd arrive in the busy Port Akdeniz in Antalya, Turkey. Some way from his destination, but the right country at least. His father was still alive, he wanted to believe. So too was his uncle. Aydin felt sure that one way or another, he'd find some more of the answers he needed in his family's home country.

TWENTY

Mosul, Iraq

Nilay spent only three nights in the hostel in Mosul. Any more than that and she would have capitulated. It was one thing to deceive the likes of Sajad and his ISIS comrades, but the idea of deceiving Abi and the other people who were sacrificing their lives to help those less fortunate than themselves was almost too much to bear. Nilay couldn't be a drain on their already overstretched time and resources. It simply wasn't fair either to the workers, or to those women and children who genuinely needed the help. Who'd lost everything but their lives.

Which was why, on the fourth night, Nilay waited until dark before she sneaked out of the service entrance of the hostel with a holdall containing the few clothes she'd been given, and never turned back. She only hoped Abi and the other workers there wouldn't waste their time looking for her. She'd left a note, saying she was sorry, that she didn't want to be a burden. Hopefully the note would serve its purpose.

Or would Abi simply alert the Iraqi authorities? Tell them that they'd made a mistake in letting Nilay go in the first place and that she was in fact a threat? Having the security services up her arse was the last thing she needed. She'd just have to keep that potential threat in mind.

It took Nilay most of the following day to travel to the country's capital, Baghdad. Arriving on a decrepit bus that was at least sixty years old and only seemed to have two working gears, Nilay made the trip on foot in the dark from the bus terminal to the grand Baghdad Central Station. The sprawling railway station, with a columned façade set off by two soaring clock towers, had originally been built by the British, but had been extensively damaged during the US-led invasion of 2003. Renovations since then had seen the building returned to its former glory, and it remained a central hub for travel into and out of the city.

The revamped building also housed shops, restaurants, and a bank. Which was where Nilay was headed. Months ago she'd taken out a safe deposit box there. Inside the box was all of the money she had in the world, a laptop computer, her UK mobile phone, and her UK passport. It was time to become Nilay Torkal once again.

With her phone charger plugged into the socket underneath her seat, Nilay sat in a wood-panelled cafe at the station as she drank treacly coffee and read through the many messages on her phone. The vast majority were from her mother. Understandably, she had become increasingly worried over time as to what had happened to her daughter. Nilay had never told her what she was doing, only that she was heading to Turkey to take a post-graduate course in political studies. During her time with Sajad she'd managed to send the odd email home from Sajad's laptop, but she'd not spoken to her mother in months now.

In many ways, Nilay simply didn't know what she'd say. What would her mother think of what she'd done? How she'd lied and tricked people, and put herself in such danger? How she'd used not just her mind but her body to lure Sajad into a trap. It was all for a good reason — to find out what had happened to her brother and father — but would her mother understand, or support, any of that?

No. She wouldn't. Which was why Nilay couldn't tell her a word of it.

Using the cafe's WiFi, Nilay opened up Skype on her phone. She'd set up the service on the home computer so they could easily keep in touch. Her mother was a real technophobe and hated the idea of using the internet and the computer to make a phone call, which probably explained why Nilay had several dozen missed calls on her mobile, but not a single one on Skype. She pushed the button to make the voice call and held the phone to her ear as the jingly dial tone sounded out. After a prolonged wait Nilay doubted whether there would be an answer. Then finally the connection clicked through.

'Nilay!'

Nilay's body stiffened. She felt a well of tears, but fought them off as best she could.

'Is that you?'

'Yes. It's me.' No, it was no good. The tears rolled down her face. At the sound of the familiar voice, flashes of memories burned in Nilay's mind. Her mother, always so loving. All of the kisses and cuddles and comforting words she'd provided over the years.

'Where've you been? I've been so worried about you. Are you OK?'

Nilay could tell from the broken tone that her mother was sobbing. Nilay had to be strong. She couldn't give anything away.

'Of course! I'm fine,' she said, surprised at how carefree her voice sounded. 'I'm sorry I've not been in touch. It's just been so busy here.'

'Yes, you said that in your last email. But that was over a month ago.'

'How's everything at home?' She hoped the quick change of subject would do the trick of avoiding difficult questions.

A disgruntled huff. 'Not much to tell really. It's so quiet here. Will you be home soon?'

'I'm not sure yet.'

'You must have end-of-term holidays.'

'It's not really like that here. It's all research. There are no holidays.'

A long sigh. 'As long as you're OK. And enjoying yourself.'

'Yeah, I am.' Nilay shook her head at just how easy it was to lie. 'I really love it out here. And I've made loads of friends.'

'Friends, eh?'

Nilay knew what that meant. 'Don't worry. I'm far too busy for boys.'

A nervous laugh. 'Yes, I'm sure.'

An awkward silence followed. On the laptop Nilay clicked through onto the website for Believe. Scrolled through the information on the charity's activities.

'Are you still there, darling?'

'Yes, I'm still here.'

'I wish I could see you.'

'You will. I promise.'

Nilay clicked on a link on the menu bar, navigated onto the page titled 'How to get involved'. There was a diatribe about the various means of giving donations, but also a section for how to apply for vacancies. Nilay clicked on that and found herself staring at an online application form.

'I do have some news actually.'

'You do? Good news I hope?'

'It is good. The university wants me to undertake a special assignment.'

'What kind of assignment?'

'Charity work. Have you heard of Believe?'

'No. Should I have?'

'They're a humanitarian organisation. They work all over the world, helping vulnerable people.'

'Where exactly?'

Nilay could tell by the change in tone of voice that her mother was already sceptical.

'I've applied to work in Syria. The people there really need help.'

'Syria! Oh, Nilay, that sounds so dangerous.'

If only you knew, Nilay thought.

'I really want to. I really want to try to make a difference.' Another silence, filled only by the gentle sniffles of her mother.

'Are you crying?'

'You're a good person, Nilay. So good. Always thinking of others. Don't ever change.'

'I won't,' Nilay said, unable to find anything but those two choked words.

'And I'll see you soon?' The sobbing was getting worse.

'I'll make sure of it.'

'OK, I've got to go.'

The call ended and Nilay knew it was because her mother was too overcome with emotion to speak. Strangely Nilay felt immediate relief that it was over. The call had been one of the hardest she'd ever had to make. She was shaking as she put her phone down on the table. So many lies. Where did it all end? But she had no doubt there was one lie that was far worse than any other, and that she feared may come back to haunt her. She'd sworn she'd be home to see her mother. However long it took, she wanted nothing more than for that to be the truth. Yet there was a gnawing thought, growing all the time, that maybe she'd already said goodbye to her mother for the last time. Just look at how close she'd already been to death in Mosul.

Nilay did her best to push the ominous thoughts to the side. There was no more time to waste. She focused back on the form on her laptop. It took all of ten minutes to fill it in and send it off. She received an on-screen notice promising a response within forty-eight hours.

Feeling more confident, she opened up another browser window, and appraised her travel options. With any luck she'd already be in Aleppo by the time the charity reached out to her.

TWENTY-ONE

Kabul, Afghanistan

Three days had passed since Flannigan's impromptu visit. Cox hadn't heard from him at all since their disconcerting meal in the market. Was he still in Kabul? Still in Afghanistan? Or had he already shipped off to Algeria to begin Wahid's interrogation?

Cox had felt next to useless since she'd seen her boss. She couldn't concentrate on her work, even though she'd barely left the safe house. Was it a 'safe' house now? It didn't feel that way any more. She felt there were eyes on her, ears listening to her every move. It hadn't escaped her attention that Flannigan had chosen to have that meeting with her away from the safe house. Who exactly was he afraid was watching or listening?

The chime of the intercom stole Cox from her thoughts. She went to the front door and stared at the small video monitor. A curly haired man was standing on the pavement outside, looking up to the camera. Looked to be a local, given his dark skin. Or at least his origins were somewhere across the Arab peninsula.

Cox debated for a second before pressing the speaker button. 'Yes?'

'Ms Cox, Henry Flannigan sent me,' the man said. His English carried a thick accent. 'I have a package for you.'

He held up a small brown envelope.

'Post it into the box, please,' she said.

'No. It has to be hand-delivered. Flannigan insisted.'

Cox sighed.

'What's the authorisation code.'

If Flannigan truly had sent a messenger to her, he would surely have given him the unique code related to her operation. Given recent events, if he didn't have it, Cox would sound an alert. But the man calmly repeated the eight-digit code of numbers and letters.

'Can I come up now?'

Cox remained unconvinced, but she couldn't let her new-found paranoia paralyse her life, or her work. She pressed on the button to buzz him in. Then spun round and scooted to the bedroom. She grabbed the Glock handgun from under her pillow and tucked it into the back of her jeans.

There was a soft rap on the door. Cox moved over, staying to one side of the frame, not putting her face anywhere near the spyhole.

'Give me that code again?' she said, then quickly shifted position, as quietly as she could so she was on the other side of the door from where she'd spoken.

The man, sounding calm and collected, once again recited the code. No hint of duress. No deliberate mistake in the code to warn her that anything was untoward.

She carefully unbolted the door and stepped back, one hand behind her, ready to grab her gun.

'Come in,' she said.

The man opened the door. Clocked her and pushed his hands into the air, as if sensing her tension.

'My name's Balal. I have this for you.'

He indicated the envelope in his hand.

'Close the door.'

Not turning away from her, Balal did so.

'What is it?' Cox asked.

'A thumb drive.'

'That's it?'

'No.'

Balal looked around the room. As if checking it was safe to speak. He tossed the envelope over to the sideboard a couple of feet away. It gently clattered to a stop.

'We need to talk,' he said. 'But first how about a drink?'

'No. I'm fine. Thank you. Let's just do the talking.'

'Then perhaps we can sit?'

'I'm fine standing.'

Balal let out a disgruntled sigh.

'I don't mean to be rude,' Cox said. 'But there's a very good reason for my lack of hospitality.'

'And what would that be?'

Cox didn't bother to answer the question.

'Seriously, Rachel, you need to look at that drive. It's about Aydin Torkal.'

Cox's brain whirred, but she wasn't backing down that easily.

'I'll look when you're gone.'

The casual look on Balal's face was wearing thin. Clearly this wasn't how he'd expected the meeting to go.

'You need me to access the drive.'

'Then tell me the code.'

'I can't do that.'

Cox scoffed. She whipped out the gun. Gripped the handle with both hands. Pointed the barrel to Balal's chest. He didn't flinch. Didn't look at all bothered by the sight of the weapon.

'Turn round and put your hands on the wall, above your head.'

Balal sighed and shook his head, but did as he was told. Cox cautiously moved forward, then did a quick search with one hand, the other still holding the gun. She felt around his waist. Around his sides. The inside of his legs. His ankles. No gun. No other weapons.

Cox stepped back, returned to a double grip on the gun.

'Take the drive from the envelope,' she said.

Balal turned and gave a slight nod. He crab-stepped to the sideboard. His eyes flicked between the envelope and Cox as he slowly drew out the small silvery thumb drive. He held it up for Cox to see.

'My laptop's in the office,' Cox said. 'This way.' She jerked the gun to her left. Balal slowly stepped in the direction she indicated.

'Keep your hands where I can see them,' she said. She was sure she saw Balal roll his eyes.

He pushed down on the handle to the office and stepped inside, Cox two paces behind. The smell of wood oil filled her nose, like it always did.

Balal moved to the laptop. Pressed on the mousepad to wake the machine.

'What's your password?'

'Move away,' Cox said.

Balal did so, but shook his head again, as though fed up with her paranoia. Cox moved over and pushed her thumb onto the pad, Balal still in her peripheral vision. The screen unlocked. Cox went to straighten up.

'I don't think that worked properly,' Balal said, nodding to the screen. 'See?'

Cox didn't even look fully at the screen. Just moved her gaze an inch so the laptop was in the corner of her eye. It was the split-second distraction Balal needed. Even though she'd been damn sure the move was coming, she still couldn't react quickly enough.

She spun, arcing the gun as Balal rushed for her. No more warnings, she pulled on the trigger. The gun blasted, the

111

sound was almost deafening in the confined space. She'd pulled too soon. Heard the thunk as the bullet lodged in the far wall. Got ready to pull again. Balal clattered into her. Pushed the gun up and away as Cox fired again. Another miss. Now, at close quarters, the gun was useless. But Cox was no slouch at grappling.

Balal tried to manoeuvre Cox into a choke hold, but she spun and swiped her leg up, pulling one of Balal's legs into the air and sending him off balance. He already had one arm locked onto hers and as he went tumbling to the floor, he took her with him. Her arm twisted painfully behind her. She shouted out. The gun bounced away.

On the ground, it didn't take long for Balal's size and strength to make the difference. One arm wrapped around her, he managed to pin her arms to her sides.

She bucked and writhed, trying to escape the hold. After a few seconds of effort, his grip loosened. She could do it. She upped the ante, gave it everything she could as she tried to break free.

But then realised her mistake – why his grip has loosened – when she felt the jab in her neck. Cold liquid surged into her veins. The icy sensation drifted down her spine, and into her arms. Balal pulled the syringe from her neck then renewed his grip with his other hand.

No, there was no escape now.

Cox did what she could to carry on the fight, but it was no use. Before long her eyelids were closing. What, or who, she'd wake up to she had no idea.

TWENTY-TWO

Cox gasped and her eyes blinked open, her head sprang upright. She gulped, taking in a mixture of air and water, realised her head and neck and shoulders were sopping wet. Standing in front of her with an empty plastic bucket in his hands was Balal.

'You piece of shit!' Cox croaked, before coughing and spluttering.

Balal remained unmoved by her response, his face passive. He said nothing as Cox got her breathing under control, and took in her surroundings. She was sitting on a basic wooden chair, her hands secured behind her. She felt around with her fingers. Was sure it was just thick rope holding her. She was still wearing the same clothes as back at the safe house. How long she'd been out for, where she now was, remained open questions.

In a strange way, the position she found herself in was far better than she'd expected.

Balal put the bucket on the floor and sat down in the chair at the opposite end of the wooden table in the middle of the otherwise empty room. Cox looked around. Concrete floor. Low ceiling. Four white-painted walls. At least they'd been white at one point, but now large patches were yellow and brown. No windows. One paint-peeling green wood door. A security camera in one corner of the room, red light blinking. Given the floor, the walls, the ceiling, the cool temperature and the smell of damp, Cox's guess was they were underground. Whether in the city still or some off-the-grid site in the middle of nowhere, she had no idea.

'Who are you?' Cox asked.

'I told you. My name's Balal.' No emotion in his voice.

'Then who do you work for?'

'I told you that too.'

'Bullshit.'

Flannigan wouldn't do this to her. Balal reached into his pocket. Placed the silvery thumb drive onto the table. Tapped it with his finger. Cox scoffed.

'We do need to talk about what's on there.'

'I thought that's what we were attempting to do back in Kabul. Before you fucking tranquillised me.'

Cox deliberately dropped in the place name to try and fish a reaction from her host. But he was ice-cold.

'You mean, before you tried to shoot me?' he said. 'I'm not sure how you would have explained that one to Flannigan.'

'And I'm not sure how you're going to explain to him that you've kidnapped his agent.'

Balal held up a finger. 'Give me a minute.'

He moved over to the door. Twisted the handle and opened. Cox was surprised to notice it was unlocked. Balal slipped out, only giving Cox a brief glimpse of the bland corridor outside for a second before he shut the door behind him.

Cox looked up to the camera again. Then around the room. Then back to the door.

Yes, she was a prisoner here, for whatever reason, but it was hardly maximum security. If she could get her wrists free, she could just make a run for it.

No. Not yet. She had no idea what was on the other side of that door.

The choice was taken away from her seconds later when Balal returned, a black laptop in his hands. It looked to be the same model as Cox had. He placed the machine onto the table and flipped open the lid. Picked up the thumb drive and placed it into the machine's USB port. He twisted the laptop so they could both see the screen, then he used his thumbprint to wake the computer up – was the type of machine and its inbuilt security a confirmation he really was with MI6?

Cox looked from the screen to Balal. His cold stare was fixed on her. He clasped his hands together on the table.

'Four days ago there was a raid at the offices of a company called ATS in Alexandria, Egypt. ATS is a satellite company that works for MI6.'

'So I've been told.'

'We believe that raid was carried out by Aydin Torkal.'

'So I've been told.'

'Ms Cox, do you know where Aydin Torkal is?'

'I've been through all this before. Though last time I was at least treated to dinner.'

'Answer the question.'

'No.'

'No you won't answer, or no is your answer?'

'I don't know where he is!'

'Do you know why he would attempt to steal data from ATS?'

Attempt to? Cox didn't question the choice of words, just made a mental note. 'No.'

'The following day, when Torkal tried to access the encrypted data he'd stolen, a trigger was automatically sent to our recovery team.'

'*Our* recovery team?'

Balal said nothing to her clarification question.

'Two agents tracked the signal to an apartment in central Cairo. They encountered a man there who we now strongly believe to be Aydin Torkal.'

Even before he'd said it, the fact that they were sitting in the room like they were suggested to Cox that Aydin had once again escaped. Was she pleased about that?

'Unfortunately, in the ensuing chase, one of our agents was killed by Torkal. In quite a disturbing fashion.'

Balal averted his eyes to the laptop. He clicked away, opening up files on the thumb drive. He turned the screen a few degrees so Cox had a clearer view. She wished he hadn't as she was left staring at pictures of a bloodied corpse. A man's head and shoulders, blood pouring from the black hole that used to be an eye, a huge gash in his neck.

'Following a brief chase, Torkal and our agent, Graham Castle, ended up in a scuffle in a hotel room. *That* is what happened to Castle. Torkal managed to escape from the hotel by lighting a fire in the room and disappearing in the melee.'

Balal took pause. Cox really didn't know what to say. Was Aydin capable of such a brutal killing? Of course he was. He'd been trained to be a killer. Yet a large part of her wanted to believe it wasn't him. Or if it was, that he had a good reason for what he'd done.

'After, as the police searched for him, Torkal took shelter in the basement of a general store a mile or so from the scene. Police received a tip-off the following morning. Police forensics have tested blood samples found there. It's definitely Torkal. And from what we've heard from witnesses, he's badly injured. But he hasn't been seen since.'

Cox shook her head. 'What are you expecting me to say to all of this?'

'Ms Cox, Torkal is highly dangerous. You know that from past experience. For whatever reason, he's now attacking our agency. He has to be stopped.'

'I haven't seen or heard from him for over twelve months. I don't see what this has to do with me. Why you've drugged me and brought me here. Wherever the hell it is.'

Balal glared at Cox but said nothing – a sign of irritation at Cox's continued denials? He clicked away on the laptop again. Cox went numb when she saw the two emails that popped up on screen. The brief message from *AT*. Her failed response.

But how the hell had Balal and whoever he worked for got hold of that? Had they been monitoring her accounts? For how long? Cox's temperature was rising. Had they ever trusted her?

'How did you get that?' she said.

'That's hardly the most important question, under the circumstances.'

'It's the most important question to me.'

'But not to me, or my superiors. Or yours.'

'I've no idea who sent that email, I—'

'AT? Come on, Rachel, it doesn't take a genius to figure that one out.'

'So now Aydin Torkal is the only person in the world with those initials? It could be anyone! I received one email. You can see for yourself how coded it is. I've no idea what it means. Yes, I admit, I thought perhaps it was Aydin. I was intrigued that he was reaching out to me. That's why I sent the response. But as you'll see, it never even went through. I have no idea who sent the damn thing to me, and I don't know where Aydin is.'

'Aydin Torkal sent the email.'

'You don't know that!'

'Yes. I do. Because the email to you was found in the meta-data on the hard drive in his Cairo apartment. Remember, I did tell you we tracked him there just a few days ago.'

Cox opened her mouth but quickly took back her response. That still didn't explain how they'd found the failed email she'd tried to send in return. But, if what Balal was saying was true, then the confirmation that it was Aydin trying to reach out was of huge significance to her. Why was he doing that?

'Have you heard of Shadow Hand?' Balal asked.

Cox sighed. 'I've seen two references to it in my entire life. Once on that email, and once a few days ago in documents I received from my boss. Just like you, he told me nothing about what it meant or what the fuck any of this is about.'

Cox didn't bother to add that over the last couple of days she'd performed several detailed searches for the term within MI6 databases she had access to. The searches had drawn nothing but blanks anyway. Perhaps Balal already knew all that.

'What this is about is quite clear. It's about finding Aydin Torkal, and bringing his latest deadly rampage to a halt.'

'I've told you everything I know. If you want my help further, then perhaps you need to be honest with me about what's happening, and why I've been brought here, like this.'

There was a knock on the door. Balal didn't say anything as he scooped up his laptop and headed over. He opened the door and there was a brief exchange with whoever was on the other side before he moved out of sight.

When Cox saw who was there, she could hardly breathe. After everything they'd been through together.

Henry Flannigan.

TWENTY-THREE

'You shitbag!' Cox shouted as a mixture of anger and despair erupted inside her. 'Why?'

She felt like launching herself at him and gouging his eyes out.

'Nice to see you too,' he said, coming over and taking the seat opposite.

'Nice? Yeah, really bloody nice. Is this how you treat all of your agents now?'

'No. It's not.' His tone was hard, and as confrontational as hers. 'Just the agents who seem to be operating with a dual purpose.'

'Dual purpose? Have you listened to a word I said?'

'Every. Single. One.'

'I've been nothing but loyal to you.'

Flannigan snorted to that, only further riling Cox.

'So let me spell it out to you,' Flannigan said. 'You received that email four days ago. You told neither me nor anyone else about it. You sat across a table in a cafe with me three days ago while I asked questions about Torkal and you never once mentioned it.'

Cox bit her lip. She knew there was no point in arguing that one.

'I gave you a transcript of a document from the moments leading up to Wahid murdering a fellow agent of yours. The last words spoken by Neumayer were Shadow Hand. It seems to me those two words very likely got him killed. Those same two words appeared in the email to you from Torkal, yet once again you chose to say *nothing* to me about it.'

Cox took a long inhale trying to compose her thoughts.

'And you're expecting me to treat you like you're one of my loyal agents? This isn't a fucking country club we're working for.'

'I'm not working with Torkal. And I really have no idea what Shadow Hand is.'

'I'd really like to believe that,' Flannigan said. 'But I'm just not sure I believe a word that comes out of your mouth any more.'

Cox shook her head in disbelief. 'And what do you know? If you're so damn clued in, then you tell me what Shadow Hand is? What has Aydin got mixed up in that's already seen two agents killed and you turning on your own people in response?'

Flannigan glared at Cox. She'd have loved to know what he was thinking in that moment.

'I'll say one thing for you, Cox. I admire your resolve.'

'My resolve? Were you hoping I'd be on my knees by now begging you for mercy?'

'The fact your reaction is the opposite is quite telling.'

Cox clenched down on her lip to stop her biting back.

'Look, Cox, I'm going to make this very clear to you, so I hope you're listening carefully. I don't trust you.'

'Yeah, thanks.'

'In fact, I don't think I ever properly can again.' The words cut right into her, even if she could understand his point. She'd been loyal to MI6 – to *him* – for years. Could

120

she ever recover what was now lost? 'But I also don't trust anyone right now within the damn organisation. Torkal has started something. Whatever Shadow Hand is or was, people are already dying because of it, and I'm not being dramatic when I say I'm wondering who's next. Me? You?'

'Well I'm the one who's been kidnapped and held captive in a grimy basement, so I'd say you're faring better than me so far.'

'Your patter is wasted on me, Cox. You might think this is a game, but I certainly do not.'

Flannigan reached into his pocket and pulled out a small digital audio player. Cox stared at the inanimate object as though it held great power. Flannigan pressed a button on the side and the audio crackled to life with static. After a few seconds the sound of breathing came through the tinny speaker. Two sets of breaths. One heavy, erratic, the other calm and measured.

Flannigan, a sour look on his face, sat back in his chair, arms folded, his stare fixed on Cox. The heavy breathing on the audio slowed. Then was replaced by a mocking laugh.

'*Are you done?*' came the smooth voice. Wahid.

Cox opened her mouth to speak but Flannigan held up a finger to stop her.

'*I think you know the answer to that one,*' came the response from an unfamiliar man. Wahid's interrogator, Cox assumed, though it didn't sound like Wahid was particularly troubled by what they'd done to him so far. '*Take him away.*'

Shuffling sounds.

'*Wait . . . Just, wait.*'

Silence, except for the ever-present static.

'*I have a question for you.*'

This time it was the interrogator's turn to give a mocking laugh.

121

'Do you know where my brother is?' Wahid asked. 'Talatashar?'

'Aydin Torkal? Who gives a shit about that runt. He's not in here. You are.'

'Who gives a shit? I'd say you should.'

'And why's that?'

'My brother made a big mistake, helping you people, and he will be punished. And every day that goes by with you protecting him . . .'

'Who says we're protecting him?'

'Then where is he?'

No answer.

'My brother needs to be brought to justice, and if you won't do it, then we'll have to do it ourselves.'

'Glad to hear it. One less scumbag on the streets.'

'No, there'll be far more casualties than that. My brother has to be punished. Maybe you have him, maybe you don't, but you have to give him back to my people. Otherwise more blood will flow.'

'Is that a threat?'

A couple of seconds of silence.

'Liverpool was just the start.'

More silence. Cox could imagine the turmoil in the interrogator's mind at Wahid's revelation.

'There will be more attacks, I can promise you that. And soon.'

'Tell me what you know about Liverpool.'

'Actually, I think I'm done. Now, you can take me away.'

The sound of banging and clattering broke out, men shouting. A cry of pain. Flannigan leaned forward and clicked the button to turn the player off. He stared at Cox as they sat in silence.

'What do you want me to say?' Cox asked.

'No one has directly claimed responsibility for Liverpool—'

'Has a suspect even been identified?'

'I can't answer that.'

'Can't or won't?'

'That's irrelevant. We have to believe Wahid's threat is real, and that his people are behind the Liverpool attack.'

'How could Wahid possibly even know what his group's plans are now?'

Flannigan said nothing, but his unfriendly glare told Cox a lot. She got it. Whatever other intel they had, SIS believed that with Aydin on the loose, Wahid's people had already begun a renewed terror campaign in the West. But was the capture and punishment of Aydin, who'd ruined their plans before, really their goal, or simply a convenient excuse?

In many ways, it didn't really matter. The fact was Flannigan, and others too, now saw Cox not just as a scapegoat, but as a potential causal factor both in the attack in Liverpool, and whatever further attacks were to come. As far as they were concerned, she'd aided and abetted Aydin in his escape. But really, she didn't have any blood on her hands, however much Flannigan wanted her to think that.

'When was that recorded?' Cox asked.

'That's not relevant.'

'Of course it is. Do you have any intel yet on what other attacks are coming or when?'

'OK, let me rephrase. It's not relevant to *you*. We believe the threat of further attacks is credible, that's all that matters. You lied about being in contact with Torkal. You messed up.'

Cox huffed. She really didn't know what to say to that.

'You have one chance to save your career, your *life* from here. I could quite easily have you whisked away to Zed site to spend the rest of your sorry days being torn apart like Wahid.'

Cox winced at the thought. Did Flannigan really think he had a sufficient cause to do that? *Would* he?

'*But,* I still see you as an asset, of sorts. For whatever reason, Torkal chose to reach out to you. I don't know what he's up to, I don't know where he is, but I do know one thing. We have to get to him, and you, better than anyone, can help me to find him. If you don't . . . then it's the end the line for you.'

TWENTY-FOUR

Aleppo, Syria

The face of Abi Garrett burned bright in Nilay's mind each day she'd been in Aleppo. It was Abi who Nilay had modelled her new 'self' on. Nilay had admired her contemporary from the moment she'd first met her, and Abi's unerring focus on helping others had without doubt left a lasting impression. Although Nilay being in war-torn Syria held dual purpose, that didn't mean she couldn't still do her damnedest to be the good Samaritan she was pretending to be. Which was why, in the eight weeks she'd been in the Syrian city, she'd never shirked her responsibilities for Believe, for whom she was now a low-paid worker.

She'd spent the last three hours of the day doing her best to comfort a young woman and her two sons – aged two and five – who'd hitchhiked several hundred miles to Aleppo from a village in the hinterlands of ISIS-controlled Syria. Two weeks previously the woman's husband had been shot in the head in the middle of the street as part of a planned execution of ten people who ISIS had accused of plotting against it. After his execution the woman, Haya, had been subjected to brutal treatment. Beaten in the streets, stripped naked, sexually assaulted multiple times by numerous men. Her children had witnessed it all.

Somehow Haya had managed to smuggle herself and her boys away from the village one night, on foot. But her horror story hadn't ended there. With no money, and wanting to stay away from watchful ISIS eyes, she'd had no choice but to prostitute herself in order to make the journey to Aleppo. Doing so had seemed, to her, to be the quickest and safest way of securing onward travel.

Arriving in the capital, the woman and her sons looked like ghosts, their features pale, their eyes hollow, seemingly with no feeling or life beyond. All of the children's natural youthful exuberance and joy had been sucked out of them.

Their story was harrowing and horrifying, though not at all unusual. In a way, although she'd never say this out loud, Nilay could scarcely believe Haya's ordeal was worth it − Aleppo was hardly paradise, yet the woman was overwhelmed with relief at having made it to somewhere that she considered 'safe', and Nilay would do anything and everything she could to comfort them and give Haya and her children hope.

The time she'd spent with Haya in the retreat in downtown Aleppo was still preying on Nilay's mind as she walked inside her building and climbed the polished stone stairs to her apartment. She tried to take Haya out of her mind as she moved up. She had a busy night ahead. Even weary after a day 'out in the field', she spent most nights researching on her computer, every day getting closer to her goal of finding out what had happened to her brother.

In a curious way, Nilay had found that it was exactly people like Haya who she needed to speak to in order to learn the truth. With Sajad, she had almost been too close. The Farm, and all that went with it, had touched so many lives, and those who had been left behind, the friends and families, had so many stories to tell. Nilay provided them all with an encouraging ear, taking in what they knew, and slowly building a bigger picture.

She'd already come to learn that Aydin was just one of fifteen young boys who'd been taken from their homes to a secret location − believed to be in Afghanistan. The Farm as a place referred to

126

that location, though colloquially people talked about the Farm more widely as an extensive organisation. It was those fifteen boys that Nilay now concentrated on. Through her work over the last two months Nilay had names, possible identities, for eight of the fifteen. But the boys' disappearances had been many years ago. No one had heard of them since. There were plenty of whispers, and stories, but what was real and what was make-believe? And where were those boys – men – now?

Where was Aydin?

That clutter of thoughts was still crashing through Nilay's mind as she reached her floor. She walked along the corridor, fishing in her bag for her key. She reached the door and put the key into the lock. She paused, then turned when she thought she heard a shuffle behind her, back near the stairs. With the thoughts of violence and kidnapping already playing in her mind, she immediately felt jittery, but no one was there.

Taking a deep breath, trying to calm her nerves, she pulled the key from the lock and pushed open the door. Still half-glancing along the corridor as she stepped forward, the last thing she'd expected was for the threat to be on the inside . . .

She caught sight of the dark-clothed figure standing in her hallway out of the corner of her eye. The man burst forward. Nilay gulped in shock. Her arm jerked up. The key in her hand held out as a makeshift blade as she reflexively tried to stab out at the intruder bearing down on her.

Her defence was easily countered. The figure snapped her arm away. The key clattered to the floor. The man grabbed her. Held her arms at bay, thwarting her pathetic attempts at escape. A second man appeared behind her. They tussled as Nilay bucked and fought with everything she had, but their arms were thick and strong. The men talked quickly, but calmly. Giving each other instructions. It struck her as strange that they spoke to each other in English, with broad American accents.

Despite her flailing attempts to hold them off, they took her legs out from beneath her and she plummeted helplessly to the wooden floor. A knee jabbed into her back, pinning her down. They quickly clasped her wrists together. Cuffs? Cable ties?

With Nilay's fight all but gone, the half-baked thought of her attackers' origin was still crashing in her mind as the rough fabric sack was wrenched over her head.

TWENTY-FIVE

If Nilay had been pleasantly surprised by the relative comfort and luxury afforded her when she'd been taken by the Iraqi forces in Mosul, the experience at the hands of the Americans was at the other end of the scale. With the hood over her head the two men forcibly dragged her down the stairs of her apartment building. Her legs and her back smacked off the hard steps continuously all the way down. At the bottom the two beefy men threw her into a waiting vehicle. Some sort of van, Nilay assumed, judging by the hard metal floor she was thrown onto and then had to lie on for the duration of the bumpy ride that followed. She guessed they were heading out of the city, though where to exactly she didn't know. No one spoke a word. Nilay, despite the numerous questions thrashing in her mind, was too scared to speak.

Eventually the vehicle stopped and Nilay was once again rough-handed as thick hands dragged her from the van and her body thumped down onto the ground. The kick of dust as she landed suggested they were perhaps in the rural hinterland desert. Someone grabbed her ankles, dragged her across the dirt. Nilay screamed – in fright as much as the pain from her skin scraping on the ground.

Hefty arms hauled her to her feet.

'Walk,' a gruff voice said. 'Yeah?'

Nilay thought she nodded in agreement but couldn't be sure. The man grabbed her arm. Or was it a second man? Or a third man? Who the hell was out there? A gentle tug on her arm got her moving. After a few steps the change in temperature and smell from dry and dusty to cool and dank told her they'd entered a building of some sort. Her soft footsteps echoed.

'There're some steps coming up.'

Nilay said nothing, just tentatively put her foot out in front of her and felt for the stair. Going down, rather than up. Nilay gulped as she descended. The temperature fell further, the dampness grew with each step. Eventually the echoes subsided slightly and Nilay guessed they'd entered a larger room.

'Sit down.'

Nilay didn't fight it as a hand on her shoulder guided her onto the cold hard chair.

Without warning the sack was dragged from her head and she squinted at the sudden intrusion of brightness. It took her eyes a few seconds to adjust to what was only a single, dangling bulb doing its best to light up the low-ceilinged room that had bare stone walls and an uneven dirt floor. Nilay flinched as her focus properly cleared and she realised there was a black-clad man standing a few feet in front of her, arms folded over his chest, his head covered with a balaclava.

'Don't move,' he said, before turning on his heel and heading for the door which he slammed shut behind him.

Nilay shivered, both with cold and terror. She whipped her head left and right, there was no one else in the room behind her. Not that she could take much relief from that. She already guessed what was coming next. She'd seen enough, had heard enough of the tactics used to interrogate suspects whether it be the Americans, the English, the Iraqis, ISIS, the Syrian government or whoever.

Nilay was only in the room for a couple of minutes before the door opened and the black-clad man was there once again. But *was it in fact the same one or a different man altogether? He was carrying a small wooden chair and a portable table which he propped up in front of Nilay, before once again turning and heading out of the door. He didn't close it this time. Instead, a moment later, a man who may well have been his twin emerged through the doorway. Somehow, even though he had a similar frame and was dressed head to toe in black, Nilay sensed he was a different person. Perhaps in the way he moved. Not as assured in his step, as though he was carrying an injury. He came into the room. The door remained open. He took a seat. Let out a big sigh. Then took off his balaclava, slowly, as if savouring the moment of the big reveal.*

The man underneath the mask was far from a monster. His rounded face was covered in a salt and pepper beard. He had a large, flat nose, big green eyes. He looked . . . friendly, almost fatherly.

'I'll explain this to you only one time,' the man said in a guttural voice that made Nilay's insides vibrate. His accent was once again American – one of the southern states, Nilay thought. 'As far as the world is concerned, you may as well be dead already. No one will come looking for you. No one will find you here. And you'll stay in our company as long as it takes.'

Nilay tried her best to stay strong, but she let out a whimper before she bit down on her lip. There was no reaction at all in the man's face to her obvious panic.

'I only ask one thing of you. One thing and you can get yourself out of this. You need to talk. You need to answer my questions. All of them. You got that?'

Nilay nodded.

'Good. Then we'll start with your name. And where you're from.'

Nilay thought about that one for a moment. They of course already knew who she was, surely? She couldn't give them the

131

same bullshit she'd given back in Iraq about being from Turkey. But why were the Americans doing this to her in the first place? Because of Sajad and ISIS? Or because of the questions she'd been asking in Syria about her brother and father?

'I'm Nilay Torkal. From England.' Her voice sounded way calmer than she'd expected.

The man nodded, as though satisfied that she'd chosen to talk right off the bat. 'Good. That was nice and simple, right? Let's just carry on that way. And what are you doing in Aleppo?'

'I work for a charity! Why are you doing this to me?'

A slight flinch on the man's face – perhaps because of the unexpected strength in her tone. She got it. She wasn't there to ask the questions. No matter how simple or justified the question was. And even though her act of defiance made her feel stronger, the fact was she had no reason to hold back on these people if they were genuinely working for the American army or government. But was that the real story? They certainly hadn't given anything away yet about who they were or what their agenda was.

The man slipped a photo from his pocket. A candid shot on photographic paper. Nilay recognised it immediately. She'd taken it.

'Tell me how you know this man.'

The photo was of Sajad. But how could she possibly tell that story? The one where she'd infiltrated ISIS and married one of their soldiers, simply to gain access to people who knew of her brother's fate. What did that make her exactly? Was she still on the side of the West to have done something like that? Her brother, if he was even still alive, had been taken away to be trained as a terrorist. For whatever reason, her father had put that life on him. Here she was, years later, having abandoned her London home to marry an ISIS soldier. Would the Americans believe for one second that she was in any way still on their side?

The man thumped his fist down onto the table, causing Nilay to jump. 'Do you know this man?'

Nilay opened her mouth to speak, but something inside stopped her now. Tears rolled down her cheeks. She looked squarely into the eyes of the man in front of her whose agitation was growing by the second. She wondered what he'd come at her with next. She didn't want to play games, but she was simply too scared, she didn't know what to do.

Before either of them could say another word, another man, balaclava over his head, strode into the room and leaned over the bearded man so he could whisper in his ear. The bearded man gave a simple nod in response, then got up from his chair. He headed out of the door without saying another word. The second man moved behind Nilay. She already knew what was about to happen, even before the sack was pulled over her head again.

The man grabbed her arm, pulled her to feet.

'Where are you taking me?' Her voice was now breaking.

The man tried to pull her along, but Nilay held firm.

'I said where are you taking me!'

Her voice a high-pitched shriek that made her throat sting.

There was a moment's pause. Nilay wondered what that meant. Then a fist was thrown into her gut. She couldn't see it coming, had no way to prepare for the blow. The knuckles dug into her belly, knocked the wind out of her. She doubled over and her head went into a spin.

'You can walk, or I can drag you out of here. Your choice.'

Nilay took several deep breaths, trying to get her breathing under control. She straightened up. The man grabbed her arm again. Gave a gentle tug.

'So?'

Nilay said nothing, just took a tentative step. Then another, then another. Whatever was happening to her, there was simply no point in starting a fight that she couldn't possibly win.

TWENTY-SIX

Antalya, Turkey

Aydin didn't move from the safety of the lifeboat for the entire crossing from Port Said to Port Akdeniz on the outskirts of Antalya in the south of Turkey. The two-day journey saw the ship traverse one of the most hostile regions in the world, edging past the Gaza Strip, Israel, Lebanon and war-torn Syria, yet the trip passed without incident.

Aydin had never been to Port Akdeniz, but as he peeked his head out between the hull of the lifeboat and the fabric cover, it could well have been any port in the world. Another sprawling industrial space much the same as Port Said. Arriving at night, Aydin already had the perfect cover for leaving the ship, and not long after arrival, he was traipsing away from the port alongside a wide highway, sticking to the bone-dry grass verge for cover.

His energy reserves remained hugely depleted, and every step was an effort. Other than the snacks he'd stolen in Cairo, he'd had no other food. Despite the morphine, his wounds were still causing great discomfort and he knew he needed to stop to redress them. The thought of tearing off the tape, however, was far from welcome.

At least in Turkey he wasn't a wanted man. Well, not because of what had happened in Egpyt at least. That meant he didn't have to move about only in the shadows of night, stealing what he needed. So his first call when he arrived in the centre of Antalya was to a twenty-four-hour pharmacy, where he bought more painkillers, some antiseptic, some surgical dressing, and other genuine medical kit. Not a meat syringe in sight.

With his new purchases, Aydin next made his way to the city's main bus terminal where he'd catch a bus for the eleven-hour trip to the nation's capital. He stepped from the night and into the busy enclosed waiting area that was built with an abundance of 1960s-style concrete slabs, and after buying his ticket for the eleven p.m. bus he first ate at a cafe before making his way to the toilets.

The stench of piss and shit and vomit was overbearing as soon as Aydin opened the door. There was a short and scrawny man with a mop half-heartedly wiping the floor by the sinks, but apparently his job didn't require him to actually enter the cubicles at all. Not that it was his fault that the men who'd used the facilities were disgusting animals.

On the fifth try Aydin finally found a cubicle that wasn't smeared with crap and he locked the door then wrenched down his trousers and took off his jacket and t-shirt. The wound on his leg was causing the most problem with movement. Not only was it big, but it was in an awkward position, stretching across his muscle. Whenever he took a step he felt the skin and flesh on either side of the gash separating. He rubbed some alcohol-based hand sanitiser he'd bought in the pharmacy over the tape on each of the three wounds then waited a couple of minutes.

The alcohol, in theory, would absorb through the tape, and help to dissolve the adhesive. When he was ready, Aydin bit down on the thick strap of his backpack, then in one quick motion tore the tape from his leg. There was a short, sharp stab of pain, but it was nothing like when he'd poured the sugar into the open wound two days previously. Underneath the tape, the gash was a mess of pink flesh and white and black pus. Aydin did his best to scrape out the gunk from the wound, his leg shaking uncontrollably as he did so. At least, he noticed, there was no odour of rotten flesh. Not yet, anyway.

After applying more sugar and antiseptic, it was time for the needle and thread. It wasn't the first time Aydin had stitched his own skin, but that didn't make the process any easier. He once again clenched down as hard as he could on the thick fabric strap. His leg once again shook and jolted each time he pierced the skin with the sharpened metal point. Taking short pauses whenever he felt delirious from pain, he'd soon worked over the wound on both his leg and his arm, which he dressed with bandages from the pharmacy. There was no way he could stitch the gash on his side, but he tried his best to clean it out, and at least now he could provide a more appropriate dressing.

When he was finally finished, he felt jaded and both mentally and physically exhausted. He gingerly made his way back out to the terminal and checked the clock on the wall above him. Half an hour to go. Aydin took a seat in the corner, looking in, and waited.

Arriving in Istanbul the following morning, Aydin wouldn't have said he felt refreshed exactly, but he was certain the few hours' sleep on the overnight bus had done him some good – certainly it was a whole lot more restful than the cold and bobbing lifeboat he'd endured on the Mediterranean.

He stared out of his window at the skyline of the historic city as they headed across the Bosphorus strait, leaving Asia behind. It was the first time Aydin had been on European soil in over twelve months. In a strange way it made him feel powerful to be back, as though he'd once again entered the wolves' lair, completely undetected.

Or did the authorities know he was there? There was always that slim possibility.

Back on more familiar territory, it didn't take long for Aydin to make his way through the city on public transport to reach his destination. He stepped from the bus and stood by the side of the road as the diesel engine groaned and pulled the weighty vehicle out of sight. Aydin crossed the street and made his way up the narrow tree-lined side road where the sporadic houses were set well back behind high walls, fences and hedges, almost completely screening them from passers-by.

Aydin took the discreet turn between two tall date palms and found himself in front of the arched brown-painted metal security gates to his uncle's luxurious home. The last time Aydin had been, he'd tied up his uncle to interrogate him, and to find out what he knew about the Farm. Aydin had got no real answers that day. For one, Rachel Cox had turned up, and although he'd outmanoeuvred her and had her tied up next to his uncle, a raid by the Turkish police's special operations department – the PÖH – had soon brought a halt to Aydin's European rampage. Though he had eventually escaped. And now he was back to finish what he'd started.

Staring at the gates, he wondered exactly how this visit would end. Without a tactical armed raid, he hoped.

But as he stared, Aydin got the first glimpse that not all was rosy at his uncle's home. The last time he'd been, the whole grounds, the house too, were immaculate. Looking now, at the scratches on the gates, the peeling paint at the edges, the grime across the bottom where rain splashes had kicked up dirt, the signs of lack of care and wear and tear were clear.

Aydin gazed across to the white wall that ran either side of the gates. Before, manicured colourful bushes and flowers had spilled over the top of the wall, but now it was a wilderness, the wall barely visible behind overgrown foliage that grew up it, over it, all around it.

Aydin pushed through the thick undergrowth along the side of the wall. The idea had never been to knock. He came to a spot where an overhanging tree branch protruded sideways towards the wall. Aydin scaled it, and then jumped onto the top of the wall.

He frowned. The gardens below him, so picturesque before, were now a weed-filled mess. The perfect lawns were a patchwork of green and brown strands, over two feet high. Weeds, as tall as six feet, were everywhere. The house was barely visible from where he was.

Aydin jumped down, grimacing as a shock of pain leaped up his leg. He pushed the pain aside, then moved on through the undergrowth, onto the yellow gravel driveway that too was now overrun by weeds. The whole scene reminded Aydin of a post-apocalyptic movie. The once glorious Roman-style white villa in front of him was in serious disrepair. Shutters hung off their hinges. Windows were smashed in. Not just signs that the place was uninhabited, but evidence it had been trashed. But why, and by whom?

As he moved, Aydin took his newly acquired knife from his backpack and held it at the ready as he cautiously stepped to the front door which was already ajar. What was he about to walk in on?

He used the tip of the knife to push the door further open. The air inside the villa was cool and musty. And deathly quiet. He moved into the echoey space, his feet gently tapping on the terracotta tiles. Some items of large furniture remained inside, though it was all upturned or fabrics ripped or wood

broken, and all of the personal belongings – artwork, orna-
ments, pictures – were either missing or smashed to pieces
on the floor.

One thing was clear; there was no sign that anyone had
been living there for some months, given the thick layer of
dust that covered everything.

Aydin continued to scour the home. Moved through into
the garden room where last time he'd found his uncle reading.
The view to what used to be a cascade of water features in
the garden outside was now more like looking into a jungle.

A creak behind him. Aydin sank down and spun round,
pulling the knife up, ready to slash. There was no one there,
just a small lizard scuttling up the white wall, looking for a
cool place to escape the blazing heat outside.

Aydin got back to his feet. Looked through cabinets and
drawers. Found nothing of interest. He headed on to the
bedrooms. Paused for a moment when he reached his uncle's
room, where last time he'd tackled Rachel Cox to the ground
by slamming her own gun against her skull. Despite that,
she'd still ended up helping him. She surely would again,
wouldn't she?

Aydin was about to leave the room when something caught
his eye. A tall oak wardrobe in the corner of the room. Its
double doors were wide open revealing the empty carcass.
The back panel of the wardrobe was loose, hanging inward.
Aydin moved over. Jabbed the panel with his finger. The wood
wobbled back and forth. He put the knife down, grabbed the
edges of the wood, realised it was attached to sliders – or had
been at least, but the top edge had come away. He reattached
the panel into position, then pushed it across. He broke out
into a smile when he saw what was on the other side.

Aydin pushed the discreet button on the wall and there
was a clunk and then a four-foot-high cut-out section of the

wall wheezed inwards and slid to the side to reveal a panic room. Soft lighting lit up automatically on the inside, casting the small space in a white glow. A quick glance was all that was needed to reveal the room was empty, but the broken wardrobe panel suggested perhaps it had been used at one point. The series of events of what had happened in the house started to fall into place in Aydin's mind.

He briefly scanned inside the panic room. Found water, some food supplies, which he took advantage of. There was nothing else valuable in there. No safe, no cash or jewellery, no documents. Not any more.

Aydin had just one last room to search before he left, and he already had a good idea where he'd go after that.

He moved through into the dark wood-panelled home office. Much like the rest of the house it was in a state. Files and papers lay strewn on the floor and on top of the large mahogany desk. All electronic equipment had been removed. Aydin collated some of the papers. Just scraps really, there was nothing of real interest. Whatever the ransackers had been searching for, they'd found. All that was left was remnants of routine household correspondence – utility bills and the like.

Though Aydin allowed himself a small smile when he found an invoice for Bella Casa Homecare Services. He hadn't remembered her name, but his ageing uncle had a home nurse with him the last time. She'd ended up hogtied along with his aunt, though Aydin had no quarrel with either of them. Now though, Aydin realised, as he looked at the invoice that gave the nurse's name as Esma, she was perhaps one of the few people who knew what had happened to Kamil Torkal.

Invoice in hand, Aydin made his way for the door.

TWENTY-SEVEN

Aydin arrived in the Kasimpasa district of Istanbul not long after midday. The neighbourhood, once a heart of ship-building in the city, had in latter years seen industry move away, leading to the slow decline of the area and its buildings with a seemingly endless expanse of run-down low-rise homes spreading into the distance. It was depressing, though he knew he'd seen far worse places in supposedly more affluent cities, including his city of birth, London.

The three-storey wood and brick townhouse that he stopped outside had a mishmash of air-conditioning units projecting from its windows. The whole thing looked strangely lopsided, though Aydin couldn't figure out if it had been built like that or if the building, or one of its neighbours, was suffering from a bad case of subsidence. Having spied on the property from across the street, and noticed the figure moving in the window on the top floor, he decided to head across to the front door.

Aydin slipped the torsion wrench from his pocket and quickly picked the simple lock as the overhead air-conditioning units whirred away. He stepped into the communal corridor, and made for the tiled staircase.

Out of breath from the climb, his leg aching badly, he came to the door for the top-floor apartment. Another

141

straightforward lock to pick. The level of security was poor, though not startling. With his tools and skills, Aydin could be inside the apartment within seconds, regardless of whether or not the occupants wanted him there. But this time he'd rather just knock.

Three simple taps, then Aydin stood and waited. He heard soft footsteps the other side. There was no spyhole, so Aydin was happy to stand front and centre. The door inched open. Two brown eyes peeked out. Esma had only seen Aydin once before. That time he'd hogtied her and stuffed her into a cupboard while he went about tearing off his uncle's toenails. He was hardly expecting a warm reception when she saw his face. Which was why, when she looked into his eyes, he thrust his foot into the doorway to stop her slamming the door shut, then barged in, grabbed her, and smothered her face with his hand to hold back her screams.

'What do you want from me?' Esma asked, her face hollow, her body sunk down in the threadbare fabric sofa.

Aydin remained on his feet, keeping a close watch on his host. Not that he expected her to attack him. He hardly thought she had a weapon of any sort stashed down the side of the sofa, nor did he believe she'd attempt to jump up and tackle him. Her mobile phone lay on the coffee table in front of her.

'I'm not going to hurt you,' Aydin said, trying to sound as sincere as possible. Which was mostly true. He certainly didn't *want* to hurt her.

He briefly looked around the modest space. The open-plan room had a tiny kitchenette with decades-old cabinets, a single sofa facing a small portable TV, a glass dining table with space enough for only two chairs. The one bedroom across the way had a single bed, a closet shower room in the corner.

It was clear Esma – a matronly lady, in her fifties, Aydin guessed – lived alone.

'Why don't you make us some coffee?' Aydin said.

'I don't have any coffee.'

'Tea then. Whatever you normally drink.'

Esma looked unsure. Aydin wanted her to feel comfortable, and the distraction of making the drinks – doing something normal in her own home – would help ease her mind.

'Please?' he said.

Esma humphed, then got up and plodded to the kitchen. Aydin watched attentively – partly out of interest, partly to make sure she didn't do anything stupid like grab a knife or an unseen phone. She filled the larger of two kettles with water and set it on the stove, stacking a smaller kettle – together called a çaydanlık – on top. She placed two spoons of loose tea leaves into the top pot, then waited for the water to boil.

'How do you have it?' she asked, not looking to him.

'*Tavşan kanı*,' Aydin said, asking for it medium strength, though the literal translation of his words was rabbit's blood.

She glanced around, a look of disquiet on her face, but then got back to work. When the water in the lower kettle was boiling she poured some out into the top kettle then left it to brew while she fetched the glass cups and china saucers.

'Milk or sugar?' she asked.

'Sugar, please.'

She poured out two teas – a deep brownish-red colour – then dropped a cube of beet sugar into each glass. She picked up the two saucers and headed back over.

'Thank you,' Aydin said as he took a saucer from her.

Esma sat down and Aydin took a long inhale of tea vapour then a small sip of the hot sweet liquid that immediately soothed his insides.

'What happened to you?' Esma asked.

143

She looked at Aydin's leg. Then his side. He looked down. Realised that patches of blood were beginning to seep through his clothes again. It'd been over twelve hours since he'd dressed his wounds back in Antalya. It looked like he hadn't done such a great job.

'I'm fine,' he said, though he knew he was feeling anything but. The morphine and other painkillers were keeping the edge off, but the toll of the wounds was beginning to tell once again, both on his body and his mind. Whether that was because they were now infected, or just because his body's energy reserves were fully directed to staving off infection, and repairing the damaged tissue, he couldn't be sure.

Either way he knew the best course of action was for him to find somewhere to properly recuperate. But that would take too much time. He wasn't sure he wanted to sit and wait for his enemies to descend.

'You don't look fine,' Esma said. 'I am a nurse, remember. You look . . . terrible. Have you got a fever?'

'What happened to my uncle?' Aydin said.

The abrupt change of subject, and Aydin's harsh tone, caused Esma to flinch. She bowed her head.

'Tell me,' he said. 'I came a long way to speak to him.'

When she lifted her head up, he saw her eyes had welled with tears, though in contrast there was a certain resolve on her face.

'They took him away,' she said.

'They?'

'I don't know who they were.'

Aydin thought back to the villa. The panic room.

'You were there?' he said.

A tear escaped her eye. She gulped. A slight nod.

'They didn't see me.'

'Because you used the panic room. Behind the wardrobe.'

144

Aydin studied her features. She looked a little surprised by what he knew.

'I went to the house today. It's a mess. No one has been there for months.'

Esma shook her head, opened her mouth but didn't say anything at first. Aydin took another larger sip of his tea. He noticed Esma hadn't touched hers at all.

'It was just a normal afternoon,' she said, looking down to the floor. 'Your aunt was in the garden. Pruning. It was a glorious day. So bright and quiet and serene.'

Aydin said nothing when she paused. Just waited for her to carry on the recollection.

'I was with Kamil in the garden room. There was a chime from the intercom. A delivery van was there with the new armoire your aunt ordered . . . except it wasn't the delivery at all.'

She sobbed. But Aydin wasn't feeling her emotion. He wanted her to give him more.

'Tell me what happened next.'

She looked put out by his lack of sympathy. 'Your aunt heard the door. She was so excited. She came inside to answer it, and I only went to the toilet. Then I heard the shouting. The banging. I knew something was wrong.' She locked eyes with Aydin. 'After last time, you know.'

Aydin said nothing.

'I ran from the toilet to the bedroom. Kamil had told me about the panic room. We'd talked about it after that day you turned up. The plan was for us all to go there if there was ever any trouble. But . . . they didn't make it. Perhaps your uncle knew I was in there. He never told them.'

'Did you see anything? Hear any of what was said?'

'I could only see what was on the monitor in the panic room. But it's a tiny screen. There were four of them, at least. They looked like soldiers, all dressed in black, with big guns.'

145

'And what did you hear? Before you ran into the panic room?'

'I told you. Shouting. Screaming.'

'What were the men shouting?'

'I don't know! My English isn't that good.'

Aydin paused mid-sip.

'English?'

'Yes. They were English.'

'You're sure?'

'Yes, I'm sure. I know the sound of the language well enough, even if I don't know the words.'

'So this wasn't the PÖH?'

'No, of course not!'

She looked at Aydin as though he were dense. He barely noticed, his brain was chugging away so fast. Was it MI6 who'd taken his aunt and uncle?

Aydin finished his tea and put the cup and saucer down on the coffee table.

'How long did you stay inside for?'

'Not long. Two hours maybe. Just until I was sure they were gone.'

'And you called the police?'

'Of course. I couldn't call from the panic room because the system went down. But as soon as I was away from there I called.'

'What did they say?'

She shrugged. 'They started an investigation, but I was told a few days later that they had no information to go on, there was no evidence of foul play, and perhaps they'd just run away. That was the end of it.'

Aydin thought for a few moments. He wondered if someone had put pressure on her to keep quiet. She'd not been disappeared by anyone, which was one thing, but if she'd gone to the Turkish police then they at least knew she'd been in the house. What exactly had the police done with her story? Had they started an investigation at all? Had *they* been silenced?

More importantly, where the hell was Kamil Torkal now?

'Two hours,' he said. He held a hand up to his head. It was throbbing with random thoughts. But he also felt dizzy all of a sudden. He put his hand out to the wall, waiting for the moment to pass.

'Two hours?' Esma said.

'You said you were inside the panic room for two hours. But the house has been cleared out. Virtually every personal item removed. How long were the men there for?'

'Five minutes. No more than that. They grabbed your aunt and uncle. Swept the house one time, then left. That was it. They took nothing.'

Which was another oddity in the story of the events of that day. If what Esma said was true, a second team had been sent back to the house to clear it out. When? And was it the same people or a different group altogether?

Aydin squinted. The pounding in his head was getting worse.

He again looked down to Esma's untouched tea on the coffee table.

'Are you OK?' she said, craning her neck.

Aydin tried to answer, but couldn't find the strength. He went to move forward. He needed fresh air. He made it a half-step before his legs collapsed underneath him. He landed on the worn-out rug with a thud. His eyes briefly locked with Esma's before they fell shut, and he drifted into unconsciousness.

TWENTY-EIGHT

Dubai, UAE

Cox was lying on a metal bench in the sprawling Dubai International Airport when she saw what had happened. She was trying to sleep, but the terminal was too noisy and the bench too uncomfortable to do so. So instead she'd just been lying there, eyes half closed, but also half watching the screens in front of her. One was the departures board, which showed that her onward flight to Egypt remained indefinitely delayed. The other screen was silently showing CNN, with Arabic subtitles across the bottom which kept getting in the way of the scrolling information bar of the news station. Still, Cox didn't need to see the info bar to understand what she was looking at.

She sat up in her seat. Picked her phone from her bag. Saw there was already a message from Flannigan ten minutes before, asking for a white line call. That was impossible. She replied as such. Not ten seconds later her phone was ringing. A withheld number.

'What happened?' Cox said.

'Can you speak?' Flannigan responded.

'I'm in the airport,' was her non-committal answer.

There was certainly no one within earshot.

'Well, it'll have to do. I'm in a meeting room at Vauxhall Cross with Roger Miles, Caroline Branding and Bob Stokes.'

Cox winced. Miles was Flannigan's boss. He'd never liked Cox. Branding and Stokes were the heads of MI5 and MI6. The bigwigs. The last time Cox had anything to do with them was after she'd helped Aydin escape from MI6 custody the year before. However that had panned out, in their eyes she was hardly a shining example of what an MI6 agent should be.

'What's going on?' Cox asked.

'What have you heard?' Flannigan said.

Cox looked back to the screen.

'I'm watching it on the news. An arson attack on a packed mosque in Bordeaux. Dozens believed dead.'

'And warring factions from both the Muslim and non-Muslim world, protesting and clashing with each other everywhere else in France,' Flannigan added.

Cox thought back to Kabul; the audio of Wahid and his interrogator. His thinly veiled threat.

'But this isn't—'

'What you're not seeing on the news is what pre-empted that attack,' Miles butted in with his upper-class accent, his cold tone riling Cox. Was this call just so they could all point the finger at her some more? 'Henry?'

A sigh from Flannigan. 'From what we've gathered so far, two young males strapped with explosives tried, and failed, to blow themselves up on a busy train at Bordeaux's main station. When their devices failed they scarpered, but they were chased by . . . *concerned* citizens. Quite how it escalated . . . the upshot is, the two men fled to a mosque where prayer was in full swing. The doors were locked to stop the growing crowd outside from getting to them. Someone on the outside started a fire. You've seen the rest.'

Cox held her head in her hands. Tensions had remained high across Europe since the attacks the previous year. Small-scale and largely unplanned retaliations against Muslims had been reported in several countries in the immediate aftermath, but nothing on this scale.

'We're already hearing on our wires that far right groups in the UK are celebrating this,' Branding said, 'and we're expecting further retaliations here in the UK, particularly after Liverpool.'

'There are already protests and counter-protests and clashes with police taking place in Paris and Belgium,' Miles added. 'The whole bloody continent is about ready to explode.'

Cox shut her eyes, as if doing so would block out the whole mess.

'And we still have to expect that Wahid's group have more attacks planned,' Stokes chipped in. 'We need to stop them. And we need to find Torkal.'

'This isn't a time for playing the blame game, though,' Flannigan added, and Cox had to admit she was greatly relieved to hear that, given how the conversation had gone thus far. 'We've now had contact with someone claiming to be part of Wahid's group. That's one of the many reasons why this call is taking place.'

'What did they say?'

'That Liverpool and Bordeaux are just the start. That they'll get revenge for what happened today, and that we have to hand Aydin over or the attacks will continue.'

Cox had her eyes on the news broadcast when the aerial footage of the smouldering mosque was replaced by a close-up headshot of Aydin Torkal.

'No,' she said.

'No, what?' Flannigan said.

'I'm watching the news right now. It's Aydin.'

Flannigan sighed. 'There was nothing we could do. A message claiming responsibility was posted on the internet. The whole world knows who carried out the attacks, and that they'll continue as long as Torkal is running free.'

'The press will love that,' Cox said 'Everyone will blame Aydin all over again. He'll be the most hated man in the world.'

'And most people would say he just about deserves it,' Flannigan said.

'OK, that's enough tit for tat,' Miles said. 'Miss Cox, this might be news to you, but we do have more information on the Liverpool attack we can share with you.'

'I'm listening.'

But was this new information? Or had they been holding out on her until now?

'We have a good indication now of the type of device used in Liverpool, and of the person who used it.'

'And?

'And, well, it's crude. About as basic as it gets. A small pressure cooker. A nitrate-based low explosive. Not that any of that is going to help us locate Aydin, but it's useful intel at least.'

'What about the bomber?'

'Intriguingly, Liverpool wasn't a suicide, though Bordeaux certainly would have been, if the bombers hadn't failed. No *Allahu Akbar* in Liverpool though. Perhaps the most surprising thing is we're sure the Liverpool bomber was a Caucasian male with no previous record.'

'So? That doesn't mean—'

'Miss Cox, I'm simply giving you the intel we have,' Miles said, his tone abrupt, but then so was hers. 'We have CCTV shots we believe are of the culprit, but we're yet to ID him. I'm just giving you the facts.'

'So what exactly are you trying to say?'

'That not everything adds up here,' Flannigan said. 'Liverpool is a vastly different MO to what Aydin and his brothers were looking to do last year. There may be a significance to that.'

'No. They were looking to kill innocent civilians. That was their aim then, and it's their aim now. And they've achieved it.'

'Same aim, yes, but different MO.'

'Liverpool and Bordeaux. Not London and Paris. The same as last time, they're hitting targets that are less well protected, where people feel safer.'

'OK, yes, I get that, but—'

'Sorry, I'm just thinking out loud. I get what you're saying. They've moved on. They've a whole new method now. New tactics, new recruits.'

'And we need to stop them before there are any more attacks like this,' Stokes said.

'We'll get Aydin,' Cox said with absolute conviction.

'I really hope so,' Miles said. 'Though I'm beginning to wonder whether just doing that is going to be enough.'

And Cox felt sure she knew what he meant by that. Catching Aydin was one thing, but doing so wouldn't stop the fanatics, nor would it help ease the bubbling cultural and religious tensions. The people behind the Farm and its deadly graduates were still out there, and they were winning. They were the ones that Cox and SIS had to find. Until they did, there would only be further attacks, and further deaths. Cox had to do everything to make sure that didn't happen.

TWENTY-NINE

Aleppo, Syria

Quite how long Nilay endured the torture that followed, she had no idea. It felt like endless days, but perhaps was only a few agonising hours. She'd heard so many stories of the many techniques used in interrogation by the intelligence agencies – both legal and illegal – but to be put through it was so much worse than she could ever have imagined.

As they'd walked away from the interview room, a pair of thick noise-cancelling headphones had been placed over her head. At first the headphones were silent, and the noise-cancelling effect had simply meant her own breaths and heartbeat echoed in her head. But soon the white noise came. Blaring designed only to wear down her senses. It worked. As well as the relentless bombardment of her ears, every so often she was forced into different positions. Sitting, crouching, lying, arms held up, arms held to the side, arms in front. Nilay didn't once try to fight it. She had no intention of finding out what would happen if she did.

Whenever the noise was turned off, she'd be left with some angry grunt yelling at her, telling her her life was over, that she was scum, that she'd never see the light of day again.

That cycle was repeated over and over until her body ached so much she could barely move, and her head was a throbbing mess, as if her brain was bouncing inside her head.

Then, finally, it was over. The white noise stopped. The head-phones were removed. No shouting, but her ears rang incessantly. Then unseen hands pulled her into a standing position – just a regular straight-up standing position, but her body was so weak and disorientated that for a while she could barely hold it and the man had to keep putting her back into place.

'This way,' the man's voice said.

Nilay was ushered along once again. When they stopped walking, the sack was taken from her head. She couldn't keep her eyes open for more than a split second, the light in the room burned into the back of her mind. Slowly, cautiously, she lifted her lids, fearful of what she'd be facing next.

What she saw came as a complete surprise.

The white-painted room had maps and posters. A Stars and Stripes was stretched over one wall. There was a bookshelf filled with thick reference books. The green cross of a first-aid kit on one of the shelves.

Nilay looked down to the figure sitting at the thick wooden desk in front of her. No mask. No black clothes. The woman, in her thirties, was pudgy with a round face and closely cropped hair. The smile on her face held a certain warmth. She was sitting behind the desk, her legs crossed.

'Please, take a seat.' Another American. 'How are you feeling?'

'Never better,' Nilay said, shakily lowering her aching body down. She let out a sigh of relief as her body relaxed into the chair. 'So you're the good cop?'

Nilay guessed that was what was happening here. Good cop, bad cop. But they didn't need that routine. They just needed to give her the chance to tell her story.

The woman smiled. 'No. I'm the doctor.'

Nilay snorted.

'Have some water,' the woman said, indicating the already filled glass on the table in front of Nilay.

Nilay took the glass and, arm trembling, lifted it to her lips. She downed the liquid in two gulps, its cool temperature causing a shiver to run right through her.

'Who are you people?'

'Isn't it obvious?'

'CIA?'

'Close enough.'

'Then what do you want from me?'

The woman got up from her seat, picked up a stethoscope from the table and came and sat on the edge of the table in front of Nilay.

'I'm just here to make sure you're OK,' she said. 'Do you mind?'

She held the stethoscope up. Nilay shook her head. The woman reached around the neck of Nilay's blouse and dropped the stethoscope inside and she winced when the cold end of the scope pressed up against the skin on her chest.

The woman listened for a few seconds then moved the scope around. When she was finished she put the stethoscope down, and continued a series of routine tests. Heart rate, blood pressure. She looked in Nilay's eyes, her ears, her throat. Took a blood sample. As far as Nilay could tell, the whole thing was some sort of charade. However long she'd been there, they surely didn't give two hoots about her physical state. It was her mental state they'd been working on after all. Still, Nilay went along with it. It was certainly a whole lot better than the room she'd just come from.

'OK, well you're all good,' the woman said when she'd finally finished.

She took the seat behind the desk again. Clasped her hands together, her brow creased as though she were deep in thought.

'You must have been through a hell of an ordeal,' she said.

'Here? You should know.'

'No. Not here. In Iraq.'

155

Nilay winced. Yeah. It was all a charade. Did this woman have any medical training at all or only training in interrogation?

'Your husband was killed there.'

Nilay scoffed.

'If there's a story to tell, you need to tell it. We just need to know the truth. You can understand how this looks, right? A young Western woman, married to a big-ass warrior. Husband gets killed, so naturally the woman, grieving, looks for a way to seek revenge.'

'You have no idea what you're talking about.'

'No? Then why don't you set it straight for me.'

Nilay really wanted to, but her brain was so confused she was struggling to know exactly where to start.

'When did you last hear from your brother?'

'When I was nine years old.' This time Nilay answered on the spot, and the woman looked slightly surprised. But the simple fact of not having seen her brother since she was a child was far easier to explain than the last few months of her life. But why were they asking about Aydin? What did they know?

'How did you meet Sajad? A young woman like you, from London, with a university degree and so much potential ahead of you. How on earth did you end up married to a key member of ISIS.'

A key member? Nilay wondered what was meant by that, though she didn't ask.

Nilay took a deep breath. 'The thing is—'

Her retelling was cut short when there was a knock on the door. The woman looked annoyed by the interruption but held up a finger then got up and headed to the door. Nilay stayed on her seat but turned her head as far as she could to see who was on the other side. The woman only opened the door a few inches, then began a hushed conversation with whoever was there. At least, the conversation started off hushed, but within a few seconds, even though she carried on whispering, Nilay could tell that the woman was pissed off about something.

The conversation stopped. The woman turned round, a deep frown on her face.

'You'll have to excuse me for a few moments.'

And with that she walked out of the door and slammed it shut behind her. Nilay heard locks turning and after that the room fell silent.

What the hell should she do?

She looked around the room. It had all the props one would expect of a doctor's office. Stethoscope, otoscope, blood pressure monitors, scales, first-aid kit. What was in there? Scissors? A scalpel?

No, it was madness to even think about trying to escape. Trying to fight against the Americans. As heavy-handed as they were, she had to believe that they were only doing their jobs. If they knew the truth about her, they'd just let her go. They weren't the bad guys. Were they?

Nilay, painfully, slowly, got up from the chair, being careful not to make any sound whatsoever. She took a half-step forward. Then another. Aiming for the first-aid kit in the bookshelves. When she took another step her eyes darted up to the corner of the ceiling in front of her. She cursed herself. How hadn't she spotted the tiny camera up there before? They were probably watching her that very second.

She heard the key turning in the lock. Her heart already drumming in her chest, she quickly back-stepped and threw herself down onto the chair, just as the door creaked open. She didn't dare to look at whoever walked in. Just hoped it was the doctor again and not the heavies to take her back to the torture room.

She heard soft footsteps.

'Nilay? Jesus, it really is you.'

157

The sound of the familiar voice sent Nilay's mind into a confused spiral. Her eyes whipped to the figure who came over to her side. She shook her head.

'No,' was all that she could say.

'I came as soon as I could. Are you OK?'

'I . . . what are you doing here?'

'I'll explain after,' Abi Garrett said. 'Come on, let's get you out of here, before the Yanks change their minds.'

Abi held a hand out to Nilay. Despite her confusion, and her growing anger, she didn't even need to think about that one. She took the hand, and got to her feet.

THIRTY

'Who the hell are you?' Nilay asked for the third time.

Abi Garrett put her foot down to send the hulking Mitsubishi Shogun through the open gates at the perimeter of the US's off-the-grid site.

'My real name is Rachel Cox. I work for the British government.'

'You lied to me.'

'Ditto.'

Nilay glared at Cox. 'What was that place?' She glanced into the side mirror to see the chainlink fence and the small low-rise building beyond it that led to the bunker complex fading into the distance. She really hoped she'd never have to see that place again, or any other place like it.

'Somewhere you're lucky to get away from.'

'You want me to thank you?'

'It might be a good idea. Without me here, exactly what do you think they would have done to you?'

'And how exactly did you know I was there?'

'How do you think?'

'You've been spying on me?'

'Did you really think you wouldn't be on our radar after where you came from?'

Nilay said nothing to that. She looked out of her window as the desert sped past outside. She felt like a fool, though Cox's was a fair question. Did she believe she'd evaded the attention of the UK and US intelligence services in escaping ISIS in Mosul and getting to Aleppo? The honest truth was yes. This wasn't really a world she belonged in, however wholeheartedly she'd thrown herself into it.

'You could have told me who you were back in Iraq,' Nilay said. 'Why didn't you?'

'Nilay, I know you're not one of them. I don't quite know how you wound up with Sajad in Mosul, but I understand what you're doing now.'

'That doesn't answer my question at all.'

'What do you want me to say? That I played you? That you're an idiot for never having spotted it?'

Cox glared at Nilay, who held her eye.

'Is that what you did? Played me?'

'You're an asset, Nilay. Sometimes assets are good, sometimes they're bad, but they all have one thing in common. Information. When I heard about your story from a source in Mosul, I knew something wasn't right. Then when I saw your picture . . .'

'What?'

'I realised who you really were.'

'Which is who?'

'Aydin Torkal's sister. I really don't know why you put yourself through what you did. But I knew I had to help you.'

'I don't get it, why do you want to help me?'

'Because of your brother. You're looking for him. And so am I. Not just him, but all of the others who were taken to the Farm.'

Nilay's heart skipped a beat at the mention of the Farm but she said nothing. The fact that this Rachel Cox was willing to talk so openly about her brother, about the Farm, was concerning. Was this just part of the same charade concocted by the Americans?

'But you can't possibly have known what I'd do next after Mosul? That I'd come to Aleppo? That I'd take a job with Believe.' Nilay paused as she thought that one through. 'Wait . . . you didn't—'

'I had to.'

'You got them to take me on?'

'I felt sure if I dropped the seed in your mind that you'd take that step, or at least one close to it.'

'How did you even know?'

Cox didn't answer that one. Had they watched her every move?

'Don't you get it?' Cox said. 'You're really good at this, Nilay. You're good at helping people here. They need you.'

'Bullshit. That's not why you got me away from that place. You're using me.'

'If that were true I would have left you to the wolves. You need to understand, the Americans figured out who you are too. They know you're the same woman who escaped from ISIS in Mosul. They have people everywhere. They think you're still connected with the caliphate, probably because now you're hassling all and sundry trying to find out information on the Farm.'

'And what do you think about me? You said some assets are good, some are bad.'

'I think, regardless, we can help each other.'

Yet another unconvincing answer from Cox. The car went silent for a long while after that. Nilay kept her eyes on the road ahead as they edged closer to the beleaguered city once more.

Abi Garrett had been a shining light in Nilay's mind for the last few weeks, but it had all been a lie. Nilay felt truly hurt, even though she knew that a large part of her disgruntlement was nothing more than embarrassment. Yet she should be grateful to Cox for getting her away from the Americans. Even if it was only to suit her own agenda, that was twice now that Cox had rescued her.

'Why are you trying to find my brother?' Nilay eventually asked.

'Do you really have to ask that? The group your brother belongs to is considered to present a serious terrorist threat, not just in this region, but in Western Europe.'

Nilay felt faint at the thought. The only image she had in her mind of her brother was of him as a nine-year-old boy. What was he now?

'My brother was just a boy. He was so . . . normal. He's not a terrorist.'

'You don't know that.'

No, maybe not. But Cox didn't know him either.

'So how many of you are there?' Nilay asked.

'How do you mean?'

'How many are on your team, looking for them?'

'You don't need to think about that.'

Nilay frowned, unsure if there was more to that story or not.

They trailed through the city streets, back onto familiar territory. Not home exactly, but something close to it. Cox pulled the Shogun up outside Nilay's apartment building. Left the engine idling.

'What now?' Nilay said.

'Why don't you go in and get some rest?'

'And after that?'

'Just carry on as normal. Nilay, I've said it already, you're doing a good job here. Keep going. Keep helping people. Keep on talking to them. You're making progress and I think we can both use each other out here.'

'Do you know where Aydin is?'

'No. I don't.'

Nilay believed her.

'But together, I think we will find him. And all the others.'

'And what then? You'll take him away to one of those sites like where I just came from, right? You'll string him up, torture him?'

Cox looked away, clearly uncomfortable with what Nilay had said. She took that to be a yes. Could Nilay let that be her brother's fate?

'I honestly don't know what comes next,' Cox said. 'We just have to find them. Before it's too late. Get some rest. You'll be safe here now. The Americans know you're working with me.'

Nilay tutted, pulled on the door handle and stepped out into the street.

'Oh, and take this,' Cox said.

Nilay leaned in and took the phone from Cox's grasp.

'Ditch your old one. It's been bugged. Your laptop too. This one is clean. I'll use it to contact you. We need to swap notes and come up with a plan.'

Nilay looked at the phone, her mind was such a mess that she really didn't know what to do or say. Cox pulled the door shut.

'I'll be in touch.'

Cox edged the car back into the road, and the diesel engine growled as the four-by-four bolted away to the end of the street. Nilay didn't move until it was out of sight.

She looked up at the building, to the window of her apartment above. How could she possibly feel safe there now? Not just after what had happened with the Americans, but after what Cox had said about her phone and laptop being bugged. What about the apartment? And who the fuck had bugged her things anyway, and when?

A large part of her wanted to turn round there and then and run away. Hide somewhere. She could even attempt to travel home to England and just forget all about her dumb quest. Was it really worth all of this?

Despite the turmoil in her mind, the irrevocable conclusion she kept coming back to again and again was yes, it was worth it. Otherwise everything that had happened already would have been for nothing. And strangely, she did trust Cox.

163

Cox. Was that even her real name or just another deceit? Nilay was sure the truth would out eventually.

She huffed then stuck the phone into the pocket of her jeans, and headed for the entrance in front of her.

THIRTY-ONE

Istanbul, Turkey

Aydin's eyes were closed, though he wasn't sleeping. He'd first woken some ten minutes before, groggy and confused and disorientated. How long he'd been out of it, he had no idea, though he was surprised at what he'd woken up to. Not some torture chamber, as he'd expected, but what looked to be a reasonably well-equipped health clinic. Not a proper hospital, it was too informal for that, too quiet too, with none of the hustle and bustle of a public hospital in a big city. His was the only bed in the room. By his right side a series of wires trailed from his body to the bank of monitors. Off to his left were metal cabinets and a large white closed cupboard. All very purposeful . . . clinical.

The reason Aydin now had his eyes closed was that he was no longer alone in the room. A heavyset man, thirties, with a tight white shirt tucked into his khaki trousers was rummaging about next to him. A doctor?

Aydin bided his time. When he'd first awoken he'd been too weak to move. He'd lain there, looking around the room, just trying to acclimatise and to figure out what was going on. Had his uncle's house nurse, Esma, drugged him? That had been his immediate thought, but then there were so many implausibilities in that; the how and the why just didn't make sense to him. And if she'd drugged him, why was he waking up on a mattress in a private health clinic with his wounds all bandaged up, rather than in a stinking cell somewhere?

As he lay there Aydin could hear the calm breaths of the man. Could hear the scratching as he scribbled away on his notepad. Could hear the intermittent blips on the monitor with every beat of his heart. Slow and steady. He'd long been trained how to relax and to control his heart rate. The doctor had no idea Aydin was awake, nor that he was about to spring a devastating attack.

The shuffle of feet. Aydin slipped an eyelid open a fraction. Just enough to see faint shadows. And to tell him that, as he thought, the man was turning to head for the door.

Aydin sprang up, out of the bed, ignoring the shock of pain that spread through his whole body at his sudden movement. It was only as he put his foot down onto the cold lino floor that Aydin realised how weak he was, how uncoordinated his limbs were. Too late, he couldn't pull out now.

He pounced on the man, wrapped an arm around his neck, and grabbed hold of the biceps on his opposite arm to pull the hold tight. He placed his other hand behind the man's head. Applied just enough force to let the man know the position he was in. If he wanted to, Aydin just needed to squeeze slightly, push the man's head forward to constrict the carotid artery against his forearm. Within seconds the lack of blood supply to the man's brain would render him unconscious. Even in his weakened state Aydin was confident he'd achieve that aim.

But he wouldn't do it straight away, he wanted to give this man the option to talk.

The man writhed, but not too much. He understood the perilous situation he was in.

'Who are you?' Aydin said, his voice calm and assured.

166

'My name's Yalcin!' the man choked. 'Yalcin Umar. I'm just a doctor. You're safe here, Aydin. We won't harm you.'

'Why am I here?'

'Esma called me! You passed out. Septic shock. You nearly died, Aydin. Please, don't be afraid.'

Afraid? It was a strange choice of words, under the circumstances. Yet Aydin knew what Umar meant.

There was a creak on the other side of the room as the door opened. Aydin took a step back, dragging Umar with him. He swivelled slightly so Umar's mass was covering his. A white uniformed nurse came into the room. Slim build, attractive face. She was holding a tray up to her chest. Food. Water. She looked across. Dropped the tray. Screamed. Went to run.

'Don't move!' Aydin snapped. 'Don't move or he's dead.'

She paused. Trembling.

'Aydin. Please. We're here to help. You need to eat. To rest.'

Aydin's legs wobbled. A stabbing pain blared in his frontal lobes. He squinted. Tensed. Hoped it would go away. It didn't. It only got worse.

Umar seemed to sense this. Consumed by pain, Aydin didn't fight as Umar suddenly jerked and pulled himself free. Aydin fell to his knees. The whole room shook and vibrated and bounced. Aydin shouted out and squeezed his eyes shut tight.

'Help me get him up!' Umar shouted.

Seconds later arms were grabbing Aydin, pulling him. He flailed, trying to get them off him, but he was too weak. They propped him up against the bed. Somehow rolled his listless body over so he was lying on the mattress on his side. Aydin kept his eyes tightly shut, but still his world kept on spinning. When he next opened his lids, the nurse was there in front of him, syringe in her hand. Aydin didn't move, couldn't, as she came forward and sank the needle into his arm. The cool liquid surged into his blood. The pain and the confusion subsided. Aydin closed his eyes . . .

When he next woke, Aydin once again struggled to keep his eyes open at first. This time though he quickly recalled where he was. Noticed he wasn't waking up alone – Umar was sitting on a metal chair across the room.

When he was lucid enough, Aydin went to sit up in the bed. Realised his wrists were tied to the metal side bars of the gurney with leather straps.

'Sorry, Aydin,' Umar said. 'But we can't have you attacking us like that.'

He didn't sound sorry at all. Aydin slumped back down onto the bed, his weary brain doing its best to figure out not just what was happening, but how he could escape.

Umar got up from the chair and came over to Aydin.

'I understand,' Umar said. He was standing just a couple of feet away. Within striking distance, if Aydin had full use of his body. Which he didn't. Yet. 'You've got a lot of questions. So let me answer some of them for you.'

Umar moved closer still. Aydin flinched as the doctor swiped away the thin white sheet that covered his body. He shivered as the cooler air hit his skin. As before, under the sheet he was wearing a light blue fabric hospital gown that was cut off at the shoulders and didn't quite reach down to his knees.

Umar first pointed to Aydin's leg. 'You did a decent enough job on this one,' Umar said. 'The stitching wasn't pretty, but at least you managed to keep the wound clean and disinfected. You'll have a nasty scar, but no lasting damage.'

Umar took a pen from the pocket of his shirt and reached out to Aydin's arm. He gently prodded the bandaged area.

'This one was not so good. I had to open it up again and clean it out properly. But it's the gash on your back that led you to being here. You had fragments inside. They could have caused you a lot of problems . . .'

Fragments. Yet another interesting choice of words. Aydin presumed Umar meant bullet fragments. He didn't seem particularly put out by the fact that the patient he'd treated had been shot. Who the hell were these people? What kind of clinic was this?

'I'm guessing because of the position of the wound, you struggled to tend to it properly yourself. The site was badly infected. If you hadn't been with Esma when you passed out you may well not have woken up again.'

Aydin said nothing to that. Umar's explanation as to what had happened in Esma's apartment seemed plausible enough. Though it still didn't explain why they were helping him, or who they were.

'We've stitched and bandaged you up properly now. The anti-virals and antibiotics have started to take effect. In a few days you should be back on your feet.'

'How long have I been here?'

'Three days now.'

Aydin winced. He'd lost so much time already.

'But you still need more rest,' Umar said, as if reading Aydin's mind. 'And to eat properly. You must be hungry.'

Really, eating was the last thing on his mind, but he had to be realistic. He wanted to be out of there as soon as possible. To do that, he had to be as strong as possible.

Aydin glanced over to his right. Under a small side table was his backpack. He'd not yet had the chance to check whether all his belongings were still there. He wondered whether anyone had looked inside. Whoever was helping him here, he couldn't risk losing the ATS hard drive. He had to find a way to get access to the data it held.

'We're in Istanbul still?' Aydin asked.

'Of course.'

'Who are you people?' Aydin asked.

'We're friends,' was Umar's simple answer.

Aydin cringed at the answer. Friends. It was a long time since he'd had any of those, and one of the last places he'd expected to find a friend or ally was in chasing down his uncle who he was sure knew more about the Farm than he had revealed.

But then Aydin had to remember that age-old saying: the enemy of my enemy is my friend.

Aydin was being hunted by the British intelligence services. He'd stolen information from them. He knew there were plenty of rebel groups around who would now see Aydin as an ally, even despite his recent past of running from and killing his own people.

'You know my name,' Aydin said.

'Esma told us.'

'You know who I am, and you still helped me. So you know I'm dangerous.'

Aydin glared at Umar, who held his gaze. The doctor didn't seem particularly put out by Aydin's words, even though not long ago Aydin had been ready to choke him.

'You need to tell me why you're helping me. What do you want from me?'

'You need to eat,' Umar said. 'There'll be plenty of time for talking.'

He turned and walked out.

Moments later the same nurse as before came back into the room, a tray once again in her hands. One eye on Aydin, she tentatively placed it down on the table next to Aydin's bed.

She pulled across the chair Umar had been sitting on moments earlier, and sat down. Then she took a forkful of the meaty stew from the plate and pushed it towards Aydin's mouth.

He shook his head. 'If you untie me, I can eat myself.'

'Not this time,' she said, a cold and stern look on her face.

Whatever. He needed the sustenance. Aydin opened his mouth and took the food. He barely chewed it before swallowing. Couldn't taste it at all. He just knew he needed to eat. He opened his mouth again.

The plate was soon empty, and Aydin's full belly bloated and gurgling. The nurse held a glass of water up to Aydin's lips and he slurped away. Some of the cold liquid ran down his chin and onto his chest. He saw the amused look on the nurse's face, as though she took some sort of pleasure from his undignified position.

She wiped his chest with a cloth, then when the glass was empty she set it down on the tray and got to her feet. She picked up the tray and moved to the door.

'Thank you,' Aydin said. The nurse paused, then continued on her way without saying a word.

Aydin was alone again, but not for long. When his next visitor arrived, Aydin was beginning to feel sleepy and woozy once again, but when he saw Esma's face in the doorway, he became more alert.

She looked at him then frowned.

'What have they done to you,' she blasted.

She stormed up to his side and unstrapped the leather from his wrists.

'I'm so sorry,' she said.

When his wrists were free, Aydin somewhat surprised himself by just lying there, rather than jumping up and tackling the middle-aged woman to make his escape, like he'd expected he might. Instead he just gently caressed the sore skin on his wrists, trying to get some feeling back into his hands.

'You've got some explaining to do,' Aydin said.

The first time he'd met Esma, he'd tied her up and thrown her into a cupboard. The second time, he'd barged into her apartment to question her. She had as much reason as anyone else to hate Aydin, to want to see him punished.

Yet she'd helped him. Or so they were claiming.

'I know your uncle didn't trust you,' Esma said. 'But I did trust him.'

It was a strange thing to say, though Aydin didn't question it.

'Do you know of your uncle's affiliations?' Esma asked.

Aydin shook his head.

'He was such a proud man, a proud Turk, but sometimes his pride got the better of him. He could be so dogmatic and single-minded.'

She looked away, frowning, as though reminiscing about something that was hard to talk about.

'How long have you known him?' Aydin asked.

'Only about five years. Anyway, the point I was trying to make was that your uncle believed in this country. And he believed in our leader, and his vision for an Islamist Turkey.'

Aydin cringed, though he wasn't sure why.

'But I first noticed the change after the coup,' Esma said.

'Attempted coup, you mean,' Aydin said, referring to the failed coup in 2016 when a group led by senior military officers had tried to overthrow the Turkish government, but had ultimately failed.

Esma laughed nervously. 'The thing was . . .' she shook her head in disbelief. 'Oh, so many lies and deceits it's hard to know where to start.'

She paused. He could tell from her increasing agitation that what she was trying to say was hard for her. But she'd opened the door here, and he had to know.

'Please, tell me.'

'The thing is, you see this place.' She looked around. 'We were part of that. Of the coup. We wanted it, we helped to set it up, had all of the plans as to what would come next. It wasn't a sudden decision, we'd been planning for years. I was sent to your uncle's house for the very purpose of spying on him.'

Aydin sat up in the bed now. The fog in his brain was quickly clearing as the potential significance of what Esma was saying dawned.

'Your uncle was on the inside of the government,' she said. 'He never suspected my true intentions, my true affiliations.'

There was a rawness to her words now. Genuine emotion, sadness, regret.

'After the coup, do you know what happened?' she asked.

'I've heard stories. Thousands of political opponents being rounded up, forced from their jobs, their homes. Hundreds locked up in jail awaiting trial.'

'Of course the military officers were the ones to fight that night, but the movement went far beyond them.'

'To people like you.'

'Exactly. We were some of the lucky ones, perhaps too unimportant to catch the eye, which is why we're still here, still plotting.'

'But what about my uncle? You were working against him?'

'Well there's the thing. Even before the action in 2016, I knew something wasn't right with him. Like I said, I was sent to spy. To gain information that would help our cause. What I found out was something quite different.'

Footsteps outside. Esma stopped and looked to the door. Aydin watched the outline of the person through the frosted glass, soon out of sight again.

'Your uncle had his secrets, you see. A spy himself, you could say.'

'He was on the inside working *against* the government?'

'More than that, Aydin. How and why, I still don't fully know, but I do know for a fact that for years your uncle was working with outside influences.'

'Outside influences? What do you mean?'

'I mean . . .' she paused again. Looked around the room. Looked to the door. Locked eyes with Aydin. 'Your uncle was a spy for the British. He was working with MI6.'

THIRTY-TWO

'That makes no sense,' Aydin said, shaking his head as his brain tried in vain to put together the pieces.

'What doesn't?'

'My uncle was no spy.'

'You didn't know him.' Her voice was stern. 'I was with him nearly every day for years.'

'He wasn't a spy. What makes you think that?'

'I don't *think* it, I know it. So maybe spy isn't the right word, but he was working with the British government. I met the man your uncle reported to several times.'

'Who?'

'I don't know his real name. He was English, called himself Mr Grey. Maybe that really was his name, maybe not.'

'Mr Grey?'

'That's what I said. He came to the house.'

'And how do you know who he worked for? Did he give you a business card?'

Esma's face screwed up in anger, and Aydin realised he'd overstepped the mark. She was helping him. He certainly believed what she was telling him was the truth as she saw it, but had she simply read the situation wrong, or read far too much into it? Possibly, but that didn't mean he needed to shoot her down. The only reason she was helping him now was because she believed his uncle was in fact working *against* the Islamists who supported the Turkish government. That he'd been working with the British, whose agenda may have been aligned with her own group's.

'I'm sorry,' he said. 'But perhaps you can appreciate what you're telling me about my uncle doesn't match with what I know.'

'You mean what you thought you knew. If he was a double-agent, playing against the Islamists, then it makes perfect sense.'

'What do you know about this Mr Grey?' Aydin asked.

'Virtually nothing. I never managed to get a picture of him, or anything like that. Of course I've had friends try to track him down and identify him, but we've never succeeded.'

'When did you last see him?'

She thought about it for a few moments. 'Not for over a year.'

'But you also said you think it was a British team who snatched my uncle?'

'I didn't say I thought that, I'm *sure* they were British. You think that doesn't make sense? But you must realise that the British, just like the Turkish, have more than one side at play within their ranks.'

Aydin certainly wouldn't dispute that one. It was one of the very reasons why his trail had led him to ATS. Did Esma know anything about that?

'I need to find this Mr Grey,' Aydin said.

Esma didn't look too sure about that.

'Can you help me?'

She got to her feet, looking nervous all of a sudden.

'I've said enough. I really should go.'

She paused, looked to Aydin, but then turned and walked out without another word.

Aydin hadn't moved from the bed more than an hour later when the young nurse came back in with yet another tray of food. Esma's words and the implications of what she'd said were still swimming in his mind as the nurse took a seat.

He saw her glance to his wrists. A startled look on her face. 'Don't worry,' he said

'I'll leave the food for you.'

Nervous, she quickly got back to her feet and headed to the door. Aydin couldn't care less. He ate the food, deep in his own thoughts. Took the collection of pills that was in the clear plastic cup next to the water glass without even thinking what the concoction could be. What he did know was that he was in better shape now than when he'd first arrived in Turkey. He'd take what they were giving him, and he'd keep working on Esma. Sooner or later he'd be fit enough to get out of there, and by that point he wanted to know everything.

Not long after he'd finished the food, with thoughts of his uncle and the mysterious Mr Grey on his mind, Aydin drifted off to sleep.

Aydin had long been used to being a light sleeper. The torment of growing up on the Farm had quickly taken its toll on him as a boy, never quite knowing what horrors would await him when he next opened his eyes. Now, as an adult, it was habit more than a reaction to an ever-present terror. A useful defence mechanism, certainly.

Even in his drug-induced state, he managed to remain partially aware of his surroundings. It meant that he was able to quickly snap from his slumber and back to reality when he sensed someone standing next to him.

Aydin's hand whipped out to his side. He grabbed the wrist of the man who was standing by the bed. Young, in his early twenties, and dressed in a blue hospital gown, the man's bloodshot eyes stared down at Aydin.

'What are you doing?' Aydin hissed.

He looked at the man's other hand. He was clutching Aydin's backpack.

'They told me about you,' he said, his words confident. He didn't seem in the least flustered. 'I had to see if it was true. If it was really you.'

'Drop the backpack.'

The man didn't.

'Drop it now.'

'I can't do that.'

'Yes you can.'

The man glanced to his other side. What was he looking for?

The next moment the man twisted his own arm round in a short sharp motion, spinning out from Aydin's grip. Together with his tone, Aydin knew this guy was no slouch, whoever the hell he was.

Prone on the bed, Aydin chose defence first, and rolled the opposite way, just as the man grabbed the heart monitor from the side and sent it crashing against the headboard.

Aydin rolled off the edge of the bed, scrambled to his feet. The monitor bounced off the bed and smashed to pieces when it hit the hard floor. The man, Aydin's backpack in his hand, decided not to stand and fight. He was rushing for the door. Aydin yanked the sensors and clips from his gown and body, darted across the room. The man sensed him but could do nothing as Aydin launched himself forward. He caught the man around his midriff and sent him stumbling forward. Both of them out of control, they hurtled towards the floor. Which would have been fine, had they not been so close to the exit. The man's head, face first, smacked sickeningly into the frame of the door. His head snapped back. Aydin thumped down on top of him and there was a crack — the man's ribs? — and an *oompf* as the air was forced from his lungs.

Aydin was ready for a grapple, was expecting it, had already planned his moves. But the man was motionless. Aydin moved off him. Glanced at the man's bloodied head. His nose was squashed into his face. There was a deep gash on his forehead, blooding pouring out. Aydin wasn't sure whether he was breathing at all. He didn't check. He decided he didn't have time.

He wrestled the backpack from the man's limp grip. Quickly checked inside. To his surprise everything was still in there.

But the man had been snooping for a reason, hadn't he? He'd said he knew who Aydin was. What was he looking for?

Aydin looked across the room. The clothes he'd worn when he'd first gone to Esma's apartment were neatly folded on a side table. He was about to grab them when he heard footsteps out in the corridor. The next moment Umar came into view, looking down at his phone as he made his way to Aydin's room.

Umar froze when he saw the man's body crumpled on the floor in front of him. He lifted his head, his terrified eyes met Aydin's.

'I didn't mean to hurt him,' Aydin said. Umar said nothing. What would he do? Aydin really hoped he wouldn't run. 'Just let me go, no one else needs to get hurt.'

Aydin realised his nervous and jittery voice wasn't exactly winning Umar over. The doctor flinched. Aydin simply couldn't take the risk. He lunged forward again. Umar thrust his arms out to protect himself. It did little to stop Aydin. He grabbed Umar's wrist, twisted around and threw his own arm around Umar's neck, putting him back into the same choke hold as the first time they'd met. This time Aydin wasn't in the mood for a warning.

'Please, no!' Umar screamed, a second before Aydin squeezed and pushed Umar's head forward, crushing the carotid artery. It took only a few seconds for Umar's body to go limp.

As soon as Umar was still, Aydin released the grip. If he held on too long there was a good chance he'd kill the doctor. He had no reason to do that. He helped Umar's body down, then darted over for his clothes.

He stripped off the hospital gown, put on his own clothes and shoes, grabbed his backpack then rushed for the door. He had a sudden thought. Went back over to Umar and prised the clipboard from his hands. He scanned the papers there, looking for the names of the medication they'd been giving him. He tore off the sheets he needed, then straightened up.

In the doorway he paused for just a moment to check the corridor outside was clear. It was. He turned back to the room. The other man was still unmoving on the floor. Umar was beginning to rouse.

'I'm sorry,' Aydin said.

Umar said nothing in response. Aydin turned and rushed out into the corridor.

THIRTY-THREE

Cairo, Turkey

Rachel Cox was shown into the hotel room by Captain Warda of the Egyptian National Police, a dour man in his forties, plain-clothed, who looked ten years older than he really was because of a persistent frown that had forged deep crevices in his face. Cox flipped the lights on. The only natural light in the room came through the small gaps between the plain chip-wood boards that sat behind broken glass and covered the window frame.

The body of Graham Castle – the SIS contractor killed by Aydin Torkal – had long since been removed, but his blood still stained the plush carpet and was splattered over the walls despite the sprinklers having in part washed it away, and despite the obvious fire damage in the room that meant black soot was smeared everywhere.

'They came through the window,' Warda said in barely decipherable English.

Cox looked over to the boarded-up window. She'd already taken a look from the outside, up to the seventh floor. It'd been one hell of a leap from the roof of the building opposite that was at least ten feet away. Quite how neither of the men had killed themselves in the process of the jump was remark-able. Well, Castle hadn't exactly fared too well shortly after, despite his heroics.

Cox walked across the room to the window, then turned and looked back over the space, trying to imagine the sequence of events, the fight, the violence that led to Castle, an English national who for all intents and purposes was nothing more than a freelance IT consultant, being stabbed to death by Aydin on the hotel room carpet.

'I guess it was lucky it was this room. Every other room on the floor was taken that day,' Warda said. 'Who knows, many others may have been injured.'

'Have your forensics teams swept this room?'

'Swept? Cleaned?'

'No. Have you taken blood samples? DNA? Fingerprints?'

'Yes, they have. Routine. But what's the point really? We know who the dead man is, and I've already had a rod inserted in me to stop me talking about who the one that got away is.'

Cox didn't question his clumsy choice of words. She got the point. Warda of course knew that Castle was somehow involved with the UK government – after all, he'd been briefed on who Cox was prior to them meeting today. He also knew that Aydin Torkal was the one who got away, although SIS had done its best to make sure that fact was confined to a close inner circle of people both in Egypt and back home, and no public announcement had yet been made that Aydin was responsible, and was now wanted for yet another death. Cox could only imagine the furore in the UK if the tabloids found out about that, given the recent bombing in Liverpool and the troubles in France and Belgium.

'Is there something you're looking for here?' Warda asked.

'I don't know,' Cox said, deep in thought.

Warda huffed his annoyance. Started tapping his foot impatiently. Checked his watch.

'You can see the body if you like?' he said.

182

Cox thought about that, but really she didn't feel it necessary. She'd never been a fan of morgues, or dead bodies. She'd seen plenty already.

'No. I'm done here. Thank you for your time.'

He raised an eyebrow, as though her visit had been a complete waste of his time. But it hadn't been a waste for her. Before going to the hotel, they'd already paid a visit to Aydin's apartment, which was now bare, having been cleaned out by SIS, and she'd painstakingly followed the trail from there and from roof top to roof top, piecing together the sequence of events that had led to Castle's death and Aydin's escape. Warda may have felt that was all unnecessary, but to Cox it was an important element in putting herself back into Aydin's mindset, which she needed to do in order to track him down. Particularly as so far it appeared he'd just vanished.

Why had he suddenly gone so quiet after his initial attempt to contact her? She'd wondered more than once whether he'd crawled into a corner somewhere and died. Or had someone else already got to him, and killed him perhaps?

'I'll be in touch if I need any more information,' Cox said.

Warda shrugged. 'You say jump, I'll ask how high.'

The time was nearly midday as Cox approached the cafe in the quaint square. The area, accessed by one of two narrow alleys, was quiet despite the time of day and the fact that it was within one of the most touristy areas of the city. To her right was a small Roman Catholic church, somewhat out of place in its surroundings. A fountain in the middle of the square was adorned with water-spitting fish, though the stonework was slimy and green and it was clear the feature hadn't had any love or care for a number of years.

There were only a small number of customers at the cheap blue plastic tables and chairs outside the cafe. It wasn't hard to spot the man Cox was there to meet. Dressed in combat trousers and a tight-fitting t-shirt, the heavily muscled man, buzz cut and all, may as well have had a sign on his head saying 'ex-army'.

'You must be Mo?' Cox said, heading over to him and taking a seat at his table without waiting for an invite.

Mo Blake, Castle's accomplice in the failed capture of Aydin, remained where he was, gave Cox a cursory acknowledgement.

'Yeah,' he said. 'You Cox?'

'I am. Thank you for meeting with me. We've got a lot to talk about.'

'I'm not so sure about that,' he said, before taking a long swig of his Coke bottle. 'There's nothing to tell that I haven't already said.'

'You think?'

'Look, Miss Cox, you know what I am. I know pretty much nothing here. I'm just a doer. I was given a job—'

'Yes, and you failed.'

Blake gave Cox a cold stare. Perhaps the look was supposed to intimidate her. It didn't.

'You're not my boss,' he said. 'I don't answer to you.'

'I'm not your boss. But right now you do answer to me. I'm in charge here now.'

'No you're not.'

Cox raised an eyebrow.

'Look, I'm not meaning to be an arsehole—'

Cox scoffed. 'But you're doing it so well so far, and we only met a minute ago.'

'Very funny. It's nothing personal, but you know how this works. I'm not like you. I'm not some fucking James Bond wannabe. I'm just a guy who does what he's told. I get a job, I do it. No questions asked. That's it. I don't have to think about the whys or whos.'

'Yeah, I get it. Plausible deniability.'

'Something like that.'

'But you're not talking to an outside party here. You're talking to me. We work for the same people.'

'No difference. I've nothing to say to you.'

'Your colleague died the other day. I'm just trying to figure out what happened.'

'He wasn't my colleague. I barely knew him.'

'Yeah, I'm sensing you're not exactly cut up about what happened.'

'The only thing I'm bothered about here is me. Don't look too good when we mess up, does it? First time it's ever happened for me.'

He huffed at his own apparent misfortune, took another gulp of his drink. A waiter came over but Cox waved him away. She got the feeling the conversation wouldn't last much longer.

They sat through a minute's uncomfortable silence. Blake remained sullen yet confident. Cox had met men like him plenty in her field. She didn't know his full history, only that at one time he'd been in the British Army, but had been snapped up by a military contractor a number of years ago. Since then the trail of who he'd worked for and what he'd done was patchy to say the least – which likely meant he'd long been used by SIS and the like to carry out questionable operations at arm's length. Cox could understand to some extent why he was reticent to open up to her about this operation, but was that more to do with an outside influence rather than his sense of a moral code?

'So who put pressure on you?'

'No one's put pressure on me.'

Though the twitch in his face suggested otherwise. Someone had already got to Blake, told him to keep his mouth shut.

'That's a load of crap. You agreed to meet me. You must have been prepared to talk then. So who got to you in between when we last spoke and now?'

Blake shrugged, uninterested in her deduction.

'So that's it? You won't talk to me about what happened?'

'No. Ask what you want, but I've nothing to say to you or anyone else about that day.' Blake checked his watch.

'You've somewhere better to be?' Cox asked.

'Yeah, actually I do.' Blake got to his feet and put some coins down on the table. 'Sorry you've wasted your time.'

He picked up a pair of sunglasses from the table, put them on, then walked away.

It took Cox twenty minutes to walk back through the bustling inner-city streets to the safe house that had been commandeered for her operation. A somewhat normal apartment on the top floor of a half-empty post-war block, the safe house was innocuous from the outside, and as she climbed the last of the stairs to arrive at her floor, even the plain outer door gave nothing away as to what lay beyond. Cox unlocked the door and stepped into the inner corridor, then shut the door behind her. Ahead was a more sturdy and more secure metal door. She pressed the intercom and stared up to where the unseen camera was located, and waited for the series of locks to be released.

Cox pushed open the door and stepped into the well-appointed space that consisted of two bedrooms, a bathroom and a large open-plan living area with a clear view of the minarets of the Al-Azhar Mosque in the near distance.

The safe house's usual sole occupant, Amir Ezzat, a British-born man in his early twenties who held dual Egyptian nationality, and was a mid-level data analyst for SIS, came into the doorway of the lounge.

186

'There's someone here for you,' Ezzat said.

'There is?'

'In the lounge.'

'Any progress?' Cox asked.

With all of Aydin's computer equipment now in their hands, Ezzat had been given responsibility for unpicking the data it contained, trying to figure out what Aydin was up to, and where he had gone.

'Some. I've found details of a few contacts. Possible leads. But it's going to take much longer.'

'OK. Fill me in properly after.'

Ezzat nodded and disappeared into the second bedroom which had been taken over by computer equipment.

Intrigued, Cox headed on into the lounge where a man she'd not met before was sitting in a leather armchair. He got to his feet. Gave her a warm smile, as though they were long-time acquaintances. In his forties, or early fifties, he was short but thick-framed, with black-rimmed designer glasses, well groomed with a heavily receding hairline, and a handsome yet hard face. Assertiveness more than arrogance.

'Pleased to meet you,' Cox said. 'And you are?'

'I'm the only person you need to speak to about this matter from here on in.' He held out a hand to Cox. 'My name's Edmund Grey.'

THIRTY-FOUR

'I understand you've just met with Mo Blake,' Grey said, taking his seat again. He indicated for Cox to sit opposite.

'I did. Not the most talkative chap in the world.'

Grey smiled. 'Yeah. You should catch him on a bad day. The thing is, he works for me, and I told him not to talk to anyone.'

'That was the impression I got.'

'He's a good asset. Never failed me before.'

'I guess he's never been up against someone like Aydin Torkal before.'

'Believe me, he certainly has. Which is why he's feeling so bruised. These guys have big egos.'

'You don't say. I don't mean to be rude, but what exactly are you doing here?'

Grey smiled again. His manner was confusing to Cox. Most of the suits she met in her job were loud and brash like Flannigan. Grey clearly had a different, and somewhat more relaxed approach. Even though it was undoubtedly more friendly, Cox wasn't sure which personality type she preferred. Or which she trusted more.

'Blake and Castle were operating under my orders. I oversee all covert ops in North Africa and the Middle East.'

'Henry Flannigan never mentioned anything about you to me.'

Grey shrugged. 'Why would he? I don't answer to Flannigan. Our paths rarely cross.'

'Then who do you answer to?'

Cox saw just a slight chink in his accommodating façade. She wondered exactly what lay beneath the friendly exterior.

'The answer to that question is an irrelevance,' he said, still measured.

'It feels pretty relevant to me.'

'OK. I can tell something's got your back up, but please, I'm not here to cause you trouble. I'm here to help. I know you're operating under your own orders, but you're just going to have to accept that those orders have now been superseded by me. Check with Flannigan or whoever else, but that's just the way it is. Like I said, nothing happens in this part of the world without me knowing about it. That's been the case for a long time, whether or not you knew about it, and however you may feel about it now.'

'Fine. Then seeing as you're the eyes and ears around here, perhaps you can tell me why Aydin Torkal decided to break into ATS last week?'

Grey sighed. 'I know the answer, but I can't tell you.'

'And I'm guessing, therefore, that you're also not going to tell me what you know about Shadow Hand?'

Another twitch on Grey's face, but he recovered remarkably well.

'How do you know about that?' Grey asked.

'What do you think my job is? I'm trained to investigate.'

Grey chewed on that one for a few moments. Cox guessed he was debating in his own mind what he was prepared to tell her. Whatever he came out with, she felt sure it would either be a lie or at most only a sliver of the truth.

'I've heard a lot about you, you know.'

189

'All bad, no doubt.'

It wasn't like she generally got along with those she reported to.

Grey chuckled. 'You do yourself a disservice. I've heard a lot of good about you. What you did . . . you saved a lot of lives. I sense you're not entirely satisfied with how events panned out, but you're a hero.'

'There are others involved in the Farm still out there.'

'Like Aydin.'

'Yes, like Aydin. But I didn't mean him.'

'You know, Aydin and his so-called *brothers* were in many ways inevitable.'

'How do you mean?'

'I mean if you poke a caged tiger often enough, then how exactly do you think it's going to react?'

'You blame the West for creating the Farm and the boys who were trained there?'

Grey shrugged. 'In a roundabout way, yes.'

'But those boys weren't animals.'

'You don't think Wahid is an animal?'

The conversation was becoming increasingly bizarre. This was a man Cox had never met until five minutes ago, yet he talked about the events of last year, about Aydin and Wahid, like it was all so personal to *him*. Where the hell had he been twelve months ago when Cox had put her life on the line to bring down Wahid and his brothers? Where had he been for the two years before that while Cox trailed around the world searching for intel on who the Thirteen were and where they were located, what their planned attacks were?

'Point taken,' Cox said. 'Yes, I think Wahid is an animal. Let me rephrase – not all of those boys were animals. You should know better than anyone not to believe everything you read in the press.'

'I presume you're talking about Aydin Torkal now. Talatashar.'

'Have you met him before?'

'No.'

'I have. He's not all bad. The papers make him out to be a monster. For months there wasn't a day that went by without some hatchet job on him, his family. But he helped us to bring down his brothers. He escaped from our grasp, but he didn't run away to live a life of solitude. He's back, and the only reason he'd risk coming out into the open is because he's found something worth finding.'

Grey nodded, though Cox didn't believe he was particularly impressed with her short speech. She was giving him nothing new.

'I guess we'll figure out what Aydin Torkal is up to when we track him down, won't we?'

'Yeah. I guess so.'

Grey chuckled again. Sat back and clasped his hands together behind his head.

'Let me tell you a little story. Did you know it was nearly twenty years ago when we first got wind of the place you now call the Farm?'

Twenty years? Cox tried not to show her reaction, but the widening smile on Grey's face suggested he knew he had her.

'Back then the Farm was nothing more than an elaborate idea. Something we knew the jihadis – Al-Qaeda at the time – wanted to implement for their long-term gain, but they didn't have the knowledge or the tactics to really put it into place back then. Not to start with anyway. But they were determined. We got wind of it when they were still planning, but they were getting closer all the time. I was tasked with investigating it. I got to the bottom of their plans before they ever got it off the ground. The ring leaders were all rounded up or quietly dispatched. We quashed it.'

Cox frowned, confused. 'But it still happened. The Farm was still set up. At the very least, thirteen boys grew up there and were sent out into the world to wreak havoc.'

'Which was my point exactly. I already said, that place was inevitable. We stopped it once, but they just went and did it again. In the same way that you stopped the attacks last year, but that hardly means you've prevented every terrorist attack forever, does it?'

Cox winced. Was he referring specifically to Liverpool or just more generally?

'Point taken,' Cox said. 'Though why is your story relevant here?'

Grey thought about that one for a moment, then sighed before he spoke. 'Because you seem to think there's something special about Aydin Torkal. And I get why that's the case. There's a bond between you two . . .' Cox blushed at those words. Embarrassed at her own reaction, her cheeks only turned redder. 'But there is *nothing* special about Torkal. Whatever you think his agenda is, he's damaged beyond repair. Really he's just like all the others. We *will* find him. You're going to help. We'll bring him to justice in our way, but the war will go on. So it's time to forget all the bullshit about who you think he is and what you think he's trying to achieve here. Concentrate on the task at hand. There's nothing deep or meaningful happening, this is just a way of life for these people. We find Torkal, we take him out. Then we move on to the next.'

Cox held her tongue. As much as she wanted to debate his caveman-like attitude to the world, she had to admit there was an element of truth in his words. Aydin was just a small element in a much bigger problem. Yet that didn't mean that whatever he was now chasing down was irrelevant. Even if Grey wasn't interested, Cox still wanted to know the truth – all of it.

There was a knock on the door. Cox and Grey both turned to Ezzat.

'I think you need to come and see this.'

Ezzat was sitting at his swivel chair in front of his bank of monitors, Grey and Cox standing over him.

'The messages themselves are all but gone, just fragments left in the hard drive's metadata. Like ghosts.'

'But you can trace where the messages came from?' Grey asked.

Ezzat rolled his head. 'Kind of. From those fragments we only get snippets of what they relate to. But I found enough to follow a lead. They seemed to be messages. Clearly Torkal wouldn't just be sending regular emails, so I went deeper. Using the Tor network I found the messaging site Torkal had visited, and matched the fragments to what I managed to figure out was the sole user he was in contact with on that site. From there I traced the real name of that person. Ruslan Garayev.'

'Russian?' Cox asked.

'Sounds it. There are plenty of people going by that name, so I need more time to search.'

'What the hell were they talking about?' Grey asked.

'I could take an educated guess. The messaging site is a known gathering place for hackers.'

'He's looking for help in getting into the ATS data,' Cox said.

'Seems the most likely explanation.'

'Any idea where Garayev is based? It could be where Aydin has gone to.'

'Don't know yet. It could take a while to unpick the mess as Garayev's left a very elaborate trail, but I will get there eventually.'

'Could it be Turkey?' Grey asked. 'Do you think he's still there?'

Cox glared at Grey. He gave her a nonchalant shrug in return.

'Since when was Aydin in Turkey?' she asked.

'Since three days ago,' Grey said, as though it was nothing.

'Why the hell didn't you tell me this already?'

Grey scoffed, for the first time his nice-guy demeanour was gone, though Cox realised her tone with him had hardly been friendly.

'You didn't ask me what I knew. You just assumed you were the one ahead of the game with all the knowledge. Like I said before, I've been living and breathing this for years. I know these people, and I might never have met Aydin Torkal before but I'm damn sure I know him too.'

'Fine. But please, can you just tell me what you know?'

'Of course. I'm not here to hold back on you.' Except where Shadow Hand is concerned, Cox thought but didn't say. 'We had surveillance in Istanbul. At the home of Torkal's uncle.'

'Kamil Torkal?'

'The one and the same.'

'You had Aydin on surveillance and you didn't bring him in?'

'Unfortunately it wasn't live surveillance. Just cameras. We didn't even know we had him until twenty-four hours after the event.'

'Which was still two days ago,' Cox said. 'Have you spoken to Kamil since?'

'No.'

'Why not?'

'Because Kamil Torkal disappeared months ago. Nobody knows where he is.'

'What, for Christ—'

'Don't even start,' Grey said, somewhat apologetically. 'I'm not trying to be difficult with you, please, I'm really not. I'm telling you what I know. I don't know why, but Kamil and his wife disappeared. They haven't been seen for months. Again, I don't know why, but Aydin chose to go to his uncle's home three days ago. He didn't stay long. After that, we've no idea.'

'Did you send anyone there, to try and trace him?' Cox asked.

'No. And I sense what you're thinking, but there's no point you going there. If he's still in Istanbul, my people will catch up with him. We need to know where he is *now*. No, scratch that, I need to know where he's going to be tomorrow so we can get there first. We need to find where this Garayev is based.'

'I can do it,' Ezzat said. 'But it may take some time.'

'No. You don't have any time. Do it now. Cox, you're on standby. You'll lead the charge when we get the location. I need you ready to move, but only when I say so. Are you good with that?'

She had to admit, she was somewhat surprised. Given the conversation thus far, she'd expected Grey to be there to close her down, but actually it looked like he was intent on keeping her out front. Which was exactly where she wanted to be. Yes, it was on Grey's terms, but still she *had* to be the one to get to Aydin first.

'Yeah,' she said. 'I'm good with that.'

THIRTY-FIVE

Baku, Azerbaijan

Now back on European soil, travelling through the modern city of Baku, Aydin had had no problems traversing the border into the Republic of Azerbaijan. His Turkish passport had already seen him safely through Turkey and into Iran, and the onward crossing into Azerbaijan had been similarly straightforward. Despite Azerbaijan's strained relations with some of its close neighbours – it was technically still at war with Armenia over the disputed Nagorno-Karabakh territory – the border at Astara was a somewhat half-hearted affair. The process of moving into Europe was as simple as Aydin arriving at the town of Astara on the Iranian side, purchasing a visa, and waiting in line for less than thirty minutes before being called through for his documents to be scrutinised. Following cursory checks by four different border officials – Aydin presumed they were each checking the visa was valid, and that he had no stamps from offending countries such as Armenia or North Korea – he was soon walking out on the Azerbaijani side through the identically named town of Astara.

Aydin had never been to the small republic before, and once in the capital a few hours later he was surprised at just how different it felt to many other countries in the region. Once part of the Soviet Union, the country had a strange mix of a modern-day Muslim state but with its recent communist past heavily evident. Not just in the buildings, but in the very mentality of the country. An atmosphere of tension remained, as though the once much-feared KGB still kept close watch on the streets, despite the fact that the country was proudly secular, unlike many of its nearest Muslim neighbours.

There was also a lot of money. Evident from the numerous modern glass-fronted skyscrapers poking into the sky here, there and everywhere, which sat at times uncomfortably with the Soviet concrete, early twentieth-century renaissance-style structures, and the ancient walled city with its many classic mosques and hamams.

With the heat of the sun beating down on him, Aydin walked along the promenade within the narrow Milli Park with the sumptuous blue of the Caspian Sea off to his right, and the burgeoning city on his left. The two-day trip from Istanbul had left him travel-weary, but had given his wounds further much needed recovery time. Together with the medication he'd stolen from the clinic in Istanbul, he was feeling close to full strength again.

He checked the time on the phone he'd purchased just a few hours before, after arriving in the city. Still thirty minutes to go.

Aydin took a left and walked out of the greenery of the park and back onto the city streets. He was soon walking past the wide steps of the grandiose Azerbaijan State Academic Opera and Ballet Theater, next to a pleasant tree-lined pedestrian street with traditional cafes and restaurants on one side and a more modern glass-fronted shopping mall on the other. Not long after, he found the cafe he was looking for, headed inside and took one of the seats by the window.

At nearly six p.m. the cafe was quiet, with only three other customers. Most of the shoppers had gone home for the day, and the evening festivities had yet to get under way. A waitress came over and Aydin ordered a coffee and a portion of dolma – minced lamb mixed with rice and fresh herbs, all wrapped in vine leaves. He spoke to the waitress in Turkish. Azeri, the official language of Azerbaijan, was itself a Turkic language. Aydin had already realised from the people he'd spoken to and overheard – as well as various road signs he'd seen, leaflets and newspapers in shops, and menus in cafes and restaurants – that there was a large degree of mutual intelligibility between the Turkish he knew and the native tongue. The waitress gave him a friendly smile and sauntered off to the kitchen with the order.

Aydin checked his watch again. Still eight minutes before the rendezvous. The man he was due to meet, Ruslan Garayev, was a Russian native who'd been living in Baku for a number of years. Aydin had never met him face to face, they knew each other only through the internet where they communicated on a deeply hidden message board frequented by hackers on the Dark Web – that part of the World Wide Web whose contents were not indexed by standard web search engines, so for the most part were non-existent as far as everyday internet users were concerned. These sites were a large part of the lives of many criminals, from paedophiles to drug dealers to jihadi wannabes. And of course there were others who just liked to do things away from the watchful eyes of others.

Garayev, whom Aydin had been in contact with for more than six months, was exactly the kind of man Aydin needed. Plenty of hackers worked for profit primarily, rather than for a political or religious cause, but still there were few who would help with Aydin's task – which was effectively to work against both the British intelligence services and the jihadi organisations he'd run from, putting him in a somewhat unusual position when searching for allies.

Perhaps the Russian authorities themselves, always happy to stir the pot where the West was concerned, would have champed at the bit to help someone like Aydin, but he had no desire to prostitute himself to a foreign government – doing so could only ever end badly for himself. Garayev too had fallen out of favour with those loyal to the Kremlin, hence his self-imposed exile to Azerbaijan. Aydin certainly wouldn't go so far as to say he trusted Garayev, but he did need help, and Garayev had the skill set to do that.

Another more nervous check of his watch. One minute past six now. The waitress brought the food and coffee over. The dolma smelled sublime – the lemony scent made Aydin's insides gurgle impatiently. He took a mouthful then stared outside at the sporadic passers-by, looking for the lone man he was expecting. His own searches had pulled up a sparse profile of Garayev so he had a vague idea of the man he was looking for.

The time moved on past six ten. Still no sign of Garayev. Aydin took the last mouthful of dolma then pulled out his laptop. No WiFi signal, so he had no way of checking if Garayev had sent a message to cancel or to delay. Frustrated, he put the computer away and again stared out of the window.

Movement off to Aydin's right caught his eye. The only other patrons who remained inside the cafe, a couple in their forties, had finished their food and were heading for the door. Aydin caught the man's eye for a split second . . . no, that couldn't be Garayev, surely? The couple walked out, headed left and were soon out of sight.

Over by the counter the cafe's phone rang. At the noise Aydin instinctively looked over and saw the waitress pick up the receiver. He couldn't hear what she said but after a few seconds her face turned, a deep frown on her forehead – confusion. She looked over to Aydin. Held the phone out to him.

'It's for you.'

'What? Who is it?' he said.

'I've no idea.'

Aydin glanced outside again. There was no one in sight. He picked up his backpack, where he'd stashed a pocket knife he'd bought in a hardware store, and gingerly headed over to the counter.

'Come on, hurry up,' the waitress said, as though impatient despite there being no other customers to tend to.

Aydin didn't respond. Just took the receiver and placed it to his ear as he half-turned to look back out to the front.

'Did you have the dolma?'

A disguised voice. Aydin's heart rate increased a couple of notches. He thought again about the couple who'd just walked out. No, it surely couldn't be them. But Garayev had somehow seen Aydin.

'The best in Baku,' Aydin said. 'You're late.'

'No. I was right on time. You lied to me. I told you to come alone.'

Aydin frowned. His brain worked overtime. 'I am alone.'

'You lied. You'll never hear from me again. Try to contact me and I'll pass everything I know to your enemies.'

Aydin opened his mouth to retort, but soon realised the line was already dead.

THIRTY-SIX

Aydin slammed the phone onto its cradle and glared at the waitress. Was she part of whatever game Garayev was playing? But then her reaction to the surprise phone call seemed genuine enough. Plus what the hell did Garayev mean about Aydin lying?

'Who's in there?' Aydin said, his tone snarky, pointing to the door to the kitchen.

The waitress looked a little uneasy at Aydin's hostile manner.

'Just the chef,' she stammered.

'Is there a way out there?'

'Y-yes, to the alley.'

Aydin thought for a second. No. He wasn't running. Neither did he believe Garayev had somehow been in the cafe and slunk out that way. Aydin hadn't seen anyone but the waitress go in there.

Which only left one other option. Aydin slapped down some money on the counter.

'Thank you,' he said, his tone at odds with his words.

The waitress gave a slight nod as Aydin turned and moved for the door. He took a cautious step outside. Not that he expected a sniper team to be aiming at him, or for there to be a sudden onslaught of armed police, but something was wrong here, and until he knew what, he'd have to be on high alert.

He quickly scanned the area and felt a slight pang of satisfaction. The only building that had a clean line of sight to where he'd been sitting was the shopping mall, but from where he was it was just the back entrance of the building – a three-storey plain brick wall with just a few blacked-out windows, behind which Aydin presumed were store rooms or maintenance rooms. Garayev hadn't been spying from there. There was only one other place he could be.

As calmly as he could, Aydin walked away. If Garayev had been watching, then maybe he still was, and Aydin didn't want to give away that he'd just found his spotting location. Aydin, shaking his head in mock frustration, carried on walking down the street, past the turning for the entrance to the shopping mall, then took a right down the next alley and burst into a sprint. He raced down to the end, took another right, then another in quick succession, and soon came back to the main entrance to the shopping mall from the opposite direction. Slowing to a brisk walk he headed inside and across the polished mock-marble floor to an escalator.

He took the steps two at a time before heading onto the next elevator to the final storey of shops. Looking overhead he followed the signs for the fire exit until he came to a pair of plain-looking grey doors. After glancing around he pushed the doors open and walked out onto a concrete stairwell. Empty. He bounded up the stairs and crashed out onto the expansive flat roof of the building. Could see no one. But there was no other exit from the roof. If Garayev had already scarpered, had Aydin already passed him in the mall without even knowing it?

There were three large air-conditioning vents on the roof. Aydin could see one was in prime position at the side facing the cafe. Aydin took the knife out and held it at the ready as he crept forward, moving as silently as he could. When he reached the vent he sprang round it . . .

No one there. He glanced over the edge of the roof, saw the cafe below. Looked back to the vent and saw there was a phone gaffer-taped to the metal.

Feeling his anger rise further, Aydin ripped the phone away just as it burst into a hideous melody. He answered the phone.

'What is this?'

'Good to see you're on the ball,' came that same disguised voice.

Aydin moved back to the edge of the roof. Down below, outside the cafe, was a man dressed in jeans and a black bomber jacket. He had a cap on and aviator sunglasses, so little could be seen of his face. Aydin was sure he would have been alerted to such a look if they'd crossed paths.

'I didn't lie to you,' Aydin said.

'I can see that now. But I wanted to test you.'

'Did I pass?'

'Almost.'

There was a light scuffling noise across the other side of the roof. Aydin darted to his side and poked his head round the metal to look back to the door. Could see no one. He looked over to the cafe again. The man was gone.

'You need to stop playing games,' Aydin said into the phone.

No response. Though the call was still connected and he was sure he could hear the faint breaths of Garayev as he walked away.

Another scuffling noise on the roof.

Garayev wasn't alone. Someone else was up there with Aydin. It wasn't Aydin who'd lied but the Russian.

'You need to stop this,' Aydin said. 'Before one of you gets hurt.'

Still no response. Knife in one hand, phone in the other, Aydin edged round the vent. There was still no sign of anyone on the roof, and only four places someone could hide — the three vents and the door.

'Are you still there?' Aydin said. Nothing. 'Last chance now.'

A slight noise behind him. Aydin spun round. Was the lurker already right around the other side of this vent?

Aydin edged forward, knife at the ready. He sprang round the corner poised to attack.

Then paused unexpectedly when he saw the figure standing there.

Which he realised almost immediately was probably a dumb thing to do, but such was his level of surprise.

Standing no more than three paces in front of him was a young woman with flowing dyed-red hair, and a whiter-than-white face. She was smirking, like she was immensely pleased with herself. Her left hand was empty. Her right hand clutched a phone. The lack of a weapon and that look on her face were probably the only things that stopped Aydin from slashing her throat on sight.

She lifted the phone to her face, indicated for Aydin to do the same.

'You passed,' came the disguised voice in his ear, an echo to the much softer voice of the lady standing in front of him.

She pulled the phone away. 'Nice to finally meet you,' she said. 'I'm Ruslan Garayev.'

THIRTY-SEVEN

Zaatari, Jordan

Nilay could scarcely breathe when they came over a ridge in the desert and the seemingly endless refugee camp below finally came into view. A sprawling grid system of tents, makeshift shelters and crude brick and stone structures, the camp was home – and increasingly a permanent one – to over 100,000 refugees from nearby Syria. Nilay hadn't been to the camp before, but had heard of its notoriety, both in terms of its size but also the increasing crime problems in the camp with gang violence, prostitution and drug-dealing all on the rise.

They arrived at the wire-mesh fence entrance to the camp where uniformed guards with their distinctive UN blue helmets stood watch. Nilay's driver and companion for the trip, Asif, a Syrian who worked for Oxfam, pulled their Jeep to a stop and showed the guards both of their IDs. After a rudimentary scan of the photos, they were waved through and Asif parked in the small clearing immediately on the inside of the camp where several other dust-covered cars and vans were lined up.

They stepped from the car. Despite the sun in the sky, the weather was surprisingly chilly with a fierce wind blasting sand and grit across the exposed area, the low-rise buildings providing little protection. Both Asif and Nilay hunkered their heads down into their scarves.

'This way,' Asif said, as they traipsed across the dirt road, and onto a wide street that was lined with a mishmash of huts and Portakabins and breeze-block buildings.

A group of young boys, seven or eight years old, came bounding out from behind one of the structures, chasing a deflated football across the road, giggling and laughing and shouting, as though they didn't have a care in the world. It was warming to see, even if Nilay knew their happiness was likely only surface deep.

'This is main street,' Asif said, as though they were walking down the wide pedestrianised pavement of a real town.

But then, in many ways, Nilay realised that this was in effect a real town now. The camp had already been in place for several years, many younger inhabitants had been born there, or probably couldn't remember life before it. And the level of facilities, although basic in their construction and delivery, was extensive. There were shacks selling fruit and vegetables and basic household goods. Coffee shops and shisha bars. A doctors' surgery, library, school buildings. There were tens of different charities and government bodies from various countries providing services from sanitation to education. Yet the whole atmosphere, even having been inside for only a few minutes, felt claustrophobic to Nilay, and surreally tense. As though the whole system, the whole community, could implode any second. People walked about with their heads down. Groups milled and whispered in hushed voices. Interaction was at a minimum, mistrust high.

'Down here,' Asif said.

Nilay followed him away from the main street and onto a narrower and more dilapidated row where the shelters were not shops or services but the most basic of homes. A group of young men, teenagers and twenty-somethings, smoking, idled on a corner, eyeing the world around them with suspicion and disdain. When one of them locked eyes with Nilay she quickly looked away, and she sensed Asif pick up his pace. They took another turn and Nilay looked over at Asif, who was just a little bit fidgety now.

He glanced at her, then over his shoulder, as if checking that the young men weren't following.

'It's the same as any town or city,' Asif said.

Nilay didn't ask what he meant by that. Did he know those men, or was he just being cautious?

After five minutes of trekking, they finally arrived at a series of grey and blue Portakabins. The door to one of the cabins had a plain piece of white paper sticky-taped to it, with UNICEF printed in bold lettering.

'The International Rescue Committee operate four shelters here for unaccompanied women and children. Unicef assists the IRC where children are involved.'

Asif opened the door and headed inside. Nilay followed. Asif greeted a moustached man in his twenties who was acting as some sort of receptionist, and then they carried on down a series of corridors until they came out in a room filled with books and games and kids' toys. Several workers were there, playing with the younger children, while the older ones got on by themselves or congregated in their own groups. Except for one boy – a young teenager with long wavy hair and sunken features who sat in a corner on his own, disconsolately, head down, looking at his feet.

Asif pointed over to the boy. 'He's expecting you.'

Nilay nodded and went over to him. He didn't move, just looked down at his feet. Nilay crouched down beside him, tried to catch his eye.

'Zaher?'

The boy still didn't move.

'My name's Nilay. It's really good to meet you.'

Nothing from the boy.

'Would you like to go for a walk? I brought you a drink.'

207

She took the can of Coke from her bag, held it up for him. The boy looked at the can, then to Nilay. Gave a shrug. She glanced back at Asif who gave her a thumbs up.

'How long have you been here?' Nilay asked Zaher as they sat on a rickety bench overlooking a clearing in the dirt that was being used as a football pitch. Lopsided metal goals, different sizes and shapes, were at either end of the dusty pitch. The kids didn't seem to mind. Somehow three games were taking place all at once.

'Nearly a month, I think,' Zaher said, taking a long swig of his can.

'You came here alone?'

'No. With my little brother. But he's dead now.'

Nilay paused. Zaher spoke with a coldness that surprised her. Had he somehow managed to lock his shock and grief away, or had he seen so many horrors that he was simply unable to express his emotions now?

'What was your brother's name?'

He gave her a hard look. 'Why do you want to talk about my brother?'

'I'm just interested to know about you.'

He scoffed. He was thirteen years old, looked a couple of years younger than that, yet his mannerisms made him seem considerably older.

Nilay spotted a group of older boys loitering at the edge of the football pitch, next to where there was a large water tower. The same group who'd had Asif intimidated earlier? Every now and then they turned their hard glares in Nilay's direction. She looked away, tried to ignore the feeling of unease.

'You lost your mum and dad on the way here?' she asked.

Zaher nodded. The story she'd heard already was that Zaher and his brother had been separated from their parents on the way to the camp when insurgents attacked their convoy. More than a dozen refugees had been killed, though all of those bodies had been identified and none were Zaher's parents. Which meant they were very possibly alive still, somewhere. Whether they were simply lost or had been kidnapped by the insurgents was anyone's guess.

Zaher and his younger brother had arrived at the camp together, but Israa, just eight years old, had died less than two weeks later after he'd contracted sepsis having originally being diagnosed with pneumonia.

Nilay could well understand why Zaher had since retreated into his shell.

'Do you know any of the other teenagers here?' Nilay asked.

'Not really. There's no one from my area here. And I don't want to make friends. I just want to find my parents, and go home.'

The latter was unlikely. His entire village had been wiped off the map.

They went silent for a few moments. Trying not to look over at the group of young men, Nilay instead focused on the football games in front of her. A young boy, maybe only four or five, was given the chance to take a penalty and the ball just about rolled over the line before all the others erupted in cheers. One of the bigger kids lifted him up like he was a trophy. Nilay smiled, but then quickly wiped it away when she saw Zaher was glaring at her.

'Why don't you just say what you came here to say,' he said.

'That's fair,' she responded. 'The thing is, I'm looking for someone too. Two people actually. My father and brother.'

'Where are you from?'

'England. But my family is Turkish.'

'Being here is the only time I've left Syria. Why do you think I'd know about them if you're English?'

'Because they both left England many years ago. My brother was taken to a place called the Farm when he was little. Have you heard of that place?'

He didn't answer, though the look of unease on his face suggested he had.

'Please, Zaher. This is really important to me.'

'If I help you, will you help me find my parents?'

'Of course. My job is to help people like you.' Though she really didn't know in this case what she could do.

'Yes, I've heard of the Farm.'

He paused. Nilay silently willed him to carry on, but realised he wasn't going to without prompting.

'Aziz al-Addad, have you heard of him too?' Nilay asked. 'People also refer to him as the Teacher.'

'Yes, I've heard of him. I've seen him.'

Nilay's heart thumped in her chest. It was more than rare to find someone not just willing to talk about al-Addad, but who had seen him too. The Teacher was notorious, one of the leaders at the Farm and one of the most wanted men in the West for his role in training insurgents and masterminding terrorist attacks, yet he remained something of an enigma. Some experts even questioned whether he existed at all – that perhaps he was a myth used to intentionally distract the West's security services.

'He came to our village,' Zaher said. 'Not where we live now, but from when I was younger, a few years ago.'

'You met him?'

'More than once.'

'Why did he come to your village?'

Zaher shrugged. 'I was only little. But I'll never forget his face, or his voice. He's just so . . . I don't know.'

'Did he come alone?'

'No. There were other men with him. Sometimes kids too.'

Nilay frowned. Why would al-Addad have kids with him? Some sort of recruitment run?

A thought struck her. She dug in her handbag and pulled out a scratched photo she had of Aydin.

210

'Have you ever seen this boy?' she asked. 'He's my brother. Was he with al-Addad and the others?'

Zaher pursed his lips. 'No. I don't think so. But it was a long time ago.'

She dug in her purse again. Found the similarly battered photo of her dad, Ergun Torkal.

'What about this man?' she asked.

Zaher's face turned, from barely amenable to outright disgust. 'Are you joking?'

'No. I'm not joking. Do you know him?'

'Of course I know him.' Zaher's face twisted in anger. 'He's my father.'

THIRTY-EIGHT

Baku, Azerbaijan

It wasn't often that Aydin was made to look and feel a fool, but Ruslan Garayev – aka Maria – had certainly done that. She hadn't given him her second name, she was simply Maria. Whether that too was bogus, Aydin didn't really care. As far as she was concerned he was called Mohammed, though she almost certainly believed that to be a false name too.

Despite her trickery, Aydin was pleasantly impressed with Maria's tactics. It was smart of her to set up the trap like that, allowing her to identify if Aydin had come to the meet with someone else, giving Maria the chance to scarper if she felt it wasn't safe, and without having to give herself away at all. She'd only turned up on the rooftop when she was certain Aydin was alone, and with him in a prone position with only one escape route should he still have tried to deceive her from there.

Located in the old town of Baku, within the ancient city walls, Maria's home was a large basement in a four-storey townhouse, nestled below a derelict shop. The upper three floors of the building were grotty-looking apartments, and from the outside of the building there was no indication that the basement level existed at all, with the only entrance being through a trapdoor within the dusty shop's store room. A perfect hideout for someone who wanted to stay off the grid – though Aydin did wonder if the windowless space was one of the reasons for her startlingly pale complexion.

'So is there really a Ruslan Garayev?' Aydin asked as he looked around the large dimly lit underground space. He'd found a profile of a man by that name, and together with what Maria had told him he'd built up a clear picture of who he believed Garayev was, and what he'd done.

'Not any more,' Maria said.

'He's dead?'

Maria nodded.

'You knew him?'

'Never met him. It's just a name.'

'No, it's more than that, it's a very detailed alias.'

'I don't have this life through telegraphing to everyone my real identity and my real story. That really would be quite dumb. In the same way you told me your name was Mohammed when it's actually Aydin Torkal.'

Aydin tensed. He'd not told her that. She spun round from her laptop monitor and gave him that satisfied smile again.

'Don't worry. Me knowing your real identity doesn't change our deal. If anything, it made me want to help you all the more. And be absolutely clear that I'd never work with anyone if I didn't know their real identity.'

Aydin said nothing.

'Tell me what you know about the security on the drive,' Maria said, picking up Aydin's hard drive from the metal table in front of her.

'I'm not as expert on these things as you,' he said, 'so I'll give you it in simple terms. I took an image of two hard drives at ATS, onto two of my own hard drives. There was nothing at all on those drives before. I bought them the day before from a regular shop. I don't believe they were bugged in any way. I hooked up one of the drives to my own equipment, and started the process of trying to break the encryption.'

'How long was it running?'

'A few hours.'

'And did you break it?'

'No.'

'Then what?'

'Then an armed team arrived at my door. I got away from them, but they now have my equipment and the other drive.'

Maria raised an eyebrow and shook her head, as though he were a dumbass.

'So?' he said.

'It's pretty obvious. I'll put this into simple terms for you. The encrypted data has an inbuilt security software. If any attempt is made to bypass the encryption by hacking it, rather than just decrypting it with the appropriate key, then the software sends a signal.'

'WiFi?'

'Could be WiFi. Could be radio. Could be all sorts of things. You said you used your own equipment. Was that equipment online?'

'No.'

'Then perhaps it could have been a radio signal. I guess it doesn't really matter. Either way, they caught you.'

'No. They caught that I was trying to read the data. They didn't catch me. So can you get into it without activating the signal again?'

Maria sighed. 'This isn't just about having equipment that's disconnected from the internet. You'd need to operate in an environment that lets literally no kind of electronic or radio or radiation signals in or out. A very deliberately constructed bunker, lead insulation, all that.'

'And do you have that?' Aydin asked hopefully.

Maria winked at him, looked across the room to the closed metal door at the far end. 'Of course I do.'

Aydin slept on the velvety brown sofa in Maria's basement while she worked away through the night, inside her purpose-built bunker the other side of the grey metal door. Together with the whirr of computer equipment and the buzz of electricity, the too-short sofa Aydin was lying on was at best uncomfortable, yet at some time after midnight he'd finally managed to drift into a semi-deep sleep, only properly waking not long after six a.m.

Not that there was any indication in the windowless room that it was now morning outside. Aydin, still dressed, moved out of the open-plan living space into the small kitchen and poured himself a glass of water. He downed it, set the glass on the worktop, then headed back to the closed thick metal door. He knocked. After a few moments the door opened slightly to reveal little of the darkened space beyond. Maria's bloodshot eyes appeared in the gap. She looked weary, though was bouncy and fidgety – too much caffeine from energy drinks, Aydin presumed.

'How's progress?' Aydin asked.

'It's only been a few hours.' Her tone was flat and far from friendly.

'I'll go and buy some breakfast. Do you want anything?'

'Just coffee.'

She closed the door.

Aydin shrugged. He wouldn't second-guess her work ethic. As long as she got him access to the ATS data, that was all that mattered. He grabbed some notes from his backpack and made his way to the door.

Behind him he heard the lab door creak open again.

'The entry code is six, six, three, six, five, nine, one, eight,' she said.

'Thanks,' Aydin said. He already knew the number. She'd tried her best to hide her fingers with her other hand as she'd typed the number into the keypad when they'd arrived the previous evening, but Aydin had still been able to tell the code simply by the relative positions of the carpals in her hand as her fingers stretched out for the keys. Another learned trick of his.

'Oh, and something to eat,' she said. 'Whatever you're having.'

Aydin smiled, opened the door, and headed up the stairs.

An hour later, having struggled to find anywhere open at such an early time, Aydin returned with two long black coffees and a selection of sweet pastries. Perhaps the sugar rush would help Maria to push through a little longer before the inevitable crash.

He was surprised – pleasantly so – to see Maria sitting on the sofa when he opened the basement door.

'You're done?' he asked.

'Done?' Her face screwed up. 'I can take a damn break can't I?'

Aydin closed the door. 'Yeah of course. Sorry.'

Her face broke into a smile. 'You're so easy to fool. Of course I'm done. Want to take a look?'

It took another hour inside the soundproof and radiation-proof and every-other-proof-Aydin-could-think-of room for Maria to show him through the hierarchy of folders within the drive of stolen data from ATS. Although the encryption was broken, many of the individual folders and documents were password protected, and some held their own secondary encryption, but Maria's hefty equipment was already working its way through the tens of thousands of files deciphering all of that.

'We can begin the search process now,' Maria said. 'The system will simply add in other encrypted documents as and when access is gained.'

Aydin was well used to techniques for drilling into large volumes of electronic data, catalogued or otherwise. Searching through the documents for specific keywords was the quickest way to hone in on useful data, but that process was fraught with difficulties – if people used coded words for example – and more often than not searching for keywords would spit out huge numbers of false positives – documents that had those words but that were entirely irrelevant. Still, using keywords to search was a lot better than having to look through each and every file.

'Start with these,' Aydin said. 'Shadow Hand. Ergun Torkal, Kamil Torkal, Nilay Torkal. The Farm. Aziz al-Addad.' He paused to think for a moment. 'Rachel Cox. And Mr Grey.'

'Mr Grey? That's pretty vague. In fact, all of it's pretty vague.'

'It is. But I'd rather start wide than narrow down too far straight away and then miss something.'

Maria sighed. 'OK. Here goes.'

She typed away at lightning speed and after just a few seconds hit the return key triumphantly.

'Should only take a few seconds,' she said.

Sure enough, seconds later there was an electric ping and a small message box appeared on the main screen. Over twenty thousand documents contained one of the keywords or a close derivative.

Aydin groaned.

'Don't worry. Let me try a few things.'

Aydin watched, out of his depth, as Maria's fingers blurred on the keyboard. She switched from one screen to another, utilising each of the four in front of her seemingly at random. Aydin, far from a slouch when it came to technology, was lost.

After a few minutes Maria paused, as if thinking, but then rather than carrying on she turned to Aydin.

'OK, this is looking a bit better now. Three thousand docs with multiple word hits, confined to only twenty-six top level folders. I've also been able to categorise by date created, date last modified, country of origin, and the user, where that's given. You've got documents of various types, but also emails.'

Aydin stared at the four screens, looking at the charts and graphs of results, all neatly categorised and laid out ready for review. He really didn't know what to say. It would have taken him hours, maybe more than a day, to do what Maria had just done in minutes.

'So where to start?' she asked.

'I need to know about Ergun Torkal.'

'Your father?' Maria said.

Aydin gave her a look.

'Sorry,' she said.

But he guessed she wasn't really. She was a born snooper. Which was why he was there.

'Yes. He was my father. I need to know about him. The story is that he was killed by an American drone strike. I need to understand why. What links did he have to terrorist cells? What links did he have to a place called the Farm? And I need to know where the Farm is.'

'You don't know?' Maria asked, as if he was stupid.

'Do you?'

'No. But I didn't spend nearly half of my life living there.'

Aydin had nothing to say to that.

Maria typed away again. What followed was an at times painful back and forth as they scoured through folders and documents, trying to hone in on areas of the data that held relevant information. Using the dates Aydin had remembered, it didn't take too long to find redacted memos discussing the drone strike that had supposedly killed Ergun Torkal. Everything looked exactly as Aydin had heard it, yet he still couldn't quite believe the story was as simple as it was being made to look.

'I'm really not sure what you're expecting to find here,' Maria said, sounding increasingly frustrated. Aydin glanced to the clock. They'd been working away without a break for over three hours and had found nothing that Aydin didn't already know. 'Your father was in that building. The building was completely destroyed. You've seen the aerial footage yourself now.'

'But they never found his body.'

'Because there was nothing to find!'

'I'm sorry, but I just don't believe it. I don't know why my father took me to al-Addad when I was a boy, but I can't believe he was part of the Farm. That he was a terrorist. You never met him.'

'And you were just a child when you last saw him, with a child's view of the world.'

'I've met evil. My father was not it.'

'What date did you leave London?'

'Wait!' Aydin shouted, when he spotted something on the screen. Maria stopped what she was doing. 'No. Go back. The last document.'

Maria clicked on the mouse and a scanned document, a letter on SIS headed paper, came back onto the screen.

'It's just the official sign-off for the drone strike,' Maria said. 'If you look at the date this actually came after the event. It was just housekeeping, making sure the authorisations were properly recorded.'

'I know that. But look at the second paragraph. It refers to another document. SH2007-043.'

Was SH short for Shadow Hand? Aydin wondered.

'OK, let me check.'

Seconds later Maria had pulled up several versions of the document. Each was heavily redacted with swathes of black, on some pages only a couple of words on each paragraph remained. Yet somehow, those few words still told a story. A story Aydin didn't want to read.

'Ergun Torkal . . . head of recruitment . . .' Maria said, reading out loud. 'ET identified candidates. AA provided vetting . . . fifteen boys . . . the Farm.'

Maria turned to Aydin. He couldn't look at her. His father, head of recruitment for the Farm? That didn't make sense. He'd never seen his father again after the day he was left in the hands of Aziz al-Addad, aka the Teacher. Yet here it was, in the official records of the British intelligence services. Aydin's father had not just known about the Farm, he'd been one of the few men who'd created it.

Maria carried on scrolling at speed. Aydin tried to take in what he could. He spotted a reference to an EG. It seemed to refer to a person – a British agent. The cogs in Aydin's mind turned.

'Go back again.'

Maria scrolled up.

'No. Back to the other document. The authorisation for the drone strike.'

A couple of quick clicks and Aydin was looking at the authorisation document again.

'Go down to the bottom.'

Maria did so. She reached the last page where the document ended with the signature of an SIS officer. The name of the official wasn't printed, just stated as 'Level 5 officer', beneath the scrawled signature.

'What do you think that says?' Aydin asked, though he already felt he knew himself what it was.

'It looks like Edward, or Edmund Grey.'

'Mr Grey. EG. And I think it's Edmund.'

Maria looked to Aydin as if to say *so what?*

'Edmund Grey had my father killed.' The same man who Esma had insisted his uncle Kamil was working with at MI6. 'Restart the search. Focus only on him. I want to know everything about him.'

THIRTY-NINE

Aleppo, Syria

It was dark when Nilay made it back to her apartment building in Aleppo. Not only was she tired, but she was frustrated from her latest trip into Jordan – the third time she'd been in as many weeks. Today's trip to the Zaatari refugee camp had proven to be a waste of time. Zaher was no longer there. She'd searched for him for more than three hours. No one knew where he'd gone, or even seemed to care too much. How could a thirteen-year-old boy just disappear without a trace?

Well, Nilay kind of knew better than most how people could just disappear, but still, where had he gone? And why?

Still distracted, Nilay turned the key in the lock. Pushed open the door. Only realised as she was stepping forward that the lights were already on in the apartment. A wave of panic washed over her, but then, through the hall, she spotted the outline of the figure in the armchair in the lounge ahead of her.

'You're back,' Rachel Cox said.

Nilay growled. 'I really wish you wouldn't do that.' She shut the door behind her, put her bag down and took off her shoes.

'Do what?'

'Sneak into my apartment. Have you no respect for my privacy?'

'I thought you'd rather I come inside and wait than have your neighbours spot a government spy hanging about outside your door.'

Cox did have a point there.

Nilay walked through into the lounge and took the sofa opposite Cox.

'How long have you been here?'

'Almost two hours. I was beginning to think there was a problem.'

'There's always a problem.'

'Are you going to tell me about it?'

'Maybe. But let me fix some coffee first. I need the caffeine.'

Nilay got to her feet and headed to the kitchenette where she put a filled kettle of water to boil on the hob. Cox stayed where she was. Nilay got out a small glass cup for herself and a larger mug for Cox.

'I'm guessing you want one too?' Nilay said, not bothering to look at Cox.

'You know me too well.'

Nilay wondered about that. What was their relationship now, exactly? Over the last few weeks she'd certainly grown closer to the MI6 agent. Were they friends? In many ways they were. Despite her annoyance now, Nilay usually enjoyed Cox's company, and they shared a strange set of common interests — like hunting for terrorists. If work — of sorts — hadn't thrown their lives together then in many ways Cox was exactly the type of person that Nilay could have held as a genuine close friend. But the spy in Cox was always there, just beneath the surface, no matter how hard she tried to appear normal.

Like breaking into Nilay's apartment, for example.

Nilay finished off the drinks and took them back over into the lounge, placing Cox's long coffee on the small wooden table in the centre of the room. She took her seat again.

'So?' Cox said, after Nilay had taken a sip of her thick and strong espresso.

'He's gone.'

Cox shook her head in exasperation.

'Gone where?'

'No one knows. Or even when exactly he went. It could have been any time over the last two weeks.'

'I'm sorry,' Cox said after a short pause.

Sorry about what? Nilay wondered. She'd asked Cox if she could do anything to try to protect Zaher. To bring him back to the city and keep watch on him there. If Cox wanted an asset who was close to people involved with the Farm then surely Zaher had been it. Cox had said she would help, but it had all been too little too late.

'We'll find him again,' Cox said.

Nilay said nothing. Had someone already got to Zaher? She felt that the more she dug into the Farm, the more watchful eyes came her way. On her first trip to Zaatari there'd been that group of young men giving her the evil eye. On her second trip to Zaatari she'd felt even more heavily scrutinised, had been genuinely scared as she'd walked the streets of the camp. It was entirely possible that the camp held spies who were feeding back to the myriad terrorist groups operating in the area.

Had someone taken Zaher? Or even killed him already?

'He probably left to look for his family,' Cox added.

His family. Nilay thought about questioning the choice of words, but didn't. With Cox's help they'd done their best to pick apart the pieces of Zaher's identity, tried to figure out exactly who his mother and father were. He'd been adamant that the picture of Nilay's father was also his own dad. Which made them at least half-brother and sister. She'd never mentioned that to Zaher, she didn't know what benefit it could have.

Was it true? Cox had seemed doubtful, though had gone along with it. They hadn't found any concrete evidence that either proved or disproved the link, but in her heart, Nilay wanted it

224

to be true. Because it meant her father was very possibly still alive. But why had he gone to Syria to start a new family? What was his link to Aziz al-Addad and the Farm? Those were the big questions that still needed answering.

'Have you found anything new?' Nilay asked, setting her empty cup down on the table, and wanting to steer the conversation away from herself.

'No,' Cox said, answering almost immediately.

Nilay wasn't sure she believed that, but she'd learned not to push. Cox told her what she wanted, when she wanted. Once again, the spy in her always won out.

'I'm sure he's alive,' Nilay said.

'Zaher, or your dad?'

'Both, I hope. But I meant my dad. There's more to this story than we're seeing.'

'Yeah, I know what you mean about that.'

'I wish we knew what happened right back at the start. How did my dad even know about the Farm? About al-Addad? For them to not only know each other, but to then still be in touch years later when he's got a new family in Syria, it's just . . .'

'You think that's the way it was? That your father and al-Addad still knew each other when al-Addad appeared at Zaher's home?'

'Surely it's too much of a coincidence otherwise.'

'But it's possible. And you have to accept that Zaher may simply be mistaken, either about your dad, or about al-Addad.'

'No, he's not. I believe my father is still out there, somewhere.'

Cox shook her head. Nilay frowned at the cold reaction. Did she know more than she was telling of her father?

But then, Cox wasn't the only one holding on to things.

'Do you know something you're not telling me?' Cox asked, as though she'd been party to Nilay's thoughts.

'No,' Nilay lied.

She wanted to trust Cox, but knew that she never could fully. They both had their own agendas after all. On her second meeting with Zaher, he'd given her the name of a man, a family friend, who the boy believed lived near Aleppo. It was possible Zaher had even left the camp in Jordan to track him down. Regardless, he was a contact that Nilay would keep to herself for now, until she'd taken the lead as far as she could.

Was it a coincidence that Zaher had disappeared just a few weeks after Nilay had told Cox about him? She hoped so, but there was always that slim possibility that Cox was really operating at completely different purposes to Nilay. That she had somehow been behind Zaher's disappearance and was working against Nilay, and had been all along. She couldn't and wouldn't jeopardise another lead so flippantly. She'd tell Cox in good time, if the lead turned out to be fruitful, but she needed to figure that one out for herself first.

'Seriously, Nilay, what's up?' Cox said, snapping Nilay from her thoughts.

Nilay smiled. 'Nothing at all. It's just been a long day.'

'You know I can only protect you if you're straight with me,' Cox said, clearly not yet ready to drop it.

'I know that. I'm really tired, you know.'

Cox sighed, drained the rest of her coffee then got up. 'Fair enough.'

They moved to the door. Nilay opened it.

'You won't do anything stupid will you?'

'Don't worry about me,' Nilay said.

It looked like Cox was about to say something else. In the end she just turned and headed out. Nilay shut the door and leaned back against the wall.

Don't do anything stupid.

She took her phone out of her bag. Not the one Cox had given her, but the prepaid one she'd bought from a local shop three days ago, and had only used once before.

She dug in her purse for the slip of paper with the phone number on. She hadn't yet memorised it, and had deleted the previous messages she'd sent. Now, following the worrying trip to Zaatari, she needed to speed up the process.

We need to meet. As soon as you can. Tomorrow?

She clicked send. Then deleted the message once she was sure it had gone through. She stood and waited for an immediate response. It took nearly ten minutes, but she hadn't moved from the spot at all.

10 a.m. Tilel Street market.

Her fingers shaking, Nilay quickly deleted the message, Cox's words of warning still swimming in her mind.

FORTY

Nilay left her apartment just after eight a.m. The market on Tilel Street was only a twenty-minute walk, but Nilay was being ultra-cautious today. She knew the Americans had previously bugged her, felt sure that Cox too was somehow still keeping covert tabs on her. If there was anyone with eyes on her as she left the apartment for her clandestine rendezvous, she wanted to at least do her best to lose them.

So what, she'd had no training in surveillance or counter-surveillance, but she felt she knew the city streets as well as anyone else. She took a twisting route, through the labyrinth of the old town, giving any stalker little chance of keeping on her tail, and staying on alert for anyone who seemed out of place. As she finally approached Tilel Street at ten minutes to ten, her legs were beginning to feel weary from the long and brisk walk, though her mind remained alert.

She bought a coffee from a street seller who gave her the stale concoction in a tiny white paper cup. Nilay, looking all around her at the stalls selling rugs and soaps and incense and other local items, took a sip of the coffee then moved away, her eyes remaining busy as she scanned the burgeoning crowd.

The message she'd received had given no exact location. Nilay was confident she'd find who she was looking for. Zaher had described

Nadim Somi to her in great detail, and she'd had an acquaintance who was adept at hacking – someone she trusted, as much as she could – do a quick search and draw up a picture of him.

According to Zaher, Somi was an acquaintance of his father's – her father's. A local leader of a rebel group that, more recently, had been all but wiped out by ISIS, Somi had met al-Addad in the past. Had even hosted the Teacher when he'd visited Zaher's home village. At least that was what he'd claimed. If it was true – it had to be – Somi would be the first person she'd met who had first-hand knowledge of al-Addad and the Farm.

She casually strolled along the street, pretending to take interest in the market stalls, but really looking around her at the people.

Two men, in their twenties, standing by a building entrance behind a stall, caught her eye. They were standing close to each other, talking, but their eyes were shifty, looking this way and that.

One of the men spotted Nilay, then quickly looked away. But not before giving his friend the slightest nudge.

She'd seen that right, hadn't she?

Nilay picked up her pace, trying to mingle in with the dense crowd a little more. She looked back over her shoulder. Only one of the men remained.

Where was the other one?

Her nerves growing, Nilay's eyes darted around. There was no sign of him. Then as she looked over her other shoulder, she was sure she saw a woman ducking quickly out of sight behind a large rug hanging on a stall.

No, Nilay didn't like this at all. She was sure it wasn't just paranoia.

Nilay returned her focus to the front. She moved with more purpose. Took out her phone. No calls or messages. The time was nine fifty-eight. Up ahead the end of the market was getting closer. In a gap between the stalls off to her left, three cafes sat side by side, their pavement terraces busy with people eating

229

breakfast and drinking coffee and tea. Nilay spotted Nadim Somi, standing by the menu board for one of the cafes. He, unlike Nilay, looked absolutely calm. He spotted Nilay when she was five steps from him. She thought about smiling, about saying something in greeting. But before she could, with a deadpan face, he simply shook his head then looked down to his phone.

Heart bursting in her chest, Nilay changed course, carried on walking towards the edge of the market. The phone buzzed in her hand. Without a break in her step she looked down at the message.

Eyes on you. Can't meet here.

She deleted the message. Looked behind her to see Somi casually walking away in the opposite direction. A woman in a blue headscarf joined his side as he moved into the crowds. The same woman Nilay had moments ago thought was spying on her?

Still no sign of that man though, nor of his friend now.

It didn't really matter. Something was wrong. Whether it was MI6, the Americans, or worse, someone was watching. Or was it in fact Somi who'd set her up?

With thoughts of what had happened to her the last time she'd been locked up by the CIA, she just wanted to get out of there and back to her apartment in one piece.

She looked back ahead. Bumped into a middle-aged couple.

'I'm so sorry,' Nilay said in a strained voice, when she saw the annoyed looks on their faces. They grumbled under their breaths before stepping aside.

There were only a few more stalls now before the end of the market. Nilay heard a noise up ahead. A high-pitched engine whining, getting louder by the second. The crowds ahead murmured. Then people began to separate. Beyond them Nilay could see the speeding moped, heading relentlessly towards the crowd, a teenage boy, no helmet on, riding. His thick green jacket bulged all around him.

230

People in the crowd shouted. At the driver, or at each other?

Nilay felt she knew what was coming, even before the boy took one hand off the handlebars and reached down to his side. As he pulled the small wired device up, Nilay turned and tried to run, but the crowds behind were too thick.

'Allahu Akbar!' came the shout.

Nilay braced herself, closed her eyes, just a split second before the devastating explosion erupted.

FORTY-ONE

Baku, Azerbaijan

After a couple more hours of helping Aydin to search through the vast swathes of stolen data, Maria had taken a long-overdue break. With the ATS data largely decrypted and Aydin becoming more used to Maria's customised search software, he really didn't need her anyway, nor did he want her to know about what he was uncovering. In many ways the knowledge could put her in an even more perilous position.

There was a knock on the lab door. Aydin's eyes flicked to the clock. It was nearly seven p.m. He'd been working non-stop since just after midday, without food or water. His eyes in the darkened room were heavy, his mind foggy. But he would carry on as long as it took, or until he collapsed from exhaustion, whichever came sooner.

He got up and opened the door. Maria was there, looking far brighter than she had a few hours before.

'Why don't you take a break. We can go and get some food.'

'No. I need to keep going.'

'Shall I bring you something back?'

'Please.'

She paused for a moment. Aydin fidgeted. He just wanted to get back to it.

'Have you found anything more about your father and sister?'

'Nothing useful yet,' Aydin said, which wasn't exactly truthful, but he wasn't sure what else to say. Maria shrugged and turned away. Aydin closed the door and took his seat again.

The fact was, the further he dived into the ATS data, the murkier his understanding of the Farm became. He'd long held out hope that his father had somehow been forced into giving his son away, either blackmailed or put under some other threat that was impossible to ignore. That was the only explanation in Aydin's mind that could tally with the man that he'd known as a boy. But there was simply no evidence so far to show that was the case. On the other hand, it was becoming increasingly clear to Aydin that perhaps his father had a much greater role in the Farm than Aydin had ever imagined. Was Ergun Torkal actually one of the men who helped to set the whole thing up?

That would certainly explain why years later Mr Grey and SIS had targeted Ergun in their efforts to wipe out an Al-Qaeda cell. The biggest problem Aydin had was figuring out how he felt about that. Here he was on a rampage to kill everyone involved in the Farm, and to stop them from recruiting more young boys for their twisted purposes. If his father was one of those who had created that ghastly place, then Aydin should have been pleased to know that Ergun Torkal was dead, and had had his comeuppance.

Yet the thought that his father was the bad guy still seemed so outlandish to Aydin. As a young boy, their family had been pretty much as normal as any other back in London. Yes, they were a Turkish family living in England, so Aydin was quite different to most of the other boys and girls at his school. There were plenty of other Muslims, but most came from Pakistan, and they'd always looked at Aydin differently, he'd never quite been part of their crowd. Neither had the white kids liked him much, or the Asian or black children.

Like many inner-city schools in London, the kids had come from so many different cultures and backgrounds, yet he'd never felt a part of any particular group there.

But the point was, his family was still *normal*. Mum, dad, brother, sister. They did normal family things like going to the cinema, or to an amusement park. They went on holidays, and weekend breaks together in the UK and abroad. They practised their religion both at home and in the mosque, but it was never an overbearing burden on their lives.

Yet Ergun Torkal had definitely changed, in those months leading up to him taking Aydin away. Had become more insular. Had started babbling more about *Allah's way*, and what a good Muslim should and shouldn't do. That change in Ergun had coincided first with him losing his low-paid labour job at a local factory, which had undoubtedly left him disgruntled with British life, but also with the arrival of a new imam at their mosque.

Yet there remained a big difference between a man finding religion, for whatever reason, and him being some sort of mastermind behind a terrorist group that had very nearly brought the world to its knees. That just didn't ring true, despite whatever evidence Aydin was now seeing.

Shadow Hand. He'd previously found that cryptic name to refer to the operation run by SIS to target the terrorist groups believed to be responsible for the Farm. An operation that had ultimately seen his father killed, supposedly, in a drone strike. It now appeared something quite different. Shadow Hand was actually the title originally given by the jihadis for the project to *create* the Farm. And it appeared Ergun Torkal was one of the key men who'd orchestrated the whole thing.

Aydin thumped his hands down onto the table as a wave of anger and self-loathing rushed through him. He got up from the chair. Despite what he'd said to Maria, he needed some air. He opened the door and stepped out into the living space, jolted when he saw that Maria was still there hovering over her computer screen on the table.

'I thought you'd gone already,' Aydin said.

She looked up. Her face creased in anger.

'What is it?'

Aydin moved over to her. Looked at the screen which was split into four segments, each one showing a blue-and-grey live camera feed – from the shop and street up above. Two dark-clothed figures roamed.

'Someone found us?' Aydin said, shocked.

'No,' Maria said, the anger in her tone clear. 'Someone found *you*.'

FORTY-TWO

'That's not possible,' Aydin bit back.

'Except it's happening. So it is possible.'

Maria glared at him as he stared at the two figures on the screen, moving cautiously through the shop above, handguns in their grips.

'Any bright ideas?' Maria asked.

'I'll go up there.'

'I said bright ideas. That's a really stupid one. We don't have any guns. We don't know how many more of them are up there, and outside.'

Fair points. Though Aydin still fancied his chances.

'They know we're here,' Maria said. 'But they don't know how to find the entrance.'

Aydin guessed she was right, judging by how the two men were currently looking in the wrong place, but they wouldn't give up easily. The hatch for the basement was cleverly hidden underneath a large storage cupboard with a false bottom – the men would find it eventually. And if they called in backup in the meantime, then the odds of an escape would only worsen. Right now it was two against one. Two against two if Maria was prepared to help.

'They're heading out of the store room,' Aydin said, which

meant they were getting colder. 'In ten seconds we'll go up together. We'll attack from behind.'

Maria tutted. 'I already said no to that.'

'Then what do you suggest?'

'I could always give you up to save my own ass.'

Aydin glanced to Maria, saw the slight smirk on her face. It was a strange time to joke. Though really, what loyalty did she owe him? Especially as somehow he'd led the authorities to her door. How?

Unless she'd already stabbed him in the back by bringing them there . . .

'There's another way,' she said.

'Another way what?'

'Out of here.'

She turned round and headed into the lab. Aydin followed her, stood in the doorway. She dug in a drawer and took out Aydin's hard drive.

'Take it with you.' She threw it over.

'That can't be how they found us. You said yourself, this room lets nothing out.'

'Maybe it's not how they found us, but that's yours. I don't want it. You need it. I wiped the tracking software. The data is all decrypted too. You can search it whenever, wherever now.'

'Thank you.'

She tapped on the keyboard. Aydin saw the flashes on the screens as folders began closing and disappearing.

'What are you doing!'

'What do you think? It's a kill switch. I'm deleting all evidence that you were ever here. I don't need any of it. I'm not part of whatever you're doing.'

The screens went black. Maria pushed past Aydin who was frozen to the spot. All of the work he'd just done . . .

'Come on, you have to go.'

There was nothing he could do about it now. He snapped into focus and followed her through to the kitchenette. She heaved the fridge-freezer to the side. Opened up a concealed panel on the wall. She inputted an eight-digit code and the hidden door, flush with the wall, only four feet high, clunked open.

Maria stepped to the side. 'Go,' she said.

'You're coming with me.'

'No. I'm not.'

'Those men are going to get in here one way or another.'

'And when they do all they'll find here is me and a bunch of computers with blank hard drives. It's you they want, not me. What do you think they're going to do?'

Aydin didn't bother to answer that question. He knew well the extreme lengths the intelligence agencies of the West would go to in order to achieve their aims.

There was a banging from across the other side of the basement. The men had found the hatch. But they still needed to find a way to get past Maria's security.

'Head along the corridor,' she said, talking more hurriedly. 'You'll come up in the basement of the building across the street.'

Another banging sound. Then a mechanical wheeze. Maria's wide eyes said everything. Somehow the men were already inside.

Aydin grabbed Maria's arm. 'You're coming with me.'

She wrenched it away. Lifted her heel and drove Aydin back. He smacked his head off the wall. Saw stars. She bundled him through the low doorway. Slammed her hand onto the keypad and the door clunked shut.

'No!' Aydin shouted.

It took his eyes a couple of seconds to adjust to the dim light in the narrow corridor that was barely six feet high.

Soft white LED lights along the bottom edges of the walls indicated the way ahead. But Aydin stayed where he was, feeling around the outside of the doorway, looking for a way to open it up to get back to Maria.

He'd take out the two men, then he and Maria could run. He wouldn't leave her behind. Not only because doing so was a liability to himself, but because she didn't deserve whatever treatment was coming her way. It was his fault she was involved.

He paused when he heard muffled voices the other side of the door. Maria, sounding calm, almost nonchalant. A much more gruff male voice. English, but with an unidentifiable foreign accent.

'Where is he?' the man's voice boomed.

'Where's who?'

'Aydin Torkal.'

Maria's jovial response wasn't quite decipherable.

The stifled sound of a single gunshot caused Aydin to jolt in surprise. A thud. For a beat he wondered who had shot who. Had Maria concealed a weapon? But then there should have been two shots if she'd taken them out.

The deep male voices echoed again. More muted now as they gave each other instructions. Aydin slumped. Realised he was shaking. With anger.

As much as he knew he needed to scarper, a large part of him was trying to talk his better judgement into heading back round to the shop to take out those two bastards. In fact, no, he didn't want to just kill them. He wanted to spend some time with them. Forcing them to give up what they knew.

Aydin clenched his fists so tightly that his fingernails dug into and cut his skin. Head brimming with rage, he turned and traipsed along the dank corridor. Soon found himself heading up crumbling stone steps. There was a wooden trapdoor at the top. No lock, but the warped wood meant the structure was wedged shut against the frame and Aydin had to pound it three times with his shoulder before it finally released. As he lifted the door up a plume of dust and grit cascaded down and caught in his eyes and mouth and nostrils. He spluttered, wiped at his eyes.

He lifted his body out into what appeared to be a maintenance room for a disused apartment building – an old industrial-sized boiler unit, pipes, electric circuit boards. Bare metal shelving. The room was dark except for the slivers of light giving the outline of a door across the far side. Aydin moved over, his eyesight clearing from the grit with each step he took.

The room's door, much like the trapdoor, was wedged shut and clearly hadn't been opened for some time, but Aydin managed to force it open and stumbled out into the building's dusty foyer. The double doors at the front entrance off to his right were partly boarded up. Aydin looked across the other way and realised there was also a back service entrance. That route would take him further away from Maria's hideout. Or should he go and confront the two men?

Sense got the better of him. Aydin moved to the back door and emerged onto an enclosed alleyway that had just one entrance. He headed for it. At the ready for an ambush at any moment, his eyes darted left, right, up and down. No sign of anyone.

He reached the end of the alley and pulled up against the brick wall of the building he'd emerged from. Stole a glance at the street outside.

A few pedestrians. Parked cars. Mopeds. No one suspicious caught his eye. Aydin took one more peek, looking over to the building that housed Maria's basement. With the anger still coursing through him, Aydin somehow managed to tear himself away, and moved in the opposite direction.

He walked quickly. Kept his head down, though eyes busy. Every time he passed a pedestrian or heard a car or motorbike approach, he tensed up, ready to uncoil. But no attack came.

Aydin was soon out of the downtrodden residential area and back among the more glitzy shops and restaurants where he'd first met Maria. The streets were busier. Easier to get lost in. Though with more people around as potential threats, Aydin was also feeling increasingly anxious – every look he received from a passer-by raised his suspicions further.

He spotted a busy crossroads in the distance. What he needed was to get out of the city. Public transport would be the easiest method, though stealing a car or motorbike the quickest. He hadn't yet decided which option he'd take.

As the crossroads got nearer, he did a quick take over both shoulders. Frowned. There were two men behind him who'd also been there the last two times he'd looked. Not walking together, but several yards apart. There was nothing alerting about them, other than the fact they'd followed him round three corners now.

Aydin picked up his pace. He didn't know Baku well, but this certainly wasn't the first time he'd had to try and lose a tail. Walking at speed, he took a series of quick turns, while at the same time trying his best not to appear flustered, to avoid tipping the two men off. When he next hit a long, straight pavement, he walked on for a few yards before glancing over his shoulder. No sign of either of the men now.

He carried on walking another twenty yards, looked behind him again. Still not there. All clear still after another twenty.

Aydin relaxed just a little, slowed his pace. Had he lost them that easily?

Then up ahead he spotted a man, head down, leaning against the wall of a mobile phone shop. He was glued to his phone, but then gave Aydin the sneakiest of peeks, before quickly glancing across the street where another man was standing in position outside a cafe. Not the same men as before either. Exactly how many people were out there?

Somewhere further behind him, Aydin heard the throb of a high-powered car engine. He looked behind and saw a large silver Audi coming his way. The car, having turned onto the road at speed, slowed.

They were trying to box him in. Perhaps him not knowing the city streets was going to be his downfall. They'd cornered him.

There were no more turns up ahead before Aydin reached the man outside the phone shop. He spotted the entrance to an alley, or possibly just one of the traditional narrow streets that was common in the nearby old town, about twenty yards beyond the man outside the cafe across the way.

Without looking, Aydin stepped out into the road.

He noticed the man by the shop flinch at the unexpected move.

The guy by the cafe looked up too.

The Audi slowed further — perhaps the driver not sure whether he wanted to mow Aydin down out in the open or not.

Aydin made a beeline for the guy by the cafe. He kept looking up, then back down to his phone, as if trying to decide at what point he'd break cover. Probably in two minds as to whether Aydin really was heading straight for him, or if he was just crossing the road, blissfully unaware.

The point he chose was too late. Aydin was only three steps away from him, and he was still looking down, trying his best to appear like he was just milling. If he'd reacted to the threat of Aydin sooner, he'd have given himself a much better chance.

There was a shout behind Aydin. Possibly from the guy by the shop, or from the occupants of the car. A warning.

An instruction. Whatever it was, it caused the guy by the shop to suddenly spring into action. He reached behind and pulled a gun from the waistband of his jeans. But Aydin was already too close.

He bounded the last three steps to the man, grabbed his wrist and twisted round, coming up behind him. He smacked his elbow down and heard the crack as the bones in the man's lower arm snapped. Aydin grabbed the gun from the limp grip, fired warning shots across the street before letting go of the man's stricken arm. He thumped the gun down onto the back of the man's neck, causing chaos in the bundle of nerves there, and the man crumpled.

Aydin didn't wait for the body to hit the deck. He was already running. He heard the roar behind as the driver of the Audi thumped on the accelerator. Aydin sprinted. Fired off two more shots behind him without looking. He just had to hope any pedestrians had already taken cover.

He took the left turn sharply, into what turned out to be a narrow street, hoping the last-minute change of direction would momentarily flummox the Audi driver. The screeching tyres suggested maybe it had.

Aydin pumped his arms and legs as he headed down the twisting street that contained rows of shops selling curios and knick-knacks. There was no way the Audi could fit down there. The opening and closing of car doors and the shouting behind him told him the driver had realised that too. Aydin fancied his chances much more in a foot chase than he did against the car.

A second later two gunshots boomed, and the whizz and crack as the speeding bullets narrowly missed him and sank into the stone walls next to him caused Aydin to duck and stumble. He was far from in the clear. He glanced behind. Saw three men giving chase. No sign of the Audi at the end of the street, but he was sure he could still hear its roaring engine nearby. Most likely the driver was racing around to intercept Aydin further down.

Aydin fired off two more warning shots without taking proper aim. Horrified pedestrians in front screamed and took cover. Except for the odd one or two who simply froze to the spot, eyes wide.

'Move!' Aydin screamed, waving the gun at them.

Some did, some didn't. He shoved a startled man out of the way, sending him clattering into wicker tables and chairs outside a small cafe, leading to heightened panic among the diners. Hopefully the melee that followed would give Aydin just a moment's breathing space from the chasing pack.

Aydin followed the street round a bend to the right, but thirty yards ahead the street came to an abrupt end where it crossed with what looked like a much busier road. The Audi would surely be coming to that junction any second. Though Aydin couldn't exactly turn round now, and there were no other turns to take.

He looked behind again. Slowed in his step just a little so that he could more properly take aim this time. Fired off one shot that caught the frontrunner of the three chasers in his side. He shouted and stumbled forward, clattering to the cobbles.

Another shot came Aydin's way. The bullet missed him by only inches and skimmed along the wall next to him, spitting grit into his face.

Aydin coughed and wiped his eyes with his arm. Heard screeching tyres up ahead. Was sure it was the Audi he'd see any second now . . .

Instead he saw a black van crunch to a stop at the top of the street, cutting him off. Aydin cursed his bad luck. There was an entire hit squad after him.

The side door of the van slid open. Out-positioned, Aydin cowered and lifted his gun, ready to fire.

Then a man appeared on foot, at the corner up ahead. An assault rifle in his arms. Two targets in front, two behind. Aydin couldn't possibly take them all out. He opened fire on the van, even though he had no sight of a target inside. The man with the rifle opened fire too. A scream erupted from one of the men behind Aydin, and he realised in that moment that he wasn't the target.

Confused, Aydin sprinted forward as he emptied the last few bullets of the magazine. He had no idea who or what he hit, if anything. But a flash of fire from inside the van told him he'd failed to eliminate whatever threat was inside.

A stab of pain in Aydin's leg. Another flash. Another stab, this time in his shoulder.

Running on nothing but adrenaline, Aydin let out a battle cry as he ran. Another yelp from behind him as the last of the chasers was sent down. Then gunfire from somewhere out of sight on the main road. The man with the rifle turned and fired off in that direction. At the Audi?

The van was only two yards in front of Aydin. The outline of the shooter inside was now visible. But it was quickly dawning on him that with each step he took, another element of strength and focus disappeared from his body and mind.

He realised why when he looked down. Saw the dart poking out of his thigh. Tranquillisers.

His body had more or less given up on him when he looked back up to see the black-gloved hands reaching out from the van. They grabbed him around the shoulders and pulled. A shove from behind – the rifle man? – and Aydin flopped forward and crashed onto the metal floor of the van.

The door was slid shut, encasing him in darkness. The engine revved and Aydin's body slid back along the van floor as the vehicle took off at speed. His eyes adjusted to the darkness, but he was quickly drifting. His body had deserted him. His eyelids drooped shut and he had to wrench them open again.

Unable to move, he tried to focus on the dark figure looming over him.

'Aydin? You're OK.'

A strangely familiar voice, though Aydin's delirious brain couldn't quite place it. Not until they turned a corner and a flash of sunlight coming in through the van's front window lit up the man's face. Aydin hadn't seen him in years. In fact he looked so different to how he remembered. Yet there was no doubt who it was.

Ergun Torkal. His father.

'Aydin?' he said.

Aydin said nothing. He couldn't. His eyelids closed and everything turned black.

FORTY-THREE

Cox listened as the sound of rattling gunfire crackled in her earbud. Her eyes stayed fixed on the small screen in front of her in the comms truck, as she watched the four camera feeds from Red Team, chasing Aydin on the streets outside.

'He's got help!' came the shout in her ear. 'We're taking heavy fire!'

'Have you still got eyes on Torkal?' Cox shouted.

'What? Yes. But . . .'

There was a brief pause then a shout of pain. Cox watched as the video feed from Red One — the assault team leader — tumbled, then went still with a view of the sky above.

'Red One?' Cox said. 'Red One, are you still online?'

No response.

'Red two?'

No response.

'Red three!'

'Ma'am, he got away.' Red Three was out of breath. 'A black van, I—'

Cox tore the headset off and screamed in anger as she tossed it against the back doors of the truck. The flimsy device broke into pieces. Emily Denton, sitting next to Cox, looked on in

247

disbelief. At Cox's behaviour, or at the shit-parade occurring outside the truck, Cox wasn't sure.

'Have you got a visual? Cox asked her.

Denton nodded. Looked back at her own screen. Cox looked too. An overhead video capture from Denton's drone of the speeding black van, as it made its way down a wide highway towards the coastal road.

'Don't you dare lose it,' Cox said.

Cox looked at the broken headset on the floor. Shook her head at her own careless reaction. She went to pick up her phone, but it was already ringing by the time her fingers touched it. Whether it would be Grey or Flannigan, she didn't know, but either way she was sure she was about to receive one hell of a tirade. Even though Cox had been given responsibility for coordinating the team on the ground, both Grey and Flannigan had listened in to the failed capture of Aydin remotely.

'Yes?' Cox said.

'If you've lost him—'

Flannigan. 'We've got eyes on him still,' Cox said. She looked to Denton for reassurance. Denton nodded.

'And what about my men?' Grey asked.

Cox groaned. So they were both on the line.

'If you weren't harassing me I'd be able to check.'

'Get it cleaned up. Now. You know damn well we don't have clearance from the Azerbaijanis for this operation. If any of you are caught, we're not coming to get you.'

Caught? Cox wasn't sure any of Red Team – Grey's men – were even alive, but she bit her tongue to stop her snapping back.

'Cox, are you still there?' Flannigan asked.

'I need to go,' she said, before ending the call.

How dare they threaten her like that? It was the idiots from Red Team who'd decided to open fire and kill Aydin's hacker friend, against her orders. Had then opened fire on Aydin in the street, once again against her orders. What the hell was going on?

Cox looked to Denton's screen again.

'Still on the move,' Denton said, without prompting.

There was a knock on the truck's doors. Cox looked to the CCTV screen and saw who it was. She groaned, scooted over and opened the doors up. The man standing outside was Red Four. One of the two men who'd gained access to Maria's basement. With the help of the Data Ops team at GCHQ – basically hackers themselves – it had taken a little over a day to trace the Deep Web messages between Aydin and his online acquaintance, Ruslan Garayev, to the basement of the apartment in Baku. Cox had been fifty-fifty as to whether Aydin would actually be there, and the confirmation of that had only come a couple of minutes after Maria had been shot in the head, as Aydin made his escape on foot. How had such a simple operation turned to shit so quickly?

'Was it you?' Cox snapped.

'Me?'

'Who shot that woman in the head for no fucking reason?'

'She was reaching for something!'

'Then punch her in the damn face. She's no use to anyone dead, is she?'

Red Four snorted. 'Fuck her. We've got two of ours down out there.'

'Are you actually stupid? Wait, don't answer that. Just get out of my bloody sight and clean up the mess.'

She shoved Red Four out of the way and pulled closed the doors.

'Talk about a clusterfuck,' Cox said. 'You're still following?'

Denton, looking more unsure now, nodded.

'Right. We're going to follow.'

'Follow?'

'Just don't lose them.'

Cox moved past Denton, opened the inner door at the end and climbed over into the driver's seat.

'What about Red Team?' Denton shouted over.

'They caused this mess, they can sort it out themselves,' Cox said.

In many ways she hoped the local police would round up the useless sods before they managed to collect their dead comrades and head off into the shadows. She certainly wouldn't help them in their efforts.

Cox fired up the truck's thumping engine and pulled out into the road. She spotted Red Four outside, running down the street. He glared as Cox headed on past. She followed the path Aydin's pursuers had earlier taken. Soon hit the backup of traffic. A hundred yards in the distance the silver Audi was visible, half on the road, half on the pavement, smoke billowing from its crumpled front end.

A police car was already there, blue lights flashing. Further on Cox saw two officers on foot, running towards the scene. She guessed that within minutes more uniforms would descend. The police would put a cordon right across the street.

They couldn't go that way, and no point in getting too close. Cox hit the brakes. Took a right turn.

'What are you doing?' Denton shouted. 'We can't just leave Red Team out there!'

'Wrong. What we can't do is let our target get away. I came here for one reason only. Aydin Torkal. And I'm not leaving without him.'

FORTY-FOUR

Aydin's eyes shot open, his body lurched up as he took an intake of air so big it made his lungs feel like they would explode.

No. It hadn't been a dream. No apparition or hallucination caused by the tranquilliser. The man sitting in front of him on the bench of the van really was Ergun Torkal.

He held a syringe in his hand. Adrenaline, or some other cocktail of drugs, had roused Aydin from his induced sleep. Aydin did wonder why his father had chosen to do that.

'It's not safe yet,' Ergun said, as if in answer to Aydin's unasked question. 'We need to get you out of Baku.'

Aydin stared at his father as the conflicting concoction of emotions worked its way through him. The van went over a bump in the road and Aydin's body jolted. His father grimaced as his head bounced off the wall of the van.

'Sorry!' the driver shouted, without turning round.

'I've been tracking you for a few days now,' Ergun said. 'But it seems I'm not the only one. MI6 has eyes everywhere. If we can get out of Baku, we can lie low. Then when the heat dies down, we can get you out of the country.'

Aydin had imagined seeing his father again so many times over the years, but now, in the moment, he was mute. His father's words mostly washed right over him. Strangely, all he could think about was his voice and accent. Many years older now, his father's voice was huskier, warmer. His accent was quite alien though. He used to speak English with a strange mixture of Cockney and Turkish. Now, any British element had all but gone.

'Aydin, are you listening to me?'

'Talatashar,' Aydin said.

'What?'

'Talatashar. That's my name now. That's the name they gave me at the Farm. The only name I've been known by for years. I'm not a boy, or a man, I'm just a number. Because of you.'

'I know you probably hate me. Probably have so many questions, and in time—'

'No. Just one question. Why?'

Another bump in the road. Then a sharp right turn. Ergun held on to the bench to stop himself sliding about. Aydin didn't bother to hold on to anything and his body tumbled to the side again.

With the momentary distraction Aydin's question seemed to lose most of its significance.

'Whatever you think you know, it's—'

'They killed them. Mother. Nilay. *Your* people killed them both. You're the reason they're dead.'

Aydin was sure he saw his father's eyes well with tears for just a moment, before his resolve took over once again.

'Not my people, Aydin. There are too many lies, too many secrets. But I'll tell you the truth. All of it.'

Another sharp turn. Aydin went flying across the van away from Ergun.

'You sent me to that place,' Aydin said, his teeth gritted. His legs and arms twitched as anger bubbled away beneath the surface. 'You knew what they'd do to me there.'

'No.' Ergun shook his head, emotion now getting the better of him. He looked like he would break down. 'That's not how it was.'

But Aydin had heard enough. He couldn't contain the beast inside any longer. He jumped up, dived for Ergun. The two of them clattered down onto the van's rutted floor with a thump, knocking the wind from Ergun.

Aydin clasped his hands around his father's neck and squeezed.

'You killed them!' he screamed. 'Your own wife and daughter!'

'It wasn't me!' Ergun somehow managed to splutter. 'None of it was me! I was trying to do the right thing.'

'Get off him!' shouted the driver, half turning before taking his eyes back to the road. A honking horn out of sight. The driver tugged on the wheel and the van swerved.

Aydin slid to the side, but his grip on his father's neck never faltered.

'Tell me where they are,' Aydin said. 'Where is the Teacher? The Farm. Tell me or I'll kill you right here!'

'I said get off him!' the driver screamed.

Another swerve. More honking horns.

'I don't know!'

'Liar!'

'I don't. But I know a man who does. He's—'

'I warned you!' came the shout from the driver.

He slammed on the brakes. A moment later there was a crashing impact as the van collided with something – another vehicle? A wall? Aydin tried his best to hold on but he went flying forward and had to release the grip on his father's neck to put his hands out in front, and prevent his face from smashing into the back of the driver's seat.

Ergun recoiled, pushed himself towards the back of the van. Aydin pulled himself upright, just as the driver unclipped his seatbelt. Aydin spotted the weapon on the passenger side.

The assault rifle. Both men went for it. Aydin got there first. Wrestled the barrel around.

'No, Aydin!'

He pulled the trigger. A burst of fire erupted. The driver's body shuddered as bullets tore into him. Blood splattered out the back of him and onto the van's windscreen.

'Aydin, stop!'

Aydin spun round. Pointed the rifle to his father's chest. Ergun Torkal, on his knees, looked on helplessly.

'I want to help you. Please, you have to believe me.'

'Tell me where they are. The Farm. I'm going there, and I'm going to kill them all.'

'I'll tell you everything I know, but please put the gun down. We have to get out of here.'

Aydin glanced around. Ergun was probably right. Whoever had been sent to capture Aydin and Maria was still out there. Through the blood-covered windscreen it was hard to tell where they were now. A bridge perhaps? But the steam rising up from the front of the van suggested they needed a new vehicle to get away.

'Open the doors,' Aydin said.

Aydin spotted a handgun on the footwell of the front passenger seat. One eye on his father, one hand on the rifle still, he leaned over and grabbed it. He put the handgun in his waistband and pulled the backpack over his shoulders as his father opened the doors to the van.

Yes, it was a bridge. Four lanes of traffic. Moving slowly in both directions because of the crash caused by the van that was blocking two lanes.

'Get out,' Aydin said.

Ergun tentatively did so. Aydin climbed out after him. Heard the mechanical whirring overhead. Looked up. Saw the miniature drone.

254

'Shit, they know we're here,' Aydin said.

Screeching tyres somewhere beyond the stopped cars in front of them. Two men jumped out, from about five vehicles back. Pulled automatic weapons up. Aydin glanced momentarily at his father. The shocked look on his face suggested they weren't his crew.

'Down!' Ergun shouted.

Aydin dived for cover behind the bonnet of the car in front of them. Gunfire boomed. The strap of Aydin's backpack snapped as he rolled along the ground and the bag slid away from him. Ergun couldn't move quick enough. Bullets smacked into him and he stuttered back, hit the van and collapsed to the floor.

For a moment Aydin was numb as he stared at the bullet-ridden body of his father. He was still breathing, but he was bleeding all over, the pool of red beneath his body widening by the second.

The screams of the family in the car Aydin was crouched by drew him from his trance. He jumped up, fired shots back at the two men.

Aydin took over again. Looked to Ergun, who'd tilted his head to his son.

What should he do? Try to save him? Moments ago he'd been ready to choke the life from Ergun Torkal himself. But to have him taken away by someone else . . .

Aydin took a half step forward, towards his father. The ping as a bullet scraped the metalwork of the car Aydin was by caused him to scurry back. Another two shots came his way. One of the bullets thumped into the backpack on the ground. Aydin looked at the bag in desperation. Could he make a grab for it? He still needed that ATS drive.

'Aydin.' Ergun's voice was weak and gruff. Aydin looked to his father.

'Remember this.' Ergun rattled off a series of numbers. What was this? A code?

'That's the Farm.'

Coordinates?

Ergun pulled a handgun from behind him. Aydin hadn't even realised he was armed. He lifted the gun up half-heartedly, he was already so weak. Another rattle of gunfire and Ergun's body pulsed, and then his head lolled.

'No!'

Aydin turned away. Couldn't bear to look.

'Get out of the car!' he ordered the young male driver of the car in front of him. He and his female companion did as they were told. They both slid out of the driver's side and ran across the bridge for cover.

Aydin scrambled into the car. One last glance at his father. Doing his best to lock away the emotion, Aydin pushed the car into gear and edged it forward to get a glimpse beyond the van. The crash had consumed several cars on the busy bridge, and with the shooters behind him it meant each of the lanes was quickly clogging up with traffic as people jumped from their cars and ran for cover. Aydin couldn't escape going forward either. There was no room for the car. Then he saw exactly what he needed.

He pushed his foot onto the accelerator and the car burst forward. It smacked into the back corner of the crashed van, shoving the heap of metal out of the way just enough, though the car took a fair amount of damage in the process. Aydin raced along the edge of the bridge, banging and scraping against the packed cars in front as long as he could until the car was battered and wedged in against the barriers at the side of the bridge.

Aydin, rifle in hand, let out a burst of fire, cracking the windscreen to pieces. He used his heel to smash through and tear the glass away then crawled out, slid along the bonnet, and across the next car to where he'd spotted a motorbike on its side – its driver likely sheltering from the melee somewhere nearby.

Aydin picked the bike up. Noticed the driver about ten yards away with two other people, crouched down behind a minivan.

'Keys!' Aydin yelled, pulling up the rifle. A second later the keys were bouncing across the pavement towards him.

He dropped the rifle, jumped on. Turned the ignition. The sports bike whined into life. Aydin pulled the throttle gently and spun the bike round, then tugged sharply and the bike shot forward. He weaved round the van. Saw the two shooters almost immediately, edging forward, weapons still trained on the area around Ergun.

They saw Aydin. He pulled out the handgun. Did his best to steer with one hand as he pulled the trigger. One of the gunmen collapsed to the ground. The other ducked down. With only one hand to control, and the punchy recoil of the gun, the bike wobbled viciously and Aydin was forced to drop the weapon to grab hold of the handlebars and bring the machine back under control.

Still, the shots he'd fired had done enough. The gunman bobbed up again. Aydin drove straight for him. The element of surprise, along with his speed, was enough and the gunman dived out of the way.

Aydin cleared the man, but he was far from free. He weaved methodically in and out of the log-jammed cars, could see the end of the bridge a couple of hundred yards ahead. Among the packed vehicles in front he spotted a large silver van. His eyes focused on the driver behind the glass. She was staring right at him. Rachel Cox.

She stepped from the vehicle. Stood right in Aydin's path. She seemed to be caught in two minds as to what to do. Rachel Cox wasn't Aydin's enemy. But was he hers?

She lifted her hand up. Pulled her other hand over so that the gun was gripped in both hands.

'Aydin, stop!' she shouted.

Aydin tugged harder on the throttle. The engine's revs peaked as the bike lurched forward towards her.

'Please, stop!'

Aydin lowered his head. They were only fifteen yards apart. She wouldn't shoot him, he kept telling himself over and over.

And she didn't. Though she also didn't look like she would move, and Aydin had no way of getting past her other than through her.

'Move!' he screamed as he raced the final few yards towards her.

She lowered the gun slightly. He saw the panic in her eyes. But she wasn't going anywhere.

Aydin let go of the throttle. But he had no time to stop before he hit her. There was only one other way out. He jerked on the handlebars. The bike's tyres screeched and skidded on the tarmac as the machine was sent on a hard left.

Aydin let go of the handlebars, lifted his hands to his face to brace himself for the impact . . .

The bike's front wheel smashed into the concrete barrier at the side of the bridge. The bike flipped up, catapulted Aydin over the top. His legs banged into the concrete as he hurtled over the edge, sending him plummeting down to the glistening water far below.

FORTY-FIVE

Aydin was still tumbling out of control when he hit the water. His head and his back took the brunt of the blow. He flailed under the surface, trying to get his body under control, trying not to gag or gasp as the cold water made his muscles spasm and sent his heart into a panic.

It took him a few seconds to find his balance, his sense of orientation, and he looked up to see the shimmering outline of the bridge far above. He kicked his legs, swept his arms and pushed his body along until he was sure he was out of sight of anyone – the shooters? – looking over the edge of the road, then finally surfaced.

He took huge lungfuls of air, gasped, sending his heart into a renewed hysteria that made his brain fuzzy. He slapped his leaden body down onto the concrete plinth of the bridge support to recover.

His body shivered violently, though with the warm outside air he wasn't in the least worried about his wet clothes or the onset of hypothermia. What he was worried about were the people above. He could hear shouting. Sirens. Before long there'd be a swarm of people descending to the water to look for him.

Aydin quickly glanced around, and spotted a small tugboat a hundred yards from him arduously pulling a barge loaded with yellow and red industrial containers. Aydin took a deep breath to ready himself then ducked his body back into the water, leaving just his head bobbing on the surface. When the tugboat was adjacent to him under the bridge, Aydin took another deep breath and dived under the surface.

Not wanting to risk coming up for air while out in the open, he swam under the water as quickly as he could, but soon found himself in the wake of the tugboat and had to battle furiously against the rippling waves.

His lungs burned. His limbs ached from lactic acid. He could see the barge through the swirling water, just a few yards in front. Aydin slowed up, waited for the barge to pass, and couldn't help but expel a mouthful of air. The bubbles quickly became lost in the already frothing water in front of him. His lungs ached all the more from the release, and it was a growing struggle not to breathe out fully and then suck the water back in.

When he sensed the hulk of the barge was almost past, Aydin kicked further down and pumped his limbs with every last ounce of strength he had to swim under and around the barge over to the other side. He pushed up and bobbed out of the water just two yards from the barge, on the opposite side to where Cox and the shooters had been on the bridge. He breathed heavily as he swam the short distance to the barge and grabbed hold of the thick rope by its side, used to tie the fenders in place.

Finally he relaxed his body, and let his limbs slump down, feeling the burn all over as his muscles were finally released from their effort. He kept his head just above the water, only enough to allow him to breathe, out of view of the lurkers on the bridge above.

After a few minutes, realising no one had spotted him, he sighed in relief. Though really, he had little to be relieved about, other than the fact that he was still breathing. He'd just lost everything. Maria was dead. The ATS data was gone, back into the hands of Cox and MI6. He'd lost his weapons, his passports, his money.

He'd lost his father.

Pulled along in the chilly water, his body aching and sore and depleted, he'd never felt more vulnerable and alone in his life.

Nor more consumed with determination to complete what he'd started.

Several hours later, with darkness fully descended, Aydin was back in the centre of Baku. Having managed to pickpocket enough cash to buy some new clothes and feed himself, he was at least feeling revitalised in body. It might have seemed a more sensible option to many for Aydin to run as far and as fast from Baku as he could, but that wouldn't have achieved his aim. Rachel Cox and MI6 were in Baku. Aydin was determined to find out more about what they were doing. In particular he wanted to find out exactly how his father had come to be there.

Even hours later, the bridge where Aydin had earlier made his escape remained closed by a police blockade. Aydin didn't get too close. He had no doubt he was now wanted not just by MI6, but by the local police too. And what about his father's people? Were there more of them too?

Who *were* his father's people anyway?

Either way, Aydin had only returned to the scene for one reason. Rachel Cox. Cox and MI6 had hunted Aydin down. In Egypt. Now in Azerbaijan. It was time for him to turn the tables. Did they believe him dead from his spectacular crash over the bridge? Without a body, it was doubtful, though the team of police divers that Aydin had seen suggested his death was at least a possibility that the authorities were trying to confirm or rule out.

Aydin didn't see Cox at the scene. What he did see were the ambulances to take away the dead bodies. Even after everything he'd come to learn about his father's involvement in the Farm, Aydin was confused and resentful that MI6 had shot him dead.

Cox wasn't at the scene, but there were two conspicuously light-skinned and casually dressed men. Certainly not Azerbaijani police, even though the two men were mingling with some of the many uniformed officers. Associates of Cox, Aydin decided. Either MI6 agents, or at the least diplomats trying to smooth over relations with the locals.

Which was why Aydin followed the men when they later left the scene, and trailed them across the city to a business hotel on the waterfront. The street outside the hotel was quiet in the dark night. Aydin set himself up in the small unlit park opposite, the gentle crashing of waves behind him filling his ears as he lay in wait.

FORTY-SIX

Cox guessed at one time the hotel's 'presidential' suite would have been considered upmarket, and plush, but the world had moved on in the twenty-plus years since the expansive space had last been decorated. More specifically, Baku had moved on. The influx of foreign investment due to the country's vast oil reserves had seen many more modern and more luxury hotels open up, but MI6 budgets only went so far.

Cox looked around. The floral carpet was threadbare. The scratched wooden furniture was beyond rustic. The old-style TV cabinet complete with pull-out tray looked plain ridiculous with a flatscreen squeezed inside it.

Anyway, no one was sleeping there tonight. Instead, the room was taken over by a whole team of agents and analysts from MI6, busy cataloguing and searching the equipment seized from Ruslan Garayev's basement, and other evidence from the various scenes of destruction left through the city as Aydin Torkal had made an unlikely escape, aided and abetted by an improbable companion – Ergun Torkal, his father.

Edmund Grey had arrived in Baku just over an hour ago. Cox had already spoken to him on the phone a lot in the intervening hours, not to mention the plethora of phone calls with Flannigan, who remained in England. Though knowing

263

him well, Cox half expected him to knock on the door any moment.

Cox was sitting on the edge of the bed, quietly watching Grey as he hovered over Emily Denton who was busy tapping away at a keyboard on a foldable table that was acting as the centrepiece of a hastily knocked-up computer lab.

Cox remained intrigued by Grey's upbeat manner. Much of his Red Team had been decimated in the carnage earlier in the day. Two of them were dead. Another was in hospital. They'd lost Aydin, and his father and accomplice were dead. Maria, aka Ruslan Garayev, was also dead. The local police were up their backsides about the whole mess, and there would no doubt be diplomatic repercussions to follow.

Really, they'd got so little to show for the day's events. So what was with Grey and his persistent good mood? It'd riled Cox when she'd first met him in Cairo too. What did it take to wipe that damn smile from his face?

She shook her head. What did it say about her that she felt more comfortable around her hard-nosed and belligerent boss, Flannigan, than she did around a guy with charisma and warmth, like Grey?

Cox looked away when she realised Grey was staring at her. He muttered something to Denton then straightened up and came over.

'Penny for your thoughts,' he said.

'I was thinking of asking you the same thing.'

'My thoughts? Today wasn't ideal, but it was still progress.'

'Not quite what Flannigan said to me earlier. Apparently the Azerbaijani PM has already been on the phone to Downing Street asking for an explanation of why we were conducting an armed raid in their capital.'

'So, who gives a shit about politics? I certainly don't. We just do our jobs.'

264

'We were supposed to be running a covert op here.'

'Ops go wrong. Ops go in completely different directions to how we plan and expect them to. Like how Ergun Torkal came back from the dead to try and get to his son today. The key is in how we react to these things.'

'We lost Aydin. We lost Ergun too.'

'But we got a whole lot more. We recovered the data Aydin stole from ATS. I doubt very much he's managed to keep a copy anywhere else – he didn't have access to that data until Garayev helped him, and her drives were all wiped clean. We haven't achieved all of our aims here yet, but we will.'

Cox didn't know what to say.

'You've had a hell of day. Why don't you call it quits and get some sleep? We'll still be here in the morning.'

'I can't sleep now. Aydin's still out there.'

'Unless he's down at the bottom of the Caspian Sea already.'

'You believe that?'

'No. Not really. But seriously, take a break. You've done your bit for now.'

Cox's phone vibrated in her hand. She looked at the screen. Sighed.

'Tell him to sod off,' Grey said. 'You answer to me for this op, not him.'

That might have been true, yet Cox couldn't just switch off her loyalty to Flannigan. Perhaps she was just a glutton for punishment, she thought.

'I'll just take a couple of hours then. But I'm not sleeping through.'

Grey smiled and shrugged. 'Whatever suits. Just be ready to move again if we need you. We've still got eyes and ears on the streets looking for Torkal.'

The phone stopped ringing. Cox grabbed her handbag and headed for the door. She walked along the corridor to her room. Had the keycard in one hand, her phone in the other ready to call Flannigan back.

No, she needed fresh air for this. She'd been stuck in the hotel for hours.

She moved down the corridor, past the two suited men by the lifts. Not exactly conspicuous, but then sometimes security was better when it was visible.

Cox made her way down in the lift and out of the clunking revolving doors of the hotel to the street outside. With a clear sky above, the night air was significantly milder than earlier in the day. Cox shivered, though the cool air in her lungs helped reawaken her brain.

She took the phone and pressed the call button, then inhaled a lungful of industrial air, the westerly wind making it thick with fumes from the oil refineries that lined the city's waterfront.

'I thought you were ignoring me,' Flannigan said. He sounded pissed off. As always.

'Why would I do that?'

'I'm just off the phone with Miles, he's got the foreign secretary hounding him over this mess.'

Grey's words reverberated in her mind. *Who gives a shit about politics.* Apparently Flannigan did. And Miles.

'It wasn't my fault,' Cox added.

'Then whose? You were op commander.'

'Red Team didn't listen to a word I said.'

'It wasn't that long ago one of your ops went south in Kabul too. Blue Team ring any bells? Almost a carbon bloody copy of the shit from today.'

'Jesus, listen to yourself. That was completely different. Something wasn't right today. It wasn't just that the op didn't go to plan . . .'

Cox's line of thought trailed off.

'Then what?'

'It was almost as though Red Team were operating under a different command. They weren't just reacting to the situation, they were following different orders altogether.'

'What on earth are you talking about?'

'There was no reason for them to kill Garayev. No reason to engage Aydin in the street the way they did. Then, when we had sight of Aydin with the drone, my decision was to follow quietly. Red Team, or what was left of them, once again blasted their way through. They're the reason we had no chance of keeping the local police out of this, why politicians are now arguing the toss over who sent us here and who's to blame. And they killed Ergun Torkal for no reason. We could have had him and Garayev in custody tonight.'

'They were still *your* team,' Flannigan said.

'No. They're Edmund Grey's team.'

Cox felt a presence behind her. She sidestepped and turned, expecting it to be a passer-by, or someone looking to enter the hotel. When she saw who it was, her heart nearly burst out of her chest.

'I've got to go,' Cox said. Wide-eyed, she pulled the phone from her ear.

'Nice to see you again,' Aydin Torkal said.

FORTY-SEVEN

Aydin's hands remained in the pocket of his hoody. The only weapon he was carrying was the basic pocket knife he'd bought earlier. He didn't believe Cox was armed. But he knew that the people with her inside the hotel likely were.

'Aydin, what are you doing here?'

'Is he up there?'

Cox frowned. 'Who?'

'Edmund Grey. I heard you mention him on the phone. Is he up there?'

'No,' Cox said. Aydin knew that was a lie. Her eyes narrowed. 'Why are you asking about Grey?'

'He's the one who signed off on the drone strike that killed my father. Or supposedly killed him anyway. Did he tell you that?'

The confused look on Cox's face told Aydin she had no idea what he was talking about.

'If they know you're here—'

'Where else can I go? You people have already taken everything I had.'

'I don't know what your plan is, but people are getting hurt, killed, Aydin. It's time to stop.'

'People are getting killed? Yeah, like Maria. Like my father. Like my uncle.'

'Your uncle?'

'You didn't know? Heavies from MI6 took him and my aunt a few months ago. Most likely they're dead now too.'

'Why would you think that?'

'He was an MI6 asset.'

'That's ridiculous—'

'No. It's not. I've seen the intel myself. It's all on the information stored at ATS. You want to know who his handler was? Edmund Grey.'

Cox shook her head, clearly flummoxed by Aydin's revelations.

'The pieces of the puzzle starting to fall into place yet?' he said. 'Someone on your end is cleaning up shop. Look what happened today. Maybe you don't know about it, but maybe you do. Grey seems to have his dirty fingers everywhere I turn.'

'Are you saying Grey is a double agent?'

'No. I'm saying he's not telling you the truth about what he knows. And whatever the truth is, it's getting people close to me killed.'

Aydin's eyes darted behind Cox when a man and woman emerged through the hotel's doors. Cox looked round too. The couple paid them no attention, just quietly walked off in the opposite direction. Aydin shuffled back a couple of steps so they were closer to the street corner, out of direct line of the hotel entrance and the beams of lights from its lanterns.

'I need the ATS data back,' Aydin said.

'That's impossible. And even if it was possible I'm not sure I'd do it.'

Aydin sighed. 'Remember what you said to me in Birmingham last year? You said you'd help me. I need to get to the Farm and finish this. Round up everyone involved. Close that place down for good.'

'I'm not quite sure I said I'd help you.'

'Dammit, Cox, what are you doing here? What do you want from all of this?'

The fact she didn't answer straight away surprised him. When had her outlook changed, and why?

'You've seen the news, Aydin, you must have,' she said. 'The attack in Liverpool. What happened in France too.'

'You blame me for that?' he asked, angered with the way she'd said it.

'No. But plenty of other people do. And I'm sure there'll be more attacks, more deaths, if you keep running. Come in with me. We can protect you.'

'There's no way you could possibly guarantee that.'

'If you don't, more people will die.'

Aydin gritted his teeth. 'Don't you dare put that on me. I can end this. Everything is on that drive. Get it to me, and I'll finish this. I'll find them and I'll kill them all.'

'I can't do it.'

'Then tell me what you can do.'

Cox rubbed her forehead for a few seconds. Aydin looked around nervously. He'd already been out in the open longer than intended. But he'd not thought it would take so long to get something from Cox. It riled him that she seemed to trust him so little after everything. Though, the fact that she was standing there having the conversation with him and not running back inside to Grey and the others had to stand for something.

'Come on, Cox. I'm asking for your help. Please? You know I'm not one of them. I'm trying to stop the bad guys here, same as you.'

'But you're killing *good* guys Aydin. The man in Cairo. He was just a contractor, ex-army. My team today . . .'

'How do you know they were good? And what do you expect me to do when men with guns come after me?'

270

Cox shook her head in despair. 'I can't get you the ATS drive. But tell me what I'm looking for on there. I'll find it.'

Aydin sighed. 'Shadow Hand. Find out everything you can. It was the operation to bring the Farm into existence. Grey and his crew investigated it years back, before the Farm even started. Why do you think he had my father targeted all those years ago? My dad was one of the people who helped set up the Farm.'

Cox shook her head. Genuine confusion, Aydin believed. 'This makes no sense.'

'Exactly. Which is why you need to find the truth.'

'I will.'

'And that's why you have to get me that drive back.'

Cox sighed. But Aydin wasn't going to let her say no. He took a hard drive from his pocket and put his hand out to Cox.

'It's exactly the same model. Just swap them out. No one will know.'

'Of course they'll bloody know when they open it up and its blank!'

'But it won't come back to you.'

'And then what?'

'My father was a ghost. You thought he'd been dead for years yet he managed to get here, to me, without you even knowing he was still alive.'

'He did. What are you saying?'

'I still don't know where he's been all these years, but I do know where he came from to get here.'

'How?'

He'd told her enough already.

'Just get me the drive. You've two hours.'

'I can't do it!'

'You either get it for me, or I take it.'

Cox scoffed at that, though Aydin was deadly serious.

'Qum Island. There's a jetty on the southern side, directly opposite the entrance road. Meet me there in two hours. Come alone. Or you'll never see me again.'

The sound of footsteps echoed across the pavement behind Cox. She spun round to look. Aydin took his chance. He slunk back into the shadows. By the time Cox turned back round, he was already out of sight.

FORTY-EIGHT

Cox traipsed back up the stairs to the top floor of the hotel, deciding the extra exercise would get the blood flowing to her brain better, and help her to make sense of what had just happened.

Just like the first time she'd met Aydin, which felt like a lifetime ago, she couldn't place why but, despite everything else, a large part of her *wanted* to help him. Deep down she truly believed that he was trying to do the right thing. That the fact he was so hell-bent on bringing down the people responsible for the Farm meant that he was, to all intents and purposes, on the same side as she was.

Was he all good? No. Was he dangerous? Yes. But often in real life matters weren't so simple as good versus evil. One thing she did know, was that the Teacher and the others at the Farm *were* evil. They had to be found and stopped.

Conflicting thoughts were still clattering in her mind when Cox opened the door to her room. She made sure the self-closing door was properly shut and locked before she moved through the narrow corridor, past the bathroom. When she spotted the man in the armchair by the window in the bedroom, she was halfway to drawing the gun from her handbag before she paused.

'Grey, what the hell?'

'Sorry, I didn't mean to startle you.'

He didn't look in the least bothered. He took a sip from the tumbler he was holding. Scotch or brandy from her mini-bar.

'Want one?' he asked.

'Not really. I'm not sure I'm done working for the night yet.'

'No. Me neither. Where've you been?'

'Just enjoying some fresh air.'

'Yeah, hardly very fresh out there tonight though, is it? Just the way the wind blows around here sometimes.'

Did he already know?

'Seriously,' he said. 'I know it's been a heavy day but what's up? You're stiffer than a corpse.'

'I wasn't expecting anyone in here, that's all.'

He raised an eyebrow. Downed the rest of the caramel liquid and set the glass down.

'I have to say, you intrigue me.'

He left the unusual comment dangling. His face was neutral, his tone flat. Clear cracks in his usual upbeat demeanour. For some reason it unsettled her. Or was that just because she knew she'd just been doing wrong by speaking with Aydin on the sly?

'Was that a compliment?' Cox asked.

'Not really. I've been in this job a very long time—'

'You told me that before.'

'Yes. I did, didn't I? And over the years I've learned to read people very well. I can spot their true intentions within seconds. Figure out exactly what they're about, who they are, where their loyalties lie. Normally. But with you . . .'

'With me what?'

'Exactly.'

Grey got to his feet. Cox's heart thudded in her chest as he walked towards her, a strange glint in his eye. She was

274

in two minds as to whether he was about to reach out and strangle her or kiss her.

She moved to the side and he shuffled past, heading for the door.

'Did you know that Ergun Torkal was still alive?' Cox asked.

Grey stopped, a step away from the door. He didn't turn round. Perhaps he didn't want Cox to see his face as he lied.

'No,' he said.

'What is Shadow Hand?'

Grey sighed. Now he turned round.

'The fact you're asking me the same questions all over again, suggests to me you already think you know the answer.'

'If MI6 knew about the Farm years ago, then why was that information buried?' Cox asked.

'Buried?'

'I thought I'd uncovered the whole story about the Farm, about the fifteen boys who were taken there. The thirteen sleepers who graduated and tried to blow up half of Europe last year. But you knew about that place before it was even set up.'

'No. I said I knew of places like it. And we did our best to stop it happening.'

'Then what was Shadow Hand? That was the project to create the Farm way back, wasn't it? You put in place an op to stop it. Years later you were still chasing down Ergun Torkal for his role in it all. You organised a drone strike to take him and his group out. But you failed. You failed to kill him then, and you failed to stop the Farm.'

'Then perhaps that's your answer.'

'No, that's not an answer. It still doesn't explain—'

'I suggest you get some rest, Rachel. It's going to be a busy day tomorrow.'

And with that Grey turned, opened the door and walked out.

An hour later, Cox finally built up the courage to leave her room. The time was just past eleven. When she reached the doors to the suite she knocked and waited. The doors were opened by a man she didn't recognise.

'Miss Cox,' he said, stepping to the side.

She didn't question who he was, or how he knew her. She went in. Saw there were still four other people milling about, less than half the number who'd been in earlier. Denton was still there, by the bank of ever-growing computer equipment. Cox approached her.

'How's progress?' Cox asked.

Denton didn't bother to look up from what she was doing.

'Garayev did a decent job of wiping everything she had. I've tried my best to see if there's anything at all that we can recover but I'm just not sure it's possible.'

'Perhaps you should give up for the night.'

Denton gave her a scolding look.

'Grey told me not to stop until I was certain.'

'Of course he did.'

Another look.

'What about the drive that Aydin Torkal had?' Cox asked.

Denton glanced to her left where the drive was inside a plastic bag, an evidence sticker slapped across the black plastic surface of the device.

'Grey's made it clear the information on there isn't for all eyes. The main thing is that it's back in our hands.'

'A bit strange that it's just left out in plain sight then.'

'Why? Who's gonna take it? Besides, I do still need to do work on it. But not yet. Grey wants me to analyse the meta-data to see if we can figure out what Torkal has seen. But that process could take days.'

Cox went over and picked up the bag. Denton gave her a quick look but then took her eyes back to the screen. Cox looked around her, then turned the drive over in her hands as though musing about something.

'What the hell did Torkal want with this, do you think?'

'Beats me. Like I said. We got it back.'

'How many people have died just for this little plastic box?'

Denton stopped what she was doing. Looked up at Cox who paused. She smiled meekly, put the bag back down.

'Sorry. Been a long day. Just spouting nonsense out loud.'

'Was there something you wanted me to help you with?'

'No. You're busy enough already. I just wanted to check to make sure everything was OK. But make sure you get some rest before morning.'

Denton looked away, back to her work. 'I'll try.'

'Night then,' Cox said.

'Yeah.'

She turned and headed back to the door. Her heart thumping in her chest. Aydin's ATS drive weighing heavy in her jeans pocket.

Cox initially went back to her room, opened then shut the door and leaned back against the wall, chest heaving. She took the hard drive from her pocket. There was a line of sticky residue from where she'd peeled away the evidence label. She just hoped it would remain stuck onto the empty drive she'd put back into the bag.

A sudden thought struck her. Was the drive Aydin had given her really empty? Perhaps it contained some sort of malware. She could scarcely believe she'd acted so foolhardily. What she'd done wasn't just stupid, it was outright treason.

At least the queen wasn't in the business of lopping off heads any more, she thought. Well, no, but the government did like to entertain its enemies at places like Zed site. Cox felt a sudden burst of panic at the thought. But there was no going back. She quickly changed, grabbed her bag that contained only her gun and the hard drive, then walked out of her room.

The same two suited men were still on guard by the lifts. They eyed her up suspiciously. Would they report that she'd left her room to Grey?

'You guys don't know where the nearest all night pharmacy is, do you?' she asked, as casually as she could. 'I need . . . you know . . . women's supplies.'

The one guard gave the other an uncomfortable look. His cheeks flushed slightly as though what she'd said was somehow embarrassing to them.

'Sorry, ma'am, never been here before,' the straight-faced guard said.

His red-faced friend shook his head sheepishly.

'No worries,' Cox said. 'Reception'll know.'

She left the two guards to it, got in the lift and pressed the button. When she was outside the hotel Cox did her best to recce the dark streets outside, making sure there was no one lurking. Then she took a careful route across the city to the single-track road that led to Qum Island, her eyes busy as she scoped for signs of anyone following her.

The road from the city and across the water to Qum Island was built up out of the sea on a bank of sand, and was lit by sporadic dull orange streetlights. It was eerily quiet as Cox traipsed across. At least the straight-as-an-arrow road gave her a perfect view behind her, back to the dazzling lights of the city. There was no way anyone could follow her across on foot without her seeing.

It took Cox nearly twenty minutes to walk along the road. Not a single vehicle passed her in either direction in that

278

time. As she approached the island it was clear there was little there. No houses, or offices, or hotels, or shops, it was entirely industrial with warehousing, and nondescript factories, a quarry?

The whole place was isolated and deserted at night-time. The only signs of life were sporadic small security huts with dim lights on inside. Cox made her way across the thin strip of land, keeping to cover where she could to avoid the attention of any guards on duty, heading on through an empty car park, past warehouses, over dunes, until she came to the far side of the island where there was a large jetty jutting into the inky water.

She made her way down to the jetty, stopped at the gated entrance and looked all around. There wasn't even any lighting here, and the lapping water in front of her was eerily black under the moonlight.

Cox took a deep breath then stepped across the barrier and onto the wooden walkway. She stopped by the first boat she came to. A small wooden vessel, no canopy, a single outboard motor.

She looked all around again. There was no one anywhere in sight. She realised she was shaking. From cold? No, she was scared.

She turned back to the entrance to the jetty. Nearly jumped out of her skin when she saw the dark silhouette standing right in front of her.

'Fuck's sake, Aydin!'

'You got it?' he asked, no emotion.

'Are you trying to give me a damn heart attack?'

'Have you got it?' he asked, more sternly.

'Would I have come all this way if I didn't? And yes, before you ask, I'm alone.'

'Why would I ask you that? I already know you are. I followed *you* here.'

Cox frowned. Was that true? How could he possibly have done that without her seeing him?

'Show me,' he said.

Cox pulled her bag in front of her and dug inside. Her hand brushed the grip of the Glock. Left it alone. She pulled out the hard drive. Stuck her hand out towards Aydin.

'Just take it and go,' she said. 'Do you realise how much trouble I'll be in if I get caught?'

'Actually, yes. I do,' he said. He took the hard drive from her and put it into his jeans pocket. 'Which is why you're coming with me.'

Before she could do anything, Aydin grabbed her and shoved her over the edge. She landed with a thud in the hull of the boat, gently bobbing on the water below.

FORTY-NINE

Faro, Portugal

Emilio Cortez checked his watch. Quarter to five. He supposed he had time for one more trip.

'Yes, OK, get in,' he said to the suited English man standing outside the hotel entrance.

Cortez pressed the button on his key fob to flip open the boot lid of his Skoda Octavia, and the passenger placed his two suitcases inside, closed the boot then took the back seat on the passenger side.

'How much will it be?' the English man asked as Cortez indicated and edged the car out into the road. No attempt at speaking the language. The same as most Brits. Not that Cortez could complain. It was the tourists who effectively provided him his job.

'On the meter,' said Cortez. 'About thirty euros.'

He glanced at the man in the rear-view mirror. The man nodded then went back to staring out the window.

'Do you think you could close that,' the man said. 'I've had enough of the heat now. Prefer the air con.'

Cortez shrugged. Pressed the button and the window glided up. Personally he'd rather have the fresh coastal air, it helped keep him feeling awake, but so what.

'You're in Faro on business?' Cortez asked.

'Unfortunately, yes.'

'It's a shame. The Algarve is beautiful. You should come again with your family.'

The man gave a slightly unfriendly look. Whatever. Cortez had no clue why. His eyes were back on the road; he wouldn't bother trying any more small talk. Instead he turned his thoughts to the plans for later on that evening. He'd told Julia he'd be home by five thirty, in time to go to his daughter's swimming gala. There was no chance he'd make that now, but with a bit of luck he'd only be a few minutes late. He thought about calling to pre-warn Julia but there was no point. He'd just blame the traffic for the delay.

They approached the airport, bustling with taxis and mini-buses and coaches dropping off.

'Which airline are you?'

'Ryanair,' the man said.

Not that it made much difference. It was basically a free-for-fall outside the departures entrance and Cortez, after a short wait, managed to squeeze the Octavia in between two other taxis, partly blocking the one behind him. He'd only be stopped for a few seconds.

Cortez looked at the meter. Twenty-four euros. He turned to the man who was waving a ten and a twenty at him.

'You can keep the change. But can you write me a receipt?'

'Sure.'

Cortez flipped the boot lid, then grabbed his pad as the man got out and went to the back for his things. The car rocked on its suspension when the passenger slammed the boot lid shut, and a second later he was back at the window.

'Have a safe trip,' Cortez said, passing the man the receipt.

'*Obrigado*,' the man said, though it was barely decipherable. At least he'd made a tiny effort.

The man walked away, wheeling his cabin baggage behind him. Cortez frowned. The horn on the taxi behind blared. He looked in his wing mirror and saw the driver gesticulating angrily. Cortez looked back to his passenger, already moving through the glass doors of departures. No, he wasn't mistaken. The guy had definitely put two bags in the boot at the hotel.

'Wait!' Cortez shouted, jumping from the car.

The man didn't hear him, but plenty of other people did, stopping to stare. That was modern life in airports. Everyone always just that little bit on edge.

Cortez left his door open as he bounded up to the terminal entrance. The guy was nowhere in sight, already lost in the crowds inside. The horn blared behind him. Then came the angry shouts of the driver. Cortez turned. The guy was mouthing off at him, using every expletive he could think of.

'Sim, vai-te foder!' Cortez shouted at him.

The anger in Cortez's voice knocked the guy back in his place. Cortez went to the boot. Opened it up. Sure enough there was a large black suitcase in there still.

'Stupid English,' he said.

He went to grab the handle. Heard a crackling of static. Like a phone trying to connect.

'No way,' he muttered to himself, a split second before the bomb erupted and tore the Skoda, Emilio Cortez, and everyone else around into pieces.

FIFTY

Herat, Afghanistan

Cox wasn't sure whether she was more horrified at, or more in awe of, Aydin Torkal's natural instinct for survival. His ability to get by in the world against all odds, without allies or resource, and all under the watchful eyes of the West's security services, was jaw-dropping.

She guessed there was a very good reason why he and his twelve sleeper brothers had come so close to fulfilling their devastating attacks in Europe the previous year. In fact, without his help, they almost certainly wouldn't have been stopped. She wasn't quite sure what it would take now to stop Aydin in his quest for revenge.

Of course *she* could stop him. For some reason, she wasn't sure that was the right answer.

'You're not hungry?' he asked, snapping her from her thoughts. He pointed down to the bread on her lap, laid on a thin muslin cloth.

She smiled at him. Picked the bread up, took a mouthful.

It had taken them nearly three days to reach the third largest city in Afghanistan – a seemingly never-ending trip, first across the Caspian Sea to Turkmenistan, followed by train, car, and walking through the vast Central Asian country, and across the rocky border into Afghanistan.

The border crossing had been the strangest part for Cox. Working for MI6, she'd crossed plenty of borders under false pretences, but at least there'd always been some level of officiality to it. Not this time, though. During the three days with Ayidn not an hour had gone by that she hadn't thought about trying to break free, somehow tackling Aydin to the ground and trying to get away. About shouting for help. As they crossed the border on foot at night, rather than feeling anxious she'd be arrested for being a spy, some part of her had actually hoped that border guards would spring out from the rocks and take them into custody.

That hadn't happened, and Cox was left to ponder her next move: how she could get away; where she would go. Yet somehow she didn't think of herself as Aydin's prisoner.

Despite the numerous people they'd come across who'd helped them on their way – whether as unsuspecting victims of Aydin's criminality, or as unsuspecting harbourers of fugitives – it had felt like they'd had no contact with the real world. No phones, computers, or internet. It demonstrated to Cox just how dependent modern life had become on technology. Perhaps that was why Aydin found it so easy to live like a ghost – he wasn't afraid to get back to the basics.

But that had been the last three days. The next three days looked quite different. Aydin's plan wasn't to lie low, after all. Which was why in Herat, rather than slumming it under blankets in the chilly desert, or huddling together in the freezing corner of a rickety freight car on a mile-long train, they'd checked into a hotel. A pretty basic – and in most respects decrepit – hotel, but nonetheless their room had four walls, a roof, a bed, and running water.

But the thing they needed most they still didn't yet have: a computer with an internet connection. It was the only way for Aydin to gain access to the data he'd stolen – or more accurately, *Cox* had stolen.

Aydin laid the large map on the wooden floor of the bedroom. He stared at it for a few moments, running a finger across its surface as he tried to pinpoint a location. Cox ate her bread silently, watching.

Aydin's finger stopped. 'It's here,' he said. He looked up at her. 'These are the coordinates my father gave me. The Farm: it's here.'

Cox didn't know what to say. Was it true?

'If we find a car, it's less than two days' travel. We should head there in the morning, once we get all the supplies we need.'

'Supplies?'

He gave her a look, but didn't answer the question.

'What are you hoping to find there?' Cox asked.

Aydin thought before answering. 'It doesn't matter. I just know I have to go. Even if it's nothing but an empty shell now, I have to go back. And if it's still in use . . . I can't let more boys suffer like I did.'

He scooped up the map, crudely folded it back into shape then placed it on the worn-out dressing table. He flipped open the lid of the ageing second-hand laptop that they'd bought from a market stall earlier that morning for four thousand Afghanis. It was as basic as a modern laptop got, but it would do its job.

Aydin pressed the standby button and the laptop groaned into life. It took several minutes before the Windows desktop had loaded and the machine was ready to go. Aydin took the ATS drive, connected one end of a USB cable to the drive, then put the opposite end next to the port on the laptop. He paused. Looked over to Cox.

'You'll never know if you don't try,' she said.

Aydin pushed the cable into the port and Cox braced herself, as if the SWAT team would descend any second, like it had done for Aydin back in Cairo. This time nothing. The little blue light on the hard drive blinked to show that it had powered on. Cox finished her bread as Aydin typed away in silence. When she was finished she got up and went over to him, looked over his shoulder at the screen.

'This is what I know so far,' he said. 'There's much more on here we still need to see. It's going to take a long time to find everything without any proper search software, but it's a start. Hopefully now you'll believe me.'

Cox stared at the screen. The heavily redacted document detailing MI6's operation to quash Shadow Hand. Cox reached forward and Aydin moved his fingers from the mousepad. Cox scrolled, taking in what she could. The purpose of the operation, the names of some of the known targets – Ergun Torkal included. The name of the man responsible for the op – Edmund Grey.

Cox realised Aydin was staring up at her.

'So?' he said.

'I wouldn't have come all this way if I didn't believe you.'

'It's not only about believing what I said about Grey.'

'Then what?'

Aydin didn't say anything to that. Just got up from the seat.

'Why don't you take a look at the other documents I've opened. I'm going for a shower.'

When the sound of gushing water filtered across the room, Cox went into the laptop's settings and connected to the hotel's free WiFi. She opened up a search page. Her fingers hovered over the keyboard, as if she was typing out the message in thin air. She looked back to the bathroom door. Then to the screen. She could get into her private email account in seconds. Could fire off an email to Flannigan. But what would she say? A cry for help? Or an explanation as to what Aydin had found? A divulgence of his plans? Perhaps all three.

Before she could talk herself out of it she typed away, hit enter and was inside her account. She stared at the cluster of unread emails. The sight of the mostly junk that she'd normally delete without even reading made her feel strange. As though she couldn't quite believe the person sitting in the hotel room in Herat with a wanted fugitive was the same woman who usually trawled through that nonsense crap several times every day. For what end? Maybe she wasn't the same person now.

The sound of water stopped. Cox's heart thudded. She turned to the door. Then back to the screen. Did she have time?

Too risky, she decided.

She went to close the browser but then her eyes caught on the subject of one of the unread emails. One of several from Flannigan. *Faro bombing* was all that was written in the header.

Cox clicked on the email which contained only a link to a BBC news article. She clicked the link. Stared in disbelief at the headline and the pictures accompanying it. Heard the bathroom door open behind her.

'What are you doing!' Aydin blasted. He stormed across the room, face like thunder. Cox didn't move, didn't even flinch.

Aydin slowed up when he saw what she was looking at.

'They think I'm responsible,' Cox said, staring at the picture of herself, unable to move. 'They're calling me a terrorist. How is this even possible?'

She turned to Aydin. Could tell he was gritting his teeth in anger. In contrast, she was numb.

He didn't answer her question. He didn't need to. She already felt she knew the answer.

FIFTY-ONE

A tear rolled down Cox's cheek, dropped from her chin and onto the wooden desktop. She didn't wipe at the salty smears on her face, just stared at the news article on the laptop screen.

'Now you know what it feels like,' Aydin said.

His heartless tone took away an edge of the anguish Cox was feeling, replaced instead with anger.

'If you hadn't pushed me into that fucking boat!' she shouted, shooting up from the chair.

Aydin took a step back, creating a safe distance between them.

'Then what?' he said. 'You think that bomb was all because of you? That's not how this works. They'd have been planning that explosion for weeks, possibly months. Just because your face is in the headlines doesn't mean you're responsible for those deaths.'

'No, but the whole world thinks I am. I'm your accomplice. It says one of *my* assets is the bomber!'

'And how do you know that's not the truth?'

Cox was ready to bite back again but stopped herself. Was that possible? That the bomber really was one of her old assets? There were plenty of people she'd known on the inside within terrorist groups. People who were irrevocably tainted by their past actions or by association, people who were misguided and conflicted as to which path to take. People like Aydin. But Cox didn't believe that was the case here for a second. MI6 had put her name to that attack to heap pressure on her. But who at MI6? What was their end game now?

'I bet you've worked with plenty of people who either played you or turned their backs on you, either willingly or by force,' Aydin said.

'That's bullshit and you know it,' Cox said. 'This is because of *you*. I'm only on the wrong side now because of your actions in bringing me here.'

'So what? You think handing me over to the British authorities would stop the Teacher and the others?'

'No, but it would at least stop my name being dragged through the mud.'

Aydin scoffed. 'Then perhaps I misjudged you. I thought stopping terrorists meant more to you than just winning plaudits.'

'Fuck you.'

Aydin turned away and sat down on the floor. Cox knew he was angry too, but his ill-feeling wasn't directed at her. Just like hers wasn't really directed at him. Aydin was little more than a pawn in the deadly game concocted by his masters. Now she was a pawn too. But whose game was it exactly?

'This doesn't change anything,' Aydin said.

'For me it bloody does!'

'Get over yourself! We can't stop now. Whoever is doing this, I can guarantee there'll be more attacks. Unless we stop al-Addad and the others.'

'Then what do we do?'

'We go ahead as planned. First up is the market. Once we have all the supplies we can leave here and head for the Farm. The sooner we do that, the sooner this will all be over.'

Cox said nothing.

'It's not like you have a choice now, Rachel. Your own people have turned against you. I'm the only person in the world you can trust from here.'

And the worse thing was, she knew he was right.

Cox wandered around the market and the surrounding shops in something of a trance. Aydin's shopping list was all in his head, Cox was nothing more than a carthorse for him. The methodical nature in the way he moved about the place, finding the various apparently indiscriminate items was startling. Aydin hadn't explicitly stated his intentions, but the picture was becoming clear enough. Metal pipes. Storm matches. Fireworks. Nails. Electrical wires. Glass bottles. Detergent. All the ingredients needed to make improvised explosives. Cox was becoming weaker at the knees with each step they took.

Tracking down the Farm and the people behind it was one thing, but was he even planning on giving anyone on that site a chance, or was he just going to try and obliterate them all? Could Cox really be a party to what Aydin was planning?

No. The answer was she couldn't. But she also couldn't bring herself to run now. Having seen what Aydin was capable of, she really didn't want to be one of his enemies. Plus, Aydin was right. She didn't know who she could trust, so running back to her old life was not possible right now. She needed to think smarter.

'Just one more shop to go,' Aydin said, turning around to Cox who was walking a yard behind him.

'Sure,' she said, giving him as convincing a smile as she could.

The blue and white and grey tarpaulins of the ramshackle stalls flapped in the breeze as they headed on past a gap in the market to where there was a cafe selling pastries and other desserts.

Aydin turned and smiled. 'You want one?'

'Your choice,' Cox said, 'I'll wait outside with the things.'

Aydin initially looked uncertain at that, but they were lugging three bulging fabric bags between them, together with a trolley suitcase and Aydin's backpack.

'If I was going to run, I'd have done it already,' she said.

He shook his head, dropped the bags he was carrying by Cox's side, then turned and went through the door to wait in line inside. There were a good half a dozen people in front of him. Cox would have a few minutes. Though she could hardly move far from the spot as Aydin could still see her from where he was.

Cox looked around her. She was right on the edge of the bustling market stalls where locals eagerly jostled with each other for position. Just a few yards further back and she'd be within the melee. She glanced over to the cafe again, through the glass. Aydin turned, locked eyes with her for a second before the pudgy man in the queue behind him shuffled slightly and blocked the view.

Cox, heart rate steadily rising, picked up the bags, grabbed the handle of the suitcase and took a half step back. Then another. Then another.

She put the things back down. Turned to look at the crowd around her again. No one was paying her any attention. Every now and then the odd person or two would break from the hustle and bustle either to head for the cafe, or to go around the back of the stalls to avoid the crowds. Cox just needed to wait for the right candidate. She again glanced over to the cafe. Saw the back of Aydin's head. He stepped forward, further down the line, further into the cafe, and was out of sight from Cox.

She looked to her right. Saw exactly what she was looking for. As the woman went scuttling by, Cox stepped to the side abruptly, stuck her foot out for the briefest flash, enough to send the poor woman clattering to the ground. The bags she was carrying went flying, fruit and vegetables rolled along the paving slabs, her handbag came loose, spilling its contents.

'I'm so sorry!' Cox said in Arabic, looking horrified, and she hurriedly went to the woman to help pull her back to her feet.

There were murmurs and grumbles from the people around them.

'Here, let me help you,' Cox said. She put her hand under the woman's arm but the woman jerked away.

'Get off me.'

'It was an accident, I'm sorry,' Cox said. She began to scoop the woman's shopping back into the bags.

'Hey, you!' Cox turned. Two men, short, squat, in their forties or fifties were glaring at Cox. 'What are you doing!'

'It was an accident. I knocked her. I'm sorry.'

'That wasn't an accident,' someone else shouted.

'What are you doing here?' someone else called.

All of a sudden there was a growing group of people circling around Cox. They shouted and called at her. Others all around stopped to take notice. The noise and anger in the crowd quickly rose. Cox's light skin and her clear foreign accent the biggest problems it seemed.

Another man stepped forward to help the woman up. She didn't resist his efforts.

'I'm sorry,' Cox said, holding her hands up in apology, and straightening up.

'Get out of here!' someone shouted. Cox wasn't sure whether it was intended as confrontational or simply good advice.

Then someone shoved her in the back. She stumbled forward. A couple of cheers from the crowd. Raised shouts. Cox could sense what would come next. Egging themselves on, the crowd were whipping themselves into a frenzy. Desperately she looked over to the cafe. Saw Aydin storming out.

'Hey!' he boomed. 'Get away from her.'

Aydin wasn't much to look at. Not particularly tall and not particularly well built, he certainly wasn't imposing in stature, but something about the anger and the command in his voice was enough to cause the crowd around Cox to take pause.

'Move away from her. Now!'

Aydin stomped forward. The crowd parted to let him through.

'She's with me.'

He picked up the bags. Cox grabbed the suitcase.

'I said move!' Aydin shouted. A few of the crowd murmured and turned their backs, satisfied that the fun was over. Others stood their ground, as though weighing up whether they wanted to pursue the confrontation.

Aydin didn't give them the chance. He turned and quickly headed away, and the people in front moved aside one by one to let him pass. Angry looks on their faces, but no one bothering to challenge him. Cox moved in step behind, head down. She knew one wrong look could cause the whole scene to blow up in her face.

She only relaxed when they turned away from the market and hit a much quieter street in the direction of their hotel.

As they scurried along, Cox looked behind her a few more times, making sure none of the mob were following.

'Thank you,' Cox said.

She could tell Aydin was pissed off with her from the way his jaw was clenched.

'I saw what you did,' he said.

Cox's heart lurched again. Aydin flicked her a look.

'What did you get?' he asked.

'I'm not just a passenger here. I can help too.'

'Is that the first time you've pickpocketed someone?'

'Actually, no,' Cox said. Which was the truth, though she had to admit she'd learned a fair amount from observing Aydin over the last few days. Talent wasn't quite the right word to describe his undoubted prowess for stealing from people without them knowing, but it was close.

'So what did you get?'

Cox dug into her pocket. Her fingers grabbed the small bundle of notes. She lifted them out just enough for Aydin to see. His face showed no reaction at all.

'I thought we could always use more money.'

He said nothing, just looked into the distance.

Cox pushed the notes back into her pocket. Her fingers brushed against the hard form of the newly acquired mobile phone. She couldn't help a momentary glance to Aydin. He was paying her no attention, but did he already know?

She was sure time would tell.

FIFTY-TWO

The journey from Herat and into the desolate mountains that made up the outer edges of the Hindu Kush was tiring but trouble free. The hours on the road, filled with little by way of chat, gave Aydin plenty of time to ponder. He knew Cox remained uneasy with him. With the position he'd effectively forced on her. In some ways he was still unsure himself why he'd taken the decision to throw her into the boat in Baku. Was a part of it simply because he was tired of being so isolated and alone?

Possibly, yes. Though she'd hardly been the best of company the last few days. The biggest reason he'd brought her along for the journey was because he needed her help, in more ways than one. Firstly, the added hands would be a big benefit when the time finally came to lay siege on the Farm. But, most importantly, Aydin knew taking Cox would help to draw out exactly who was who within MI6, in particular who was operating at cross purposes – which was clearly evident given the way Cox had been drawn in to the latest terrorist bombing campaign in Europe.

'We're gonna need to stop soon,' Cox said.

Aydin glanced at her, saw her squirming.

'Come on,' she said. 'We've been driving non-stop for nearly four hours. You must need a break too?'

'We're less than an hour away now.'

'So we're just going to rock right up there straight away?'

'I've waited long enough for this.'

Cox looked out of her window.

'But I still need to stop.'

Aydin didn't respond. He looked out of the rear-view mirror. The twisting road through a valley in the mountains meant for large parts they couldn't see very far in front or behind, but as he looked now there was a clear view some half a mile into the distance behind. Not a vehicle in sight. Nor had one passed them in the opposite direction for well over half an hour.

'A quick rest stop,' he said. 'Very quick.'

He eased off the accelerator and after a few seconds slowly pushed the brake. He veered from the tarmac road onto the rocky rubble by the side, and the view behind was soon lost in grey dust kicked up from the tyres. He brought the Jeep to a stop and they both stepped out from the car into the sunshine.

The temperature in the desert was warm, not hot, but the wind blasting between the desolate mountains either side of them was fierce and kicked up grit and dust. Aydin turned away when a strong gust smacked into him. He shielded his face and spied on Cox as she crept a few yards away. She squatted down behind a rock, facing away from him. He kept his eyes on what he could see of her. Not that he expected her to make a run now – in the desert there really was nowhere to go.

Landlocked Afghanistan had for centuries been of strategic importance as a crossroads for many major trade routes, including the historic Silk Road connecting East with West for well over two thousand years. But, as Aydin looked around the barren landscape, he could see exactly why so few invaders had successfully overcome the local tribes through the years. Even without their knowledge of the land and their guerrilla tactics, the terrain was unforgiving and hostile.

Cox straightened up then turned and walked back over to the Jeep. Got in without saying a word. Aydin retreated to the driver's seat and they were soon back on the empty road.

They didn't have use of sat-nav for their journey, relying instead on a compass and the map Aydin had bought not long after they'd first arrived in Herat. A few miles after their latest stop, the tarmac road ended and was replaced by a dirt track that snaked around the mountainous land in front.

As they edged closer and closer to their destination, Aydin's nerves began to build. Every small town or settlement they passed, or viewed from a distance, created an uneasy silence in the cabin as if they were both braced for an unexpected attack. What would the locals think if they stopped the Jeep? Did the people around here know about the Farm and support it?

'Do you recognise any of these places?' Cox asked.

'Not exactly. That range up ahead on the left, judging by how far away we are now, I think the Farm will be just the other side. But I've never seen the mountain from this angle before.'

He could feel Cox's eyes on him. He glanced over, then back to the road. He thought about explaining his answer, but decided against it. The fact was he was only a boy when he'd been taken to the Farm, and the life created for him and the other boys by the elders was based on the acceptance that the Farm was the be-all and end-all. If they were to know where it was, how close it was to civilisation, if they were to have any outside communication with the world, then the whole mystery and power of the place would have disintegrated. He only left the Farm on a small number of occasions in all the years he stayed there. Recruitment drives, and their obligatory pilgrimage to Mecca for the Hajj. But they were always blindfolded before they left, and hours before they arrived back.

Until recently Aydin hadn't even known for sure what country the Farm was in.

They sat in the car in awkward silence. He could feel Cox's eyes on him still.

'I'm sorry for what they did to you,' she said. 'No child deserves what you went through.'

Aydin glanced at Cox. Couldn't quite read what the look on her face meant.

'The saddest thing isn't what they've made me into. In many ways I've come to terms with that. The saddest part is not knowing what kind of person, what kind of man, I would otherwise have been.'

'Who do you like to think you would have been?'

'To be honest, I try not to think about it. No good can come from dreaming like that.'

'Of course it can. You're still young. You lost your childhood in that place but you've got a lot of life ahead of you. You can still be the person you should have been. You can lead a good life.'

Aydin snorted and he saw the look of offence in Cox's eyes. 'The problem is, I'm not sure I would have been a good person. The things I've done . . . some of it comes too easily. Maybe this really was the path God intended for me.'

Aydin sensed Cox was about to say something else in response, but then they rounded the next corner, round the edge of a mountain, and in the distance the land opened out in a wide and long plain. Aydin's heart raced in his chest. His hands clammy on the steering wheel as he stared ahead, several miles away, where the form of low-rise buildings was barely visible on the horizon,

'Is that it?' Cox asked.

Aydin took a deep intake of air, trying to calm the mash of emotions that clattered about inside him.

'Yes. I think it is,' he said. 'We're finally here. That's the Farm.'

FIFTY-THREE

The falling sun behind Cox and Aydin cast long shadows as they made their way on foot across the rocky outcrops. Having spotted the Farm from the dirt track road, Aydin had turned the Jeep back round and headed for the mountain, driving off-road to reach a spot in the hills overlooking the plains below, but that was in cover from the Farm way in the distance. Nightfall would soon arrive, and with it would come much cooler temperatures. They had blankets in the Jeep and enough water and basic foods to keep them steady for three or four days, though now they'd arrived, Aydin would rather act sooner than later.

They came to a stop behind a large cluster of jagged grey rocks. Aydin's legs ached from the hilly traipse from the Jeep which had taken the best part of an hour. He pulled the binoculars from his backpack, then reached up over the rocks to spy on the buildings further in the distance.

'What do you see?' Cox asked.

Aydin didn't answer. His brain was too busy trying to take it all in. This was no trick of the eye, he'd really found it. But as he stared at the familiar buildings he'd once known as home, the dusty courtyard where he and the others had trained in all manner of combat, where he first pulled the trigger of a gun, where he'd first killed a man, Aydin felt no real satisfaction at having finally tracked the place down. He only felt immense sadness, and a growing yearning to get bloody revenge.

'Aydin? Are you listening to me?' Cox shook his arm to snap him from his morose thoughts. 'Do you see anyone there. Is it still occupied?'

Aydin shifted the binoculars left and right, trying to focus and to think strategically, rather than filling his head with the pain of the past.

The buildings he saw had changed little. The main central complex – a single-storey labyrinth of stone and wood construction, with white-painted walls – remained exactly as he remembered it. The fact the paint looked clean and fresh despite the battering he knew the building took from the elements suggested its upkeep was ongoing. The series of smaller outbuildings dotted around the compound were largely the same as he remembered, though Aydin noticed a couple of new ones too. What they were used for he had no clue.

The main entrance to the compound – tall wooden gates – had a stone wall trailing off from either side, but much of the perimeter of the compound was simple picket fences, or the back wall of the main building. Still, the position of the front wall meant Aydin didn't have a clear view of exactly who or what was directly beyond the entrance. One thing he could see quite clearly though . . .

'I see vehicles,' Aydin said. 'A four-by-four. Two vans. A truck.'

Aydin took the binoculars away from his face and looked over to Cox.

'They're here,' he said. 'We're going in. Tonight.'

FIFTY-FOUR

Cox shivered and pulled the blanket further around her shoulders. Thousands of stars glistened in the clear sky above, completely unobstructed from light pollution on the ground, with the only illumination in sight the blue flickering flames of their camping stove and the soft orange glow of electric lights coming from the Farm far in the distance. Cox watched Aydin with something close to disbelief. The level of concentration, of skill, of nerve continued to startle her.

He finished screwing the plastic cap onto the last of the metal pipes and carefully laid it down on the ground next to the others. Each was crammed with explosives stripped from the fireworks and storm matches, together with nails to act as lethal shrapnel. The devices were crude. The explosives under normal circumstances were weak and would cause little damage on their own. Yet Cox knew that packed together inside the steel tubes, the pressure created when the explosives ignited would be sufficient to cause an almighty racket, and to kill or severely injure anyone unlucky enough to be caught close by.

Aydin looked up at Cox.

'That's all of them.'

He picked up the pad of paper from the open boot of the

Jeep and came over and sat on the rock beside her. He began doodling on the paper with a pencil.

'This is the main building here,' he said, pointing to the crude shape in the centre of the page. 'It contains the living quarters for the students, the teachers, the guards, as well as classrooms, labs. It's the hub. I have to get inside. I'll go in through the side, passing through this courtyard at the western end.'

'I'm glad you said I, not we.'

'But I do need your help. On the outside. You're my eyes and ears. I don't know how many people will be in there. If the students will be boys or teenagers or young men. If they'll fight too or take the chance to run or hide. Typically we'd only have a small number of actual guards at night. Perhaps four to six. Maybe the same number of elders. It's not like anyone knew the place was there, and if they did who the hell would be stupid enough to attack it?'

Cox said nothing.

'So basically you could have over twenty people in there,' she said. 'How can you possibly expect to get through them all on your own? You don't have a single gun.'

'I don't need a gun. I've got a knife. There're six pipe bombs, I'll lay them around the perimeter . . .'

Cox closed her eyes, shook her head in disbelief.

'. . . They're for distraction as much as anything. I'll control them all—'

'How?'

'Radio. The cap on each device contains an electrical firing circuit. I'll carry the transmitter. I haven't had enough time to separately rig them, so one push will trigger the firing pulse in all of them. You tell me what you can. How many people you see, where, what weapons they have. And if any backup arrives.'

Cox was trembling. She tried to convince herself it was only the cold. It certainly wasn't that she was unused to siege operations, but with MI6 she'd never questioned whether what she was doing was the right thing.

But then wasn't *this* the right thing? The Farm was a legitimate target. The enemy was inside that compound, and had to be taken down. The fact she was working with Aydin, and not a crew of ex-military meatheads, was of little difference.

'I've got three Molotov cocktails too,' Aydin said, referring to the glass bottles that he'd packed with a mixture of paraffin and detergent – an incendiary mixture that with the greasy detergent would stick to anything it touched once ignited. 'I'll carry them on my belt and use them as and when needed.'

'And what do I get? Other than a radio and blanket?'

'You want a weapon?'

'You don't think I need one?'

'There's a spare pocket knife. You can have that. And you have the Jeep. If I get into trouble, you run.'

'You mean that?'

'Absolutely. I have to do this. I know I may not come out of there alive, but it has to be me. If I fail, then you run. You tell the world about this place.'

Aydin put his hand on her shoulder. Gave her a determined look. She nodded.

'OK,' she said.

Aydin got to his feet. He went back over to the bombs. Packed the pipes into a backpack. Clipped the glass bottles into a utility belt which he clasped around his waist.

'Come on then.'

Cox got up, kept the blanket around her. She moved over to Aydin and he handed her the multitool pocket knife and a radio handset. Cox grabbed an empty backpack from the Jeep and put the things inside. Took a bottle of water, then packed up the rest of the equipment they didn't need into the back of the Jeep and locked it up.

They set off side by side across the sand and rocks. Neither of them spoke a word as they walked through the darkness.

They were only a few hundred yards from the Farm, growing larger in the near distance with each step they took, when Aydin reached out an arm to bring Cox to a halt.

'This is close enough for you. Head up into the hill on the left.'

Cox nodded. Aydin pulled a balaclava over his face. When he stepped to the side, out of the blueish glare of the moon and into the shadows behind the rocks they were standing by, he all but disappeared from view.

'Good luck,' he said.

'You too,' Cox replied. Her voice sounded shaky. She hoped her nerves wouldn't rub off on him.

She heard the crunching as Aydin turned and walked off into the distance. She didn't move, just stared straight ahead in the direction she thought he'd gone. Kept her breathing slow and regular so she could concentrate on the sound of his footsteps. Other than the trembling in her body, she didn't move at all until his footsteps had faded away.

Then she slowly, carefully pulled the mobile phone from her pocket. Pressed the button to power it on. It took a few moments for the home screen to load. The battery had only five per cent charge remaining. She looked to the top left-hand corner of the screen. Saw she still had the faintest of signals – where from, she had no idea. Did the Farm have its own antennae? Would the people inside be able to track the signal from her phone?

Too late to worry about that now. Using one hand to cover the screen so as to not let the light escape, she quickly typed out the message.

Alpha en route. Arrival approx 10 mins. Beware explosives around perimeter, out of my control. Incendiary devices on Alpha, no guns. 5% battery. Request advice on required action?

Cox pressed the button and the message silently disappeared into the ether. The third that she'd now sent since leaving Herat. So far she'd received nothing in response. She had no clue what that meant.

She let out a big sigh. Then turned away to find a spotting position.

FIFTY-FIVE

Aydin looked around the darkness that surrounded him. Could see no one. Could hear no one. The faint moonlight was enough to give him the most basic of outlines of the buildings in front of him, but he was using his memory of the area to guide him as much as he was his sight. As he'd approached the compound from afar there'd been an orange glow coming from two of the main building's windows, but from where Aydin was now positioned on the western side, there was nothing.

He clambered over the five-foot-high wooden fence, into the square recreational yard, the ground of which was lined with compacted sand. As his feet crunched across the familiar surface, a whole host of memories swam in his mind. He could hear the Teacher's orders, his angry shouts, his heckles. His cackle when he showed his authority by brutally punishing the boys. Aydin had been his favoured plaything – or so it had felt at the time.

Just the smell of the place – what was it? – caused memories to flash in Aydin's mind. He had to stop, and squeeze his eyes shut to try to force the unwelcome thoughts away.

When he opened his eyes again he paused, staring up to the space between the side door he was aiming for and the roofline above. There was the faintest flickering red light there he now realised. A camera.

Aydin cursed himself. How had he not seen that before? There certainly hadn't been CCTV when he'd last been at the Farm. In the dead of night, he just had to hope there was no one watching the feed live. Surely if there was, he would already be under attack.

Aydin crouched low. Pulled the radio handset out. He hadn't yet had any contact with Cox since he'd left her up in the hills. He'd carefully laid all of the pipe bombs out since then and was now caught in two minds as to what his next move should be. One option was to blow the bombs straight away. The ruckus would likely cause whoever was inside to reveal themselves. But the other option was to leave the explosives in place, and make a more stealthy approach. Use the bombs to contain anyone trying to escape, or to hold off reinforcements.

'Cox,' Aydin whispered into the handset. A crackle of static but no response. 'Cox, are you there?'

More static. No response. What the hell was going on?

Aydin looked around him again. Up to the spot where he'd left her. Could see nothing up there. Had someone already found her? But then why wasn't the alarm raised? He really couldn't believe that she'd have taken the chance to run now.

'Cox?'

No response. Too late for him to turn back. Whatever had happened to her, he was on his own.

Aydin crept forward on his haunches. He took the serrated combat knife in his hand, holding it at the ready, in case of a surprise attack. He reached the door without incident. Looked up to the camera above him. Could tell that the camera was pointing into the yard still – the lens remained focused in the near distance. There was no one spying on him.

He looked to the door. Two locks – a deadbolt and a lever mortice. He could pick through both, but he knew

309

that in the past there were bolts on the inside too, so little sense trying to go in that way. Instead he crept along to the window just a few yards away that opened out into a store room. The single pane window had hinges on one side, and a simple clasp lock.

Aydin sheathed his knife and pulled the backpack off his shoulders. Took out the three-foot crowbar. Inserted the claw end round the edge where the window lock was located. In one sharp movement he heaved on the end of the bar, pivoting it round and eliciting a short, sharp crack as the lock gave way and the edge of the window sprang loose. Aydin paused, waiting for a reaction to the noise.

Nothing.

One last look around him, then Aydin placed the crowbar in the backpack, slung the bag over his shoulders, took the knife out again then silently slunk in through the open window. He landed on the concrete floor hands first, his body slithering in behind him until he was on all fours in the darkened space. He crept forward, past shelving containing cleaning and other domestic products. Came to the door. Tried the handle. Unlocked.

Aydin pushed the door open a few inches. The corridor outside was lit with low wattage LEDs, giving a soft white glow. Aydin stepped out from the storage room and as quietly as he could shut the door. Stopped to listen again. The faintest murmurs from somewhere in the distance. Voices? A TV?

He moved along to where the living quarters were located. The familiar musty smell of the place fired a cascade of memories – he tried his best to block them out.

In the past, there had been six rooms for the boys, all along one corridor at the opposite end of the building to where he'd entered. The guards and elders shared a space in a side annexe adjacent to the main entrance. What Aydin would come to first was the guards' rest room where those on duty would spend their time when they weren't doing their rounds.

As Aydin carried on through the labyrinth, passing closed doors where he'd been taught so much – religion, history, warfare, chemistry, engineering, he was sure he could hear echoes from his past. The sounds of him and his brothers as young boys having their innocence snatched away from them. Aydin realised he was shaking. He was sure it wasn't fear or stress, just his rising anger.

He turned a corner. Real-world sounds took on more focus now. A radio or TV, he realised. Aydin slowed, taking one small step at a time, his body pressed up against the cool stone wall. He passed the turn that led to the boys' rooms. Glanced down the corridor. All of the doors were shut tight. No sign of anyone outside in the corridor at all.

He carried on, the sound of the voices grew louder with each step. Definitely a TV, he decided. He pulled up against the doorframe to the guards' rest room. Stole a glance inside. The TV was playing some comedy show he didn't recognise. The grainy image and terrible canned laughter suggested the programme was older than he was. But there was no one else inside the room.

Then Aydin spotted something. A bank of four monitors. Green and black images on each. The feeds from the outside CCTV cameras. He was too far away to get a proper look, but he was sure as he'd first glanced he'd seen movement on one of the cameras. One with a view to the main entrance.

Noises behind him. Shuffling feet and muted voices.

Aydin spun round and darted across the corridor to pull up against the wall opposite. The footsteps continued, getting closer all the time. Two men. Coming down past the boys' rooms. Aydin slipped the backpack from his shoulders. Carefully removed the Molotov cocktails from his belt, then,

311

knife in hand, slunk across the wall to the junction from where the men would emerge at any moment. They would surely be coming back to the rest room, and he would have no choice but to fight them, whoever they were.

Thin voices joined the footsteps. Aydin recognised one. Qarsh, the Arabic word for shark. The name given to him by the boys at the Farm because of his sharp nose, beady eyes and his thirst for blood. A big man. Probably the last person Aydin welcomed the idea of going head to head with. Was there another way?

His fingers fell into his pocket. The trigger for the bombs . . .

Too late, the left boot of one of the men came into view. Aydin had to act first. He spun round a hundred and eighty degrees, brought his elbow up. Using the added force from the momentum of the spin he crashed his elbow into the man's neck, the exact spot Aydin had aimed for. The sharp bone crunched into the man's windpipe and he fell backward onto the floor clutching at his throat, rasping for breath.

Aydin realised the man on the floor wearing the familiar blue fatigues wasn't Qarsh at all. In fact, he had no clue who the man was.

Just then he caught sight of Qarsh off to the side. As a boy, Qarsh had seemed like a giant, but now he was only inches taller than Aydin.

Qarsh locked eyes with his prey. A look of recognition. A confused look of fury on his face. Aydin readied himself as Qarsh lunged forward. He grabbed Aydin around the neck, lifted him clean off his feet, and then burst forward and slammed Aydin up against the wall. Aydin pinned in place, Qarsh used his free arm to hold the knife at bay, as the intruder squirmed and choked.

'*You*,' Qarsh said, his anger turning to a strange and crooked smile. 'Welcome home, Talatashar.'

Qarsh leaned back then drove his head into Aydin's. The head-butt caught Aydin at the bridge of his nose. His vision blurred. His head lolled. He wasn't given even a second to recover. Qarsh threw his head forward again. The second blow even more vicious than the first. Blood poured down Aydin's face. He coughed and spluttered, trying to breathe, but the grip on his neck was too tight. Through his blurred vision, all he could see was the blood-smeared head of Qarsh, contrasted by the white teeth of his horrible grin.

'The only question is, should I finish you off, or take you to the Teacher?' Qarsh craned his neck. 'Would you like to see him?'

'Yes,' Aydin croaked.

His answer seemed to flummox Qarsh momentarily. Aydin mustered everything he could. He hauled his knee up. Caught Qarsh in the groin. The big man groaned but his vice-like grip on Aydin's arm and neck didn't let up at all. Aydin hit him again. Qarsh snarled. The hand around Aydin's neck squeezed harder still. Aydin was on the brink . . .

One last try. He lifted both his knees, curled his legs up as high as he could. Using the wall behind him as a springboard he heaved out with his heels, driving them into Qarsh's waist. Despite his strength, the big man stumbled a half-step back. His grip slipped from Aydin's wrist just a fraction.

It was all he needed.

Aydin pulled his arm free and drove the knife into Qarsh's neck. The blade sank deep inside until Aydin's fist was pressed up against Qarsh's skin. The Shark groaned then roared in anger. Aydin pulled the knife away and thick, red blood gushed out. Qarsh wobbled. Somehow the grip on Aydin's neck became tighter still. Aydin gulped and gasped for breath, not sure what else he could do.

Then Qarsh's eyes rolled. His free hand went up to his neck, in a pathetic attempt to stem the flow. There was no

313

way that was going to work. He stumbled back. Aydin came away from the wall. His toes scraped the ground but Qarsh still had hold of his neck. He writhed, trying to get free. No use. Qarsh plummeted backward, taking Aydin with him.

They landed in a bloody heap on the floor. Aydin's face pressed up against Qarsh's chest. Aydin, gasping for air, his brain fuzzy and distant, wrestled free, pulled himself up. Looked down. Qarsh squirmed for just a few more seconds as blood continued to gush. Then he went still. He was dead.

But no time for rest or for reminiscence. Another familiar voice brought Aydin back to reality.

'Mustafa, do you hear me?' came the voice of the Teacher, from the radio of the first guard.

He was still on the floor. Hissing and wheezing as he tried to breathe through his crushed windpipe, his whole body shaking violently. Aydin didn't fancy his chances. Yet he made a move for the radio. Aydin darted over, drove the heel of his boot into the man's face, shutting him up for good. He picked the radio out of the man's belt.

'Mustafa? Are you there? I saw lights outside. Check the cameras.'

Aydin spun round. Squelched through the blood pool, past Qarsh and to the rest room. He went inside, over to the monitors. Scanned across them. Sure enough, on each of the four screens he could see dark-clothed men – combat dress. Carbines held in their hands. Night-vision goggles over their eyes. Creeping forward towards the Farm.

He picked his radio out of his pocket.

'Cox, what's going on?'

Nothing.

'Cox, are you there? I see men coming to the Farm. Who the hell are they?'

No answer.

Aydin felt he knew. MI6. Or their militant cronies, at least. Had Cox, despite everything, betrayed him?

There was only one thing left to do. Aydin put the radio down on the side. Took the transmitter from his pocket. Kept his eyes on the screens as he pushed the button, then braced himself for the explosions.

FIFTY-SIX

Cox jumped when the explosions erupted around the perimeter of the Farm. The shockwave, even from where she was still hiding, blasted into her face and knocked her back. She heard shouting and screaming in the distance.

'Aydin!' Cox shouted into the radio. 'Aydin what the hell is going on? Why aren't you answering?'

'Fancy meeting you here, Rachel,' came the voice from behind her.

Cox spun round. Anger rather than surprise consumed her when she saw Edmund Grey standing there. An armed crony by his side.

'What the—'

He waved her question away. 'You asked for help. I'm it.'

But she hadn't asked *him*. The messages she'd sent had all been to Flannigan. Yes, she'd wanted a team on site to back Aydin up, but she already highly doubted that was what was happening.

'You've scrambled my comms,' she said, holding the radio up.

'No. I've scrambled *their* comms.' He pointed over to the Farm.

Somehow Aydin's transmitter had still been able to blow the pipe bombs though. Cox guessed that was a good thing, but wasn't really sure.

'You've got to tell your men not to hurt Torkal. He's not one of them.'

Grey said nothing to that.

'Please? Tell me you're not going to kill him.'

'We're going to do our best to take whoever we can. But if they choose to fight back . . , there's really nothing I can do about that.'

'What is wrong with you?'

He shook his head nonchalantly. 'Miss Cox, I'm just doing my job. It's a shame you seem to have forgotten how to do yours.'

Cox had nothing to say to that. She flinched when a further boom came from below, followed by the rattle of automatic gunfire. Grey smiled at her.

'Where's the ATS drive you stole?'

Cox huffed.

'You don't need to fight me. You'll have plenty of enemies now, don't add me to the list. Where's the drive?'

'Is that all this is about? Covering your tracks?'

'For once, just do as you're told.'

The man next to Grey lifted his weapon, pointed it to Cox. She shook her head in disbelief.

'It's in the Jeep,' she said, pointing behind Grey. 'About a mile that way.'

'No. It's not. We already checked there.'

Cox frowned. 'Then I've no idea where it is . . . Unless . . . Aydin took it.'

'Why would he do that?'

'I don't bloody know!'

Grey sighed. 'Well come on, about time we got down there too.'

Cox hesitated. Was he going to give her the choice? What would he do if she said no? Grey looked to his man. Nodded. The man dropped the weapon down.

Cox sighed in relief. Grey looked amused.

'After you,' she said.

Grey laughed. He took a handgun from the holster on his hip and lifted it up to Cox.

'No. After you, I insist.'

FIFTY-SEVEN

When the pipe bombs exploded the whole building around Aydin shook. Walls and ceilings creaked. Dust fell from above and filled the air. Almost immediately there was shouting from within the compound – guards instructing each other, readying themselves, boys in their rooms waking from their sleep to terror, panicking. Aydin could hear their bedroom doors rattling as they tried to escape.

Then the sound of a door banging open. Heavy feet on the ground. A key in a lock. Aydin sneaked out of the rest room and back to the junction where Qarsh and his friend were lying on the floor. He peeked round the corner and saw another guard hurriedly opening the boys' rooms, shepherding them out. Dressed only in vests and underwear the boys scurried barefooted along the corridor, heads down. Most of them were all of five feet high. Maybe eleven or twelve years old. Aydin felt weak at the knees just watching them.

The one saving grace was those boys weren't up to fighting tonight.

'Get them to the truck!' came a booming voice.

The Teacher. Coming round the corner further down from the boys' rooms. Aydin whipped his head back into cover. For the first time his heart was thumping in his chest. Anxiety.

Seeing Qarsh was one thing, but the Teacher, the cause of so much grief and torment for Aydin and the others . . .

He'd not seen al-Addad in the flesh for years and he looked just as menacing now as he always had done. In many ways Aydin was in awe of the man, in most other ways he remained petrified of him.

Caught up in his own moment, Aydin forgot about the armed intruders on the outside. A huge bang down the hallway brought him back to reality. A charge, set to blow open a door or window. A second later stampeding feet echoed along the corridors.

Two black-clad figures scurried round the corner into the corridor where Aydin had earlier come from. He was still pulling the backpack over his shoulders. Was completely out-positioned. He picked up one of the Molotov cocktails from the floor. Scraped the storm match attached to the bottle across the rough wall to ignite it, then hurled the bottle as hard as he could down the corridor.

The glass hit the floor and shattered and a ball of fire spread out. The heatwave smacked into Aydin's face. He threw himself to the ground as the flames leaped towards him in the confined space. One of the two men screamed – set alight? – while the other opened fire with a high-powered automatic weapon.

Aydin huddled on the floor. After a few seconds the gunfire stopped. Aydin looked up. Further down the corridor the flames were still leaping high into the air. The assault team weren't coming through that way. Aydin grabbed the other two bottles and peeked again round the other corner. All of the doors to the boys' rooms were now open. The last of the children pounded away, heading for the front entrance. Aydin had no choice but to follow.

He stepped over the bodies of the two dead guards, then ran along the corridor. More gunfire from outside. More shouting. Who had the upper hand, Aydin couldn't tell, but having taken out two of the Farm's guards himself, most likely it was the SWAT team who had the manpower advantage.

Aydin passed by his own old bedroom, didn't dare look inside. He had to remain focused. He slowed as he rounded each corner to avoid running head-on into an ambush.

Soon the open main entrance was in his sight, the sound of gunfire growing all the time. Outside in the darkness, flames leaped about, smoke billowed. He saw a plain-clothed man scurry across in front of the open doorway. One of the elders? A blast of gunfire and the man collapsed to the ground. There was screaming and shouting everywhere. As Aydin edged closer he saw bodies splayed on the ground. Few of them the black-clad assault team. It was a bloodbath out there. MI6 weren't there to capture, they were there to execute everyone.

The exit was fifteen yards ahead, but Aydin wasn't going out that way. Instead he stopped by a closed door on his left that led into the Farm's main mess hall. The door was unlocked. Aydin opened the door and stepped into the darkened room. Saw a shape moving across the other side, between two tables.

Aydin flinched, but could tell from his size and shape that it was a boy. Aydin moved forward quickly, came to a stop halfway through the room.

'Boy,' Aydin whispered. 'Don't you move from there. Stay there as long as you possibly can. You understand?'

Nothing.

Aydin had tried at least. He moved away from his position, over to a window. Slowly lifted his body up to peep out. Saw the children being crammed into a waiting military-style truck, two armed guards giving covering fire as another man shepherded them onboard.

The other man was the Teacher . . .

Soon the kids were all inside. The Teacher climbed into the front passenger seat. Aydin couldn't let them get away.

He turned and picked up a chair and swung it with venom at the window. It smashed to pieces, leaving several jagged edges in the pane. With all the commotion outside, no one took the slightest bit of notice.

Aydin knocked the largest of the glass shards out of the frame then scrambled out, pulled himself up against the outside wall to take in the scene. What was left of the SWAT team were all hunkered across on the western side of the open courtyard. What was left of the Farm's guards – far fewer – were all on the eastern side, with the exit right by them. The main gates already blown wide open – charges set by the SWAT team most likely.

Were there still more of the MI6 team on the outside, though?

The truck's engine roared into life. Its brake lights flicked on, then off and its wheels began to roll. With the escape imminent, two dark figures bobbed up on Aydin's right. Opened fire on the departing truck. The last of the Farm's guards still on his feet, trying to protect the truck, took several hits and plummeted to the ground.

The SWAT team edged forward as the truck made its way for the gates.

Aydin couldn't let the Teacher get away. But he also couldn't hurt those kids.

He pulled one of the bottles off his belt, used a lighter to light the storm match. The sparkle of fire grabbed the attention of the assault team. Aydin hurled the bottle towards them. Flames leaped up in to the sky when it smashed on the ground. He lit the match of the last bottle, lobbed it across. The spread of flames more or less blocked off the assault team, though with nothing around it for the fire to consume other than sand, the blaze wouldn't last long.

The explosions did at least give Aydin, and the truck, momentary respite from the automatic gunfire. Aydin took the chance. He sprinted forward for the truck. If he could get inside . . .

Then there was a hiss off to his right. Aydin whipped his head round as he raced along. Saw the trail of fire heading his way. Knew exactly what it was.

As the projectile whizzed past his head, Aydin flung himself to the ground. The RPG landed by the truck's back tyre. The explosion lifted the huge hulk of metal clean off the ground and it came crashing back down again on its side.

There was fire and flames everywhere. The heat was almost unbearable. Aydin went to pick himself up. His body heavy, his head distant. Just the effects of the nearby explosion or had he been hit by something – a bullet, shrapnel?

He tried to pull himself to his knees. Heard the screaming of the boys in the burning truck. Those who were still alive at least. Men were shouting and rushing all around him. Trying to help, or were they just there to take out the stragglers?

Aydin, still on his side, looked over to what was left of the truck's mangled cabin. Saw two black-clad figures climb on top to wrench open the door. One pointed his weapon inside while the other fished in and hauled someone out. A man.

The man was rolled off the cabin and landed in a heap on the ground below. The armed men jumped down. Grabbed the man who was conscious but barely moving. Aydin saw his bloodied face. The Teacher. The men began to drag him away. Aydin couldn't let them have him.

'No!'

Aydin found the strength to get to his feet. Hobbled along towards the men.

'Don't move!' came the shout from behind him. English. 'Don't you fucking move.'

Aydin stopped. Half-turned so he could see. One of the assault team, with the barrel of an M4 carbine trained on Aydin's head.

'Whoah, whoah!' came another voice, and through the darkness stepped another man. Edmund Grey.

'It's OK, I've got this one. Go and help the others.'

He pointed off to the truck. The mercenary nodded and scurried away. Aydin glared at Grey but said nothing.

'Aydin, we finally get to meet face to face,' Grey said.

Aydin held his tongue. Soon realised Grey being there wasn't the worst of it when another figure stepped forward into view from behind him, lit up by the flames of the nearby fires.

Rachel Cox.

FIFTY-EIGHT

Aydin looked down to Grey's hand. He was holding a handgun, though the barrel was pointed to the floor.

'So what now?' Aydin asked. 'You take us all away and bury us in the desert?'

Grey laughed as though Aydin was being mind-numbingly stupid.

'It's OK, Aydin. It's over,' Cox said. 'We're going to get you out of here.'

'You lied to me.'

He saw hurt in her eyes, though it was him who'd been betrayed. Aydin could hear the sound of diesel engines and thick tyres kicking up dirt, growing louder by the second. He looked over his shoulder, saw the headlights of the approaching vehicles through the blown-out main gates.

'We're taking the others to a local detention centre,' Grey said.

Aydin laughed. He didn't fancy the chances of those kids in MI6 hands.

'But you're coming with us,' Cox said.

Aydin looked to Grey for reassurance. Grey nodded, then turned round.

'Come on, this way.'

Grey began to move off, back across the grounds the way Aydin had originally come in from. Aydin followed. Cox walked by his side. They were soon away from the carnage by the front gates. Heading into darkness.

There were more cries of anguish from behind them. Gunfire. Grey briefly turned round to look over his shoulder. Aydin looked to Cox. What was that look she gave in return? Apology? Acquiescence?

Aydin heard the *whoop-whoop* of a helicopter's rotors. The beam of its bright searchlight became visible over the crest of the hill in front of them. Seconds later the craft was above them, slowly descending.

Out of the darkness to Aydin's left, one of the assault team came forward, M4 in his hands. Grey slowed. So too did Aydin and Cox, always staying a couple of steps behind – space to move.

Grey turned.

'I need the ATS drive,' Grey said.

It wasn't clear if he was speaking to Aydin or Cox.

'Give me the drive and then we all get out of here.'

Aydin looked to Cox who gave him a pleading look.

'Aydin?' she said.

Aydin focused on the helicopter. As it neared the ground the blast of air from its rotors whipped up sand all around them. When it was a few yards away, in the darkness Aydin spotted the armed man hanging off the edge of the open back cabin.

'The drive!' Grey shouted, above the din.

'I lost it days ago,' Aydin said.

Grey huffed, looked seriously pissed off. The helicopter gently touched down. The rotors kept spinning. Hand up to protect his face, Grey turned to the craft. There was an unspoken command given to the armed commando. Aydin could tell by the way the guy on board nodded.

326

Or perhaps Aydin was just being paranoid. Better paranoid than dead, though.

Aydin sprang to his side. Grey ducked down as the man on the helicopter lifted his weapon.

'No!' Cox screamed. It was unclear who her instruction was to.

Aydin grabbed the muzzle of the M4 in the hands of the guy next to him and spun round, kicking his legs out from under him. The guy fell to the floor, Aydin snatched the weapon from his grasp, fired two shots into his legs, stomped on his face, then dived out of the way as the man on the chopper opened fire.

Bullets raked the ground, spitting up more sand. Aydin, rolling for safety, held down on the trigger of the M4 and a spray of bullets erupted. He caught the guy in the helicopter, but hit the fuselage at the same time. Black smoke billowed. Aydin looked over to Grey, scrambling to his feet. Then to the pilot. Realising the position, the pilot tugged on the cyclic stick and the helicopter began to lift away.

'Aydin, stop!' Cox shouted. 'Please.'

Aydin paused. He could see Cox out of the corner of his eye. In a heap on the ground. Grey turned. Aydin fired off another shot that caught Grey in his foot and he fell to the floor screaming.

Aydin rattled off more bullets at the departing helicopter and the pilot lost control. The craft tilted, swept sideways away from them. The rotors scraped the ground, snapped off and went flying across the yard. The whole thing came to a crashing stop on the dusty ground. Thick black smoke plumed up.

Aydin moved to Grey. Used his foot to kick him back down into the dirt. Grey rolled over, looked up at Aydin disconsolately.

'You people,' Grey said, all niceties disposed. 'No matter how much I try to help, you only throw it back in my face.'

'You killed my father,' Aydin said, the flood of sadness far greater than he expected.

'Like hell I did.'

'You *tried* to kill him. That drone strike, I know it was you.'

'He was part of an Al-Qaeda cell! My job is to take out pieces of shit like that.'

'Bullshit.'

'You've seen the evidence yourself!'

'I have. Evidence that you knew of the Farm for years but did nothing about it. Why?'

'Did nothing about it? I've been trying for years to bring this place down.'

'It's not true,' Aydin said, shaking his head.

'Aydin, please, not like this,' Cox said. She was off to Aydin's right. On her feet. Her hands by her sides. Except they weren't empty any more. In one she now had a handgun. Where had that come from?

'And if you're looking for someone to blame, you may want to look a bit closer to home,' Grey said, a snide grin on his face, despite his predicament.

'What are you talking about?'

'Rachel Cox. MI6 spy. How do you think my team came to be here tonight. She betrayed you.'

'Aydin, don't listen to him,' Cox said.

'Think about it,' Grey said, a slight smile returning as the reality dawned on Aydin. 'She set you up tonight, and she's set you up before, too.'

Aydin looked to Cox. She was more rattled now. Her hand twitched.

'Don't even think about it!' Aydin boomed, switching the M4 barrel to Cox. She flinched.

'Aydin, I haven't betrayed you. I called in backup to help you here. You have to believe me.'

'And what about in Baku?' Grey said, shuffling back and slowly getting to his feet. He looked over to the helicopter. The pilot was still in his seat. Unconscious or dead? 'Who was op commander that day, when Maria was gunned down? When your father was gunned down?'

'It wasn't my fault!' Cox screamed.

'Bit of a coincidence, no?' Grey said.

'They weren't operating under my orders! Aydin, please believe me.'

'But he doesn't believe you,' Grey said. 'How could he after what you've done.'

'I've done nothing wrong!'

'Then what about Nilay?'

Now Cox looked panicked. Her eyes darted about.

'What about Nilay?' Aydin snarled.

He was trying so hard to focus, but his eyes were welling with tears as he thought of all the pain and misery. His father, his mother, his sister. They'd all been killed. He'd long blamed al-Addad for it all, but was that the truth?

'Did Cox not tell you what happened that day?'

'Rachel?' Aydin said.

He noticed tears were now streaming down her face.

'Nilay was my friend,' Cox said.

'Friend? You let her walk into a trap. You knew the bad guys were on to her. She was your asset. You were watching her every move but you allowed her to walk to her death because you thought it might get you a good lead.'

Cox shook her head. 'It's not true,' she said.

'Then what is true?' Aydin asked.

'Yes, I was watching her! She was getting so close to finding answers. The same answers you've been searching for. About your father, about this place. And *she* was lying to *me*! I had her followed that day but there was nothing I could do to stop it.'

329

'Are you really going to believe that?' Grey asked. He still sounded so cocky. Way too cocky.

'Wait,' Cox said. A resolve broke out on her face. 'Aydin, think about it. How does Grey even know all this? I hadn't even met him until a few days ago.'

Aydin's eyes were back on Grey now. He spun the barrel of the gun back to him, causing him to lift his arms in the air. Aydin took a step back to give him more distance from Cox. He couldn't trust either of these two. Were they both playing him?

'Don't let her mind-fuck you, Aydin.'

'You want the truth, Aydin?' Cox said. 'Grey is the only person who knows it. Tell us about Shadow Hand.'

Grey scoffed. 'Now's not exactly a good time for pointless reminiscence.'

'We got it all wrong,' Cox said.

'Got *what* wrong?' Aydin asked.

'Remember you said your uncle was an MI6 asset. You told me that yourself. What if your father was too.'

'That makes no sense.'

'It's the only explanation that does make sense. Grey was handler to them both. Shadow Hand wasn't an Al-Qaeda project to start a jihadi group. Shadow Hand was MI6 all along. It was supposed to be a counter-terrorism op. Sleepers embedded into jihadist groups, but who were really feeding back to MI6.'

Aydin, baring his teeth like a dog, took two determined steps towards Grey now, his finger twitched on the trigger.

'Wait, wait,' Grey said, looking more panicked.

'Your father thought he was putting you into a life to help *fight* terror, not to be a part of it,' Cox said. 'Maybe Grey has always been corrupt. Or perhaps something else went wrong, but Shadow Hand was hijacked by the real bad guys. Grey

330

and his SWAT teams have been trying their hardest to clean up ever since. Just look at tonight.'

'Enough of this nonsense!' Grey blasted. 'We need to get out of here before reinforcements arrive.'

'Aydin, listen to me, I—'

'No. I'm done with listening to you two. Just one question, Grey.'

Grey looked unsure.

'Tonight was your op.'

'Correct.'

'Those men were operating under your orders.'

'They *are*.'

'Why did your men blow up that truck? They knew kids were in there.'

Grey bit down as he searched for a response. His hesitation was enough for Aydin.

'No!' Cox screamed.

Too late. Aydin pulled the trigger. The bullet hit Grey in his knee. He crumpled back to the ground, screaming in pain.

'I asked you a question,' Aydin said, stepping forward. He pressed the barrel to Grey's head. 'One last chance to tell me the truth.'

'OK!' Grey screamed. 'I'll tell you.'

Aydin paused.

'Cox is right. Shadow Hand was our counter-terror op.'

Aydin flicked his eyes to Cox, then back to Grey.

'And?'

'And it's true your father was working with us back then. He helped to set it up. But you were wrong about one thing.'

'What?'

'Your uncle. He wasn't an MI6 asset, like Ergun. And I wasn't his handler. He *was* MI6. An agent. He was responsible for Shadow Hand. But he betrayed us all. He—'

'You killed him too?'

'No! Nobody knows where he is. He's hiding. You want to find the man responsible for *all* of this, it's Kamil Torkal.'

'You're lying.'

Aydin got ready to pull the trigger. Movement to his right. Aydin went to turn the gun but could already see the weapon pointed towards him.

'Not like this, Aydin,' Cox said.

'We've been in this position before.'

'And last time I shot you. To stop you killing Wahid.'

Aydin said nothing to that.

'Just drop the gun, Aydin. Grey will talk. We need him to talk.'

It was the last thing Aydin wanted to do. He was there to punish those responsible for the Farm, for ruining his life. But was Grey really the bad guy? There was so much duplicity on all sides that Aydin really couldn't be sure.

What other choice did he have?

He lowered the M4. Tossed it over to Cox. It skimmed along the dirt next to her. She lowered her weapon too.

Grey laughed.

Aydin turned, snarling, and thudded his boot down onto Grey's face.

'Not subtle. But at least you shut him up,' Cox said.

'Now what?' Aydin asked.

'Now we get out of here.'

FIFTY-NINE

Zed site, Algeria

Cox knocked on the door then waited.

'Come in,' shouted Flannigan from inside.

Cox opened the door and stepped into the office. Well, office was a kind way to describe the makeshift space. The walls on three sides and the ceiling were unfinished plywood boards. The other wall was bare rock. Electric cables hung all about the place. Flannigan was sitting behind a cheap-looking desk, focused on his laptop.

'Sir,' Cox said.

'Ah, you're here.' Flannigan got to his feet, gave a half smile. 'I finally persuaded you.'

'It's not my favoured location, but—'

'But you couldn't resist, right? We've now got two of the most high-profile terrorists in the world in this bunker . . .'

He said it with genuine pride, which made Cox all the more uncomfortable.

'. . . and that's in no small part due to you, Plain Jane.'

Cox winced at his words. It was only a few days ago that her face had been plastered on the newspapers as a wanted terrorist accomplice. Now it was back to being the hero once again. Neither public role suited her particularly well. Flannigan had never apologised for her name having been smeared like that, but, she guessed, neither had she apologised for absconding with classified data in order to help a known fugitive.

'Is he here too?' Flannigan asked.

'He's waiting outside.'

Flannigan mulled that one for a few seconds, as though he wasn't sure whether he approved, and wasn't sure whether he wanted to be introduced or not. This time it wasn't up to him.

'Take a seat,' Flannigan said.

'No. It's fine. I'm not going to stay long. I just want to know . . .'

'Yeah?'

'What comes next for me?'

'How do you mean?'

Cox couldn't quite explain it.

'I know you're bruised by all this,' Flannigan said.

'I just don't know who to trust any more.'

'That's the world we operate in.'

'I'm not sure it's the world I want to operate in.'

'You can still be part of this. Take some time off. The world will keep ticking over. Bad guys will keep springing up. You'll soon realise where you're meant to be.'

'That's the problem, though, right? I don't even know who the bad guys are any more.'

'You mean Grey?'

'Among others.'

Flannigan sighed, shook his head.

'If peace cannot be maintained with honour, it's no longer peace,' Cox said.

'John Russell?'

'I've no idea. But it's quite apt here, don't you think? Grey's not going to stand trial. He's not even been forced from his job.'

'That's because as far as the top brass is concerned he did his job.'

'After fucking up Shadow Hand he's killed people at will just to cover his own mistakes.'

'Says you. He's a level five operative, one of the most senior covert agents we have. It's his job to do the dirty work.'

Cox shook her head in disbelief.

'I'm not saying he's lily-white,' Flannigan said, 'but the way it's been given to me, Grey had authority for every action he took.'

'What about the bombs in Liverpool and Faro?'

Flannigan's face turned sour. 'There's no evidence he was responsible for that.'

'No evidence? The culprits were both English nationals, MI6 assets, known to have links to him!'

'Links? Like you have links to people who have killed and caused chaos around the globe, you mean?'

'So you believe that story about Kamil Torkal? That he was the MI6 agent tasked with setting up Shadow Hand but then betrayed us all. That Grey was just the good Samaritan trying to stop it? Where's the bloody evidence for that?'

'It's consistent with what we know.'

'It's steeped in dirty secrets and misinformation and one man's word against everyone else's.'

'Look, Cox,' Flannigan said, his tone more authoritative now. A clear sign his patience was wearing thin. 'Grey is not your concern any more. Rest assured someone somewhere will be analysing every action he's ever taken. They'll be searching for answers as to how Shadow Hand, if it was an MI6 op, morphed into something evil and how we lost all control over it. Whether that was down to Grey or Ergun Torkal, or his brother, perhaps we'll never know now. But it's not your job to pick it apart. Understood?'

'Yeah. You've made the point quite clear. You don't give a shit about the truth. Just about not ruffling the feathers of those above you.'

'OK, I think we're done here.'

Cox humphed, turned for the door.

'Oh, and Cox?'

She paused.

'Our guys tore apart the Farm. That Jeep you and Aydin travelled in. The hotel you stayed at in Harat. They never did find the ATS data.'

Cox smiled to herself. 'Worried the truth might still come back to bite us?'

Flannigan said nothing more. Cox opened the door and walked out.

She made her way down the grimy corridors to the small waiting area where Aydin was sitting, alone, looking down at his feet.

'You ready?' Cox asked.

'I'm not sure,' he said. 'I still can't quite believe you pulled this off.'

'I might not be in the good books exactly, but I've got some leverage after what they did to me, believe me.'

Aydin huffed. 'I've been thinking about this for days. I convinced you I just wanted to confront him, to speak to him face to face but really I've been thinking how I could kill him here . . .' Cox flinched but said nothing. 'I thought it's what I needed. What had to happen before I could move on.'

'And now?'

'And now that I'm here, I'm glad al-Addad is in this place. It's nothing more than he deserves. Same for Wahid.'

'Come on,' Cox said. She held her hand out. Aydin took it and got to his feet.

They moved to the door across from them and Cox opened it. Aydin stepped through. Stared through the glass to the man on the other side. Tied to a chair, he was naked except for a pair of dirty boxer shorts. His skin was grimy and bloody and covered in beads of sweat. A sack was over his head. Cox knocked on the window and the green-fatigued man standing next to the prisoner lifted the sack away.

Aydin stared into the darting eyes of Aziz al-Addad, the Teacher. He still carried a certain resolve though the defeat in his face was clear.

For a few moments Aydin didn't move.

'Aydin? Are you ready?'

He didn't answer. Couldn't.

'Aydin?'

'No.'

'No?'

'I can't do it.'

Cox sighed, though part of her was relieved, especially after what Aydin had said moments earlier.

'I'm sorry,' he said. 'I don't need to speak to him. Nothing he could say would make me feel better. Seeing him like this is enough.'

'You're sure.'

'I'm sure. Just get me out of this place. Please.'

SIXTY

Aydin drove the Toyota through the open gates of the compound and parked up in the dirt. The evidence of the carnage that had taken place just a few weeks before was still plain to see – burned-out vehicles, black smears in the sand and on the walls of the buildings. Bullet casings on the ground. Aydin stepped out into the heat. Took in the smell of the place. Headed for the now boarded-up entrance. He prised a wooden board away and stepped into the darkened corridor. Headed on past the mess hall where tables were overturned, remnants of food packets and tins across the floor. He carried on down to the living quarters. Moved into the room that he'd shared with his brother, Itnashar, for several years. His brother, his best friend, who Aydin had killed in an apartment in Bruges the previous year.

Aydin looked around the now empty room. He could hear Itnashar's voice. Could recall the times they'd laughed together – far fewer times than they'd cried themselves to sleep at night.

He wondered what misery the new recruits at the Farm had endured before their eventual capture by MI6. Five boys had died that night. Nine had been taken into custody. According to Cox the plan was to find their families and send them home, but for now they all remained in the hands of the British government somewhere. No longer a threat, but what life would they have?

Aydin stepped back out into the corridor, walked on down, past the spot where he'd killed Qarsh. The now blackened stain on the floor the only evidence of what had happened there.

He moved into the rest room. It had been stripped bare by MI6. So too had the labs, the classrooms. They'd taken everything that wasn't bolted down.

There was nothing left for Aydin to see inside. He was done with the Farm for good.

He headed on outside into the sun. Walked through the recreation yard, doing his best to block out the voices in his head. He clambered over the fence and used the position of the sun to head south-west, back in the direction he'd come in from on that fateful night.

After twenty minutes he came to the spot in the hills, next to a jagged rock that jutted outwards and somehow looked to him like a gorilla's face. The number of times he'd stood by the barred windows of his room and stared at that rock from afar. He checked around him. Satisfied no one was in sight he used the trowel in his backpack to claw away at the dirt at the base of the rock. Several inches down, the trowel hit something hard. Aydin dug his fingers in, lifted the small black box out.

He blew and brushed the sand away, leaving only a small rectangular strip where the grit remained stuck to the plastic casing – remnants of a sticker.

Aydin straightened up, looking at the inanimate object in his hand. Where was his uncle now? Was he really the mastermind behind everything that was the Farm, or just another scapegoat? Had his own father been in cahoots, or just betrayed by those closest to him like so many others?

And what about Edmund Grey? Rachel Cox? Nilay?

So many lies. So many secrets. So many people already dead. So many answers still out there somewhere.

Aydin wiped a tear from his eye. He placed the hard drive into his backpack, turned, and headed for the car.

FIND OUT HOW IT ALL ENDS IN THE THIRD AND
FINAL BOOK IN THE **SLEEPER 13** TRILOGY

IMPOSTER 13

Coming 2020 . . .

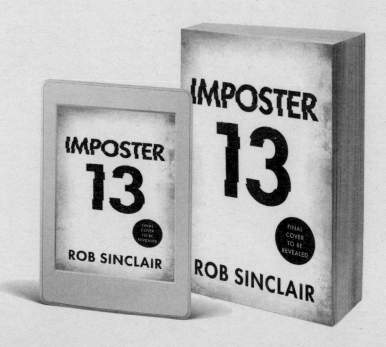